A wild horse,
a broken man,
a family in ruins and a
woman with the power to heal....

The Horsemaster's Daughter

Susan Wiggs

MIRA

ISBN 1-55166-534-4

THE HORSEMASTER'S DAUGHTER

Copyright © 1999 by Susan Wiggs.

All rights reserved. Except for use in any review, the reproduction or utilization of this work in whole or in part in any form by any electronic, mechanical or other means, now known or hereafter invented, including xerography, photocopying and recording, or in any information storage or retrieval system, is forbidden without the written permission of the publisher, MIRA Books, 225 Duncan Mill Road, Don Mills, Ontario, Canada M3B 3K9.

All characters in this book have no existence outside the imagination of the author and have no relation whatsoever to anyone bearing the same name or names. They are not even distantly inspired by any individual known or unknown to the author, and all incidents are pure invention.

MIRA and the Star Colophon are trademarks used under license and registered in Australia, New Zealand, Philippines, United States Patent and Trademark Office and in other countries.

Visit us at www.mirabooks.com

Printed in U.S.A.

For Reed Alexander Brown
and Jamie Gatton, lifelong friends
With love and gratitude

And for Nicholas J. Klist,
my beloved father–
I will always be "the engineer's daughter"

My thanks as always to the steadfast
Joyce, Christina, Betty and Barb; to my wonderful
editors Dianne Moggy, Amy Moore-Benson and
Martha Keenan; and to the supercharged librarian
Pat Mason, who leaves no stone (or sand dollar)
unturned in the quest for story facts.
Any mistakes are my own, but for the inclusion
of such perfect details as mating ospreys
and suicidal piping plovers,
I'm indebted to Pat.

Part One

The isle is full of noises,
Sounds and sweet airs, that give delight, and hurt not.
—William Shakespeare, *The Tempest,* III, ii

Part One

One

*Mockjack Bay, Virginia
April 1854*

Hunter Calhoun started drinking early that day. Yet the sweet fire of the clear, sharp whiskey failed to bring on the oblivion he thirsted for. Lord above, he needed that blurred, blissful state. Needed to feel nothing for a while. Because what he felt was a lot worse than nothing.

Gazing out a window at the sluggish, glass-still waters of the bay, he noticed that the buoy was sinking and a few more planks had rotted off the dock. The plantation had no proper harbor but a decent anchorage—not that it mattered now.

"That poor Hunter Calhoun," folks called him when they thought he was too drunk to notice. They always spoke of him with a mixture of pity and relief—pity, that the misfortune had happened to him, and relief, that it had not happened to them. In general, women thought it romantic and tragic that he'd lost his wife in such a spectacular fashion; the men were slightly disdainful and superior—*they'd* never let that sort of disaster befall *their* womenfolk.

Calhoun glared down into his whiskey glass, willing the amber liquid to numb him before he talked himself out of what he knew he must do. He experienced a strange, whimsical fantasy: the whiskey was a pool he could dive into, headfirst. *If the ocean was whiskey and I was a duck, I'd swim to the bottom and never come up.*

A sound of disgust from the adjoining room alerted him that he'd sung the lines of the old ditty aloud.

"Don't go clucking your tongue at me, Miz Nancy," he called out. "I can sing. A man has every right to sing in his own house."

"Humph. You call that singing? I thought the neighbors' hounds just treed a coon." The gentle clack of her knitting needles punctuated the statement.

He finished his drink with a long swig, and oh-so-silently set his glass on the age-scarred sideboard.

"Don't matter how quiet you try to be," Nancy called. "I know you been at the spirits." A moment later she stepped through the open pocket doors and came into the shabby parlor, her cane tapping along the floor until it encountered the threadbare carpet. Her African face, wizened by years she had never learned to count, held equal measures of patience and exasperation. Her eyes, clouded with blindness, seemed to peer into a deeper part of him even he didn't see. Nancy had the uncanny ability to track his progress through a room, or worse, to track his very thoughts sometimes.

"Humph," she said again, this time with a self-righteous snort. "How you going to shoot a gun if you all full up with Jim Hooker's whiskey?"

Hunter gave a humorless laugh, poured another drink and gulped it down. She was the only person he knew who could actually hear a man drinking. "Drunk or sober, Nancy, have you ever known me to miss a target?"

Setting his empty glass on the smoke-stained mantel, he said, "Excuse me. I've got something I have to do." He paused to fill his silver hip flask with more whiskey. Nancy waited in silence, but he felt the cold bluster of her temper as if she'd scolded him aloud.

It was too much to hope she wouldn't follow him. He could hear the busy *tap-tap* of her cane as she shuffled along behind him, down the central hall toward the back of the big house. In his parents' day, the gun room had been a hive of activity on hunt mornings, when neighbors from all over Northampton County came to call. Now the room contained only the most necessary of firearms—a Le Mats revolver, a percussion shotgun and a Winchester repeating rifle. He went to the gun cabinet and took down the Winchester, cocking open the side loading gate to make sure it was well oiled.

It was. He had known this moment was coming. In preparation, he had lit himself with whiskey, but suddenly strong drink wasn't enough.

He looped a deerskin sack of .44-40 cartridges to his belt, then stood for a moment at the window, staring out the wavy glass at the broad gardens of Albion. Dogwood and rhododendron grew profusely at the verges, though the flower beds had a weedy, untended look.

"You best get a move on," said Nancy. "Miz Beaumont took the children off to lessons at Bonterre for the day, and you want this dirty business done 'fore they get back."

"I reckon I do." He flinched, picturing his son Blue's silent censure when the boy learned what had happened in his absence. Blue had suffered so much loss already, and

here his own father was about to take something else from
him.

A wave of self-loathing washed over Hunter. Earlier
that morning, he had sat down to breakfast with the children, putting jam on Belinda's biscuit and pouring the
cream for Blue, pretending—God, always pretending—
that things were right between them.

With her strange, unerring sense of direction, Nancy
joined him at the window and caught hold of his arm.
"I'm real sorry, son. I'm just as sorry as I can be," she
said, gently fingering a rip in the sleeve of his shirt.

"I know you are, honey." He stared down at the dark,
papery-dry hand, the knuckles gnarled and shiny with
rheumatism. That hand had soothed his feverish brow
when he was a baby and dried his little-boy tears. It had
mended his breeches with a lightning flash of the needle,
and, when the occasion warranted it, delivered a smack to
his backside a time or two, though never without drawing
him into a hug afterward.

And when he had signed the manumission papers to set
her free, that trembling hand had cupped his cheek, her
touch more eloquent than the words she could not sum-
mon.

Nancy's mothering hand couldn't soothe him now. His
nervous fingers strayed to the slim hip flask in his pocket,
but he didn't take it out. Nothing could soothe him this
morning.

"I'll be back by and by, honey," he said to Nancy, then
stepped out on the veranda.

Setting his jaw, he jerked open the gate of the rifle and
loaded the cartridges. Then he hitched back his shoulders
and strode down the steps to the walkway. The brilliant
Virginia morning mocked him with its bright promise.
Thready high clouds veined the April sky, and sunlight

flooded extravagantly down through the twisted live oaks of Albion. The long misty acres rose up into the sloping green hills.

At one time the tidewater plantation had been as busy as a small village. Tobacco fields had covered hundreds of acres; the cultivation and curing of the leaves had occupied hundreds of hands. Now everything had changed. All that remained were Hunter and his children, a small staff of misfits and a dream that was about to be shattered.

Not for the first time, he contemplated giving up, selling out. Would a prospective buyer notice the chipping paint on the soaring columns that flanked the entranceway? Would he see the brambles and creeper that encroached on the once-pristine lawn?

Would a buyer see the work and sweat that had gone into the riding hall, the round pen and lunging ring, the barns and paddocks and the only mile oval racing track in the county? Would the mares and foals in the hills show themselves? Would a stranger be dazzled by Albion's wild promise, or disappointed by its failed glory?

He simply didn't know. These days, he had no answers.

He sucked in a deep breath, tasting the cool green tang of the Spartina grass that fringed the marshes by the bay. The weight of the Winchester pressed insistently on his shoulder. His strides kicked up droplets of dew as he walked, dampening the toes of his scuffed riding boots. No matter, there would be no riding today.

A cluster of farm buildings lay in quiet morning shadow. A stone boat of thick planks laid over heavy runner beams had been brought out in readiness for the dead body.

A high-pitched whinny broke the silence, and on the farthest hill to the west, the herd appeared, moving like a banner of silk across the spring meadows. No cart horses or farm plugs these, but Thoroughbreds. Against the green-draped landscape, they were magnificent and primal, their loping forms stretching into one entity, like a mythical beast, as they traversed the hill. As always, Hunter's heart caught at the sight of them.

At one time the racehorses that had beggared his fortunes had also brought him true happiness. The enterprise was the beginning of his hope and the end to the troubles that had shadowed the years since he'd inherited Albion. But after Lacey's death, he'd turned away from the dream, for a dream seemed too auspicious a thing to have when your world was falling apart.

Still, through everything, his affinity for the unusual horses remained a powerful force. Most days, "Hunter's Folly" as the neighbors called them, were the only things in his world that made sense.

Putting two fingers to his lips, he loosed three shrill whistles. The lead stallion—once declared unridable, which was why Hunter rode him—broke away from the herd and headed down at an angle, answering the summons with his customary mixture of obedience and disdain. Hunter walked over to the fence and treated the horse to a piece of barley sugar. "There you are, Julius," he said quietly. "How's my old boy?"

From the time he was very young, and had no inkling of the troubles ahead of him, Hunter Calhoun had possessed a God-given way with racehorses—the more spirited, the better. The stallion called Julius had been his triumph, the most remarkable Thoroughbred Virginia had ever seen.

But Julius had run his course and could no longer race or stand stud. He finished his barley sugar and nudged at the pouch of cartridges on Hunter's belt.

"That's not for you," Hunter said, stepping away from

the fence. "Though Lord knows, some breeders would put you down since you no longer earn your keep."

Julius lifted his big, dumb head in a nod and flapped his lips. Hunter tried to smile, but his mind lingered on less pleasant matters. He'd best not put this off any longer. With the rifle over his shoulder, he walked to the cluster of barns and arenas.

At first glance, the paddock appeared deserted. Just for a moment Hunter's spirits lifted. Perhaps he didn't have to do this at all. Perhaps it had all been a mistake, a horrible mistake—

A low rumble of rage came from the green darkness beneath a sweeping branch of live oak. In the shadows at the corner of the pen, a malevolent gleam flickered. Approaching the weathered cedar fence rails, Hunter pretended not to notice. He watched obliquely, and from a corner of his eye he saw the quivering of a filthy patch of hide, caked with mud and manure.

The nightmare lived yet.

He took a step closer to the paddock. If the beast stayed cornered, they wouldn't have to drag it far to load the carcass onto the stone boat. If Hunter's shot was true, there wouldn't be too much of a mess.

And the shot would be true, for the bite of the morning air had evaporated every drop of whiskey Hunter had consumed. Icy sobriety overcame him. Nothing stood between him and the pain.

He should be swift, have done with it. But for some perverse reason he took his time, surrounded by the false serenity of the shady paddock and stables. No trace of the mare's blood marred the sandy surface of the paddock. The crazed pacing of the stallion had kicked up the sand, covering over the stain.

Hunter squeezed his eyes shut, remembering the way

the stallion had attacked the broodmare, racing toward her with his mouth wide open, sinking his teeth into her flank and hanging on like a mountain lion on the hunt. The deafening squeals of the mare had gone on and on, echoing across the flat water of the nearby bay, finally stopping when the mad stallion fought her to the ground, causing her foreleg to snap. Only by swinging six-foot bludgeons had Hunter and the grooms been able to beat the stallion off and back him into the paddock.

It had been too late for the mare, though.

No one had dared to come near the fence, not since that night.

Hunter had been so excited about the stallion's arrival. More important, the idea of importing a racehorse from Ireland had captivated his son Blue, and for the first time since his mother's death, Blue's eyes had shown a spark of interest. When he learned the fate of the stallion, the boy would probably retreat once again into his silent, impenetrable world.

The acquisition of the champion Thoroughbred was supposed to have turned the tide of Hunter's fortunes. Instead, it had dug him even deeper into disaster.

The beast—called Sir Finnegan—had been brought off the ship wearing an eight-pound iron muzzle. Offended by the cruel measure, Hunter had removed the muzzle immediately—and nearly lost a hand for his pains. The stallion had gone on the attack. He reared time and time again, screaming, strong teeth snapping at the air. The chafing of the muzzle had created raw, running sores on the beast's head, making him look as ugly as his temper.

"He's just spirited," Hunter had remarked, and like a fool he had brought the mare in season to the paddock. In addition to ruining the mare, the stallion had nearly killed a groom, a hired man from Norfolk. More predator than horse, Finn had rushed the man back against the fence, then slashed out viciously. Rearing, striking, bellowing, the stallion had focused his fury on the groom. If Hunter hadn't distracted the horse with a bludgeon blow, the stallion would have murdered the man.

Now the stallion's breath heated the air, making little puffs of fog. His eye, filled with an iron-hard malevolence, rolled back. The shallow veins beneath the surface of his skin formed angry, distended rivulets, and the hide itself quivered as if to cast off flies.

Cold purpose enclosed Hunter like a crust of ice. Emptying his mind of everything save the task at hand, he braced one leg on the lowest fence rail. Then he slung the other leg up and over, steadying himself there while he jammed the butt of the rifle against his shoulder.

The stallion exploded. A furious energy stiffened his back, and in a great wave of movement he reared. Filth-clotted hooves raked the air. Hugely muscled haunches bunched in his thighs, supporting his great weight. A shriek of pure equine wrath broke the quiet.

A hard knot formed in Hunter's chest. Even crazed and covered in muck, the horse was magnificent. Buried beneath the madness, the fire and heart that had made this horse the swiftest in Ireland still beat strong.

All of Hunter's fortunes rested with this magnificent, ruined animal.

He should have drunk more whiskey.

Grimly, he once again set the butt of the rifle against his shoulder and waited for the horse to settle. But the blood of champions flowed in this stallion's veins and he had enormous reserves of stamina, despite the grueling sea voyage from Ireland.

After a time, the horse dropped his front feet to the

ground. He hung his head, sides bellowing in and out, the banked fires of malevolence still burning in his eyes.

Hunter took aim. A single shot between the eyes and it would all be over.

He took in one long breath, then let half of it out. His forefinger tightened, squeezing slowly and steadily on the trigger. In the notch of the rifle's site, the stallion stood hanging his head. Puffs of dust scudded outward as the horse exhaled through his distended nostrils.

"Mr. Hunter, sir!" yelled a voice across the lawn. "Wait!"

Hunter's concentration shattered. The stallion swung his head toward the noise and his front feet pawed the ground. Gritting his teeth in frustration, Hunter lowered the gun.

"What the hell is it, Noah?"

The mulatto boy was out of breath from running, and his eager face ran with sweat. His breeches were soaked from the knees down. He'd probably just left the launch at the plantation dock.

Noah's one passion in life was horses, not tobacco nor even, thus far, girls. Though only sixteen, he was regarded as a local expert at breeding and racing, and his small stature made him a talented and sought-after jockey. He had been nearly as excited as Hunter over the arrival of Finn, the Irish Thoroughbred.

"You mustn't put him down, sir. I know of a way to save him." Noah's face was pale and taut with earnestness.

Exasperated, Hunter climbed off the fence. "Noah, it's not possible, you know that. I've had the best trainers in Virginia down to have a look at him."

"But I heard tell of someone—"

"Son, there's no hope. Every one of the experts I consulted assured me the horse is ruined." He gestured at the shadowy dark beast in the pen. "His mind is gone. He probably injured himself during a storm at sea, so he could be ruined for racing anyway. No one can get close enough to examine him. I'm sorry," Hunter said. "I hate like hell that I have to do this."

"Then don't—"

"Damn it, you think I want to, boy? If this horse had a broken leg, you wouldn't want him to suffer. You'd want me to put him down, wouldn't you?"

"Yes, sir." Noah stared at the ground, his bare foot stabbing at the grass. "But listen—I been trying to tell you something."

"All right," Hunter said, setting the rifle aside, muzzle down. Each time he looked at Noah, he felt a piercing tenderness, for the boy was his kinsman. The son of Hunter's young cousin and an African laundress, Noah had grown up at Albion. He was an everyday reminder of the sweetness of first love—and of the bitter aftermath of forbidden passion. "Of course I'll listen, but my mind is made up."

"I was in Eastwick, at the drovers' club there, and I heard tell of a man at the eastern shore who can gentle any horse."

"I believe I heard from his advance man," Hunter said cynically, angry that someone would play upon the youth's hopes. "Would he be the one with the magical healing powder? Or maybe he's the one who wanted to sell me a book of incantations."

"No, this is for real. Honest and true!"

Hunter hesitated. Were it anyone save Noah he would dismiss the idea out of hand. But this was Noah, the boy he had educated when no school would have him, a horseman who had proved time and again that he had the head and heart for the business of racing horses.

Hunter took a long, hard look at the stallion. Once his dream, now his nightmare. Then he shouldered the rifle and walked with Noah away from the paddock. The ripening sun brought out the sweetness of lilacs and hyacinths in the air.

"His name is Henry Flyte, and he was horsemaster to Lord Derby in England. Grandson of *the* Lord Derby," he added, referring to the famous Englishman who had inaugurated the first running of the Derby Stakes at Epsom more than half a century before. "Henry Flyte trained Aleazar."

Hunter came to attention. The story of Aleazar was known throughout racing. The three-year-old had been bred out of the Royal Studs, but was declared unridable by the best trainers and jockeys in England. Then, seemingly out of the blue, Lord Derby had raced him at Epsom. The stallion had broken every record in memory, and Derby gave full credit to a trainer whose unusual methods had worked wonders on the horse. There followed some tragedy and upheaval, but it all happened when Hunter was a boy and he remembered no details.

"And the claim is," Hunter said, "this wonder of a trainer lives in Virginia now."

"It's what the drovers are saying." Noah shifted from foot to foot, clearly agitated. "Been here for years. They say he keeps to himself. He lives on an island across the marsh from Eastwick."

The low islands were lawless, dangerous places where shipwrecks happened, and not always by accident. The favored haunts of pirates and fugitives, the long, shifting islands had become the stuff of legend, featured in spooky bedtime stories and tall tavern tales.

Noah took a rolled pamphlet from his hip pocket and shoved it at Hunter. "His name's listed here in the *Far-*

mers' Register.'' He stabbed his finger at an article called
"The Horsemaster of Flyte Island." "Claims he tames
wild ponies for riding and farmwork."

"Why would such a gifted trainer leave Lord Derby's
Thoroughbreds for a herd of wild ponies?"

"I don't know," said Noah.

Hunter flipped through the yellowing pages. "This *Register* is two years old. How do you know the horsemaster
is still there?"

"How do you know he's not?" Noah's solemn, handsome face was drawn taut with intensity and pleading.
"He can save this stallion," Noah added. "I know it, I
do!"

"Son, a miracle wouldn't save this stallion." Hunter
turned back toward the paddock, angry that he was letting
himself be swayed by this earnest, hopeful youth. Earnestness and hope were alien notions to Hunter—for good
reason.

"Don't matter whether you put him down today or wait
until tomorrow," Noah persisted, an edge of anger in his
voice. "We got to go see the horsemaster."

"He'd have a chance to kill again." Hunter lengthened
his strides, thinking of the broodmare, dead because of the
crazed stallion's punishing hooves and wolf-like mouth.
He thought of the hired groom slumped against the well
house, cradling a crushed hand but thanking God he'd
been spared his life. "And what makes you think this
horsemaster would come to Albion for the sake of this
Thoroughbred?"

Noah hesitated. "They say he won't travel."

Hunter let loose with a bark of laughter. "Even better.
You're saying I have to go to him?"

Noah danced ahead in his agitation. "It could be done,
sir. I've thought and thought on it. You and I can drive

the horse into the squeeze and I'll get him blindfolded and muzzled. Then we'll get the drover's scow, the one with the pen. It's shallow draft. It can dock right here at Albion so we can use the penning chutes, and at high tide it can be poled over to the horsemaster's island."

The drover's scow plied between the low-browed peninsula that reached like a long, stroking finger down the eastern side of Chesapeake Bay and the mainland. Herds of horses, sheep and cattle grew fat on the rich salt grasses of the peninsula and islands, and each season drovers came eastward to pen them and bring them back across the water to market. But the drovers worked with tame livestock, not demonically possessed horses.

"It can work, sir," Noah said, his voice rising with desperation. "I know it can."

"Step aside, son," Hunter said in exasperation. "This is hard enough without you calling up all sorts of false hopes."

"Shoot him and you'll have a dead horse for certain. I ain't digging no grave for him," Noah said defiantly. "Take him to the horsemaster and you'll get your champion back. *Sir.*"

Hunter eyed the horse with its nervously twitching skin, all caked with mud and filth. The agent in Ireland had praised this stallion's coat and conformation, the depth of his chest and the breathtaking sight of him running at top speed. The horse had, the agent claimed, that elusive quality known as "heart."

"There's nothing but madness in this beast," Hunter said.

"Can you be sure of that?" Noah looked not at him but at the horse. Every muscle in the youth's compact, slender body was tense, as if he wanted to leap into the paddock and tame the beast himself. "Can you be sure entirely? Look at that beauty."

"I can be damned sure this horse killed an expensive mare and he'd do the same to you or me if we let him. He's ruined, Noah. I don't want that to be so, but it is."

Noah's head came up sharply as he confronted Hunter. "I never did ask you for much. You been good to me, I ain't denying that, and I count myself lucky. But now I got something to ask. Do this for me, sir. Sure as I'm your cousin's born son, give this horse a chance."

Not prone to displays of emotion, Noah swung away and snuffled, wiping his face on his voluminous sleeve. He faced the horse in the paddock.

Hunter's hand closed around the rifle stock. The oiled barrel had grown warm with the coming of the day.

And then he too looked at the stallion.

Two

Eliza Flyte's favorite time of day was evening, when the light of the setting sun fused the sea and sky into a single wash of color. The flood tide turned the salt marshes into a green, floating kingdom with the shorebirds gliding silently by to roost for the night. A breeze rippled through the beach grass and sea oats, and frogs and crickets started up, marking the end of another day.

At such moments, when the beauty of nature burst with such force across the island, she felt she had all the riches of the world. She liked the unspoiled wilderness and the safety of being completely alone.

She stood at the shore of the island, shading her eyes against the coppery glare of sun on sea, and watched the flight of the wild swans that had taken up residence in the reeds along the freshwater estuary that seeped into the Atlantic. Every bird in the sky, it seemed, chose to roost in these parts. She knew why they came, for this was a place apart from everything else, separated by time and tide and the mists that fogged it in so that it appeared to be drifting, unanchored to the rest of the world.

It was a safe haven for creatures whose only defenses were flight and camouflage.

The cry of the departing swans always sounded inexplicably sad. Eliza imagined the piercing *obligato* to be some terrible wordless lament for a lost mate, and the sound never failed to make her shiver.

She was about to turn away from the shore, to step over the tangle of trumpet vines and the dunes clad in beach heather, when another movement caught her eye. She noticed a flicker, low on the diffuse waterline, and she paused, squinting, holding herself tense, ready to flee.

Something was there, in the distance, coming from the lee shore. At first she thought it was a whale. She had seen one once, a finback strayed in from the briny deep to beach itself and die with a horrible exhausted shudder on the strand. For weeks afterward she had avoided the stinking blue-tinged carcass, and when a wild autumn storm skirred in and sucked the carnage back out to sea, she had wept with relief.

But she realized as it drew near that this new apparition was no whale. It was the drover's scow.

She recognized the low profile of the wooden craft from the old days, when her father would bring horses from the annual penning on Chincoteague Island. But no drover had visited Flyte Island recently. There was nothing here for him, nothing at all, and there hadn't been in a very long time.

A man worked on the deck of the scow, his brawny form silhouetted against the sky. Alarm spread through Eliza in a swift, silent wildfire, radiating out along limbs and spine and scalp, seemingly to the very tips of her hair. She responded with the same instinct as the wild ponies that ranged across the island. Her nostrils filled with the scent of danger, a thrill of panic quivered across her skin, and she fled.

She sprinted up the beach, vaulting over the wrack line

choked with refuse from the sea. Her bare feet were sound-less on the dunes, and she covered a hundred yards before reason took hold and she slowed her pace. In a grove of whispering cedar trees, she stopped running. Still breathing hard, she scrambled up the curved scarp of a dune that had been bitten away by the tides. The vantage point gave her a clear view of the shore.

What would a drover want here? Did he think to graze his sheep or goats on the island? It was well-known that the grazing was poor, and could only support a handful of animals. What wild ponies there were would not welcome an intrusion. Aggressive and territorial, the herd would close ranks against any outsider.

The ponies would be up on the high ground for the night, huddled together for protection. Sometimes when Eliza watched them, she felt a tug of yearning, for the animals lived in a herd, their society regulated by the turn-ing of the seasons and the sense of social order that seemed ingrained in the mares.

By watching the herd, Eliza had learned long ago that some animals were meant to live in groups. Living alone was unnatural, and the single, unconnected individual never survived for long. Perhaps people, like horses, were meant to live together too. But despite her loneliness, Eliza had never found any humans she wanted to live with.

She edged back out to the lip of the dune where it dropped off sharply to form a cliff. Her gaze tracked a meander of the marsh current. The tide had risen so that only the tips of the cordgrass showed, marking a passage deep enough for a flat-bottom vessel. The barge, rigged with two canvas sails, lurched awkwardly up the beach, propelled by a gust of wind and helped along by the drover's long pole. Then the craft beached itself upon a shoal of fine sand and crushed shell.

She wondered how in heaven's name he intended to correct such a haphazard landing. The pole came up, touching the top of the mast, and with a windy sigh the sails collapsed onto the deck, covering the tall-sided narrow pen in the middle.

Eliza stood perfectly still in the sweeping shadows of evening and watched while her heart sent her another message of danger. It took all of her will not to flee deeper into hiding.

A lone figure stood aboard the shallow-draft scow. The golden fire of sunset outlined his form in a strange flaming nimbus. He was a tall, broad-shouldered man wearing fitted trousers and a blousy shirt with sleeves so generously cut that they blew in the breeze. She could make out his silhouette, a sharp-edged shadow against the coppery sky, but was unable to discern his features. He seemed unnaturally big, a threat, as he cast down the two bowlines and stepped into the thigh-deep surf to secure the lines to an ancient, worn stump of heartwood.

Eliza mustered her courage on a breath of marsh-scented air, then descended the dune in a tumble of crumbling sand. She strode out to the beach, unconsciously tightening the rope that held her smock cinched around her waist.

The boatman struggled with the sails, pulling them to one side of the pen. He unhitched a long wooden plank, creating a walkway to shore. His movements were sharp and angry.

A frightened whinny came from the pen.

The sound raked over her senses, calling to her like the song of a siren. Her every instinct screamed warnings but that sound, above all others, cut through her timidity and brought her out of the shadows. She forced herself to go nearer the intruder. He straightened, rubbing at the small of his back. The movement alarmed her, and she fell still, waiting. She could hear him muttering under his breath. He had a low, mellow voice that seemed curiously at odds with the barely restrained violence of his movements as he hauled on the canvas.

From the tall-sided pen she could hear a thump, then another. And finally a low, eerie growl, unmistakably equine.

She hurried the rest of the way to the beach and stepped barefoot through the wrack line, where changing varieties of flotsam were heaved up by the tide. The tattered hem of her dress swirled in the surf.

"Are you lost?" she asked, raising her voice over the roar of the sea.

His shoulders jerked up in surprise. He turned to glare at her. She could tell he was glaring even though the sun behind him obscured his features. Shading her eyes and squinting, she was able to catch a glimpse of his face, and for a moment she felt disoriented, adrift, confused, because it was such a striking, cleanly made face. In her entire life she had met few people, but she knew that here was a man who happened to be gifted with an excess of beauty. He looked like Prince Ferdinand in her illustrated *Tempest*.

For some reason that disturbed her more than anything else she'd seen so far. With a face as idealized as any artist's fancy, he made a romantic sight; despite the circumstances, he possessed the sort of unsmiling demeanor of a man of great dignity and stature. He regarded her with a haughty aloofness, as if he lived in a kingdom not of this world.

But when he spoke, she knew he was very much of this world. "Is this Flyte Island?" he demanded, rude as any two-legged profane creature known as a man.

"It is," she said.

"Then I'm not lost." He yanked on the bowlines, testing them. "Who the hell are you?"

She cast a worried eye at the pen on the scow. "Who's asking?"

His shoulders, remarkably expressive for such a nondescript part of the anatomy, lifted stiffly in annoyance. He turned to her once again, a shock of fair hair plastered with sweat to his brow.

"My name is Hunter Calhoun, of Albion Plantation on Mockjack Bay." He paused, watching her face as if the name was supposed to mean something to her.

"Hunter. That's a sort of horse, isn't it?"

"It happens to be my name. I am master of Albion." His eyes—they were a strange, crystalline blue—narrowed as his gaze swept over her. At a thud from the barge, his brow sank into a scowl. "I've come to see the horsemaster, Henry Flyte."

The sandy earth beneath her feet shifted. Even now, after so much time had passed, the mere mention of the name disturbed her. He had been her world, the gentle-souled man who had been her father. He'd filled each day with wonder and wisdom, making her feel safe and loved. And then one day, without warning, he was gone forever. Gone in a raging blast of violence that haunted her still.

She felt such a choking wave of grief that for a moment she couldn't speak. Her throat locked around words too painful to utter.

"Are you simple, girl?" the intruder asked impatiently. "I'm looking for Henry Flyte."

"He's gone," she said, her small horrified admission stark in the salt-laden quiet of twilight. "Dead."

A word she'd never heard before burst from the man.

From the stormy expression on his face, she judged it was an oath.

"When?" he demanded.

"It's been nearly a year." Her pain gave way to anger. Who was this intruder to order her about and make demands, to pry into her private world? "So you'd best be off whilst the tide's up," she added, "else you'll be stranded till moon tide."

"He's been dead a year, and no one knew?"

She flinched. "Those that matter knew."

Hunter Calhoun swore again. He took out a hip flask, took a swig and swore a third time. "Who else lives here?"

"A small herd of wild ponies, up in the woods. Three hens, a milch cow, a dog and four cats, last I counted. More birds than there are stars."

"I don't mean livestock. Where's your family?"

A wave of resentment rose high, crested. "I don't have one."

"You're all alone here?"

She didn't answer. He drank more whiskey. Then, bending down, he fetched a long-barreled rifle. The scent of danger sharpened. Was he going to shoot her?

"What do you mean to do with that?" she asked.

He didn't answer. Instead, he cocked the gun and lifted the barrel toward the latch of the pen. With horror, she realized his intent. "Stop it," she said sharply. Animals were sacred to her, and she wouldn't stand by and see one slaughtered. "Don't you—"

"I've a mad horse aboard," he interrupted. "You'd best move aside, because when I open the gate, he'll escape, and I'll take him out."

Eliza stood her ground.

Scowling, Calhoun lowered the gun. "Without Mr.

Flyte's help, the beast is a mortal danger to anyone and anything. He's got to be put down, and it's best done here, in this godforsaken place.'' His haughty glare encompassed the marsh. Ever-softening light spread over the low ground, the placid water reflecting the rise of dunes and the forest beyond.

He paused for another drink of whiskey. Eliza scrambled aboard and grabbed the gun, using her finger to pry the shot out of the pan. "This godforsaken place, as you call it, is my home, and I'll thank you not to be leaving your carrion on the shore."

He wrenched the gun away, elbowing her aside with a hard, impatient nudge. He lifted the heavy latch to the pen. "Stand aside now. This horse is a killer."

Eliza burst into action, planting herself in front of the pen, her back flat against the gate. She could hear the heavy breath of the horse within, and she fancied she could feel its heat. The smells of hay and manure brought back waves of remembrance from the days when her father was alive. She let her emptiness fill up with fury.

"Who in God's name are you, that you think you can simply do murder right here in front of me?"

"Who the hell are you that you think you can stop me?" As he spoke, he touched the barrel of the gun to her shoulder, where a long tangle of her hair escaped its carelessly done single braid.

Though she'd unloaded the rifle, she stood frozen with fear. In an obscenely gentle caress, he used the barrel of the gun to move aside the lock of hair and the edge of her blouse with it, baring her shoulder.

"Darling," said Hunter Calhoun with a low, false endearment in his voice, "I've had a long, trying day. I'm armed with a deadly weapon. You don't want to cross me, not now."

She ignored him and battled the fear, closing her eyes as the sweet fecund aroma of horse and the sense of a big animal's warmth reached her, entered her, plunging down to her heart. She hadn't worked with a horse since her father had died, and she had sworn she never would again. But the magic was still there, the potency, the wanting.

She should walk away now, let him shoot this hapless beast and finish his whiskey flask. Her father's magical way with horses, legendary on two continents, had got him killed. Ignorant, superstitious men had gone on a witch-hunt after him.

But there was something the world didn't know. The magic had not died with Henry Flyte.

"Step aside, miss," Calhoun said brusquely.

She opened her eyes, put her hands on the cool gun barrel and shoved it aside. Then she turned and peered through the gaps in the pen siding. She caught vague glimpses, obscured by the movement of the scow and by the twilight shadows, of a proud head, arched neck and a cruel iron muzzle. An old rag blindfolded the animal. Moist sores ran with pus that coursed down the horse's cheeks, and he swayed with a sunken-ribbed hunger. The sight tore at her heart, and the pain she felt was the animal's pain. Rage at Hunter Calhoun made her bold.

"Was this horse mad before or after you muzzled and starved him?" she demanded.

"Look, I came here hoping to save him."

"Well done," she said sarcastically.

"It's no fault of mine he's in this condition," Hunter Calhoun said. "He came off the ship from Ireland crazed by a storm at sea. Killed a mare and nearly did in a groom before we were able to stop him."

"What did you need a horse from Ireland for anyway?"

"For racing and breeding."

The precise things that had given her father his start. Racing had elevated the horse, but it had also been responsible for unforgivable abuses.

"And you're absolutely certain this horse is ruined." Even as she made the comment, she realized his opinion didn't matter to her. She sensed the horse's fear—but she also knew that the fear could be penetrated.

"Look, I'm good with horses," said Calhoun. "Always have been. I can ride anything with hair, I swear it."

"Lovely."

"Horses are my life. This is the first one I haven't been able to handle."

"So you're going to shoot it. Do you deal with all your problems that way?"

"Damn it, I won't stand around and debate this with you, woman."

She turned away from him and peered through the slats of the pen. She saw the filth-caked coat shudder. An ear twitched, angling toward her. And then she felt it. An awareness. A connection. The stallion could feel her presence. He sensed she was different from the brute who had blinded and muzzled him.

She clutched the rough wood of the pen, battling her own instincts. Her need to reach out, to heal, was acute. For a moment, she felt very close to her father, who had taught her to respect all living things. The horse made a sound low in his throat, and in an odd way he seemed to be pushing her, forcing her toward a decision that could mean nothing but trouble.

The dilemma lay before her, demanding a course of action. If she healed this horse, she would unmask herself to the world. As they had in her father's day, ambitious trainers and jockeys would come calling, begging her to rehabilitate their badly trained stallions, and in the next breath condemning her as a necromancer.

"Get away. Now!" Hunter Calhoun tried to shoulder her aside. "You think I like doing this? I just want it to be over—"

"I can help you." The words rushed out of her, unchecked by reason. The sensible response would be to turn her back on this stranger and his abused stallion. But when it came to horses she had no will of her own.

Calhoun gave a short, sharp laugh, and in the pen the horse huffed out a startled breath.

"You can help?" he demanded.

Eliza felt torn. By revealing her secret ability, she would end her own self-exile. She would make herself vulnerable to the same ignorant prejudice that had killed her father. She wanted to curse this poor, damaged horse for forcing her to choose. Yet another part of her wanted to discover how the animal had been hurt, to bring him out into the light.

She took another look at the furious muzzled creature in the shadowy pen. Her special affinity, which had always been a part of her, gave her a glimpse of the tortured confusion that muddled the horse's mind. A wave of compassion swept over her.

"Aye." She used the old-country affirmative of her father.

"The horsemaster is dead. You said so yourself."

"I did. But his craft is still very much alive." She made herself look the intruder square in the eye. "I am Eliza Flyte. The horsemaster's daughter."

Three

❧❧❧

Hunter didn't know whether to laugh or curse. It was a minor wonder he had actually made it to this godforsaken place. Having grown up on a tidewater bay, he was a good seaman and knew the shoals and currents, but making the crossing to the barrier islands with a wild horse aboard a clumsy scow had not been easy.

Now that he had finally reached the island, this ragamuffin of a female claimed Henry Flyte was her father. Her late father. Unless Hunter wanted to go traipsing off around the island, he had no choice but to take her word for it.

"Eliza Flyte, is it?" He tasted her name, let it find its way over his tongue. It suited her, somehow. In her tattered brown smock and bare feet, she seemed wild and a bit fey, quite unlike anyone he had ever met before. A darkling girl, possibly of slave or Indian stock, she had a flawless complexion enhanced by the silkiness of her long eyelashes and the blue-toned sweep of her indigo-black hair. She had eyes of some indeterminate color beneath two dramatic slashes of eyebrow. The expression on the pale oval of her face was a mixture of annoyance and compassion—annoyance at him, and compassion for the murderous stallion in the pen.

When the breeze blew the dress against her legs, he saw that this was no girl. She lifted her face to the light, and he noted a woman's maturity in the clear, fine-boned features. And in her strangely light eyes, eyes the color of mist on the water, he saw a look that was a thousand years old.

She stood no more than thirteen hands high, the top of her head barely reaching his shoulder. Yet she claimed she could tame this horse.

She was a liar, a cheater, a marshland bumpkin taking advantage of him.

"How much do you want for your services?" he asked suspiciously.

She frowned, then said, "The life of this horse, no more."

"Right." He snorted in disbelief.

"Why would I lie?" she asked peevishly. "Do you think I came out here expecting to meet some whiskeyed-up planter and the horse he beat half to death?"

"I never—" He stopped himself. It was pointless to argue. He needed to do what he should have done first thing that morning instead of listening to Noah. He eyed the landing. The scow was positioned just right for the horse to exit down the ramp to the hard-packed sand of the long, lonely beach. Hunter could simply take aim, shoot and leave the carcass lying on the beach to be taken out with the next tide.

"So let's have a look at him," the woman said, a brisk bossiness in her voice now. She reached for the latch of the pen.

He pushed her hand away. "Haven't you heard a word I've said?" he demanded. "This animal is dangerous.

Now, stand aside." He grabbed his rifle and rammed the butt against his shoulder. "I need a moment to reload—"

A distinct sound interrupted him. He looked up in time to see his cartridges spin through the air, stark against the twilight sky, before plopping into the water about fifty yards out.

His first thought was one of amazement. He had never seen a woman throw so far. His second was one of fury. "No wonder you live like a hermit on this island. You're completely mad."

She flinched, a strangely animalistic movement, as if he had struck her physically. Then she glared at him, pain hardening into an anger to match his. "You are the one who can't seem to hear. You won't be shooting this horse."

He anticipated her move and stepped in front of the gate. She made a sound of exasperation and bent down. Complete disbelief held him immobile just long enough for her to grab him around the ankle. She pulled up sharply, surprising him with her strength. Arms wheeling in the empty air, he fell backward over the gunwale of the scow and landed in the chilly shallows.

While he sat, half stunned, in the silty muck, she climbed up and spoke quietly to the horse. Then she reached over the side of the pen and untied the blindfold. The iron muzzle fell with a thunk. She lifted the latch of the gate, drew aside the bolt and opened the pen.

Cursing, Hunter sprang up. The stallion clattered down the ramp, frantic hooves throwing up a spume of blue-green water. The animal raced ashore, a sleek dark shadow moving with amazing speed. Hunter's anger drained away as he stood knee-deep in water and saw, for the first time, the full power of the horse.

In a wave of strength and grace, the stallion ran across

the ribbon of the beach, loping along as if made of water, one movement flowing seamlessly into the next. The length of his stride and his quickness convinced Hunter that if the sea storm had not driven this horse to madness, he would have been a champion beyond compare.

Still, Finn's owners had sold him cheaply. Too cheaply. Perhaps he was mad from the start, and the agent in Ireland had failed to see that.

Something scuttled up Hunter's leg. He jumped, brushing at a pair of quick, busy crabs. Then he waded ashore, the heavy sand sucking at his boots. He still had murder on his mind, but the stallion was out of range. He would murder *her*.

Eliza Flyte watched him, her mouth quirking suspiciously close to laughter.

If she laughed, he would do worse than simple murder.

She laughed.

And he did nothing but drip, and rage. And glare at her. And despite the insanity of the situation, he laughed too.

He laughed because there was nothing left to do. Because he was a widower with two children he didn't know how to love, and a fortune he wasn't able to repair. Because he was considered a rebel among his peers. Because he was raised to be a wealthy Virginia planter and he had become something entirely different. Because losing the stallion would be the final nail in his coffin.

The thought sobered him utterly. The horse would die in the wilderness. Finn was a stable-bred horse that had been raised as artificially as an orchid in a glass house. The purchasing agent in Ireland had sworn the yard did all but chew the Thoroughbred's food for him. Such a creature had no notion of how to survive in the wild. The humane thing to do would be to hunt the poor animal down and put it out of its misery, but the very idea turned Hunter's stomach sour.

"Well," he said to the strange woman, who had finally managed to conquer her mirth and stood watching him expectantly. "You've certainly solved my problem for me. The horse'll starve and thirst to death on this island all on his own."

Her smile disappeared. Only when it was gone did he realize how attractive she was. She had full, moist lips and straight teeth, and a twinkle in her eye that hinted at a merry intelligence.

"I said I would tame him, and tame him I shall." She had a weird accent, a combination of Virginia's lazy drawl and something foreign, from the small shires of England, he guessed.

He regarded the chestnut shadow in the distance. The stallion was tossing his head and trotting to and fro, pausing now and then to browse in the odd spiky grasses that fringed the marsh.

"I see," he said sarcastically. "And I suppose after he gets tired of being on his own, he'll simply come knocking at your door."

"You're close to the truth," she said. "Horses are herd animals. They naturally want to join with you. It's their nature. Their instinct."

"He'll kill anything he encounters," he promised her. "You've let Satan out of hell."

She fixed him with an enigmatic stare. "Why do you assume his madness is a permanent state? That it can't be healed?"

His mind flickered to events of the past and then recoiled. "Experience has taught me so."

"Not me." She started walking away.

"Where are you going?" he called after her.

"Home. It's nearly dark and I'm hungry for my supper."

The mere mention of food made his stomach cramp with need. He'd had nothing but whiskey all day, and at last the hunger had caught up with him. He eyed the scow and then the evening sky. It was too late to sail for home tonight. He was marooned on this wind-harried island with the most bizarre young woman he had ever met.

"I'd be obliged for a meal," he said.

"I didn't hear myself invite you," she retorted, her voice growing as faint as her form in the distance.

He hurried to catch up to her. "I've money to pay."

She kept walking, didn't even glance at him. "I don't want your money."

He touched her arm. She yanked it away so quickly that she nearly stumbled over the vines snaking across the sand dunes. "Skittish, aren't you?" he asked, torn between feeling intrigued and annoyed.

"Why should I trust you?" she fired back. "You're a stranger. You've brought me a wounded horse, which you claim is not your fault, but how do I know you didn't beat him until he went insane?"

Hunter was nearly out of patience. He planted himself in front of her, stopping her. "You took one look at the horse," he said, "and you went all weird and misty-eyed, like you could read his mind. Take a look at me, Eliza Flyte." He glared down at her. "Take a real good look and tell me you see a man who beats horses and crosses dangerous waters in an old scow just for sport."

Her eyes narrowed, and in the flickering twilight he fancied he could feel her scrutiny probing at him. In the long, tense silence, broken only by the shudder of the wind and the lapping of the waves, he resisted the urge to squirm like a schoolboy.

"I don't know what I'm seeing," she said quietly. She gestured at the scow. "Have you any personal belongings you'll be needing for the night?"

"For the night?"

"You know, things. You're sleeping on the porch where I can keep an eye on you. So if you need something from your boat, get it now."

"There's only my gun," he said. "And without shot, it's no good to me at all."

She made no apology. "Come, then. You'll want to dry your clothes."

"I'll sleep on the boat," he said.

"The mosquitoes will drive you mad," she promised him. "And I have no experience restoring a man to sanity. Just horses."

Four

Eliza felt sick with nervousness as she made her way over the dunes to the path that led to the house. Since her father's death, no one had come to the island.

Henry Flyte had built the house more than twenty years ago. He had made it of materials salvaged from shipwrecks, and indeed it resembled a ship in some respects, with an observation deck on the roof and spindly rails around the porch. The dwelling had two rooms and a sleeping loft where she had passed each night since she was old enough to climb the ladder. Set upon cedar blocks, the house had a lime-and-lath chimney and sparse furniture, most of it salvage goods or fishing flotsam. An iron stove and a dry sink comprised the kitchen.

He had built it for her—a home. A refuge, a place of safety after he had fled the chaos of the royal racing circuits in England. Eliza had always suspected his self-exile had something to do with the circumstances of her birth, but he never spoke of it, and he'd died before she could wrest the whole story from him.

Now she lived alone in the house he had made with his own hands and shingled with layers of cypress. It had never been a beautiful home, not like the ones in the illustrations in their prized collection of printed engravings. But it was the place Eliza had always associated with love and comfort and safety. When she thought of home, she could imagine no other place but this.

Yet as she brought this angry, damp stranger home, she could not help but feel violated in some fundamental way, intruded upon. This aristocratic planter would judge her by what he saw, and while she shouldn't care what he thought of her, she found that she did.

Following the curving path, shaded by myrtles, they came to the old barn first. The burned-out stalls and paddock looked haunted, the charred timbers like an enormous black skeleton against the night sky.

"You had a fire here?" Hunter Calhoun asked. His voice sounded overly loud, almost profane, in the stillness.

"Aye."

"Was it recent?"

"Last year."

"Is that how your father died, then?"

She hesitated. He had been dead before the fires had started. But to spare herself further explanation, she nodded and said again, "Aye."

She led him around the end of the once-busy arena where her father's voice used to croon to the horses, coaxing them to perform in ways most men swore was impossible. A short sandy track led to the house built up on pier and beam to take advantage of the breezes and to protect it from high water in case of a flood.

A weathered picket fence surrounded her kitchen garden, tenderly green with new shoots and sprouts of beans, squash, corn, tomatoes, melons. Peering through the gloom, Eliza could just make out the friendly bulk of Claribel placidly chewing her cud. The milch cow flicked one ear to acknowledge them. She was down for the night, sleeping beneath an old maple tree with branches that swept low to the ground. From the henhouse came the soft clucking of Ariel, Iris and Ceres, the biddies settling for the night.

"You don't have trouble with cougars or wolves?" Hunter Calhoun asked.

"I've seen a few. But they don't come too near."

"Why not?"

Before she could answer, a horrible sound bugled from beneath the sagging porch of the house. A shadow detached itself from the gloom and streaked toward them.

"Shit!" Calhoun swung his rifle over his shoulder, preparing to use it like a club. "You picked the wrong damn time to throw away my cartridges."

"Caliban, no!" Eliza said sharply, unable to keep the amusement from her voice. "Heel, that's a boy."

The huge beast loped to her side and collapsed at her feet, peeping and quivering in ecstatic obeisance. Belly up, he resembled a small, uncoordinated pony.

"What the hell is that?" Calhoun lowered the rifle.

"That," Eliza said, dropping to her knees to give Caliban a friendly rub, "is the reason I don't worry about wolves and cougars." She got up and patted her thigh. The huge dog lumbered up and trotted along beside her. "He's part mastiff, part Irish wolfhound. Part horse, you'd think, the way he eats."

How odd, she thought, to be talking to another person. Other than the occasional trip to the mainland for supplies, her only companions had been animals. Hearing replies and questions in response to her was disconcerting. The nervousness seemed to bunch up in her throat, and she began to wonder if it had been a mistake to bring him here, into her world. But she had a natural inclination to heal wounded creatures, and something told her this man had wounds she could not see.

"Delightful," Calhoun said dubiously. "Any other surprises?"

She forced herself to swallow past the taut anxiety as she stood up. "Not unless you count Alonso and Jane. The fawn and the doe. They're both rather timid. Oh, and the cats—"

"Four cats," he said.

She nodded, intrigued that he had actually been listening to her earlier. "Miranda, Sebastian, Antonio and Gonzalo." She counted them off on her fingers.

"Why do all these names sound so familiar to me?" he asked.

"We stole them," she said simply. "From Shakespeare."

He gave a short laugh as realization dawned on him. *"The Tempest,"* he said. "Of course."

They reached the house as night closed over the island. So near to the sea, the darkness fell fast, like a pool of black poured over the inverted bowl of the sky.

"I'll just light a lamp, then," she murmured, striking flint and steel and holding the flame to the betty lamp at the base of the porch steps. Climbing the stairs ahead of her visitor, she felt overly conscious of her bare feet and the ankle-length smock brushing against the backs of her legs. What on earth was she doing, bringing this stranger into her house? She should have left him at the shore, or better yet, driven him off entirely.

She stole a glance at him, and the large, looming shadow behind her did little to allay her fears. She had seen the worst men could do, and now this stranger was upon her. How could she be certain he wouldn't turn feral on her?

"Why are you looking at me like that?" he asked.

"Because I don't trust you," she blurted out.

He laughed. "Woman, I don't blame you a bit. I haven't done a damned thing to earn your trust. But remember, you haven't earned mine either."

Affronted, she opened her mouth to protest, but he held up a hand. "You claim you're my only hope of helping the stallion. I've yet to see it. All you need to know right now is that I've got no possible interest in harming you."

She quelled a shudder of fear, then raised the lamp and showed the way inside. Neatness was her natural inclination, but somehow the painstaking order of the house seemed to add to its air of empty poverty. For a wild moment, she wished for a room full of abundant clutter, the way it had been when her father was alive. Since his death, she had brought a sterile order to the house, lining the precious few books up on the shelves, the wild cherry and muscadine grape syrups and beach-plum preserves in a neat row of jars in the kitchen, the bins of supplies carefully closed and stowed.

Her hand quavered as she hung the betty on a peg and turned to face her guest. Hunter Calhoun's presence seemed to fill the austere keeping room and kitchen to overflowing. She studied him by lamplight and could well imagine him the master of a place with the grand name of Albion, ordering slaves about and sipping mint juleps while his Negro grooms and jockeys spurred and whipped his racehorses into submission.

Pinching her mouth into a pucker of disapproval, she turned away. "I'll find you something dry to put on." Without waiting for a reply, she went to the old sea crate containing her father's belongings. The scent of him lingered there as if woven into the very fibers of the fabric: cedar and soap and a faint lovely essence that had no name—it was unique to her father. She told herself she should be used to the elusive fragrance by now. She should be prepared for all the memories that rushed over her when she caught that fine, evocative scent, but as always, it took her unawares. Tears scorched her throat and her eyes, but she conquered them, breathing deep and slow until the crippling wave of grief passed.

She rummaged in the trunk, shifting the contents. Her father had owned the silk breeches and blouses of a professional racing jockey, though now the clothes were outdated by decades. On the island he had worn a workingman's garb, and she never remembered him any other way. Her hand brushed a parchment-wrapped parcel. Only once had he shown her the contents. It was the yellow silk jacket he had worn when he'd ridden Lord Derby's stallion, Aleazar, to victory in the most important race in England, so long ago.

"That was the night you were made," he had once said.

She shut her eyes, remembering his pride as he'd told her of the race. He had always promised to tell her more about her mother, and why, bearing his infant daughter in his arms, he had suddenly taken ship for America. But he had died before the tale could be told.

Darting a glance over her shoulder at Hunter Calhoun, she drew her mind away from memories. She had a stranger in the house, and it wouldn't do to turn her back on him until she discovered just what he was about. With brisk, decisive movements, she selected a pair of brown homespun trousers and a white shirt. Closing the lid of the trunk, she shoved the clothing at her guest. "Here," she said. "You can put these on and hang your own things out to dry on the porch."

"Much obliged." He took the clothes, then stood waiting.

When she made no move, he did, bending slightly forward and peeling off his wet shirt. His damp chest was broad and deep, gleaming in the lamplight. When Eliza saw it, she experienced a peculiar knot of sensation low in her belly. Embarrassed, she realized that if she didn't turn away, he would simply undress right in front of her.

"I'll see about supper," she said, yanking the half curtain across the room, separating it into two parts. Her father had put up the curtain when she had come to him one day in her fourteenth summer, terrified, convinced she was dying.

"It's your estrous cycle. You've seen this happen with the mares," he had said simply.

"You mean I'm...in season? Like a mare?"

"Not quite like that. But...similar."

She remembered, with a rush of affection, how flustered he had been.

"It means your body is that of a woman," he'd explained awkwardly. "But not your heart, my daughter," he'd added. "Not yet."

And that day he had strung up the curtain, made of an old saddle blanket pierced by an awl, for privacy.

In the small corner kitchen, she opened the iron stove and pumped the bellows at the banked embers there. Coaxing a fine wood fire under the two iron plates, she put on the coffeepot and heated the skillet. Fixing a meal for someone other than herself gave her a faint but undeniable stab of pleasure. Why was that? she wondered. Why did it please her so to have company? Because she had been alone for so long, she decided. She would have been pleased to welcome Bluebeard himself, she was that pathetic.

With a flourish, Calhoun moved aside the curtain and affected a haughty bow, like a gentleman at a cotillion dance. Not that she had ever been to a cotillion dance, but she had certainly read of them in her favorite—her only—novel.

He was, she noticed immediately, a much bigger man than her father had been. The breeches were tight, outlining every curve and bulge of strong thighs and hips. The shirt pulled taut across his shoulders, and he had rolled back the sleeves to reveal large, muscular forearms. The arms of a workingman. Odd, she thought. He was a planter. He forced slaves to do all his work for him. Yet he lacked the lazy, limp-wristed physique that came from idleness.

"In the absence of a mirror," he said, "I have to judge by your expression that it's not a perfect fit."

"Um, my father was a rather small man." She hoped Calhoun would attribute the redness of her cheeks to the heat from the stove. To herself, she couldn't deny that the sight of him created a soft melting sensation inside her. She knew she was no different than she had been an hour before, but since meeting Hunter Calhoun she felt more... aware. More alive. More womanly. Because he was so...so manly. Nature had made them that way, she told herself, so why did she feel embarrassed? Flustered?

Living as she did, she knew the ways of horses and wild animals. She'd seen a stallion cover a mare with a strength and power that left her weak with awe. She had seen the strangely compelling mating of the ospreys, the rhythmic, almost violent beating of the male, the taut-throated response of the female. She thought she understood such things, but judging by the chaotic feelings churning inside her, she knew she was totally ignorant.

Calhoun took a flask from the pocket of his wet breeches and went outside, draping the pants and shirt over the clothesline strung across one end of the porch. Then he leaned back against the weather-beaten rail and tipped the flask, taking a long, thirsty pull.

Watching him through the screen mesh door, Eliza felt a small spark of shame, and hated herself for feeling it. There was no shame in being poor, in living simply. She harmed no one. But she couldn't help wondering what this man thought of her shabby little house, the abandoned outbuildings, the swaybacked milch cow in the yard.

She put the fish on to fry and stepped outside. Calhoun didn't turn, but kept staring out at the almost-dark sky, the pinpricks of stars and the moon riding low over the water.

"You've got a fine place here," he said.

She gave a sharp laugh. "Do I, now?"

"It's mighty peaceful."

"You just said it was godforsaken."

"But I'm getting drunk. The world always looks better to me when I'm drunk." He held out the flask to her. In the cool blue light of the moon, she could see that it was made of silver, engraved with the initials H.B.C.

"No, thank you," she said.

"It's good whiskey."

"I've no taste for spirits." She folded her arms, feeling awkward.

He took a deep breath. "Something smells good."

"The fish. Come inside. It should be ready." She tried to steady her jittery hands as she served him the coffee and a plate of onions, potatoes and fillets of rockfish browned in butter. "Caught it this morning," she said.

He ate ravenously, yet with a curious refinement of manners. At least, she thought, he had good manners. He used a knife and fork rather than fingers, and didn't wipe his mouth on his sleeve. Despite his claim that he was getting drunk, he ate with steady concentration, polishing off the meal and the coffee quickly.

The kettle shrieked in the silence. Eliza jumped, then covered her reaction by getting up to brew a pot of tea. She made tea every night of her life, yet for a moment she simply stood in front of the stove, her mind a blank. Only by force of will did she remind herself to take down the packet of tea leaves from Eastwick, add them to the pot along with the boiling water and return to the table.

She gave him tea from her black basalt tea service. He picked up a shiny cup, holding it to the light. "Where the devil did you get this?"

"Father salvaged it from a wreck years ago."

He studied the mark on the underside of the pot. "This was designed by Josiah Wedgwood."

"Who's he?"

"A famous potter in England from the last century. This is probably priceless."

"I always thought it was just a teapot." She ducked her head and took a bite of her food.

"I guess you don't get many visitors," he said.

"I don't," she said simply.

"Gets lonely here, then."

His comment put her on edge again, reminding her that she was alone with a man she did not know. She chewed slowly, unwilling to admit how true his words were. When her father was alive, they'd had visitors from time to time. Folks came from far and wide, bringing their ill-trained but high-spirited horses for him to tame, and most of them left proclaiming him a miracle worker. Once a year, her father offered up a pony or two culled from the island herd. People in need of workhorses prized the ponies her father trained.

Most of the wild ponies were brutally beaten into submission by ignorant farmhands. But Henry Flyte, who had once gentled the finest racehorses in England, treated the island ponies with the same patience and care he had used with the Derby winners.

After his death, no one came. Everyone assumed that Henry Flyte had taken his magical touch to the grave with him.

Eliza alone knew there was no magic in what her father did. There was simply knowledge and gentleness and patience. He had raised her with the same principles, schooling her in the evenings and by day, teaching her the ways of horses and wild things. Her earliest memory was of lying by his side on a sand dune, their chins tickled by dusty miller leaves while they watched a herd of ponies.

"See that dappled mare?" he'd whispered. "She's in charge of the herd. Watch how she runs off that yearling stallion." The younger pony had approached with an inviting expression, mouth opened to expose the lower teeth, ears cocked forward. The mare had rebuffed the advance with a flat-eared dismissal.

Eliza had been fascinated by the display. The horses performed an elaborate, ritualistic dance. Each movement seemed to be carefully planned. Each step flowed into the next. The mare lowered her head, menacing the interloper even while capturing his attention. Each time she drove him off, he came back, contrite, ready to obey.

"That's all we need to do," Henry Flyte had explained. "Make him want to be part of our herd."

She stabbed a bite of potato with her fork. "Aye," she said to Hunter Calhoun. "Aye, it's lonely here."

"Then why do you stay?"

"I can leave anytime I want," she said defensively.

He scraped the last of the potatoes and onions from the pan. "And where would you go if you left?"

She hesitated, thinking that it would somehow diminish her dream if she confessed it to a stranger. The dream was hers and her father's. She refused to tarnish it by confessing it to this haughty off-islander.

She set down her fork. Turning the subject, she said, "What is the name of your horse?"

"Sir Finnegan. He's registered in the Dorset books that way. His damned pedigree doesn't matter now, though. I'll have to track him down and shoot him tomorrow. He's mad, and he's a menace."

"Why do you keep saying that?"

"I saw him kill, saw him cripple a good man's hand."

"But you brought him here," she pointed out. "You must have had some hope that he could be saved."

"I let my cousin's boy persuade me that your father was some sort of wizard with horses. Shouldn't have listened to him, though." He took a gulp of tea. "How big is this island, anyway?"

"Half a day's walk, end to end."

"I'll go looking for the horse in the morning," he said. "The infernal creature ran off as if the ground were on fire. Might take me a while to hunt him down."

"A creature's only lost if you don't know the right way to find him," Eliza stated.

He blinked as if her explanation startled him. "That's a hell of a thing to say."

"Let me show you something." Pushing back from the table, she raised the flame of the lantern and set it on a high shelf where she kept her books, a collection of lithographs and a packet of old farming journals. Taking down one much-thumbed tome, she set it on the old wooden crab trap she used as a table. Flipping open the heavy book, she paged through the text until she found what she was looking for. "'The horse is aware of you,'" she read aloud, "'though he doth appear indifferent, and will with a show of like indifference desire to attach to you.' That's from *On Horsemanship*."

"Xenophon's text."

She felt a cautious smile touch her lips. "You've read it?"

"In the original Greek." Haughty and boastful as a drawing-room scholar, he stood up, running his finger along the spines of her books. "I've also read Fitzherbert and John Solomon Rarey and the letters of Gambado." He angled his head to inspect more titles. "You're well-read for a—" He caught himself. "You're well-read."

"For a pauper," she said, filling in for him.

"It's unusual for any woman to quote from Xenophon."

"The texts on horsemanship were brought by my father from England."

"Where did these other books come from?" Calhoun asked.

"Father salvaged a few pieces of the King James Bible and one Shakespearean play from a shipwreck. There were many more, but the water spoiled them." She had been very small the day he'd brought the surviving volume up from the shore. She had a vivid memory of her father stringing a line across the yard and hanging the book with its pages splayed open. She'd begged him to teach her to read that day, and he had given her a smile so filled with pride and affection that the memory was imprinted forever on her heart.

That very night, he had begun reading *The Tempest* to her. The tale of a father and daughter stranded on an island after a shipwreck had become, in her mind, a gilded mirror of their lives. Her father was Prospero, the wizard, bending wind and weather to his will. She, of course, was Miranda, the beautiful young woman awaiting her true love.

We are such stuff as dreams are made of, Prospero said

in the play. And she had embraced the truth of it with her whole heart. But believing in dreams did not prepare her for the discomfiting reality of encountering a man like Hunter Calhoun.

"This other one is my newest," she said, showing him. "*Jane Eyre* was a special gift my father brought me from the mainland last year. I've read it four times already."

"I never thought much of lady novelists."

She sniffed. "Then you probably haven't thought much at all."

"And how many times have you read the Shakespeare?" Calhoun asked.

"I've lost count. *The Tempest* has been my main companion for years." She hesitated, then decided there was no harm in admitting her fanciful view of the play. "I used to imagine my father and I were Prospero and Miranda, stranded on their island." She flushed. "I used to wait on the shore after a storm had passed, to see if a prince might wash up on the beach, like Ferdinand in the story."

He leaned back, hooked his thumb into the waist of his pants and sneered at her. "Honey, believe me, I'm no prince."

"I'd never mistake you for one." She put *The Tempest* and *Jane Eyre* back on the shelf. "All I know of the world is what I've read in these books."

"How do you know they're showing you the world as it is?" he asked.

She ducked her head, conscious of his physical proximity and oddly pleased by his interested questions. "I don't know. Does it matter?"

"'Course it matters. It's not enough to understand something in the abstract. Life is meant to be lived, not read about."

She pressed her hand against the row of books, stopping when she reached *The Tempest*. "Is it better to read of Antonio's bitter envy and jealousy, or to feel it myself? What about Caliban's rage and madness? He was a perfectly miserable monster, you know."

His mouth quirked—almost a smile. "I know." He took down the fat calf-bound volume of *Jane Eyre* and flipped through the crinkly pages. "Do you never wonder what Mr. Rochester felt, being reunited with Jane after all those years?"

She gave a little laugh. "You said you didn't think much of lady novelists."

"Not the bad ones, anyway." He replaced the volume and stood back, surveying the collection. "So you have been raised by a horsemaster and his books."

"I have."

"You never missed having friends? Neighbors? Folks to call on you?"

"My friends and family are the birds and wild ponies and animals that have no fear of me." Her cheeks grew hotter still. She felt so gauche and awkward in the presence of this plantation gentleman. "You must think I'm strange."

He gave her a look that made her shiver. "I do, Miss Eliza Flyte. Indeed I do."

He made her want to run and hide. Yet at the same time, she felt compelled to stand there, caressed by his scrutiny.

The strange heat she had been feeling all evening spread through her and intensified. She had the most peculiar premonition that he was going to touch her...and that she was going to let him.

A distant equine whinny pierced the air.

Eliza felt the fine hairs on her arms lift. The lonely,

mournful wail of the stallion severed the invisible bond that had been slowly and seductively forming between her and Calhoun. She stepped sharply away from him. "You can bed down in that hammock on the porch," she said tersely. "And it's only fair to warn you—I sleep with a loaded Henry rifle at my side."

Five

When Hunter awoke the next morning, the sun was high and the crazy woman was nowhere in sight. He lay in a sailor's hammock strung across one end of a rickety porch, feeling the warm sting of the sun on his arms and smelling the fetid sweetness of the marsh at low tide.

He'd slept surprisingly well, considering the rough accommodations. She had lit a small fire in an iron brazier on the porch, laying lemon balm leaves across the coals, and the smoke kept the mosquitoes away. The night sounds—a cacophony of frogs and crickets and rollers scudding in from the Atlantic—created an odd symphony he found remarkably soothing. He usually needed a lot more whiskey to get himself to sleep.

He could hear no movement in the house, so he got up and went inside. Opening a stoneware jug in the dry sink, he discovered fresh water and took a long drink. Then he went to check his clothes, finding them stiff with salt, but dry. He dressed, his mind waking up to the fact that a peculiar woman had turned his horse loose on this deserted island, and that he had been powerless to stop her. Today he'd have to sail the scow home empty.

He tried to blame Noah, but none of this was the boy's

fault. Noah could not have known the horsemaster was dead and that his daughter had lost her wits.

Worse, he would have to face Blue. He'd have to explain to his son that he had not been able to save the stallion.

Muttering under his breath, he found his hip flask and wrenched off the cap. Empty.

"Shit," he said, then drank more water and stepped outside. If she wasn't anywhere in sight, he wasn't going to waste his time looking for her.

Broad daylight didn't improve the place. If anything, the poverty and ruin of Eliza Flyte's settlement glared even more sharply. The little broken-back house and the burned-out barn resembled a scene in the aftermath of battle—lonely, eerie, abandoned. Yet despite the desolation, a closer examination revealed that someone actually lived in this place. She had added small, halfhearted touches here and there—a jar of wildflowers on the kitchen windowsill, a glass deck prism hung from the eaves to catch the sunlight, a row of martin houses high on posts in the trampled yard.

He followed a sandy path past an old arena shaded by a tall red cypress tree. Presumably this was where the fabled horsemaster had worked his spells. Now the splintered fence rails hung askew, and thick-leafed groundsel spread lush tentacles across the ground and up the posts. Fallen beams that had once held up a sail canvas sunshade lay collapsed in the middle. A smaller arena appeared to be in better shape, the rails lashed in place and the sailcloth stretched overhead, shading a full rain barrel.

As he continued along the winding path toward the sea, Hunter wondered what he could have been thinking, allowing himself to be persuaded to bring the stallion here. What a fool's errand it had been. What a waste of time.

The horse was a menace. It needed to be shot.

It was not a duty he embraced, for the truth was, he loved horses. He always had. Against all caution, good sense and advice from well-meaning neighbors, he'd made the breeding and racing of Thoroughbreds his life.

Necessity, as much as desire, had dictated the change. His father, the master of Albion, had left the tobacco plantation to his first-born son. Hunter had expected the legacy. From the day of his birth he had been groomed for it. By the age of eight, he knew the worth of a peck of tobacco on the Richmond exchange. By the age of eleven, he knew how many pickers were needed to bring in a crop.

The only thing he hadn't been prepared for was bankruptcy. When the will was read and all the dust settled, Hunter discovered something his father had concealed for years: Albion was swamped by debt. The once-prosperous tobacco plantation teetered on the verge of collapse.

Everyone had expected him to either go down with the plantation like the captain on a sinking ship, or to cut his losses, take what he could salvage and rebuild.

But to the amazement of the Tidewater plantation society, and to the consternation of his wife and her family, he did neither. He appalled them all with his actions. Before the small-eyed, hated trader came to sell off the slaves of Albion in order to pay pressing debts, Hunter set each one of the slaves free. Hunter's father-in-law, Hugh Beaumont, had shrieked that the servants and field-workers were worth a small fortune as chattel, but nothing as free people.

What could Hunter have been thinking?

He knew setting them free was foolhardy, yet the day he signed the stack of manumission papers, Hunter had felt ten feet tall. His father-in-law had accused him of going insane, but Hunter had simply turned away and called in an estate agent to auction off some of the remote tobacco fields and furniture.

When all was done, he was left with a huge, half-empty house and a handful of ex-slaves who stayed on out of old age, infirmity or loyalty. In addition to the house, he kept the barns, the paddocks and acreage in the high meadows suitable for pasturing.

He remembered the day he'd told Lacey what he intended to do with Albion. He and his wife had sat together in the still-elegant parlor; the estate liquidators had not yet come to seize the Waterford candlesticks and chandeliers, the Heppelwhite chests, the Montcalme harpsichord and Aubusson carpets. His voice low and deep with excitement, Hunter had finally confessed his life's ambition. He told his wife that he wished to make a new start and turn Albion into a Thoroughbred breeding and racing farm.

She had laughed at him. He'd recognized the merry, girlish laugh that had captivated him when he was a boy, only this laugh had a harsh edge of desperation. "Darling, you can't mean it. Making a horse farm will take far more money than you have, and years of work. And you've just set all your laborers free."

Her lack of belief in him struck hard. He had looked down at his large, pale hands, holding them to the light and splaying the fingers wide. "Sweetheart, these hands have held the reins of the finest horseflesh in Virginia. They've cradled bottles of wine worth more than some men earn in a lifetime. They've been dealt hands of cards that won or lost a small fortune. And they've loved you with all that I am for eight years. The one thing they've never done is a day of hard, honest labor." He turned them palms up, studied his long fingers as if they belonged to someone else. "Right now, these hands are the only thing

I can truly claim as mine. So I reckon I'd better get used to the idea of doing the work myself.''

Lacey Calhoun had wept, certain her husband had lost his mind. She had begged him to consider their young children, Belinda and Blue, and what this would do to their position in society. But Hunter had stood firm. For once, he was going to go after something he truly wanted. For the first time in his life, the dream belonged to him. Not to his father or to the other planters, to his neighbors or Lacey's family, but to him.

Lacey had not understood. Hysterical, she had run from the room to pack her things. Then she'd taken the children to her father's house, refusing to see Hunter until he regained his senses.

That day had marked the end of their marriage. He hadn't noticed it at the time, of course, because he had given himself, to the last inch of his soul, to the new enterprise. He'd worked like a madman on stables, arena, round pen, racing track, starting gates. Working side by side with Noah, he had sought out broodmares and studs—bargaining, borrowing, buying, breeding and praying his luck would hold. Slowly, as time passed, things began to happen. His horses won races. He received invitations to run his horses at Clover Bottom, Metairie and Union Course. Breeders from Virginia and Maryland, Tennessee and Kentucky sought out his studs. The foals out of his mares were considered to be among the best in racing. He inaugurated an annual yearling sale at Albion.

But as he gained a hold on the racing world, he lost it on his wife. The daughter of Albion's nearest neighbor, Lacey had been groomed to be a planter's wife and had no idea how to cope with a husband who worked like a man possessed and didn't seem to care whether or not he profited from his labors. The tobacco culture, which made up her world, no longer welcomed Hunter Calhoun. Planters looked down on him, branding him a brawler, a gambler, a horse racer. If he'd grown wealthy from his enterprise, they would have changed their minds, but despite the success of his horses, the expenses always outpaced the profits. He should have known the change would be too much for Lacey. But he had been naively certain she would come to believe, as he did, that there were better ways for a man to live his life than employing slave labor to grow a weed that would make him rich.

By that time, it was too late to win Lacey back. He tried—Lord, he tried—but to no avail. His pleas and promises fell on deaf ears. His reminders of their marriage vows and their duties to the children were met with stony silence. He had humiliated her in front of the society that meant everything to her, an unforgivable offense. Never once did Lacey crack, never once did she allow herself to show a flicker of feeling for the man she had pledged to love until the day she died.

Then she had died, in the most hideous possible way, leaving the shattered wreckage of a broken family in her wake—a husband whose only solace lay in a dented silver flask of whiskey, a son whose soul had been sucked away by shock and grief and a daughter who was too young to understand anything except the fact that all the joy had gone from her life.

The prospect of repairing his fortune became the only thing that gave shape and meaning to Hunter's future. Importing the swiftest Irish Thoroughbred on record should have been the culmination of his ambitions. Deemed a bad foal-getter, Finn was undervalued, and Hunter's agent in Ireland had acquired him at a low price. Even so, it had cost him all the proceeds of his first yearling sale, and he could not afford to insure the animal through Lloyd's. He had not once paused to consider that a disaster could befall the horse on the voyage from Ireland.

By the time Hunter breasted the broad dunes facing the southeastern end of the island, he had worked himself into a black and thirsty mood. The need for whiskey sharpened to a gnawing hunger in his gut, and until he reached Albion he had no way to assuage it.

At the high tide line, he reached the scarps in the dunes, forming cliffs where heaved-up surf had clawed into the sand. The roots of sea oats dangled in a dense snarl from the underlip of the cliff. Hunter stood at the crumbling edge, scanning the shore for his scow. He could make out the shadow of a cove, and noticed that the sea changed color not far offshore, indicating a decent deepwater anchorage.

Pirates had probably haunted this place long ago. All Virginians had been raised on stories of Bluebeard, who had visited the islands, leaving at least one wife on Assateague. This island was a place where people with secrets might come. He wondered what Henry Flyte's secret had been.

As he surveyed the landscape, a movement on the beach below caught his eye.

In a dazzle of sunshine, Eliza Flyte walked along the broad ribbon of sand. Her bare feet left a trail of imprints. She moved slowly, though a curious sense of purpose marked her demeanor. She was strange indeed, with her bare ankles and tattered skirts, and thick, indigo hair pulled back in a long tail. She was as slender as a girl, and at first glance yesterday he had mistaken her for one. One look at her full breasts and curving hips had disabused him of that notion. She was no girl, but a woman. A crazy woman, alas.

In one hand she carried a loose length of rope, and she held a halter looped over her shoulder.

He was about to call out, but then he caught another movement at the edge of his field of vision. His jaw dropped. It was the stallion, a huge rust-colored shadow trailing in her wake.

A single thought streaked through his mind. The horse was a killer.

Half running, half falling down the slope of the dune, Hunter raced toward the beach. He had seen what the stallion could do. The woman had no idea of the danger she courted. Hunter wished he had his gun, but the fool woman had drowned all his shot. He had to make do with yelling, waving his arms as he ran down the hill.

Both horse and woman turned to him at the same moment. The stallion whistled and snorted, then reared and landed with front feet splayed, ready for battle. Eliza Flyte regarded Hunter with fury in her eyes. The horse tossed his head to one side, and Hunter feared he would attack her.

He redoubled his speed, pausing only to pick up a length of driftwood. He flung it with all his might at the horse. He missed, but the stallion broke and ran. Hunter released a sigh of relief, but he knew the danger wasn't past. He had to get Eliza Flyte to safety.

"This way," he yelled, grabbing her arm and pulling her toward the dunes. "For Chrissake, hurry!"

She pulled back, her strength surprising as she wrenched free of him. "Are you mad?" she demanded. "I almost—"

"I'm not the crazy one around here." He reached for her again.

She feinted away. "It took me half an hour to get him

this far,'' she snapped. ''Now you've spooked him and I'll
have to start all over again.''

He cast a look at the horse. Finn stood tensely some
yards away. His skin twitched, and his tail flicked nervously over his flanks. His nostrils were distended, eyes
wary.

''I've seen what this horse can do,'' Hunter said. ''I
won't stand by and watch him attack you.''

''He won't attack me.''

''Damn it—''

''Look.'' She edged away from him as if fearing he'd
try to touch her again. Her long hair twitched in a manner
that reminded him of the horse. ''Give me a chance with
this horse. That's all I ask. Just a chance.''

''No. It's too dangerous.''

''Please,'' she said, her anger draining away to desperation. ''I need to try. Just let me try.''

He didn't know why she moved him. What was she,
anyway, but a strange hermit woman with crazy ideas?
Yet he found himself softening, relenting. ''I'll wait
there,'' he said, pointing to a gnarled, budding tree at the
edge of the marsh. He stooped and picked up the stout
piece of driftwood. ''And if he goes on the attack, so will
I.''

''But you have to promise you won't unless I call for
your help.''

He hesitated. Then, surprising himself as well as her, he
said, ''I promise.''

She didn't smile, though her eyes shone in a way he
shouldn't have noticed, but did. ''I hope you have a lot of
patience,'' she said, hefting the rope over her shoulder.
''You're going to need it.''

Hunter waited quietly in the shadows, feeling the wind
dry the sweat on his face. He was convinced he'd have to

save Eliza Flyte from herself, from her own fool notions. He was amazed at how scared he'd been, seeing her stalked by that horse. He was even more amazed that she'd convinced him to let her try her weird training again.

Walking along the beach as if just taking a stroll, she completely disregarded both Hunter and the horse. The stallion turned at an angle, but Hunter could tell Finn was watching her with one wary eye. She continued walking, elaborately and disdainfully ignoring him. Like an inquisitive child, the stallion sidled closer.

Hunter's fist closed around the makeshift club. Instinct told him to act quickly, spook the horse, but he forced himself to stay still. And watchful.

The horse moved closer and closer, inexorably drawn to the woman walking along the empty beach. Hunter could relate to that level of curiosity even as the tension churned in his gut. He tried not to think about the hired groom almost fainting from the pain in his shattered wrist.

The horse closed in near her shoulder. She sent Hunter the swiftest of looks, warning him not to interfere. His muscles quivered with the urge to act.

Eliza turned, quite calmly, and made a shooing motion with the rope. Snakelike, the rope sailed through the air and dropped on the sand. The horse immediately shied back, pawing the sand and dipping his head in irritation.

But he didn't spook the way he had when Hunter had run at him. He wondered why Eliza would do that with the rope. Why provoke a dangerous animal? What was she thinking?

She continued walking, unconcerned. She reached a tall brake of reeds where the sand disappeared into the spongy estuary leading to the marsh. Making a wide turn, she headed back the way she had come, staying on the beach.

To Hunter's surprise, the horse followed her, though he gave her a wide berth.

After a few minutes, the stallion approached her obliquely again, and again she shooed him away, flicking the rope in his direction. She behaved like an exasperated mother flapping her apron at a wayward child. And like the wayward child, the horse never did lose interest, but kept trying to move in closer. They repeated the bizarre exchange several times more, always with the same result.

Then, with her shoulders square and her eye fixed on the horse, she moved abruptly toward the stallion.

Her motion alarmed Hunter. He took a step forward, then remembered his promise and made himself stop. Finn cantered in a tight loop, his attention fixed on her. Hunter expected him to disappear, but instead, he loped around and came back again. She kept pushing, taunting, startling him into flight over and over again. She never looked away from the horse, and the horse never looked away from her. It was an intricate dance of aggression and surrender, the partners intent on one another. The fascination was mutual.

Hunter kept expecting her to call for help, because the horse had moved in too close for comfort. Then he realized, with a start, that Eliza was controlling the situation completely. She dictated when the horse could come near, and when she wanted him to flee. There had to be a point to her actions but he couldn't quite decide what that point was. She had the posture of ritual—the fierce attention of her stare, the dignified stance of her body, the solemn flick of her arm shooing him away.

After a few minutes, her gaze underwent a subtle change. Rather than staring so intently into the horse's eyes, she looked away once. Then twice, thrice. The horse's cantering slowed. It flicked back one ear. Still he feinted, but the loops he ran were tighter; he came back more readily. His head dropped a little, and Hunter could see his jaw working.

Each time the stallion approached her, he became bolder. Each time she shooed him away, he came back again. To Hunter, it resembled a subtle flirtation of sorts. She was clearly interested, yet full of disdain. The stallion played the ardent suitor, persistent, refusing to be put off, yet not gregarious enough to force himself on her. There was a curious grace in the interplay between girl and horse.

Perhaps she was stranger, even, than Hunter had originally thought.

Then, right before his eyes, the dance changed from a wary flirtation to a tentative partnership. The stallion stayed at her side now, his muzzle practically nudging her shoulder. They walked along side by side, their pace unhurried and their steps oddly synchronized, as if they were moving together to the same silent music.

Hunter started to relax a little. The horse perceived no threat from the woman, so he posed no menace to her. When Eliza Flyte turned, the stallion turned. When she quickened her pace, so did the horse. When she slowed down, he did the same. And finally, as if it were the most natural movement in the world, she stopped walking and touched the horse, her hand resting at the side of his head.

Hunter heard her whoa across the broad stretch of beach. The horse halted. Hunter froze, held his breath. He couldn't have taken his eyes off her if he'd wanted to. But he didn't want to. He was as much her prisoner as was the horse. Finn's ears flickered but he didn't pull back, and she didn't take her hand away.

She turned her body toward the stallion, though she held her gaze faintly averted. He dropped his head, submitting with something almost like relief. His muzzle hung so low to the ground that he probably inhaled grains of sand into his nostrils. The pose of submission looked incongruous on the big horse.

The girl, like an angel, ran her hand down the length of the horse's head. Even from a distance, Hunter could see the stallion's shivered reaction to that gentle caress, and it had a strange impact on him. He felt Eliza's hand on the horse as if she had touched him. It was absurd, but he found himself so captivated by her that he wanted that caress for himself.

It was an unorthodox way to train a stallion, one Hunter had read about in the writings of the great horsemaster, John Solomon Rarey. He had never thought the method could be put to practical use, but the mystical ritual had taken place before his eyes.

She had made the stallion want her—to be near her, to be touched by her.

Hunter lowered himself to the ground, looping his hands loosely around his drawn-up knee. He wondered what she would do next.

Just then, a flock of gulls rose as one from the shallows. Their wings flashed white against the sky and they made a sound like a gust of wind. The horse panicked, rearing so high that his hooves nearly struck Eliza in the head. Hunter roared out a warning, leaping up and running toward her.

She calmly stepped away. The horse landed heavily, then twisted his big body and galloped away toward the thicket behind the dunes.

"You're crazier than the horse is," Hunter said, his nerves in shreds. "I won't have any part in this. I'm leaving with the morning tide."

Eliza appeared not to hear him as she coiled the rope

carefully. "That's enough for today anyway," she said. "There's always tomorrow. Best not to rush."

"You might not be able to find him tomorrow."

She shaded her eyes and looked up at the rise of the dunes. The stallion turned, showing his profile, and reared against the sky, a whinny erupting from deep within him. Then, with a flick of his tail, he was gone.

"He'll be back," Eliza said.

Six

Eliza set out some of last autumn's apples she'd preserved in a charcoal barrel. In the morning she slipped out
early to find that they'd been eaten. She tried to quell a
surge of excitement, reminding herself that her father's
first rule was to work at the horse's pace, peeling away
his fears layer by layer rather than trying to rush things.
There were more good horses ruined by haste than by any
sort of injury, she reminded herself.

In the half-light she inspected the training facility that
had been the hub of her father's life. It was sad, seeing it
like this, broken, burnt and neglected. He had died here,
she thought with a shudder. He had died for doing the
precise thing she was about to do.

The area inside the pen was overgrown with thistle and
cordgrass. She would have to spend the day clearing it.
Backbreaking but necessary work. Perhaps Hunter Calhoun would be of some use after all.

The thought of her unexpected visitor seemed to have
summoned him, for when she untied the halter and turned
to pull the gate, he stood there, behind her.

He discomfited her. There was no other word for it.
Wearing his own clothes rather than the ill-fitting ones

he'd worn yesterday, he managed to appear as broad and comely as a storybook prince, with the breeze in his blond hair and his sleeves rolled back to reveal the dark sun-gold of his forearms. On closer inspection she saw that a golden bristle shaded his unshaven jaw, but that didn't make him less striking. It only served to soften the edges of his finely made cheeks and jaw, and added to his appeal.

She had never heeded her own looks. She'd never taken the time to make sure her dress fit nicely or her hair was properly curled and pinned. Living on the island with her father, and lately all on her own, made such vanities seem unimportant.

But now, feeling the heat of this man's stare upon her, appearances were everything. Absolutely everything. She wanted to shrivel down into the ground like a flower too long in the sun. She found herself remembering a group of gentry that had accompanied the drovers to the island to buy ponies from her father one year. They'd made a holiday of it, much as people did on penning day up at Chincoteague to the north. She was twelve, and until that day she had not known a girl wearing breeches and hap-hazardly cropped hair would be considered anything un-usual.

But as she walked past the freshwater pond where the herd of ponies grazed, she became aware of a hush that swept over folks as she walked by, followed by a buzz of whispers when she passed.

"I never knew Henry Flyte had a boy," someone said.

The dart had sunk deep into the tender flesh of her vanity. She recalled actually flinching, feeling the sting between her shoulder blades.

"That's no boy," someone else declared. "That's the horsemaster's daughter."

That day, Eliza had stopped wearing trousers. She had

painstakingly studied a tattered copy of *Country Wives Budget* to learn how to make a dress. She let her hair grow out and tried to style it in the manner of the engraved illustrations in the journal. In subsequent years, visitors to the island still whispered about her, but not because she looked like a boy. It was because she had become a creature recognizable as female no matter what she wore. The stares and whispers carried quite a different connotation. But she never managed to fix herself up quite right. Never managed to capture the polished prettiness of a girl gently raised. And in truth, it usually didn't matter.

But when she brushed the tangle of black hair out of her eyes and looked across the field at Hunter Calhoun, it mattered.

"I was just thinking about you," she confessed.

He propped an elbow on the rail and crossed one ankle over the other. "You were?"

"This area needs clearing."

One side of his mouth slid upward. She couldn't tell if it was a grin or a sneer. "And why would that make you think of me?" he asked.

A sneer, she decided. "Because it's where your horse is going to be kept."

"I told you yesterday, I want no part of this idiotic scheme. I plan to leave—"

"You're not going to get away with just leaving him." Her thoughts, of which he could have no inkling, made her testy. If he wondered why, she'd just let him wonder. "I didn't ask you to bring him here, but now that you have, you're going to see this through."

He spread his hands in mock surrender. "It *is* through. Don't you see that? The horse is vicious, and he's scared of a flock of damn birds. Sure, you did a little parlor trick with him down on the beach, but you'll never turn that animal into a racehorse."

She glared at him. "Get a shovel."

"I just said—"

"I heard what you said. Get a shovel, Calhoun. If I'm wrong, you can—" She broke off, undecided.

"I can what?"

"You can shoot *me,* not the horse."

He laughed, but to her relief, he picked up a rusty shovel and hefted it over his shoulder. "You don't mean that."

"There's one way to find out."

"Damn, but you are a stubborn woman. What the hell gives you the idea you can turn this horse around?"

"I watched my father do it for years, and he taught me to do it on my own."

"And just what is it you think you can do for that animal?"

"Figure out why he's afraid, then show him he doesn't need to be afraid anymore." She eyed him critically. "It would help if you'd quit spooking him every time he twitches an ear."

"If it's so simple," he asked, "why don't all horsemen train by this method?"

"I don't know any other horsemen," she admitted. "My father showed me the ways of horses by taking me to see the wild ponies, season after season, year after year. If you watch close enough, you start seeing patterns in the way they act. As soon as you understand the patterns, you understand what they're saying."

"You claim to know a lot about horses, Eliza Flyte. Sounds like you gave it a fair amount of study."

"It was my life."

"Was?"

"Before my father passed."

"What is your life now?"

The question pressed at her in a painful spot. She braced herself against the hurt. No matter what, she must not let Calhoun's skepticism undermine her confidence. The horse had to learn to trust her, and if she wasn't certain of her skills, he'd sense that. "You ask hard questions, Mr. Calhoun," she said. Then she froze, and despite the rising heat of the day felt a chilly tingle of awareness.

"What is it?" he asked. "You're going all weird on me again—"

"Hush." She carefully laid aside her rake. From the corner of her eye, she spied the stallion on the beach path some distance away. "There you are, my love," she whispered. "I knew you'd come."

"What?" Calhoun scratched his head in confusion.

Eliza stifled a laugh at his ignorance, but she didn't have time to explain things to him right now.

Hunter held out for as long as he could, but at last worry got the better of him. Taking the shovel in hand to use as a weapon, he followed Eliza's footprints in the sand. No matter what she said, her scheme to pen the horse and train him was as insane as the woman herself. He had no idea why she thought she could tame a maddened, doomed horse that the best experts in the county couldn't get near.

A sharp, burning tension stabbed between his shoulders as he quickened his pace. He kept imagining her broken, bleeding, maimed by the horse. Before he knew it, he was running, and he didn't stop until he saw her.

As she had the day before, Eliza Flyte walked barefoot down the beach. And, just like yesterday, the stallion followed her. He was skittish at first, but after a while he started moving in close. She repeated the ritualistic moves—the turning, the shooing away, the staring down.

Hunter was intrigued, especially in light of what she had said about knowing what a horse was thinking by watching what he did with his body. Perhaps it was only his imagination, he thought, arguing with himself, but the horse followed her more quickly and readily than he had the day before. He stayed longer too, when she turned to touch him around the head and ears.

The docile creature, following the girl like a big trained dog, hardly resembled the murderous stallion. The horse that had exploded from the belly of the ship with fire in his eye. The horse they all said was ruined for good.

Hunter caught himself holding his breath, hoping foolishly that the girl just might be right, that Finn could be tamed, trained to race again. The notion shattered when the horse reared and ran off. This time the trigger was nothing more than the wind rippling across a tide pool, causing a brake of reeds to bend and whip. The stallion panicked as if a bomb had gone off under him. Eliza stood alone on the sand, staring off into the distance.

A parlor trick, Hunter reminded himself, trying not to feel too sorry for Eliza Flyte. Maybe she had put something in those apples she'd set out for the horse. Hunter wanted to believe, but he couldn't. He'd seen too much violence in the animal. Letting her toy with him this way only postponed the inevitable.

"I can't stay here any longer," he informed her that evening. He stood on the porch; she was in the back, finishing with the cow. A cacophony of chirping frogs filled the gathering dark. "Did you hear what I said?" he asked, raising his voice.

"I heard you."

"I have to go back to Albion," he said. "I have responsibilities—"

"You do," she agreed, coming around the side of the house with a bucket of milk. She walked so silently on bare feet, it amazed him. The women he knew made a great racket when they moved, what with their crinolines and hoop skirts brushing against everything in sight. And the women he knew talked. A lot. Most of the time Eliza Flyte was almost eerily quiet.

"Responsibilities at home," he said. He had a strange urge to tell her more, to explain about his children, but he wouldn't let himself. She disliked and distrusted him enough as it was. And he didn't know what the hell to think of her.

"And to that horse you brought across a whole ocean," she reminded him. "He didn't ask for that, you know."

"I never intended to stay this long. I swear," he said in annoyance. "I can't seem to get through to you, can I?" The craving for a drink of whiskey prickled him, making him pace in agitation and rake a splayed hand through his hair. "The damn horse is ruined. You've managed to get close to him a time or two, but that's a far cry from turning him into something a person could actually ride."

She set down the milk bucket. "We've barely begun. That horse is likely to be on the offense a good while. His wounds need to heal. He has to regain his strength and confidence. He has to learn to trust again, and that takes time."

"Give it up, Eliza—"

"You brought him here because you thought there was something worth saving," she said passionately.

"That was before I realized it's hopeless."

"I never said it wouldn't be a struggle."

"I don't have time to stand by while you lose a struggle."

"Fine." She picked up the bucket and climbed the

steps, pushing the kitchen door open with her hip. "Then watch me win."

"Right."

Yet he found himself constantly intrigued by everything about her. He felt torn, but only for a moment. Nancy and Willa looked after the children, and the Beaumonts' schoolmaster at neighboring Bonterre saw to their lessons. Blue and Belinda wouldn't miss their father if he stayed away for days or even weeks. The truth of the thought revived his thirst for whiskey. His own children hardly knew him. It scared them when he drank, and he often woke up vowing he wouldn't touch another drop, but the thirst always got the better of him. Maybe it was best for them if he was gone for a while.

"I'll strike a bargain with you," he said to Eliza through the half-open door. "You get a halter on that horse without getting yourself killed, and I'll stay for as long as it takes."

The stallion greeted Eliza with savage fury. On the long stretch of beach that had become their battleground, he stood with his mouth open and his teeth bared. He flicked his ears and tail and tossed his head.

She fixed a stare on him and forbade herself to feel disheartened by the horse's violence and distrust. Patience, she kept telling herself hour after hour. *Patience.*

The horse shrieked out a whinny and reared up. The sound of its shrill voice touched her spine with ice. She treated him with disdain, turning and walking away as if she did not care whether or not he followed. Perhaps it was the storm last night and the lingering thunder of a higher-than-usual surf, but the stallion behaved with fury today. He snorted, then plunged at her, and it took all her self-control to stand idly on the sand rather than run for cover.

She flicked the rope out. The horse flattened his ears to his head, distended his nostrils, rolled his eyes. Eliza stood firm. The stallion pawed the sand, kicking up a storm beneath his hooves. Yet even as he threatened her, even as the fear crowded in between them, she felt his indomitable spirit and knew one day she would reach him.

But not today, she thought exhaustedly after hours of trying to keep and hold his attention and trust. His whinny was more piercing than ever, and when thunder rolled and he shot away like a stone from a sling, she stood bereft, defeated, fighting the doubts that plagued her.

Taming the stallion became the most important thing in Eliza's life. She tried not to examine her reasons for this, but they were pitifully clear, probably to Hunter Calhoun as well as in her own mind. It was not just Calhoun's challenge, and her need to win the bargain they had struck, to make him stay and see this through. Nor was it any sort of softhearted nature on her part. No, her primary reason for dedicating herself to the violent, wounded horse was to bring herself closer to her father.

For some time now, she had been losing him by inches. Her father, whom she had adored with all that she was, kept slipping farther and farther away from her, and she didn't know how to get him back. One day she would realize she had forgotten what his voice sounded like when he said "good morning" to her. Then she would realize she had forgotten what his hands looked like. And the expression on his face when he told her a story, and the song he used to sing when he chopped wood for the stove. Each time a precious memory eluded her, she felt his death all over again.

Yet when she worked with the horse, she felt Henry

Flyte surround her, as if his hand guided her hand, his voice whispered in her ear and his spirit soared with her own.

So when the horse broke from her, pawed the ground with crazed savagery and ran until he foamed at the mouth, she wouldn't let herself get discouraged. The stallion was a gift in disguise, brought by a stranger. The gift from her father was more subtle, but she felt it flow through her each time she locked stares with the horse.

Hunter wondered how much longer he should pretend he believed in her. He had stopped worrying that the stallion would murder her outright. So long as he wasn't confined or restrained, Finn didn't seem to go on the attack. As hard as Eliza worked with him, however, she seemed no closer to penning him than she had that first day.

Yet she went on tirelessly, certain he would become hers to command. Hunter decided to give her just a little more time, a day or two perhaps, then return to Albion. To pass the time, he did some work around the place, repairing the pen where she swore they would train the horse once she haltered him. The mindless labor of hammering away at a damaged rail was oddly soothing—until he accidentally hammered his thumb.

Words he didn't even realize he knew poured from him in a stream of obscenity. He clapped his maimed hand between his thighs and felt the agony radiate to every nerve ending.

Eliza chose that precise moment to see what he was doing. Caliban—as ugly a dog as Hunter had ever seen—leaped and cavorted along the sandy path beside her.

"Hit yourself?" she asked simply.

Her attitude infuriated him. "I hammered my thumb. I think it's broken. That should make you happy."

"No, because if it's broken or gets infected, you won't be able to work. Come with me."

He started to say that he didn't plan to stay and work here any longer, but she had already turned from him. She led the way to the big cistern near the house and extracted a bucketful of fresh water. The big dog sat back on his haunches, the intensity of his attention seeming almost human.

"Ow," Hunter said when she plunged his hand into the bucket. "Damn, that stings."

"I know. It'll be even worse with the lye soap."

"Hey—damn it to hell, Eliza."

Caliban growled a warning. Clearly he didn't like Hunter's threatening tone to his mistress.

She showed no sympathy whatsoever as she applied a grayish, irregular cake of soap to the cut thumb, then worked the joint to prove to him it wasn't broken. Ignoring the curses that streamed out from between his clenched teeth, she fetched a tin of wormwood liniment and rubbed it into the wound. He noticed her staring at the wedding band he had never bothered to discard, but she said nothing. The ointment soothed his fiery, raw flesh, and as she wrapped his thumb in a strip of clean cloth, he grew quiet.

She regarded him through eyelashes that were remarkably long and thick. "You've stopped swearing. I suppose this means you're feeling better."

"Might mean I'm about to pass out from your tender care," he said mockingly. The truth was, he caught himself enjoying the sensation of her small hand rubbing the herbal liniment on him. Though impersonal, her touch was gentle and caring, undemanding.

She glared at him. "It wasn't my fault you pounded your thumb."

"I wouldn't have been pounding if you hadn't insisted on fixing up your pen."

"I wouldn't need the pen fixed if you hadn't brought me that horse."

"I—" He yanked his hand away from hers. "All right. So it's all my fault." Despite his amusement at sparring with her, he grew serious. "Eliza, we have to end this."

"End what?"

"The pretending. That horse isn't going to get any better."

Something flickered in her eyes—fear, rage, distrust—something that reminded him eerily of the stallion.

"You're wrong," she said in a low, angry voice. She stepped back, wiping her hands on her apron. "Come with me. Maybe you'll understand better when I show you."

Motioning for the dog to stay back, she led Hunter on a hike northward, perhaps two miles along a narrow, sandy track that wound along the edge of the loblolly pine forest and skirted the dunes. After they crossed a low, marshy area, Hunter noticed hoofprints and droppings on the path and in some of the thickets they passed.

"Stay very quiet," Eliza said, leading him around a curve in the path. "They're not terribly shy, but they are wild."

"The ponies, you mean."

She nodded. "Let's climb that dune there. Be very quiet."

He found himself lying, belly down, next to her on the slope of a dune. The spiky reeds framed a view of a broad saltwater marsh crammed with tender green shoots of cordgrass. A herd of about eighteen large ponies grazed in the distance while starlings and sparrows perched on their backs and pecked insects from their hides.

Hunter had seen herds before. But the sight of the island

horses, wild and free, moved him. It was a scene he knew he'd hold in his heart for all his days—the placid animals with their heads bent to their grazing, the salt-misted air soft around them, the white-winged gulls wheeling overhead. He glanced over at Eliza and saw that a similar wonder had suffused her face. That was her charm, he realized. Her sense of wonder, her different way of looking at things. He suddenly wished he could see the world through her eyes.

"Where did they come from?" he asked.

"My father brought a herd down, one animal at a time, from Assateague."

"I wonder how they got there."

"Pirates, some say. Others think they're descended from horses turned out to graze by settlers on the mainland. My father believed they're descended from a shipwrecked load of Spanish ponies. They were being sent to Panama to work in the mines, and every last one of them had been purposely blinded." She made a face. "So they wouldn't panic when they were lowered into the mines. Those that survived the wreck swam ashore and turned wild."

They listened for a while to the deep rhythm of the sea and the wind through the pine forest behind them. He felt surprisingly comfortable, lying in the dunes beside Eliza Flyte. It was something he wished he could do with his children—simply lie still in the sand, in the late afternoon, and watch a herd of horses. He hadn't done anything of the sort with his children, not in a very long time. Maybe not ever.

"Now watch," Eliza whispered. "That big shaggy gray is the stallion, and you'll be able to recognize the mares by the way they behave. See that yearling there, the little bay? He'll ask the mare for a grooming."

She turned out to be right. The younger horse approached the mare obliquely, head down, mouth open. The mare rebuffed him, laying back her ears. He persisted even when she reared up and threatened to bite, and after a time she accepted him, nibbling at his head, mane and neck. The exchange was remarkably similar to the interplay Hunter had seen on the beach between Eliza and the stallion.

"Funny how he keeps after her even when she's ignoring him. I reckon I've met a few Virginia belles who must've gone to the same finishing school as that mare."

She propped her chin in her hand. "What are they like—Virginia belles?"

He thought for a moment, remembering the endless dancing lessons he had endured as a boy, the stiff and awkward society balls and the tedious conversation that had droned on and on when the belles went on their annual husband hunt. "Like that mare," he said simply. "Bossy, fussy about grooming, and fascinating to youngsters and males."

She blew out an exasperated breath, scattering grains of sand. "That doesn't tell me anything."

He fell silent and watched the herd for a while. Then he reached out and skimmed his finger along Eliza Flyte's cheek in a slow, sensual caress. It felt even smoother than it looked.

She smacked his hand away and whispered, "What are you *doing?*"

"If I keep after you," he said in a teasing voice, "will you eventually give in?"

"I'll eventually box your ears." Yet despite the threat, merriment danced in her eyes, and—wonder of wonders— she was blushing.

They watched the herd until the sun lay low across the

island, plunging toward the bay in the west. Eliza stood and brushed herself off. Some of the ponies looked up, but settled back to their grazing or resting when she and Hunter started along the path. About halfway to the house, she turned into a thicket bordered by holly and red cedar.

There in the middle of the clearing stood a weathered gray stump. Carved on the trunk was the name Henry Flyte, d. 1853, and, encased in sealed glass, a painstakingly copied verse Hunter recognized from *The Tempest:*

"Full fathom five thy father lies;
Of his bones are coral made;
Those are pearls that were his eyes:
Nothing of him that doth fade
But doth suffer a sea-change
Into something rich and strange.

The image of Eliza Flyte, giving her father a solitary burial and marking the grave with the weird and beautiful verse, tore at his heart. The peaceful wonder of the afternoon had gone. "You should leave this place," he said. "Make a new life somewhere else."

She made her way back to the path. "You shouldn't feel sorry for me. I have riches beyond compare, here on this island."

"And you're content to live here for all of your days."

Just for a moment, a secretive look flashed in her eyes. "I—yes," she said hastily. "Why would I want anything else?"

"Because you're human," he said, speaking sharply. He wasn't certain why she made him angry, but she did. "You don't belong with a herd of horses. You belong with other people."

"People like you?" She sent him an insolent, sidelong glance.

"Why not?" he demanded.

"I might just choke on all that Virginia charm," she retorted, flipping her plaited hair with a toss of her head.

She made him want to stay long after common sense told him it was time to leave. Hunter watched the struggle between Eliza and the stallion with a mixture of admiration and hopelessness. There was something to be said for being stubborn enough not to give up, but how long should he let her keep denying the truth? The difficult battle of wills might go on for weeks, months, maybe even longer.

Enough was enough, he decided two days later. It was time to end the charade. He found Eliza and Finn easily enough. All he had to do was follow the stallion's piercing, bloodcurdling scream.

They were on the long south beach, the one shadowed by the tallest dunes. Hunter was not surprised to see the horse up on his hind legs, his open mouth working furiously. Below him, Eliza looked helpless, yet curiously unafraid.

The stallion's front hooves raked the air. Then he came crashing down mere yards from the woman. Up he went again, and down. Hunter imagined he could feel the ground shaking. A tight, nervous fear clutched his chest, but he told himself he'd only infuriate them both if he interfered. Though Eliza had made no progress with the horse, she had convinced Hunter that Finn would not hurt her.

The tantrum continued for a few more moments. Hunter waited on the dune until it subsided. Then the stallion planted his front hooves in the sand, and the woman reached out and touched him. The silent, familiar ritual gave the false impression that the horse was hers to command. But when she looped her soft rope over his head, he exploded again. He shook his head like a wet dog and started foaming at the mouth.

Eliza waited patiently, then started the ritual all over again. The crazed eyes of the stallion tracked her every move. The horse's nostrils quivered and his muscles twitched. Yet after a while, Hunter realized the horse was standing his ground rather than going away. The next time Eliza put the rope around his neck, he pulled his head back but kept his feet firmly planted.

This was different, Hunter realized, lowering himself to the sand and forgetting his purpose. Something was changing, even as he watched. The stallion clearly didn't like the rope, but the woman had somehow convinced him to bear it.

She went to his side, touched him gently along his neck and cheek. The horse stood frozen, alert but not alarmed. Eliza put the halter where the rope had been. She loosely placed it around his neck. Finn trembled, then broke away in a sweeping, athletic feint.

Hunter's hopes plummeted. Enough, he thought, getting up.

But then the horse stopped and turned back toward Eliza. As if she had bade him, he walked to her and stood placidly while she touched him all over, head and neck and sides and flanks. His chestnut hide quivered beneath her small, questing hand, and he kept his bright stare fixed somewhere out beyond the waves. But he let her slide the halter over his muzzle and ears.

Then she tugged on the rope. The horse snorted and snapped his back, kicking up sand. Eliza let go and waited for him to calm down. He made a rumbling sound in his throat and dropped his head. She picked up the rope and positioned herself in front of him.

The horse gave a deep sigh, dipping his head in relief and surrender. The air between horse and girl seemed to tingle with electricity, yet the tension had a different quality now. Like a wave of wind through the marsh grass, an ineffable softening came over Finn's body; he was visibly giving himself over to Eliza. This time when she started to walk, the stallion gave a nod of his noble head and followed. Hunter stood aside to let them pass. He knew he would never forget the sight of the black-haired girl leading the huge stallion along the path to the burned-out barn and paddock.

By magic, Finn had been transformed from savage to docile.

No. Not by magic. The girl had done it. The stallion's madness had been cooled by the horsemaster's daughter.

Eliza's back and shoulders ached, but she felt warm all over with pleasure in the work she had done. Leading the stallion to the round pen, she felt a rare and welcome lifting of the spirit. It was a good feeling, clean and pure, that rose and spread through her. She had found a way to understand this horse, had managed in some small part to penetrate the scrambled rage inside the confused animal's head.

Like all of his breed, he was not made to be alone. He was a social animal, born to live in a herd. Instinct had driven him to seek out her company. She had simply opened the door, and he had stepped through.

She entered the pen, noting that the stallion's withers tensed when they passed the wooden slats. The voyage across the sea had involved a pen, and that structure was part of Sir Finnegan's fright and confusion.

She had no recollection of the one time she had voyaged across the sea. According to her father, she had been only weeks old, and nursed by a Danish woman en route to Maryland. Her father spoke little of the past. Secrets lurked there, she knew, and if Henry Flyte had kept them in his heart, he had had his reasons. She just wished he had told her about her mother before he died.

In the middle of the pen, the stallion flicked his ears in nervousness. Though he stood still, he swung his head from side to side occasionally. He had come a long way from the fearful animal on the scow, though.

"Well done, Miz Flyte," said a low masculine voice. Hunter Calhoun stood outside the pen, watching her and the stallion.

She felt his approval like the warmth of the sun, and it meant so much to her. She'd had no idea that she was so hungry for this...connection. For months she had lived alone in the wilderness, content with her animals and books, never thinking she needed anything more. Yet the way Calhoun made her feel, with his words and the soft look in his eyes, made her realize how desperately lonely she had become.

She wondered if he could tell she was blushing. "Still intent on shooting him?" she asked in a teasing voice.

He walked into the round pen, latching the gate behind him. But instead of going directly to the horse, he walked over to Eliza. She was unprepared for what he did next. He reached out with great strong arms and grabbed her by the shoulders. His fierce embrace held not warmth, but intensity and desperation.

"I didn't want to shoot that horse," he whispered into her hair. "I surely didn't."

Frozen by amazement, Eliza simply stood there in his embrace. The stallion ignored them both, tugging indolently at a tuft of grass. Eliza's eyes drifted half shut, and just for a moment she thought of nothing at all. She merely let her senses turn on, much as a wild animal's do, taking in the essence of this creature holding her so tightly. The finely woven linen of his shirt felt cool and smooth against her cheek. The fabric smelled lightly salty from the sea air. His hair, long enough to brush his collar, held the clear golden color of the sun. And his skin was scented with a strangely evocative combination of sweat and salt.

His hand moved. Slowly, feeling its way, it skimmed upward over her back so that his fingers found the nape of her neck and pressed there. She felt almost compelled to tip back her head, baring her throat, completely vulnerable to him. Soft heat swirled through her, and she felt such a terrible wanting that it frightened her. Summoning all her self-control, she resisted the warm pulse of her body's needs and shoved him away.

"I told you I could help this horse," she said.

He took a step back. "I didn't believe you could break him, until I saw it with my own eyes."

She drew herself up, disliking his choice of words. "My father called it 'gentling.' Breaking a horse is a savage, dangerous practice." She watched Finn with a welling of pure affection. "It was a matter of gaining Finn's trust. He has no idea what patience and dignity and respect are, but he needs them just the same. A horse doesn't lie, Mr. Calhoun. Not ever."

"Humans lie all the time." He leaned back against the fence. Across the circle, the big chestnut horse browsed in a clump of clover. "Finn could have gone anywhere on this island," he said at length. "And the only place he wanted to be was with you."

"Don't look at me like that. It's not black magic," she said testily. She gestured toward a lean-to at the end of the paddock. "There's a scythe in that toolshed over there. You can get started on the bigger pen. It's best to have you working nearby so he can learn who his owner is. You need to clear that field, and later see about fixing that lower fence rail. It's almost rotted through."

He fixed her with a narrow-eyed stare, his earlier gratitude gone. "I don't take orders."

"I didn't think you would. You probably aren't even used to doing work."

The blisters on Hunter's hands rose before noon, and burst before one. The sun burned through the clouds and beat like a hammer of fire on his bare head as he worked. He was no stranger to this sort of labor. He had wanted to tell her that. But she wouldn't have believed him, for she considered him a lazy planter who amused himself by racing horses. Or a bungler who maimed himself with a hammer. Best to show her who he truly was. She seemed the sort of woman who believed her eyes more readily than her ears.

From the corner of his eye, he watched the stallion in the adjoining pen. The animal stood calmly in the shade. She had put soft leather hobbles around his forelegs, and he tolerated them as he had the halter.

Hunter tried not to wonder where Eliza had gone and what she was doing. But it was all he could think about. She had amazed him. In a world that held very few surprises, she had surprised him. Her bond with the horse seemed so natural. Hunter had watched with his own eyes as the barrier separating human from horse had melted away. He had seen, between girl and stallion, a touch so intimate that it was like the touch between two lovers.

Why did her manner with the horse make her so attractive to him? Hunter pondered the question as he worked, heaving scythed plants up and over the rail, his movements as methodical and regulated as a tobacco worker's. It left his mind free to think about Eliza Flyte.

With no sense of vanity or even gratitude, Hunter knew he had loved some of the most extraordinary belles in Virginia, so a barefoot island girl should not stand out in the pantheon. Yet in her own way, Eliza Flyte was extraordinary too. She was not pretty, but clear-eyed and dark-haired in a way that commanded attention. She wasn't charming. Raised by a mysterious man in the middle of nowhere, she lacked the refinements of a well-brought-up lady. She dressed poorly and spoke oddly, and yet she was the most compelling woman he had ever met. There was something about her that he recognized. Suddenly, a part of him emerged that he had never been able to bring out before. Her freshness felt brand new, made *him* feel brand new.

In the years after returning home from the University of Virginia, Hunter had been treated to a variety of women. As the elder son of the master of Albion, he had regularly reviewed a bright parade of eligible ladies all vying for his favor. Some of them were willing to do more than flirt. Some of them were prettier than a girl had a right to be—particularly Lacey Beaumont.

Fair-haired and merry-eyed, she had captured his heart and held it for longer than he should have let her. Long enough for him to convince himself that the match—arranged years before by their parents—was founded on love and trust, and that their vows actually meant something.

Disaster was the crucible that melted their marriage. Lacey had taught him the painful lesson that even the brightest love could not transform the world. Perhaps a deeper love would have held them together through the years of struggle after Albion had failed. Perhaps not. Hunter would never know. What he had begun to suspect, as time marched on and his heart grew icy and hard, was that true love was an illusion. A hoax made up by poets and dreamers.

Out here, on this wind-torn island where breakers crashed and willets wheeled, he seemed far from all the intrigue and entanglements of the past. He found that he liked being out here, on the edge of everything, where earth and sea and sky met and the lines blurred. The hugeness of the sea put his own world into perspective. Perhaps that was the appeal of the island. Perhaps that was why Eliza Flyte stayed here, her back squarely turned on the world.

Maybe she was not so crazy after all.

Seven

Eliza came to the horse pen at the end of the day. Hunter had just finished putting up the sagging sunshades and replenishing the water in the barrels. He noted with satisfaction that her eyebrows shot up when she saw that he had finished clearing both the round pen and the larger arena.

"You surprise me," she said.

"By getting so much work done?" He shouldered a garden rake and let himself out through the gate.

"And not even whining about it." When she took the rake from him, she caught a glimpse of his hand. The bandage around his thumb had long since come undone. "You've got blisters," she said.

They spoke no more as they stood side by side at the fence, looking at Finn. The stallion grazed in his pen, his muscular form outlined by the colors of the sunset.

"You'll have to use the dandy brush on him tomorrow," Eliza said. "Get all that caked mud off him."

"He'll take my hand off."

"Only if you scare him."

Hunter felt too tired to argue. He wished he had a nice jug of whiskey and a cigar. Instead, he asked the question that had been nagging at him all day. "Can the stallion be trained to race again?"

"You'll know more after you've worked with him a while."

"After I've worked with him?"

"Of course. He's your horse."

"And can he be trusted to stand stud without murdering his lover?"

She blushed. "Maybe that depends on the lover."

"How soon can he be ready to race?" He asked it too quickly, revealing himself.

She gave him an exasperated smile. "Rich planters and their horse races."

"You disapprove?"

She thought about it for a moment, pressing her finger to her lower lip. "Yes. Yes, I do."

"Of what? Rich planters or horse races?"

"Planters. And the horse races too, if the trainers are cruel. But mainly planters."

"What do you know of them?"

"Not much," she admitted, spreading her hands. "A few used to come with the drovers sometimes to get horses from my father. They always seemed haughty to me, ordering everyone around and picking snuff out of dainty little boxes. They used to talk endlessly of the Old Dominion."

"The university. It's a place of higher learning."

"Well, I don't know what they learned there. None of them ever said a thing worth listening to. Father didn't think much of them, either." She paused. "He said planters keep dozens of slaves."

"What do you know of slavery?"

"My father told me enough. And even if he hadn't, is

there anyone with a brain in his head who can honestly believe slavery is a good thing?''

"Planters." He laughed.

She censured him with a dark-eyed glare. "You find this funny?"

"What's funny is your assumption that I'm a planter."

"Aren't you?" She frowned skeptically, setting her hands on her hips and tilting her head to one side.

"Why would you think so?"

"First of all, you said so yourself. 'Hunter Calhoun, of Albion Plan-*tay*-shunn,'" she intoned, doing a dead-on parody of his deep voice and accent. She ticked off the reasons on her fingers. "You have the drawl of an Old Dominion man. Your clothes are made of fine stuff, and by a tailor's needle. I imagine you're used to having your every desire gratified. Everything about you reeks of the plantation."

He laughed again, harder. "*Brava,* Miz Flyte. A fine piece of deduction. But you're wrong."

"Then why do you talk like a planter?"

"My father was a tobacco planter. But all that changed after he died and left Albion to me."

As they talked, she led him around on the evening chores. With no modesty whatsoever, she tucked up the hem of her skirt, waded into the oyster bed and drew up a string of fresh oysters, tossing them in a bucket. He couldn't help but notice the shapely turn of her calves as she bent to rinse the oysters.

"Well?" She held a shucking knife out to him. "If you're not a planter, what are you doing with a plantation?"

She pretended not to be curious about him, but clearly she was. He concentrated on what he was doing, and the words came easily. "I became the man my father expected

me to be—a son of the Old Dominion. I had a love affair
with a laundress at the age of sixteen, and my father would
not have objected, because men of his class see nothing
wrong with bedding the servants. But I did the unthinkable.''

"What's that?" she asked, narrow-eyed with suspicion.

He had never met anyone who listened the way Eliza
did, with her whole self, as if the words being spoken
contained the secrets of the world. He wondered if that
sort of thoughtful attentiveness was something she'd
learned from watching her father's herd.

"I fell in love with the girl." He nearly winced, remembering how naive and stupid he had been. "My father
did what any good Southern father would do. He sold her
to the slave trader." He sliced savagely at an oyster shell,
severing the muscle. "I used to think about setting out to
find the girl, but, well, tradition and obedience were bred
into the bone in my family, and after attending the university—surely I don't have to tell you which one—I came
home and married my neighbor's daughter, Lacey Beaumont."

A sharp shell stabbed into the pad of his bruised thumb.
His hands had suffered such abuse in the past few days
that he almost didn't feel it. He pinched the thumb against
his forefinger until the blood stopped, then resumed working.

"And did you make the mistake of falling in love with
her too?" Eliza asked, her gaze falling to the wedding ring
he still wore.

He thought about her question and realized he didn't
know the answer, so he said, "Lacey was pretty as a magnolia blossom—"

"Was?" Eliza asked sharply.

"She died two years ago." Suddenly he felt exposed,

foolish, so he scowled, closing himself off. "And that's all I've got to say about the subject."

Eliza let down the hem of her skirt and picked up the bucket. She stopped to wash at the cistern, then went into the house and started fixing supper.

Hunter paced back and forth on the weather-beaten porch. Ordinarily, he didn't like having a woman pester him with questions about his life, his thoughts, his past. Women had a way of prying that sat ill with him. Eliza was different, though. Her questions...they didn't feel like prying. And when she walked away from him, he caught himself wanting to follow.

Just like Finn, he thought ironically, going into the house.

She barely looked at him as she scraped butter and sliced onion into the big stew pot on the stove.

Without thinking, he opened his whiskey flask, then remembered it was empty and put it away. "Damn," he muttered. "What I wouldn't give for a drink."

"What *would* you give?" she asked.

He caught her eye and turned his hands palms out, showing off his blisters, bruises and cuts. "An honest day's work?" He put on his best smile.

She stared at him, clearly unmoved. "Save the charm for your Virginia belles."

He hated it that he was so transparent. But his hopes rose as she lifted the slanting doors to the root cellar. She disappeared into the tiny crawl space, then reappeared, lugging a stoneware crock in both hands.

The sight of it nearly sent him to his knees. "Is that what I think it is?"

She set the jug on the table, took a pewter spoon and

knocked the thick wax seal off the tap on the bottom. "What do you think it is?"

A grin spread slowly across his face. "Heaven in a bottle."

She drew a tin cup of the amber liquid and handed it to him. "Salvage from a shipwreck," she said. "It's been in the cellar for years."

He took a long drink of the rum, letting its sticky warmth slide down his throat. Fireworks of welcome went off in his gut. "And you, my dear," he said, grinning even wider, "are an angel from above."

Eliza caught a drop from the tap on her finger and tasted it, making a face. "Why do you like to drink?" she asked.

He drained his cup in two gulps. That was what he needed: a drink to steady him. "So I don't have to think."

"What is it you don't want to think about?"

"All the troubles of the world," he said expansively.

"Humph." She went back to stirring the oyster stew. She clearly didn't believe a man like him could have troubles.

The rum made him maudlin, talkative. He wanted her to understand. "When my father died, I discovered he was eyeball deep in debt. He did not do me the courtesy of leaving me nothing. Instead, he left me with debts that cost nearly the entire estate to pay off." He poured another cup of rum. "I hire grooms when I can afford them, and my cousin's boy, Noah, helps with the horses. Best trainer and jockey in the county."

Eliza stopped working for a moment and held herself very still, listening with that same intensity he had noticed in her earlier. He paused, slightly aghast that he was speaking so openly of matters so private. Yet her thoughtful silence encouraged him to explain. Or maybe it was the rum.

"I've built a skinned one-mile oval for training. Got some promising Thoroughbreds in my yard, and I spent nearly all that I have on Finn. If he doesn't perform, I'm finished. This season's races and the yearling sale will determine my future. If I fail, I'll probably lose Albion." He helped himself to more of the rum, and felt himself smoothing out at last.

The oyster stew was delicious, or at least he supposed it was. He wolfed down two wide dishes of the stuff and sopped the last of it with corn bread, not pausing to savor the rich, buttery broth. Eliza ate in silence, a trait he found strange in a woman. So strange that he started to resent it. Replete with a stew of oyster and onion, and nicely lit by the rum, Hunter decided to get her to talk to him. When she had opened the cellar door, he'd noticed something else hidden there.

While she was busy clearing up after supper, he opened the narrow angled door and stepped into the crawl space.

"What are you—" Eliza bent over the open door. "Put that back," she snapped. "It's private."

"I'm just curious."

"Put it back."

He shook his head and balanced the big, oblong box on one shoulder as he climbed out of the cellar. "What's inside?" he asked, setting it down on the crab trap table.

Her cheeks grew bright red with mortification, and he chuckled. "I don't know why you're feeling so bashful," he said. "I'm the one who spilled my guts to you, telling you things I've held inside myself for years. Why? Why did I tell you I'm penniless, that I risked everything to build the horse farm?"

"Because you drank enough rum to float a boat," she snapped, grabbing for the box.

He moved protectively between her and the dusty crate.

The rum only accounted for some of his honesty. Maybe he spoke to her easily because she was a stranger—someone he would never see again after he left this island. That made her...safe. Trusted.

It was sad, in a way, that the only person he could trust his secrets to was someone he would never see again.

"Calhoun," she said, "you have no right to pry—"

Ignoring her, he lifted the clasp of the tired-looking old footlocker and flipped up the lid. Within lay an odd collection. "What's all this?" he murmured.

An exasperated sigh burst from her. "Not that it's any of your business, but those are things we salvaged from wrecked ships over the years."

Hunter took the items out, one by one—a wig, a drinking chalice with handles formed from the curved bodies of mermaids, a silver comb, a conch shell with a pearlescent pink interior, a woolen Monmouth cap, a mourning ring of gold inscribed *In memory of my beloved wife Hannah—How many hopes lie buried with thee.*

"Here, let me get the rest," she said, apparently resigned to his intrusion. "You might break something." With a curious reverence, she brought out a colorful hand-stitched counterpane. It was made of some fine stuff—silk or satin brocade—with a glossy fringe.

"When I was very small, a ship ran aground during a storm," she said. "We found the wreck in the aftermath. I don't remember it very well, but there was such a terrible feeling of loss. A desolation. In the dark, the crew and passengers couldn't find a way ashore, and they drowned." Her eyes turned soft with regret. "Every last one of them, that's what my father thought at first. Then, by some miracle, he discovered one survivor. It was a woman. He found her at sunrise in a stateroom, and she was injured and dying. We never knew her name, and she never spoke to us in English. My father recognized her language as Spanish.'' She spread the counterpane over the dining table, smoothing away the wrinkles with her hands.

''She managed to tell my father, with gestures, that she wished to be brought ashore with all her fine things.'' Eliza took out the salvaged wares, setting them on the cloth one by one. There was bone china so fine that it glowed when held to the lamp, silver forks and knives and spoons, crystal goblets, all nestled in protective layers of linen and lace. ''My father guessed that it was a dowry, for she was young and very beautiful. She touched my cheek, and her hand was so cold that I wanted to cry. Later that night she died, and my father buried her with the sailors in the high meadow behind the first row of dunes.''

''Did you ever find out who she was?''

''We never learned her name. The salvage company in Eastwick came straightaway and took the cargo—sardines and olive oil, mostly. They asked about the Spanish lady's belongings.'' Eliza gestured at the treasures. ''My father was an honest man, but he said nothing to the salvagers. When I asked him about it later, he smiled at me and said one day I'd be needing a dowry of my own, and he was sure the beautiful Spanish bride would want me to have hers.''

With a self-deprecating grin, Eliza looked down at her homespun smock and bare feet. ''Thus far, I haven't found any use for it. But—'' She broke off, stopping herself and glancing away from Hunter.

He found himself staring at the sweet, slender curve of her neck as she turned her head away. ''But what?'' he asked, almost against his will. ''Tell me what you were going to say.''

With his fingers at her jawline, he brought her gaze to

his. Her skin was petal soft, washed clean from the cistern water earlier in the day. She tensed when he touched her, and seemed so flustered that he relented and dropped his hand.

"You're as skittish as one of those wild ponies you showed me," he said, reaching into the bottom of the old chest.

"That was with her things," she said.

He opened the large, flat book. Folded inside the front cover was a map printed on yellowed paper. He raised the flame in the lamp and studied the map. The words were in Spanish, but he recognized the outward curve of the coastline. "California," he said.

"We thought that was her destination." Eliza paged through the book. "The text isn't in English, but by studying the text and the pictures, I——" She bit her lip, bashful again.

"Go on," he said, intrigued. He was having to pull this out of her.

She opened the book to a page marked with a length of black ribbon. "I know these pictures as well as the saltwater channel in front of this house. My father and I spent hours studying them. The lithographs were printed from famous paintings by an artist called Jiminez. There," she said, indicating a page in the book. "I've always wanted to go there."

He scanned the text beside the picture. "Cel——"

"Cielito," she said, correcting his pronunciation. "It's north of gold country, and the land is there for the taking. Wild horses run free for thousands of miles. My father always said we would go there one day."

"I take it you're more at home with horses than with people."

"A horse never did a thing wrong to me."

"And a person has?"

Agitated, she recoiled, as if sensing she had revealed too much. She shut the heavy book with a thud and put it back in the trunk. Hunter sensed something more was going on than the simple display of her treasures. She was telling him her dream. Like the dance she had done with the stallion on the beach that first morning, she was doing a dance with him. She would reveal something to him, and see what happened in return. Interesting.

"So when do you set sail?" he asked.

She laughed, but he heard bitterness in her laughter. "I think I'm a little late for the gold rush."

He indicated the things in the trunk. "That would be worth something."

"That poor dead bride left them with me. I'm not sure she meant to, but it seems wrong to sell her things. I'll take them with me. They were always meant to wind up in California anyway."

"And when will that be?" he persisted.

She looked him in the eye, and for a moment he wished he hadn't drunk so much.

"That depends," she said, "on what I have to do to earn the price of passage."

Eight

Eliza scrambled out of bed with a vague, disoriented sense that something was amiss. She washed and dressed quickly, and didn't bother with her hair. Then she went outside to find the porch deserted.

Had he gone? Had he taken Finn, or simply left the stallion for her to train?

Caliban came trotting up, his fringed tail swishing to and fro in friendly fashion. "So where'd he go?" Eliza murmured, distractedly scratching the dog's ears. A breeze hissed in the high trees on the lee shore, bringing with it a tingle of heat from the coming summer. The tide was out, and the long slick mudflats fidgeted with the movements of bugs and crabs. Eliza climbed up to the porch rail and balanced there to give herself a longer view, past the outbuildings and the rippling windrows of saltmeadow hay. No boat or scow lay at anchor at south shore. Instead the strand was wide and empty, the tide out far, gulls and cormorants squabbling over crabs and shellfish on the flats.

She had looked upon this sight every day of her life, but today felt different. After her father died, she had finally understood what loneliness felt like. She discovered that it was bearable so long as she didn't brood about her isolation.

But with the arrival of Hunter Calhoun, she had discovered something else. She needed to be with someone. Even if that someone was an arrogant, hard-drinking Tidewater blue blood. In his absence, she no longer felt merely lonely. She knew a sense of abandonment so vast and deep that she wondered how she could be feeling it and still be alive. It was a different sort of hurt from the hopeless agony of losing her father. This was a sort of hurt that held the heat of anger.

Why had he left without a word? Had he revealed too much of himself, telling her of his dreams and plans for the place called Albion? That was probably it, she decided. People were rarely grateful to those to whom they told their secrets.

Caliban whined impatiently, eager to get on with the day. There were weirs and crab traps to be checked, chores to do. It was silly, but she had grown used to Hunter Calhoun being present when she awoke. Sitting around and wondering about him accomplished nothing.

Claribel's milk pail wasn't in the kitchen. Eliza wondered if she could have left it out somewhere. But she never forgot the pail. She hurried outside and walked up to the meadow, listening for Claribel's bell and calling her name. The little cow always walked the same track, and the path beaten into the sandy earth was easy to follow. Like the other animals of the island, the cow had a language all her own, a silent and simple language Eliza understood. Rather than shying from her, Claribel almost always came when called.

With a strange shock Eliza saw Hunter Calhoun, carrying a bucket of milk down the cow path toward her.

"Morning," he said, his manner casual, as if this were an everyday occurrence.

"Morning," she echoed, unable to get her mouth to say anything else.

"Did your milking for you," he said gruffly.

She followed him down to the house. "I'm used to doing my own chores."

He went inside and set the bucket in the dry sink, laying a towel over the top of it. "Don't look so outraged, Miz Eliza. You know, in my time I've given cause for any number of women to take offense, but never on account of milking a cow."

She felt her cheeks redden. "I'm not offended—"

"You are." He took her hand and pulled her along with him, leading the way outside. "And I can tell you why."

She wrenched her hand away from his, but he kept walking, so she had to quicken her step to keep up. "Very well. Tell me why."

"Because you're starting to like me."

"I'm not. I don't even know you."

He slowed his pace and sent her a sidelong glance. "Honey, you know me better than almost anyone I've ever met. See, I don't talk about... What happened with Lacey and the farm and what I hope to accomplish—I'm not sure why I spoke of it to you." He thought for a moment. "You started liking me better after I told you about my terrible past."

"That's not true. I—"

"You're just relieved to hear I'm not some arrogant planter, whipping his slaves and taking their women to bed."

"I'd be relieved to hear that about anyone."

"Well, the fact is, you like me better today than you did yesterday, and tomorrow you'll like me even more."

"Why is that?"

"You'll see."

They made their way along the path to check on the stallion. Finn stood in the shade of a sweetleaf tree, drinking from the rain barrel and switching his tail rhythmically to and fro. At the sound of their approach, he stopped drinking and brought his head up sharply, long bright strands of water dripping from his muzzle.

She could see the lingering ghosts of fear and rage in him. He pricked his ears high and clamped his tail low, sucking under his haunches and lifting one foot. He was fully prepared to defend himself by kicking.

"He's about to explode," Hunter observed.

"Yes." She felt a certain satisfaction in the idea that he was paying attention to the stallion's signals.

"He seemed better yesterday, but look at him now." He touched her arm lightly, and she felt stung, unused to any man's touch.

She pulled away. "You can't rush the process. His fear was deep. Be patient."

"Show me," he said to her. "Show me how you tamed him."

Over the years, many had asked the same of her father. Only a few had genuinely wanted to learn. Looking into Hunter Calhoun's clear blue eyes, she hoped he was one of those few.

"He's willing to listen," she said. "Watch the ears." Ever so slightly, one ear turned back obliquely. "Go on into the pen. You should start working with him."

"Don't you think it's too soon to test him?"

"We'll know in a moment, won't we?"

Hunter Calhoun stood at the gate, scowling. He was peevish, balky, like an intractable plow horse. The thought made her smile. "All right, Mr. I-Can-Ride-Anything-with-Hair. Are you saying you're afraid?"

"You didn't see us getting him off the ship from Ireland. This stallion's a lit stick of dynamite."

"Just watch him," she said softly. "Feel what he's telling you."

"Honey, what he's telling me is he'd like to kick my eyes through the back of my head."

She pushed him lightly, her hand on his back. "You'll be fine. And if you're not, just—stay close to the rail."

He grumbled, but he did as she said, walking into the pen. She took a quiet joy in the morning now, for it felt like so many mornings past, when her father had been alive. The prospect of a new horse. The squeak of the bar across the gate and the solid thunk of the rail dropping into place. She had missed this. Oh, how she had missed this.

"Now, hold your shoulders square, but don't threaten him. Think about what he sees when you walk toward him. Your eyes are at the front of your head, which marks you as a predator."

"I can't do much about that," Hunter said between his teeth.

"I'm just pointing out that to a horse, you have the look and the smell of a predator. Instinct will tell him to flee from you. So you've got to convince him to want to follow you."

"In other words, he's got to see something I'm not. I don't think a horse is that smart."

"You've got to avoid threatening him. Walk slowly. Don't be intimidated, but don't intimidate."

As Hunter approached the horse, the chestnut hide quivered and the ears flattened. Hunter half turned to her, a question in his eyes.

"Watch the horse," she said. "See the way he holds himself. He distrusts you, but you have his attention."

When Hunter walked closer, she said, "Now, turn away."

"But shouldn't I—"

"I know it's not customary," she said. "But it works. Just don't act anxious or impatient when you turn."

He did as she told him and, as she knew he would, the stallion watched the man walk away. They repeated the exercise—Hunter's advance and retreat—several times, until the stallion decided to go along with the man.

Hunter Calhoun surprised her. She had expected disdain from a Virginia aristocrat. She had expected him to balk at taking advice from a woman. Yet with the stallion, he showed a remarkable patience, never trying to rush the horse as most men would. "Take the time now, or spend a longer time later," her father used to say.

For all of his bluster, she observed, Hunter had not lied about his abilities. He was good with horses. As the morning wore on, he convinced the stallion to follow him, stopping and starting at his will. Finally, by mid-morning, she said, "Try getting him to lie down."

His skeptical gaze flicked to her, but then he nodded. He understood what it meant to get a horse to lie down. It was the ultimate exercise in trust, for a horse was at his most vulnerable when lying on the ground.

Hunter took the shank of the halter and tugged it down. The horse resisted. Hunter let him resist, time and time again, not fighting him but not letting up either. He touched the horse, spoke to him in a low, compelling voice. Eliza felt entranced by the sight of Hunter's big hands skimming over the horse's hide, the sound of his dark, nonsensical whispers. Deep within her, she felt the same primal response of the horse—an awakening, a quickening. Warmth and interest. She found the picture of the blond man and the dark horse enchanting. Finally, as the sun arched up to high noon, the stallion lay down in the shade of the sweetleaf tree.

"I'll be damned," Hunter said. "It's working." He stared at her for a long moment with the oddest expression on his face. For no reason she could fathom, she blushed and looked away, holding her breath until the moment passed and he turned his attention back to the horse.

She sat on a heartwood stump and watched while Hunter tamed Finn limb by limb, inch by inch. The man's large hands rubbed the horse all over, the vulnerable spine and withers, the neck and haunches and cheeks—everywhere. The drowsy warmth of the afternoon invaded Eliza, and a curious lassitude stole over her. She kept watching those hands, those big gentle hands, touching and patting, rubbing and caressing. The horse grew more and more relaxed. Hunter took the great nodding head between his hands and shook it gently, pressing his will upon the stallion like a father to a wayward boy.

He selected an old, rusty dandy brush from the cobwebby grooming box and groomed the horse, working slowly, always talking, seeming to take a pure sensual delight in the task. The mud-caked hide was transformed, bit by bit, into a coat of polished mahogany, its color pure and dazzling to the eye. Eliza could not keep her gaze away from the spectacle, even though she felt like an intruder in a way she never had while watching her father. She grew warm and lazy with the contentment of watching a man who knew the ways of horses. A man who knew how to use his hands, and his voice, and an intimate touch to bend the creature's will.

After a long time, he gave the stallion a piece of barley sugar and left the arena. When he looked at Eliza, he laughed softly. "I take it from the expression on your face that you approve."

His laughter and his words flustered her. It was as if he had caught her in the middle of an impure thought. "Oh!" she said, brushing off her smock. "You did very well. Exactly as my father would have had you do."

He studied her for a moment. "I wish I'd known him."

The quiet statement pressed at Eliza in an unexpected place. She found she couldn't speak, so she merely nodded and gave her attention to the horse.

"Should we go on with him today?" Hunter asked.

"Later, perhaps. It's fine to keep after him, but we should let him rest too."

"Good." In one smooth movement, he peeled the shirt off over his head.

She gaped at his chest, glistening with sweat.

He laughed again, still softly. "Pardon me. I reek of horse."

Trying to recover her composure, she said, "You can draw a bath at the cistern if you like."

He sent her a long, speculative look that made her tingle in appalling places—her throat, the tips of her breasts, between her legs. She prayed that he couldn't discern the reaction by looking at her.

"I'd like," he said simply, and followed her back to the house.

Nine

It was full dark. Ordinarily Eliza would have made herself a cup of tea from the wild rose hips she'd gathered at the last of the summer and climbed into her creaky bed with a lamp and a book. But she was not alone. She had a guest, and she couldn't decide what to do with him.

At first, they'd been thrown together by circumstances and the horse's need. But now, by some mutual agreement they had not actually discussed, Hunter Calhoun had become her partner in working with the stallion, and her guest.

She had no skills as a drawing room wit. In fact, she lacked both—the drawing room and the wit. Her father once told her that in some faraway places, like Boston and Baltimore and Philadelphia, people stayed up late reading aloud to each other and discussing what they read. Perhaps she and Hunter Calhoun could do that.

As she paged through her books—she didn't know why she had to browse, since she knew the books like treasured pets—she kept thinking about how Calhoun had looked when he had finished bathing at the cistern and come to supper. There was something both touching and compelling about his thoroughness. He had washed every inch that she could see. He smelled of the hard lye soap she'd bought on one of her rare visits to the mainland. Even his fingernails were clean. His golden-yellow hair showed the furrows of his fingers where he'd combed through it, and a crystal drop of water seemed to cling to each curling end. She had the wild and probably erroneous impression that he wanted to groom himself for her, look nice for her, and the very idea made her stomach cramp with nervousness.

Over supper, Calhoun had explained how he'd come into possession of the stallion. His agent, a man whose judgment he trusted, had found Sir Finnegan on a vast estate in the west of Ireland. It was an area famous for producing the fastest horses in the world, and the stallion had grown strong on the grass that grew in the lime-rich soil. Though the stallion was known to be extraordinarily swift, his English owner deemed him a poor foal-getter and a nervous racer. Thinking to dupe an American bumpkin into a bad trade, he had been pleased to sell Finn.

"And he was right," Calhoun admitted. "He probably knew Finn was half mad, and he only got worse on the sea voyage. That's why he came cheap." Calhoun looked disgusted with himself. "I still don't know if this horse will race."

Eliza didn't want to raise his expectations too high. "My father used to say speed and sanity don't often reside in the same horse. He trained the champion Aleazar, but his fame was brief. The stallion came to a bad end. At four years old he killed a boy and was shot moments after. So there's no bloodline, just memories. And those are dying too."

After supper Calhoun had gamely offered to look after the animals—water and dried cordgrass for the cow and the horse, and dried corn for the hens—and left her to herself in the quiet cabin. Idleness sat ill with her. She simply wasn't used to sharing her duties.

She folded her arms protectively across her middle and stood in front of the bookshelves, wondering if she should offer to read to him like some young lady of Boston. But what? *Jane Eyre?* That was an unabashed romance, and Calhoun would probably mistake her intent.

A loud thump on the roof startled her. Without even thinking, she grabbed her rifle from under the bed and burst out on the porch, searching the darkness for the gleam of a cougar's predatory glare. Instead, she saw only Caliban in the light streaming through the open door, his tail swishing and tongue lolling. The big dog's attention was focused at a point over her head...on the roof.

"Mr. Calhoun?" she asked uncertainly.

"Hunter. I know you think it's a stupid name, but I'll thank you to call me that."

"What are you doing on the roof?"

She heard a metallic clink as he opened his drinking flask. Ever since she'd given him the rum, he had kept his flask filled with it. "I wanted the view from your father's observation deck."

"The wood's rotten. Falling apart."

"It'll hold. Join me."

She set down the rifle and walked out a little ways so she could see him. "How did you get up there?"

"Stood on the porch rail and pulled myself up."

His words made her picture him just that way; long strong body stretched toward the sky, his enormous muscular arms working to lever him up and over the eaves.

He held out an arm. "Stand on that puncheon and I'll help you up."

Feeling ridiculous, she climbed up to the top of the tall wooden cask—it had once contained Spanish olives in pickling brine—and balanced on the lid. His large hands reached for her, and she wasn't sure what she should do.

It didn't matter. He pulled hard. She heard a slight tearing sound as her dress caught on something. A second later, she lay on the sloping roof of the cabin.

Hunter Calhoun lay beneath her.

The moment heated every bone in her body, though her mind burst into a thousand scattered thoughts. She had never touched a man like this, even by accident. He didn't feel as hard as he looked. He had a wonderful cedary fragrance. His yellow hair was amazingly soft. All the wild sensations rushed through her with the speed of a spring breeze, and then she realized he was laughing softly, amused by the awkward pose.

And his laughter too, was as evocative as a kiss. She could feel the rush of his breath and fancied she could discern its flavor. He tasted sweet with the spiced apples they had eaten at supper.

"You're heavier than you look, girl," he said, rolling to one side.

He kept hold of one arm while she righted herself and sat up, pulling her knees to her chest. He didn't move away from her. "You were right about your father's deck. Too rickety to hold us." He pushed at the small, railed projection, made from the topmast of a wrecked ship. "Why did he build a deck up here?"

She hesitated, thinking of the hours her father had spent here. "I'm not sure. I think he liked looking out to sea. We should get down."

"Don't be in such a hurry. The pitch of the roof is shallow. I don't think you'll slide off," he said. "But these cedar shakes are dry as tinder. Don't you worry about fire?"

"No."

"One good spark from the stovepipe and the whole house could go up in a second."

"It's just a house," she said, then saw that he was grinning and shaking his head. "What?"

"You're a sorry excuse for a woman, Eliza Flyte."

"Why do you say that?"

"All the women I've ever known are devoted to their things. They couldn't stand the idea of losing anything." He took a long drink of rum, though a distant expression sobered his face. "There're women who'd give up a loved one before they'd give up the family silver."

She wanted to ask him if he was talking about his late wife, but then she realized she didn't have to ask.

"So," he said. "About this view." Setting aside the flask, he lifted an arm and with a sweeping gesture encompassed the night sky. "No wonder your father used to come up here."

She let her head drop back and looked. It was the clearest of spring nights, the display of stars so dazzling that they seemed to circle and swim in the deepest black imaginable. "I do love the stars," she said softly. "I love the stories about the constellations and how they got their names."

He chuckled. "Let me guess. Your father's stories."

"That's right. See that one there? It's called Delphinae, who shot an arrow through her lover's heart," she said. "It's truly a glimpse of heaven, especially on a night like tonight."

"When we were boys," he said, "Ryan—that's my half brother—built a lookout platform at Albion. He always wanted to go to sea, and he used to lie up there each night, studying the constellations."

"And did your brother ever go to sea?"

"He did. Sails a brig out of Boston and keeps a town

house in Norfolk. He and Isadora make port often enough to visit.''

"He travels with his wife?"

Hunter grinned. "And their two babies. I daresay Isadora gives him no choice." He settled back thoughtfully. "I never did pay much attention to the constellations and their stories. I just liked...the light, I guess. The idea that the universe is bigger than anyone can imagine, and that it's always there, even when we're not looking at the stars." After a pause, he added, "These days, I forget to look up at them for months on end."

"Why?"

He laughed quietly, mirthlessly. "Girl, you asked a mouthful. I reckon if you think about what I've told you of my life, you'd understand."

"You haven't told me that much," she said.

There was a long pause. He took a drink from his flask. "I have two children," he said.

She hoped the darkness covered her surprise. "Why didn't you say anything about them before?"

"I don't—I never know what to say about my kids. Theodore—we've always called him Blue on account of the nursery rhyme."

"Little Boy Blue, you mean."

"Yeah, that was his favorite. And Belinda."

"A boy and a girl. That's lucky."

"I wish I could believe it." He drew his knee up and rested his arm on it. "I might lose my kids for good to their grandparents. The Beaumonts don't think I'm much of a father anyway."

"Who's looking after your children right now?" she asked.

"Nancy and Willa, the housekeeper and cook." He noticed her skeptical look. "In my world," he explained, "the father is not important."

"In my world," Eliza said, "the father is everything." A wistful yearning stole over her. She waited for Hunter to tell her more, but he stayed quiet for a long time, listening to the sounds of twilight rising up over the marsh. The crickets and frogs surged to life on a great, energetic crescendo.

"I reckon I'll have to find a new wife soon—give my children a mother," he said.

"Ah." She didn't know what else to say. Resting her chin on her knees, she imagined how hard it must be for him to be missing his wife and worrying about his children and his farm. Perhaps being alone out here on the island was a blessing after all.

In her heart, she knew she'd never believe that, but she kept telling herself that she was fortunate to be free, unfettered by family ties.

"Is the viewing platform still up in that tree?" she asked.

"Yeah, but it's old, probably rotted like your father's deck. No one goes there now."

"Wouldn't your son like to climb up and look at the stars with you?"

"Blue?" His tone changed with that one syllable. "No, not Blue."

She tried to picture Hunter Calhoun's son. In her mind's eye she saw a yellow-haired boy, rosy-cheeked, robust and athletic. Merry eyes and a laughing mouth. Hunter would be the sort of father a boy would worship, she was sure of it. Yet it was strange. When Hunter spoke of his son, she found herself wondering about what he wasn't saying as much as what he was.

"Won't your children miss you if you stay here much longer?" she asked.

He laughed, and it was that humorless, bitter laugh, the one that made her feel sad. "No, honey, those kids won't miss me. I've never been much use to them."

"How can you say that? You're their father, the one they look up to, listen to, tell all their troubles to. I never knew my mother, but my father was my whole world."

"It doesn't work that way in my family. After Lacey died, her people took over with the children. Blue and Belinda spend more time at Bonterre than they do at Albion. They share a tutor there with their cousins and the neighbor kids. I can't complain. The Beaumonts are good to them." He lay back against the slope of the roof and stared up at the sky. "Yeah. They're good to my kids."

What about you? she wanted to ask. Are you good to your kids?

But she didn't know this man. She had no right to question what he did or failed to do about his children.

"Charles is good to them too," Hunter said. "He's my cousin on my father's side. He lives in Richmond, but comes out to Albion all the time. Loves the horses, and he knows about running a farm. And he likes being near his boy, Noah."

"Noah is his son?"

"Yeah. Noah's mother was a servant."

"A slave."

"Yes."

"Is Noah a slave?"

"No. He's family, and he knows it."

She thought of her father's rage and indignation when he read the journals and broadsides from the mainland. "In the eyes of the law, he's not family," she pointed out.

Hunter blew out a sigh, like a gust of weary wind. "He knows that too. I don't make the laws."

"You don't object when they're unjust, either."

"How do you know?"

She almost laughed. It was so obvious from his laconic, pleasure-seeking nature that he wouldn't bestir himself to take up a cause beyond himself and his precious Albion. "Because I think you are comfortable with matters just as they are."

"I never saw it as my mission to change the world," he admitted. "Hell, I can't even change my bad habits." He grinned fondly at his whiskey flask. His grin faded. "If folks won't tolerate a boy of mixed race, I can't force them to change. But in my eyes, Noah's family. I count myself lucky, having a family." His gaze penetrated through the darkness. "Don't you get lonely out here?"

She spread her arms, encompassing all she could see. "This is the life I've been given. My father's love was a precious gift to me, and I'd dishonor that gift by wanting more than I have."

"So you'll just stay here, settle for this?"

She watched the blaze of stars, and from the corner of her eye saw one shoot off and then fall out of existence. She could confess to Hunter Calhoun that there were days—many of them—when the simple act of breathing required too much effort. She could confess that there were some nights that she would not allow herself to sleep for fear that she'd dream of the night her father had died. But he was a stranger, so she didn't answer.

They tracked the silent, angry flight of an owl on the hunt and listened to the distant swish of the endless, destructive caress of the waves on the edge of the island. The marsh whirred with the sound of frogs and crickets, but the noise itself was a sort of silence, pervasive and never-ending.

Finally, Hunter moved his hand. He touched her shoulder, turning her to look at him. "How did your father die, Eliza? Tell me how he died."

She shivered at his touch, and from the question. A stranger, she kept telling herself. This man is a stranger. "I told you. There was a fire—"

His hand stayed where it was, although surely he could sense that her shoulder stiffened beneath his gently massaging fingers. "No," he said. "I asked you if there was a fire. You let me assume that's how he died because you didn't want to tell me the truth."

"That's not so."

His finger came up, brushed aside a lock of hair that lay across her cheek. The sensation made her shudder. "Eliza. There's nothing up here but you, me and the stars."

His statement—so simple, so true—drew a long, uneven sigh from her. "It's awful."

"All the more reason to tell me." His finger skimmed along her cheek, then traced the line of her jaw. She realized she held it clenched tight and forced herself to relax.

"Tell me now," he said, and she could imagine what that dark honey voice would do to any woman's will. Lacey Beaumont Calhoun must have been putty in the hands of this man, with his seductive voice, his compelling touch and his attention fixed on her in a way that could make a woman believe she was the most important thing on earth.

"It'll still be awful," she warned him. But she could already feel herself unbending, opening up, like Pericles's lion holding out a wounded paw, trusting the hunter to pull out the thorn.

"Tell me anyway." The questing hand moved lower,

finding the pulse at the side of her neck. It was almost as if he were touching a place inside her. It felt that deep, that intimate. She half shut her eyes and gave a small, distressed gasp.

"Don't you want me to do this?" he asked. "Don't you like me touching you?"

"I—don't know," she choked out. "You confuse me, Calhoun. In so many ways."

The starlight caught the flash of his grin. "It'll be like the horse. I'll leave you alone until you want to be with me."

Oh, Lord. It wasn't supposed to work like that on people.

"So talk to me, Eliza Flyte," he said, then took a swig of rum. And even though he was no longer touching her, she could feel the press of his attention on her, and it had almost the same devastating impact as his caress. "Tell me about the horsemaster. Tell it any way you like. We've got nothing but time."

A faraway feeling seeped into her mind, sending her back to the years she had spent with her father. She drew the story from a well of pain deep inside her, and each word emerged from that terrible dark place.

"My father and I never did count my birthdays, nor did he ever make note of the day of my birth back in England. The first time I left this island was the year of the big storm that swept away the main wharf of Eastwick, so in my mind the events are connected. My memory of helping my father catch ponies for the annual penning happened the same year as the shipwreck with the Spanish bride. That's how I remember things. It made for a certain..." She stared at the sky as if the right word might be written there. "A certain sense about the world. I believed that nothing mattered but the sea and the seasons and the work we did. I always had the feeling that we would go on like that forever, my father and me, living out our lives right here, with the animals and our books and the occasional visitor, the occasional trip to the mainland.''

"You never thought about leaving?'' he asked.

"We talked about California, but it was a dream, not a plan.'' She opened her arms as if to embrace the sky above. The stars were so numerous that they lit the roof, and she could see clearly the outline of her hands against the night. "Why would I want to leave this?''

"Because there's a whole world out there.''

"Yes. I didn't realize until I was older that my father kept trying to prepare me for changes. He used to show me where the waves bit away the dunes, and where the sand is shifting, and how there's a marsh full of stumps where a forest used to be. It's the nature of the islands to change. That's what he used to say to me. That nothing is permanent, nothing lasts. He was trying to tell me that changes were coming, but I didn't listen. Didn't want to know. And so, after a lifetime of thinking nothing would be different, I found myself with an empty cabin, a burned-out barn, and my father hanged from a beam across the covered arena where he used to train.''

A hissing sound came from Hunter Calhoun. It was as if her words burned him. She felt their sting too, even now, long after the event. She couldn't stop talking, though. Didn't want to stop. The dark well inside her had been plumbed. A floodgate had opened. All the words and feelings that she'd held in with her silence and her loneliness came pouring out.

"I remember crushing myself into a hiding place the night they came for him.''

"They—'' His voice broke on the single word. He was

a tense shadow beside her; she could feel him bracing himself for what came next.

"The men who killed him. He had only moments to warn me, and he made me promise to stay hidden and silent no matter what happened. When he went off to the barn with them, I thought it was to do some horse trading, though it was the middle of the night."

She squeezed her eyes shut. "Why didn't I think it was unusual to make deals in the middle of the night?"

"Because you weren't looking for evil." Hunter paused a moment, then asked, "You didn't recognize these men?"

"I never saw their faces. I suppose that's why they never came back for me. Even if they knew I existed, they had no fear that I'd ever be able to identify them. As far as they knew, I had nothing they wanted. As far as they knew."

She had always wondered if they would have murdered her too, because she had her father's gift with horses. Opening her eyes, she said, "I'll always remember the tread of their footsteps and the sound of their voices. Papa always said I was just like the horses—an animal that survives by fleeing. Quiet, wont to run from danger or camouflage myself in hiding rather than confront it. There was nowhere to flee that night. I managed to hide between two burlap sacks of milkweed pods, wedging myself in, praying my dark frock and dark hair blended with the night. And while I was quailing in terror, my world was transformed."

The cedar shingles had begun to press painfully into her elbows. She eased down onto her back, assuming Hunter's supine posture.

"Just like that," she said, snapping her fingers. "My father and I had a life of innocent simplicity here, and suddenly I knew only danger and isolation. My father taught me to believe in the basic decency of people, but in just a few moments I had the smell of blood and death in my nose. I learned to suspect everyone." She glanced over at Hunter. "You included." It bothered her that she felt so comfortable with him. She'd warmed to him too quickly, and for too little reason. Yet she believed strongly in instinct, and instinct told her that this man would not hurt her.

"I gathered that." Pain or anger—she wasn't sure which—reverberated in his voice.

"One moment I had my father's unconditional love. The next I had nothing. Less than nothing. When he was gone, so was the only thing in my life that mattered."

He shifted to his side, one hip against the roof. "Why did they kill him?"

"I always assumed it had to do with his gift for working with horses. Some people still think it's a black art. I imagine I'll never know for sure." She shut her eyes. "Since he was killed, I've begun to do something I never thought I'd do. I've begun to count time. Not just the years and months, but days and hours. Stupid, isn't it?"

"So how long has it been?"

"Seven months, eleven days. I've been alone ever since that night. I picked up my life as best I could. Every few months I take the dinghy to town for supplies. I've been trading herbs and mushrooms, sometimes shellfish or whatever else I can sell. I don't say much to anyone. Most folks in these parts have forgotten my name. They just call me the horsemaster's daughter."

Telling the tale had exhausted her, and she lay limp on the sloping roof, scarcely breathing, studying the powdery white light of the stars, her gaze probing the deeper black between them.

"What are you staring at?" Hunter asked.

"I'm looking, always looking for the place where my father dwells, up there among the stars."

Hunter Calhoun fell utterly silent. He didn't speak, didn't move, didn't touch her. She lay still beside him, listening to the rhythmic breathing of the night and the ocean, feeling the chill lick of the breeze passing over her body. The silence drew out, long and longer still, and then she started to worry. What had she done, baring her soul to this stranger from across the water? What had she been thinking?

Finally, nerves got the better of her and she made the first move, sitting up and scooting over so that she faced away from him.

"You know," she said, her voice gratifyingly clear and loud. "I don't really care what you think of my story, or my life and the way I live it. You asked what happened, and I answered you honestly, and now you probably don't know the first thing to say to me." Eliza heard herself speaking faster and faster, releasing still more of that flood of words that had been dammed up inside her for far too long. "I can't blame you. The story of my life since the murder would leave anyone at a loss for words, I swear. But it's what happened and there's no way I can change—"

She broke off as his hand clamped down almost violently on her shoulder. He drew her around to face him, cedar shakes crumbling with the abrupt movement. He had risen from his supine position and he appeared huge against the night sky, rearing up on his knees, the chalky starlight forming a nimbus around his breeze-mussed hair. She took this all in with a single glance, but only had time to gasp in astonishment before he bent swiftly and pressed his mouth down hard upon hers.

It took a few seconds for her to realize that this brutally sensual assault was a kiss. Her first kiss. She couldn't quite think of it in that way, for kissing was something she had only ever read about: Mr. Rochester's brief peck on Jane Eyre's wrist. This was not brief, and it wasn't a peck. He crushed his mouth down so hard that she could feel the imprint of his teeth against her lips. Though it shocked her, it didn't hurt.

A moment later she felt his tongue pushing insistently against the seam of her mouth. At the same time, he worked his thumb against her jaw as he had done earlier, only this was no friendly caress but an assault, and one she craved. With no choice but to obey, she opened her mouth, and then his tongue was in her, pushing, probing, and in the oddest way seeming to drink or feed upon whatever it was that was inside her.

She felt confused, unbalanced, and she braced her hands on the roof behind her to keep from falling somewhere she didn't want to go. He pressed his body close, and he was overwhelmingly big, warm and protective as he covered her. She heard a faint, helpless sound and realized it came from her. Protesting? Not that. Pleading? Perhaps. But for what?

The taste of him was so surprising, but not nearly as surprising as the softness of his mouth and the painful sweetness of the feelings that spread through her. A few moments before, her skin had been chilly from the sea breeze. Now she burned, she stung. She wanted.

But life had taught her to flee the unknown, and before her wanting raged out of control, she recoiled.

"What's the matter?" he asked, pulling away.

She still felt the ghost of his kiss on her lips. "Why did you do that?" she demanded.

He took another drink of rum, and his voice was lazy and careless as he said, "Because you were so alone, Eliza. Because you were so alone."

His pity infuriated her. Before he could stop her, she scrambled down the slope of the roof. Her legs went over the side and swung there, toes outstretched until she found the top of the barrel she had used to boost herself up. From there she found the porch beam and then the rail, and finally felt the hard, chill earth beneath her bare feet.

Ten

Waking late the next morning, Hunter pulled on his boots and made himself eat something—a bit of spiced apple from a jar in the kitchen. The food tasted foul in his mouth after all that rum the night before, but he knew he needed to eat. Then he left the house to search for Eliza.

He knew he had better find her and explain himself as soon as possible. Kissing her the night before had been the height of stupidity. Never mind that she had looked like a goddess, lying there in the misty starlight. Never mind that he had felt her ache of loneliness as acutely as his own base instinct. Never mind that she had roused in him a blaze of passion he'd never felt before—not for a woman, a horse or even a dream. He should have known better than to touch her, kiss her, fan the banked fires of their relationship. He'd known almost from the start that the passion was there between them. But so long as he kept a respectful distance, he didn't have to acknowledge the attraction.

Last night, reckless as a moonstruck lad, he had closed that critical, unspoken distance. Some girls were meant to be kissed, fondled and toyed with like playthings. Not Eliza. Earnest and strange, she would never treat love as a game that ended in laughter and forgetfulness. She took everything seriously, took *him* seriously. He groaned aloud. He had misled her. For all he knew, she was now thinking that *she* might be the new wife he was looking for. He never should have told her his thoughts on the matter, never should have raised her hopes, never should have taken her in his arms and kissed her as if there were something they might dare to believe in.

Furious at himself, he searched for her, intent on making certain she understood it was the rum and the moonlight that had made him take her in his arms. Nothing more. There could be nothing more, ever.

The round pen where they had tamed the stallion was empty, the gate open. He followed the footprints—the girl's small bare feet walking next to the horse's sharp hoof marks. They had left at a slow walk. He could tell by the impressions they made in the sand. He followed the trail over the dunes and down to the beach. The incoming tide had erased the prints, but Hunter spotted the girl and the horse standing knee deep in the lagoon.

What a pair they made—the black-haired girl and the tall stallion, their images reflected in the still water.

Spying him, she lifted one arm. He could not tell if she waved in anger or welcome or caution. He approached them, and the horse swung his head toward him. Eliza had put a sheepskin, with the wool side down, over the stallion's back. Two leather straps held the odd saddle in place.

"Good morning," she said as he reached the edge of the lagoon.

"What are you doing?" he asked.

"He needs to be ridden."

"Like that?" Hunter frowned skeptically. "By you?"

"Haven't you learned to trust me by now?" Without

waiting for an answer, she made a clicking sound to the horse and led him deeper into the water. The surface of the lagoon mirrored the sky, reflecting treetops and high summery clouds that rippled as the woman and the horse waded deep. "This way, if I get thrown, I won't get hurt," she explained.

"I hope you know how to swim," he cautioned, feeling himself go tense.

"I won't need to swim. Finn will be doing the swimming."

He marveled at the way she spoke to him, in the same matter-of-fact fashion that she had...before. As if their kiss last night had not happened. Or as if it didn't matter.

Her manner nonchalant, she went deeper until the horse was in up to his withers. Then he swam, and Hunter was amazed at the calm way he moved through the water. He had expected the stallion to panic.

Eliza took hold of the mane and let her legs drift up and over his back. Hunter held his breath, bracing himself for a terrible accident. The stallion shuddered, but went on with Eliza holding fast to him. She lay forward and dropped her arms around his neck, and the pose had a powerful effect on Hunter. She was the picture of surrender and trust, her body draped over the stallion, her arms around the big arched neck and her cheek against the damp hide. No lady in Hunter's world would even contemplate such a thing, yet Eliza rode without the slightest hesitation, as if swimming with a horse were the most natural thing in the world.

She didn't so much ride the horse as become a part of him, moving as he moved, breathing as he breathed, letting him go where he would instead of trying to direct him. They were one entity, neither horse nor girl but a magical melding of the two. After a while, she sat erect, and he was surprised to see that her posture on horseback was as perfect as if she had attended the Hirsute Riding Academy of Williamsburg. She held her chin up and her shoulders level and square, and with only a slight press of her knee, she turned the horse toward shore.

Stallion and rider emerged from the water in a trail of glistening sunlit droplets. The horse planted his forelegs wide, and for a moment Hunter feared he would buck her off. But instead, the horse shook himself dry like a dog. Eliza laughed and clung tight to the mane. Then she asked the stallion to walk, indicating her desire with her knees and that soft clicking sound. The damp dress clung to her, outlining her breasts and belly.

Hunter had loved touching her, and even though he knew it could lead to trouble, he wanted to do more than kiss, even now. Her posture, once again, was flawless— heels down, head up—so proper he almost forgot her ragged dress, bare feet and unkempt tail of hair clubbed back with a bit of string. He forgot that her saddle was fashioned from a sheep's hide. Upon the back of the Irish Thoroughbred, Eliza Flyte looked as regal as a queen.

They trained all day, taking turns with the work. Each exercise, each step along the way, brought the stallion closer to the champion he had been before the sea voyage. One step at a time, they reintroduced him to bit and bridle, to saddle and stirrups, and most of all to the presence and touch and authority of humans. By the end of the day, Finn was exhausted and biddable, only occasionally balky. Hunter groomed him, invigorated by the clean smell of the lagoon in Finn's hair and mane.

"Eliza," he said over his shoulder, "you're a wonder."

"I'll fix us some supper," she said.

When he turned around, he saw that she had already

left silently on the sandy path. A little disgruntled, Hunter finished the grooming. He checked the horse's feed and water, then shoveled out the arena. As he worked, he couldn't stop thinking about Eliza.

It galled him that she didn't seem as preoccupied as he was about their intimacy the night before. She had stayed focused on the horse, limiting her topic of conversation to Finn and his progress.

He didn't understand her at all. She had gone through the entire day behaving as if nothing had happened between them. It wasn't that he *wanted* her to be furious or hurt or horrified—it was that he expected no less.

Before going into the house, he put up the grooming box and washed himself at the cistern. Through the kitchen window, he could see Eliza stirring something, her face as serene and untroubled as a madonna's. Her damp hair hung down her back, and she'd changed clothes. He caught himself wanting to smell the rainwater on her skin and in her hair, to taste her lips again. Immediately he shut off the thought.

"Something smells good," he said as he stepped inside.

Eliza busied herself at the stove. Within a short time, she set the table with two mugs of cider, bowls of stewed greens and hot corn pone with butter melting over the golden-brown tops.

"Have I told you," he said, hoping to keep the conversation light, "how much I admire your cooking?"

She watched him shovel in the greens and corn pone. "Not in words."

He washed it down with a slug of cider and wiped his mouth. "My compliments. I know I'll burn in hell for saying this, but your corn pone is better than Willa's."

"You like this corn pone better?"

He took a bite and nodded. "Maybe she uses more lard or something."

"I don't use fat at all," Eliza said. "I never eat meat either."

He blinked in surprise. "You don't?"

"Of course not."

"Why not?"

"I could never be that...predatory."

"I've never heard of that," Hunter said. "Never heard of someone who didn't eat meat."

"My father wouldn't touch it either. I'll eat fish and shellfish, but never anything with fur or feathers or warm blood." She gave a shudder of distaste. "It would be like eating a...a relative."

He could understand that—sort of. She lived with animals, communicated with them in her own strange way. He could understand why she wouldn't betray the bond of trust she formed with them.

They finished their meal in a silence that, to Hunter's mind, grew louder and louder with each passing moment. He helped her wash up the dishes, and as they finished the task, darkness fell with that peculiar merciless swiftness he'd noticed the first night here. Long purple shadows streamed across the water and the marshland. The sounds of nocturnal creatures came out one by one, like the stars—the hoot of an owl, the squeal of a bat, the chirp of a thousand frogs.

His tongue and throat itched and thirsted until he almost couldn't stand it. "I think I'll have a little more of that rum," he said.

She untied the cloth she wore as an apron and draped it over the back of a chair. "Why?"

"What do you mean, why?"

"Why do you want a drink of rum?"

"It's one of the pleasures some folks enjoy."

"You enjoy it? Drinking gives you pleasure?"

"Sometimes, yes."

"But sometimes no," she persisted.

He grew exasperated and defensive. "Look, if you don't want me to drink any rum, just say so and I'll—"

"I don't want you to drink any rum," she said readily. "I shouldn't have let you have the jug."

"But—" He narrowed his eyes at her. "You're just saying that to make me angry."

"Are you angry?"

"No, goddamn it, I'm not angry." But the sexual frustration that had begun so recklessly on the roof came bubbling to the surface. "I wanted to do a lot more than kiss you last night," he said.

She brought her fists up to her chest and shuddered. He saw a flash of fascination in her eyes, but it was quickly doused by suspicion.

"What? What else did you want to do?"

"You'll never know, because it'll never happen."

"Why not?"

"Because it's not right, Eliza. I don't have a damn thing to offer you."

"What makes you think I need something from you?"

"I see it in your eyes, honey." He nearly choked on the admission. "Now, where's that rum?"

Eleven

Passion, Eliza realized, was not a thing one could easily control. That must have been what Hunter meant about seeing a great need in her eyes. No wonder passion had inspired so many sonnets and stories. No wonder Charlotte Brontë had described it as a living entity with a will of its own.

Because of the way she felt about Hunter Calhoun, she saw the world differently. Nothing would ever be the same again. The light looked clearer. The stars brighter. Food tasted more delicious. A simple birdsong suddenly sounded so sweet it made her heart hurt.

And all because he had kissed her.

As she worked with the stallion—Finn had made amazing progress, and they were practicing racing starts—she kept lapsing into long moments of dreaminess.

Seated on a heartwood stump at low tide, she watched the nervous frenzy of the crabs on the mudflats as, one by one, they fell victim to hungry seagulls. On the long yellow-brown beach, Hunter rode the stallion.

Though reasonably cooperative, Finn was a strong-willed animal and probably always had been. He balked and pranced. From time to time, he reared. He backed into a brake of sassafras trees, trying to scrape his rider off. Sweating and cursing, Hunter struggled to regain control. He was thrown several times, and soon was covered in sand.

Eliza tried not to let her amusement show, but he caught her grinning at him. "You're supposed to weep when you see me work," he grumbled. "Isn't that what the virtuous Miranda did when Ferdinand stacked the logs in *The Tempest?*"

She laughed aloud. "In case you haven't noticed, I'm not the virtuous Miranda. And forgive me, but you're no Prince of Naples."

He took a long drink of water from the jug she had brought from the house. Wiping his mouth with his sleeve, he looked off in the distance, where the tip of Cape Henry, on the mainland, melted into the sea. Three ships were passing through from Chesapeake Bay into the open waters of the Atlantic. Shipping traffic was a common sight, but one of the vessels caught her eye because it had a bright red topsail.

"I wonder what schooner that is," she mused. "I wonder why it flies a red sail."

Hunter stiffened, drawing his shoulders up to his ears. Then he shrugged elaborately. "I imagine so it can be recognized from a distance."

"You've seen it before?"

He hesitated, then said, "Yeah. I've seen it." He hauled himself to his feet and got back on the horse.

Finn was born to run; she could see that clearly. And that had been the key to finding the way out of his madness. The horse simply needed to be urged to do those things that were in his nature. Finn was so filled with energy and exuberance that he returned quickly. He had a few bad habits. She suspected they had come about as a result of inferior training in far-off Ireland. But he was an exceptionally intelligent horse, and his training was a joy.

Shaded from the late afternoon sun, she watched Hunter and the horse, and let her mind meander lazily. Hunter Calhoun had a sort of madness inside him too, she thought. It was not so obvious as the horse's had been, but she could feel it in him, seething, looking for a way out. He drank whiskey and rum to keep from feeling himself falling into the darkness, but drinking was only a temporary measure.

What had his life been like before the madness? His wife, Lacey, had been a true Virginia lady, a planter's daughter, and to hear him tell it, she had given him every happiness—as long as he was a prosperous planter.

Eliza couldn't understand why a change in wealth would turn a woman's heart.

Especially against a man like Hunter Calhoun.

She might have sat all day and into evening in this dreamy state, if she had not heard Caliban bark. The stallion shied, and Hunter had his hands full trying to settle him. A heavy crashing sound came from the woods beyond the dunes on the leeward side of the island.

Instantly alert, she scrambled to her feet.

"What's that?" Hunter asked. The stallion jarred him this way and that.

"Nothing," she said, hoping she was right. "Caliban probably treed a critter, that's all. I'll quiet him down."

As she left the beach, she tried not to hurry.

Following the sound of the dog's frenzied barking, she wended her way deep into the tall forest behind the house. Long bars of sunlight slanted down through the fir and cedar canopy, falling upon a soft carpet of rusty needles and moist-lipped mushrooms.

"Caliban, enough," she called out. "Hush now."

The big dog gave a few more barks that trailed off to agitated whining. She found him sitting back on his haunches facing a slanted deadfall. Eliza followed the dog's point and brought her hand up to stifle a scream.

High on the lichened trunk perched a man. A furious, terrified man, brandishing a baling knife. She had a swift impression of dusty black skin, shiny dark eyes, tattered clothing, bare feet.

"Who are you?" Eliza called up to him. "What do you want?"

No reply. The shining eyes narrowed and glinted with danger. The strong hand tightened on the knife sheath. Yet Eliza felt no fear of him because the fear she felt emanating *from* him was so powerful. He had the furtive posture of a man fully aware of danger.

And then she knew. He was a runaway slave, and what he wanted was as simple and as dangerous as freedom. But how had he come to be here?

"You can come down," she said. "I've called off my dog. He won't hurt you."

The man sent her a measuring glance. He didn't move.

"You can't stay there forever," Eliza pointed out. "And believe me, Caliban can, and will, if need be. He's a stubborn one. But you have my word. He won't hurt you."

The man hesitated, then clamped the blade between his teeth and started to descend. As he inched down the slanted tree trunk, distrust seethed from his every pore. She felt the same but tried not to let it show. "Do you think you could put the knife away?"

He shook his head. The dog growled, and she shushed him urgently. "I won't betray you," she said. "I won't... tell anyone."

He glared at her obliquely and took the blade from between his teeth. "How'm I s'posed to know that?"

"You've got the knife."

"You got a real big dog, missy."

This was the first time Eliza had encountered a runaway slave. His speech was strange, his manner frightened and volatile. Desperation sharpened his features. "I was told to come here," he said, mumbling the words at the ground. "Told there'd be a safe cove for waiting, and a ship in the night."

Eliza frowned. Who would have said such a thing to a man looking for freedom? Who would have made such a reckless promise? Suddenly realization swept over her. *This was something her father had done.* So many things became clear to her in that moment. Her father's habit of spending hours on the lookout walk on the roof. His occasional disappearances at night, when he must have thought she was asleep. His habit of laying in more food than the two of them could eat. His keen interest in news broadsheets from the mainland. In secret, he must have been helping slaves to freedom.

"You were supposed to meet my father, Henry Flyte," she said.

The use of the name seemed to calm the man, and he came down the rest of the way, all the while keeping his knife at the ready and his eyes on Caliban.

"My father was—he passed away," she said.

The man's shoulders drooped. She could see the spirit going out of him like a slow exhalation.

"Tell me what you expect," Eliza suggested. "Perhaps I could help you."

He shot her a dubious look. "I been told there'd be a deepwater cove, north end of the island."

"I know the place." Excitement tingled in her chest.

This new awareness of her father made her feel closer to him than ever. "There's only one proper cove with a view out to sea."

"I been told to build a fire on the beach."

"To signal the boat." She tried to keep her voice low, but it was hard. After all the months of fearing her father would fade from memory, she suddenly felt very close to him. She could picture him clearly now, his movements assured as he led fleeing men and women to a place of safety. Dear God, he must have been helping fugitives for years. How could she not have known? "I can do this," she said, praying she could be half as encouraging as her father must have been. "I can help you."

The man leaned back against the fallen tree, exhausted. He was young. Most of them were, she supposed, for how else could someone endure the terror and hardship of this secret journey? His bare arms and hands bore the scars of work and whippings. His hair was cropped short, one side infested with hayseed. He had probably passed the day hiding and sleeping in a hayrick on the mainland before making the low-tide crossing to the island. He was dangerously thin, and his skin had a deep bluish cast to it. The leg of his homespun trousers had been shredded, and sticky blood stained his ankle.

She stepped back, wondering what to do next. She knew instinctively that she must be careful to give him space, not to threaten him.

He gingerly raised the injured leg, and she feared the wound was even worse than it appeared.

"I'd better have a look at that," she said quietly.

He froze, narrowing his eyes at her.

"If you get an infection, you'll be in no shape for the rest of your journey," she added.

He gave one curt nod and followed her through the woods. But he kept his knife out.

"I'm not alone on this island," she said quietly. "The other person who is here with me won't betray you." She hoped she was right, but she didn't intend to test Hunter by telling him about the runaway. "I'm going to ask you to wait for me here while I fetch some things from the house. Then we'll see about getting you to the north shore."

She showed him where he could sit on a low flat rock about fifty yards from the house. Cedar branches swept down, concealing him from view.

"Will you stay?" she asked. When he gave no answer, she said, "Please. I only want to help."

"I'll stay." His reply was a weary whisper. He slipped the knife into his belt.

She patted her leg so Caliban would follow, and went to get some water, soap, bandages and liniment. Hunter was nowhere to be found; he was probably still working with the stallion. She set out some corn pone and freshly churned butter in case he came back early. She prayed he wouldn't question her absence or come looking for her.

She returned to the runaway, pleased to see he had not left. She gave him some cider, corn pone and a jar of beach-plum preserves, which he devoured while she examined the wounded leg. The gash was horrible. Something had encircled his lower leg and sunk deep.

"What happened?" she asked.

He took a swallow of cider. "Mantrap." He winced as she teased a thread of fabric out of the wound.

Eliza gritted her teeth. She wasn't squeamish, but the cruelty of a steel-toothed trap made her ill. Of the many things she had heard about the outside world, the custom of slavery was the most incomprehensible.

Slave, whom stripes may move, not kindness! She had read it in *The Tempest*, but who would ever think such an atrocious thing could really exist in a sane mind?

Her father had explained that slavery was legal, but unjust. He must have felt morally obligated to help defeat it by assisting the runaways.

She was amazed that she hadn't guessed the secret sooner. Her father had told her that in years long past, pirates had made use of the north shore, concealing their swift schooners offshore and racing to the mainland to plunder supplies. She should have realized that Flyte Island was ideally suited as a stop on the route to freedom. It had a deepwater moorage not far offshore, and was protected from view of the mainland by the tall rise of the leeward forest. A cove, gouged out by the sea and sheltered under the curve of a cliff in the dunes, created a secluded place to build a signal fire and wait.

She finished cleaning the wound, coated it with liniment and bandaged it. The man finished all of the food she had brought. She wished she had given him more.

"It's about a mile to the cove," she said. "Can you walk?"

The man nodded.

"It's nearly dark," she said. "We'd best go down to the water and wait." She led the way through the high parts of the forest, moving north and east over the dunes to the remote, storm-carved cove. The runaway followed slowly, stumbling now and then.

"Here," she said, putting out an arm. "You must lean on me."

He hesitated, his thin shadow tense. "You just a little bit of a thing."

"You're pretty skinny yourself."

He put an arm across her shoulders and leaned in close,

his hip alongside hers. She took care to let him favor his
injured leg as they walked together. His sweat smelled of
the fear of a man pushed to the brink of his endurance,
and his breathing sounded loud, almost frantic, in the stillness of nightfall.

Eliza felt almost overwhelmed by the closeness. The
physical contact startled her. After months of being alone,
she had encountered two men within the span of a few
days. Curiously, both men were wounded, each in a different—but undeniable—way.

The runaway's touch was impersonal, even reluctant,
that of necessity. Hunter's had never been impersonal, not
even the first time he had touched her.

Twilight had fallen by the time they reached the cove,
but Eliza knew the area well. "We can wait here." She
indicated an ancient twist of driftwood. One side of it had
been charred by fire. When? she wondered. When had her
father last helped a fugitive?

"You got to go back," the man said.

"Shouldn't I stay with you?"

"Best you don't see this. Less you knows, the better,"
he said.

Conceding his point, she handed him a tin of lucifers
for making the fire.

"Godspeed," she said, walking backward, watching
him.

The fugitive said nothing. His eyes were the eyes of a
dead man. He lifted one hand and then sat down on the
sand to wait.

Eliza lay abed that night and tried to sleep, but she could
not. Her thoughts were filled with Hunter Calhoun. He had
been exuberant at supper because of the progress the horse
had made. He'd grown merry with the rum and had not

noticed her silence or the glances she kept aiming at the door. Pleading fatigue, she had gone to bed early, and he had taken his flask to the hammock on the porch.

Now, hours later, her body wept for him. He had lost all interest in her after that one kiss. She was embarrassed each time she recalled her fumbling conversation that evening. How stupid he must have thought her. How naive.

Restless, she lit a candle and opened her favorite book. Jane Eyre's troubles seemed so much more comprehensible to her now. She wondered if that was what she was feeling—the torment of confusion Charlotte Brontë described. It certainly sounded as if poor Jane was in a fix. Mr. Rochester kept a terrible secret locked away—his mad wife, hidden in the attic. What awful secret did Hunter Calhoun conceal, back at the place called Albion?

She felt so jumpy that even Jane and Mr. Rochester couldn't keep her attention. It was the runaway. Like Hunter Calhoun, he was an unexpected visitor. And like Calhoun, he posed a danger to her solitary way of life.

She began to enumerate the things that could go wrong. The runaway might fall asleep. A noise might frighten him. The wrong ship might spot the signal and send a shore party to investigate. What had her father done on nights like this? She needed him now, needed his wisdom, his certainty.

After a few minutes she convinced herself. She had no choice but to go to the cove and wait with the fugitive.

She slipped from her bed and dressed in a hurry. Gingerly she opened the door and crept barefoot across the porch. Praying the planks would not creak, she inched over the floor, keeping an eye on the long, sagging form sleeping in the hammock.

He lay half in moonlight, half in shadow. The neutral tones created by moon and darkness gave his features the silvery smoothness of chiseled marble. His weary masculine beauty caught at her heart. In sleep, the worldly, cynical expression was gone. He merely looked vulnerable, perhaps a little sad. She thought of the engraving in her lithograph collection of the wounded Celt. That was how he looked to her. Like a fallen warrior, one who had surrendered his soul to the darkness.

She reached the edge of the porch and turned away with a self-deprecating smile. She had never had such romantic thoughts, never considered herself capable of them. That was the trouble with learning all she knew from books. The abstract was not anything like the actual experience. Her father had tried to explain this to her, but she had never understood it until now.

She never understood the pain of yearning for intimacy. Now it was a part of her.

She stepped down into the yard and heard a distant hissing sound. High over the tops of the cedars at the north end of the island, a signal flare blossomed and then descended. She picked up the hem of her skirt and ran, stubbing her toe on a root but not stopping. Caliban loped at her side.

She prayed Hunter had not awakened. Probably not. She had found him to be a sound sleeper, particularly after he drank.

He drank every night. The jug of rum that had been sitting for years in the root cellar was nearly empty. She wondered if he would go too, when the rum ran dry.

She should not be thinking of Calhoun at all, but of the fugitive.

By the time she reached the cove, the signal fire flamed high into the night. Motioning for Caliban to stay back and keep quiet, she called softly to the runaway.

"It's me," she said. "I wanted to be sure you're all right."

"I'm all right, missy. Don't know what's going to happen next."

They watched in anxious silence. The ship's stern light formed a tiny, bright pinprick in the distance. They didn't speak any more as they waited. She wished she had learned the rules from her father. But she understood why he had kept this from her. The less she knew of those who crossed the island, the better off everyone would be. Escaping slaves knew this instinctively. They mistrusted everyone, and Eliza could feel the sting of that distrust. She didn't blame the fugitive, didn't resent his silence.

A bumboat appeared gradually, blackness out of blackness. Eliza could feel anxiety seething from the runaway. "Keep to the shadows," she whispered. "I'll make certain this is no trick." She motioned with her hand, and he fell back to wait and watch. Caliban whined once, but a sharp shush from Eliza quieted the big dog.

A lone figure rowed the boat with strong, even strokes. She waded out to meet it as it slid up onto the sand. The rower turned; in the dark she couldn't see his expression. Under a knitted cap, he had light-colored hair that curled over his shoulders. He was strong but slender, not so broad as Hunter Calhoun—

Immediately she grew exasperated with herself. Was everything about Hunter Calhoun, then?

The boat beached itself in the shallow water. Caliban greeted it with a rumble of warning. The rower turned, showing a remarkably youthful face. In the firelight, his clothing looked extraordinary—a silk waistcoat of lime green, no shirt beneath. Around his waist he wore, pirate fashion, a tangerine-colored sash. Stuck in the sash were at least four weapons, including a seaman's dirk and a pistol.

"Are you the delivery I was told to collect?" the man asked softly.

She shook her head, slightly bemused by his question. In the dark, with her wild black hair and her ragged clothes, she might well resemble a runaway slave. "I'm a friend," she said simply.

The man's hand closed around the handle of the dirk. "Where is Henry Flyte?"

"He's dead. I'm his daughter."

The sharp gaze raked over her as if probing her for falsehoods. Then he said, "Everything's ready. By daybreak, we'll be in northern waters."

Even his voice, with its smooth Virginia accent, held a curiously familiar note, she thought, beginning to panic. She had to stop seeing Hunter in every man, hearing his voice in everything spoken by a man.

"Is it just one passenger?" he asked.

She nodded.

With a metallic snick, he drew the knife from his garish belt and stood up. "Then why are two men coming toward us?"

Eliza whirled around. The fugitive stood as if frozen by fear. A bigger, broader form hurried across the beach.

Dear God, Hunter Calhoun. He had followed her.

She stood immobile, thinking of words that wouldn't form on her lips. She had no idea what impulse to obey. Should she call out to Hunter and warn him of the dagger, or should she beg him to forget what he saw here?

"By the Almighty," the man in the boat murmured. He stepped out, slogged through the water and strode ashore.

Eliza braced herself, inhaling for a scream. The two men were nearly equal in size, Hunter slightly larger. They hurried toward each other like a pair of stags about to tangle antlers.

But the boatman didn't wield his knife. Instead, he put it away and spread his arms wide. While Eliza and the runaway watched in astonishment, the two big men drew each other into a bear hug.

Hunter stepped back, grinning. "It's been too long, brother," he said.

Twelve

The *Spolia Opima* was one of the most elusive secrets of the Underground Railroad. Expertly skippered by a man known only as "Mr. Swan," the sleek, swift oceangoing schooner had transported dozens of escaped slaves over the years. In certain circles the ship was spoken of in the hushed, reverent whispers reserved for legends and tall tales. It moved through the glassy night waters like a ghost ship, breaking away from the horizon to head to the next secret anchorage. Its favored haunts were the low, shifting islands of the Chesapeake and the Outer Banks, places separated and isolated by the tides. And Flyte Island, with its proximity to the mainland and its protected deepwater anchorage, was the preferred rendezvous, and had been for years. By moonlight, the waiting slaves sneaked aboard, snatched from forced servitude and taken to places in the north where they would be, if not safe, at least free.

"What a marvel," Eliza said softly as she and Hunter walked back to the house. "But I feel so foolish, with this going on between my father and your brother, and all the while I had no idea."

Hunter cast a look over his shoulder. Ryan and the runaway slave had already been swallowed by darkness. Soon they would be aboard the *Spolia Opima,* sailing north with a good headwind.

"You weren't supposed to know," he said.

"What about you?" She grabbed his arm. "You knew, didn't you? You knew when you saw that ship flying a red topsail."

"True. I didn't realize his rendezvous was this particular island, but I know what my brother has been doing." Hunter gently disengaged his arm. His heart swelled with pride for his younger half brother. Ryan Calhoun had always been reckless, vain, amusing, and ultimately driven by his convictions, no matter how dangerous or unpopular.

Eliza's reaction amused Hunter. She had been so flabbergasted to see him embrace the boatman on the beach.

"I'm telling you more than is prudent for you to know," he said. "But aiding the cause of abolition is not as unthinkable as you're making it out to be."

"You're from a Virginia family. Your father was a planter. Why would your brother be working to end slavery?"

"It's a long story. Ryan and I each rebelled against our father in different ways."

"And you approve of Ryan's work?"

"For all my faults, I do possess a small bit of human decency. If a man desires to escape bondage, it's not for me to stand in his way. Ryan always knew I'd help him if he needed it." Hunter grinned, savoring the look of shock on Ryan's face when they had met on the beach. He'd quickly explained about the Irish Thoroughbred. Ryan had subjected Eliza to a long, measuring stare, and said a curious thing, "Brother, you seem more content out here than I ever saw you at Albion."

Hunter and Eliza returned to the house. She was clearly too agitated to go back to bed right away. She built up the fire under the kettle for tea and paced back and forth, throwing inquisitive glances at Hunter.

"I've not grown antlers or a tail," he said, chuckling.

"How does the escape work, then?"

He found himself noticing her body as she paced, and thinking of how it felt to hold her in his arms. That thought led to even less appropriate thoughts. He had to force his mind back to the issue at hand.

"Ryan and his wife, Isadora, keep a town house in Norfolk. He's a legitimate shipper, has a good clean record for runs between New England and Rio de Janeiro." Noticing the puzzled expression on her face, he added, "That's in Brazil—South America. On his return runs from Rio, he makes port in Virginia and takes on his…passengers," he said cautiously. "Anyway, that is how it works, more or less."

She added a pinch of loose tea leaves to the kettle. She made her own, of rose hips and wild chamomile, and the brewing fragrance filled the small cabin. Adding a dollop of honey to a tin cup, she poured tea over it and handed it to him.

"No, thanks," he said. "I thought I'd have rum."

"You always have rum. Why is that?"

"Because there's no whiskey," he said.

She had a way of looking at him that made him feel guilty for drinking. Not accusatory. Just melancholy, perhaps. Disappointed in him.

Scowling, he said, "Fine, I'll try the tea."

She beamed at him, her cheeks coloring up with a blush. Were he a man given to flattery, he would have told her she had a beautiful smile. He would have told her that her unusual eyes, mist colored with a dark fringe of lashes, were entrancing. He would have told her that the sight of

her small, lithe body did wild things to him and that he
yearned to kiss her full, sweet lips again.

Instead, he took the cup from her and sipped the tea.
The flower-sweet taste wasn't terrible.

But it wasn't rum, either.

"So now we share a secret," he said, going out to the
porch.

"Do you only have the one?" She leaned against the
rail.

"One what?"

"One secret. I consider you to be the sort of man to
have more than one."

He laughed. "You're so strange," he said, "and I like
you so damn much."

She stared at Hunter as if he had spat frogs.

He spread his arms with elaborate innocence. "Shall I
apologize?" He laughed again, amazed that he could be
in such a good mood without the aid of strong drink.
"Let's go up to the roof and see if we can spot Ryan's
ship."

Once they had climbed aloft, Eliza was consumed by
the thought that it was here that her father had passed so
many nights looking out to sea.

"Here I thought he was just being whimsical," she murmured. "I had no idea the platform was meant for a secret
purpose."

Hunter sat on the roof beside her, drawing one knee up
to his chest and surveying the long, moonlit marshes and
the dunes beyond. "It's a hell of a view. You can see for
miles when the moon is up and the stars light the sky.
Look, there goes the schooner."

She felt a curious jolt of emotion when she saw the ship

silhouetted against the night sky. "There it goes," she whispered. "Godspeed."

He touched her hair, brushing a wisp of it away from her cheek. "What's the matter?"

"I thought I knew my father. Now, long after his death, I find out there was a whole part of his life he kept hidden from me."

"For your own good, Eliza. Abolition's a dangerous business. He probably figured the less you know, the less you'd be held accountable for if anyone came sniffing around."

"If one of Albion's slaves ran away, would you go after him?" she asked.

He surrendered the lock of her hair and leaned back on his elbows. "There are no slaves at Albion. Haven't been since my father died. Folks said I should sell them off to pay the debts, but instead I freed them all and sent them off to find their fortunes where they may."

She felt an unexpected warm wash of pleasure. "You're not just saying that."

"No. I actually did it. Only Nancy, who is old and blind, and Willa, who is old and ornery, have stayed on. The rest all went north or west."

The warmth stayed with her, mingling with other things she was starting to feel for Hunter Calhoun—pride, trust. *Wanting*. She had not forgotten that the last time they'd been on the roof, Hunter had kissed her. She wondered if he would do it again, and the sharpness of her yearning embarrassed her.

"What are you smiling about?" he asked.

"I've got a right to smile." She tried to look away, hide her face from him, for she was afraid he'd look at her and know exactly what she was thinking.

He caught her cheek in the palm of his hand and said, "I know exactly what you're thinking."

She nearly choked with surprise. "How?" she blurted.

"Because I'm thinking the same thing." Then, wasting no more time, he settled his mouth over hers and kissed her. She was lost instantly. The speed of her surrender was shameful; the eagerness of her response, shameless. She arched forward, wanting a closeness and intimacy she understood only vaguely, wanting *him* in a way that touched her every nerve ending with flame.

He stopped kissing her for a moment, long enough to pull back and stare down at her. His face lay in shadow, but she knew he could see hers in the starlight. She wondered what it was he saw there, what made him whisper her name on that quavering note and then dip down again to kiss her, long and roughly, as if some will besides his own were forcing him to do this to her.

After he said her name, just once, in a whisper, neither of them spoke again. Words had no place in whatever strange communion they shared. She wanted him; she strained toward him. This was what had kept her awake for so many nights, feeling so alone. This was what she had hungered for. She was consumed by the same primal instinct of a mare in season, the instinct that made a horse tear her flesh on sharp brambles and swim great distances to find a stallion. Now Eliza knew the feeling of needing something so badly that it didn't even matter if she wounded herself in the process.

He took hold of the hem of her smock and peeled it upward, and then did the same with her shift. She didn't cover herself, even though she knew the milky light spilled freely over her bare breasts, concealing nothing. She didn't even cover herself when he removed her drawers and lifted her onto the outspread dress, using the garment as a blan-

ket. She didn't recoil with shyness as he studied her
frankly, his eyes dark and glittering as they swept over
her. And she didn't look away when he took off his shirt
and trousers and lay on his side next to her.

He looked beautiful in the way the stallion was beautiful. His skin had a fine-grained, polished look to it, and
his musculature had the firmness of a marble sculpture.
She stared at him, all of him, too dazed to be abashed.
And then, still in the grip of the wildness inside her, she
touched.

He made a sound like the hiss of a bead of water on a
hot stove. Thinking she had hurt him, she started to pull
away, but he covered her hand with his to keep it there.

And then he touched—everywhere, invading her most
sensitive and vulnerable places, without a single word of
explanation. And the whole time he was touching her, he
watched with a frank, intent stare. He watched his fingers
circle her breasts, pulling at the tingling tips. He watched
his hand skim slowly and inexorably down her torso, trailing over the soft skin of her belly toward the nest of curls.
He watched her fall limp upon the slope of the roof and
arch the small of her back upward. Her neck grew taut as
her legs grew slack while he touched lightly, then harder.
Quickly, then slower. And he watched her look up at the
stars.

Did he know they changed color before her very eyes?
Did he know that each and every star in the sky exploded
into a rainbow-hued blossom, that the sound that leaped
from her throat was a sound of joy, even though it sounded
like pain?

She reached for him urgently. She had to taste him
again, to speak without words, because she had no idea
what words to say. She caught at his shoulders and drew
him downward, all the while reaching up with her whole

body and her whole burning will. She kissed him as he had kissed her, hard and searchingly, with a hunger that knew no satisfaction. The taste of him overwhelmed her: sweetness and sweat and something as distant and indefinable as the spaces between the stars.

Responding to her hunger, he moved closer still, so that their bodies were aligned, touching in a hundred places, the friction striking sparks in the night. Her body knew what she wanted before her mind did, and she made it happen, bringing him lower, pressing up toward him, urging and guiding him. He settled over her with a controlled gentleness, like a blanket flicked out to the wind and then drifting downward in a dreamlike motion, covering her, yet barely touching her, his flesh just skimming hers. She tipped herself up higher to receive him. With a single breath he signaled resistance and then surrender, holding back, and finally sinking down, filling her. The heat and the pain shocked her, and she felt her every muscle stiffen as she cried out. Yet when he braced his arms on either side of her and prepared to draw away, she caught at him again and held him close, closer than she could imagine. Aye, she felt the pain of their joining. Yet with an inner wisdom that came from a source she could not name, she knew what lay on the other side of that pain.

The moment he had sunk into her she had glimpsed a lightning bolt, and she knew that if she surrendered to him completely, that flash of beauty would be hers. It would belong to her like the pleasure he had shown her moments ago.

He began to move, and it was a rhythm she understood. She had seen the silent mating flutters of the shorebirds and the more violent couplings of the wild horses. She had seen the beauty and the desperation of an act as natural and as inevitable as the waves beating upon the shore. She knew this; she wanted it.

She experienced an overwhelming excess of sensation. Too much came at her at once—the taste and feel of him, the rasp of his breathing and the night sounds of the island, the misty white starlight and the pulsations deep inside her, pounding to get out. Certain she was about to explode, she squeezed her eyes shut and held tight to his shoulders, believing with all that she was that if she let go, she would drift away into nothingness.

Unrelenting passion tore through her, a wildfire burning a path through the sere landscape of her body and her heart. His caresses brought heat to cold places, light to dark corners, drew music from silence, and, most of all, reminded her that she had, until this moment, only been half alive.

Too much, it was too much, and she heard herself begging him to stop because there was no way she could fit this experience into her sedate, quiet, contemplative life. No way she could carry on after this.

But he didn't stop, even though she begged him. If anything, his strokes quickened and became more aggressive, bringing her to a state of unbearable sensitivity. Finally he froze at a peak that made him seem miles away from her, and he said, ''I'm sorry,'' in a pained whisper. Then he shuddered and lowered himself, almost falling on her, though he broke the fall with his strong, sweating arms.

He covered her completely and put his mouth down upon hers. Only now he didn't plunder with his tongue, but tasted and probed with a tenderness that made her want to whimper and weep. He kept kissing her, and between kisses he lifted his head and whispered ''I'm sorry'' into her mouth as if to blow the very essence of his words into her.

She wanted to tell him to stay like this forever, blanketing her and kissing her and speaking so tenderly. She wanted to thank him for this night, because he had shown her wonders she had never before imagined. He had shown her that she was alive, vital and filled with a need to live and go on, no matter what she had suffered in the past.

But each time she tried to speak, her throat locked up the words, and the only thing she could do was sob. It was terrible, weeping like this, making him think it was because he'd hurt her, and more terrible still when he separated from her.

The emptiness was suddenly more apparent than it had ever been before. She felt helpless, unable to speak. Putting on her shift and her dress seemed a Herculean task. Donning his own clothes, he turned away from her, leaned back on the roof and stared up at the sky. His profile was a clean line of anguish against the starlight, and she could see the working of his throat as he swallowed. She had never seen a man so filled with regret. She didn't know what to do or what to say to him, so she merely watched and waited until he turned to her.

He moved to the edge of the roof and held out his hand. She took it, and he drew her to the eaves.

Catlike in his grace, he climbed down and dropped to the ground beside her. They stood in the yard, facing one another. The tears had dried on her face, but she could feel them gathering in her eyes once again. He was so beautiful in the starlight. It was impossible to look at him and not weep.

He put out one hand, and though it felt hard and callused, his touch was insistent, like the touch he had used to tame the horse. "I think I'll take a swig of that rum after all."

Thirteen

───❧❧❧───

Hunter awoke with the bitterness of guilt and old rum in his mouth. Judging by the position of the sun, it was early still. He unfolded his long form from the hammock with utmost care. The way his head felt, it would be too easy to dump himself unceremoniously onto the porch. He wobbled a little and had to grab the railing to steady his swaying.

Each pounding pulse of the headache hammered home the message of what he had done.

He had ruined the girl who had saved his horse.

There was probably a special place in hell for him. He was probably headed there right now, he thought as he walked barefoot and muzzy-headed into the small house.

Empty. She was gone. Maybe she took the dinghy to Eastwick to cry up a lynch mob for him. Maybe she'd fled to a witch-woman in the wood who, young ladies whispered, had a magical means of ''restoring'' a woman's lost virginity.

At the cistern outside, he washed himself and tried to rinse the sour taste from his mouth. He was glad she had no mirror, for he didn't want to see his bloodshot eyes, his ashen face and the corners of his mouth turned down in self-disgust. Her accusing stare, when she saw him next, would be mirror enough.

Last night before he had left her, he should have shown a little restraint. A decent man would have done so. But any explanation would be a lie, of course. The truth was, he'd taken her because he was selfish and accustomed to taking what he wanted. And she was so damn pretty. And the way she felt when he touched her seemed to fill the aching void in his heart. Mostly, he made love to her because she was so alone.

The way she lived out here, all by herself, tending her animals and grieving for her father, nearly put Hunter out of his head with pity, and made him want to hold her close and comfort her. Still, it didn't excuse what he had done.

Making love to Eliza—Lord, he had almost lost himself inside her—had sucked all coherent thought from his head. Afterward, words had failed him and he'd had to settle for touching her cheek, touching that milk-white skin and feeling the dampness where her tears had been.

She hadn't spoken to him, but had turned away and gone to the cistern. The moon was high by then, and her face had a bluish caste as she took a cloth and dipped it in the water and bathed herself, never looking at him, never speaking, simply washing her face and her neck, her arms and her legs, up under her skirts. She had looked strangely lovely to him, so silent, so solemn, so intent on her task. But part of him knew what she was doing. She was washing away his touch, trying to regain the purity that had never been breached until that night.

After a while he could no longer look at her. It hurt too much to see this beautiful, damaged girl trying to reclaim herself after what he'd done.

He had drunk rum straight from the jug, hoping to blind himself to the image of the trusting young woman he had destroyed. Stumbling, staggering, he had somehow managed to find his way to the hammock, where he collapsed and knew no more.

Now by the harsh light of day, he had to face up to what he had done. He had to find Eliza and see if there was a way to smooth things out with her. But when he encountered her on the beach, she scarcely acknowledged him, so intent was she on riding the stallion.

"We're using the hackamore today," she said, cantering up to him. Finn whistled lightly and tossed his head. "He took to it well enough."

"Eliza—"

But she had already ridden off, urging the horse to a wild gallop that hurled sand and spray in their wake. Hunter could see that she was lost in the world of the stallion, and he knew there would be no talking to her now. Perhaps she wasn't ready to discuss last night, and this was her way of showing it. He stood watching her for a while, and as always her unusual dark beauty took his breath away. Her hair, the color of ink, thick as the stallion's mane, streamed out on the wind like a banner. Her small, lithe body moved with the gallop as if girl and horse were one.

Hunter's thoughts turned hot and wayward, and he had to force his gaze away from her. This wasn't doing any good at all. He decided to keep busy with chores. The burned-out barn needed plenty of attention, so he decided to remove the charred timbers from another part of the arena. It was hot, dirty work, and he was grateful for the occupation. The thoughts that nagged at him while he labored were not pleasant. This, after all, was the place where her father had died.

The ghost of Henry Flyte was bound to take offense at the man who had violated his only daughter. Though he knew it was foolish, Hunter kept looking over his shoulder. He found himself wondering about Henry Flyte. So adored by his daughter.

But someone had hated him enough to murder him.

That night over supper, Eliza spoke to Hunter of the stallion's progress, and her pleasure in the newly cleared corner of the arena, and the possibility of rain because the silver maple leaves had been blowing wrong-side up.

Her voice was pleasant and cordial. She sounded little different than she had...before. She sounded completely normal.

She had made love to him as if it were the most natural thing in the world.

Was it possible a woman could actually feel that way? The idea boggled his mind.

He kept trying to think of a way to bring up the subject, but he didn't know how to approach it. Truth be told, he wasn't sure exactly what had happened between them.

No, that was lying to himself. He knew exactly what had happened. He had raped her.

He knew what rape was. Not always a violent act, but always a violation.

It was true that their mating had not been savage. But he had violated her. He had stolen her innocence. No matter that she had offered it freely, as freely as the face of a flower turning to the sun. No matter that she had kept her eyes wide open, looking up at him, and that he had seen the reflection of thousands of stars in her eyes.

When it came to women, Hunter had always been careless. Quick to love them, quick to stop. But never, ever had he bedded a virgin.

Even Lacey had not been a virgin—

He pushed aside the thought of his late wife.

Maybe Eliza was untroubled. Maybe what he had done to her was so horrible that she refused to think of it or speak of it at all.

He didn't know what to think, what to say, how to act around her. He had worried the subject like a dog with a bone all day, but he'd failed to arrive at a solution. Well, he thought, if she was not going to bring up the subject, maybe he wouldn't either.

She finished tidying the kitchen, then lit her lamp and brought it to the carved wooden bench by the fireplace. Hunter's gaze tracked her around the room, and when she settled into her seat and opened *Jane Eyre,* he couldn't stand it anymore. He burst out, "Hell, I don't understand you, Eliza Flyte. I don't understand you at all."

She glanced up, blinking. "What do you mean?"

"You know damn well what I mean. I'm talking about last night."

A softness stole over her, almost like a trick of the light. Her eyes grew cloudy and unfocused, and her mouth slackened almost imperceptibly. The look made Hunter want to forget caution and manners and propriety, and ravish her all over again. He made himself stay where he was, planted like a tree in the middle of the room.

"What about last night?" she asked quietly.

"You haven't mentioned it at all."

"Was I supposed to?" From anyone else the question might have been coy, but coming from Eliza, it sounded completely guileless.

Irritated, he said, "I didn't expect you to pretend it didn't happen."

"Oh!" She shut her book. "I'm not pretending at all. I thought about it all day. Didn't you?"

Yes.

She set aside her book and hugged her knees up to her

chest. "When I woke up this morning, I felt different. In a good way, I think. As if I had been someplace completely new, and then came home to discover that the whole world had changed." Her gaze was direct, unwavering. "Did you feel that way too?"

Trapped. He felt trapped by her probing questions and by her innocent stare. What in God's name did she want from him, need from him? An apology? Dear God—a proposal?

She didn't wait for his answer, but carefully changed position on the wooden bench, lowering her knees and crossing her ankles. "When I was riding the horse today, it felt...a little uncomfortable. Not unbearable," she hastened to add. "But in a way that kept me thinking about last night."

It was all he could do to keep from leaping across the room and clamping his hand over her mouth to shut her up. Didn't she know how frank she was being, how inappropriate?

No, of course not. How could she? Raised by a man alone, she couldn't know what was proper and what wasn't. Still, some things were so obvious.

"Is that the sort of thing you expected me to do?" she asked him. "Talk about it like that? Tell you everything I've been thinking?"

"Christ, no. I meant...by doing...what we did—"

"What do you call it anyway?" she asked. "Surely there's a term for it other than mating."

Hunter sat down on the wooden crab trap across from her. He resisted the urge to put his head in his hands. Speaking of last night made him uncomfortable and peevish too, because he knew he could not allow himself to repeat the experience. He shouldn't even want to, but he couldn't help himself.

"That depends," he said in answer to her question, "on who you ask."

"I'm asking you."

How was it that this weird, rag-clad girl had such a disruptive effect on him? He was Hunter Calhoun, who had a reputation for handling beautiful women and blooded horses. Cold control had always been his stock-in-trade. Yet when he considered Eliza Flyte, he could think only of heat and surrender and a wanting so pure that he almost couldn't look at her for fear she would see the passion in his eyes.

"I could tell you some pretty rough terms for it, but in mixed company I reckon I'd call it 'making love,'" he said, forcing an easy nonchalance into his tone.

"Making love," she repeated, tasting the words as if sipping a drop of nectar from a blossom. "I like that better than simply 'mating.' Which is accurate but not terribly poetic. In biblical terms, it's 'fornication,' which is a sin." She folded her hands in her lap, fingers twisting together. "So if...last night...was a sin, that makes me an unrepentant sinner."

"Why unrepentant, Eliza?" He gaped at her, wondering if he had heard correctly. All day long he had been thinking she regretted what they had done.

"Because I'm not the least bit sorry. I loved what we did. I loved the way you made me feel. I'd do it again. You only have to say the word, and—"

"Damn it." He stood up and went to the window, staring out at the blackness of the night. "You shouldn't talk like that, Eliza. You know damn well that what we did is wrong, and that it's my fault." He forced himself to turn to her. "I took advantage of you," he said. "I could stand here all night, blaming the rum and saying I wanted to hold you on account of you being all alone, but the truth is, I took advantage of you."

"Why do you say that?" She rubbed her temples as if a headache had started there. "What was wrong with what you did?"

He couldn't believe his ears. "There are those who would call it rape, Eliza. I stole your virginity."

"You can't steal what I freely gave."

"I ruined you for any other man."

She laughed. "Do you see men lining up at my door?"

It was even remotely possible that he'd made her pregnant, he thought with a sick lurch of his stomach. And here she sat, wondering what was wrong with that.

"We acted according to our nature," she said matter-of-factly. "How can that be wrong?"

"It won't happen again," he said.

"Don't you want it to?"

"Wanting has nothing to do with it." He drew a long, deep breath, hoping absurdly to suck wisdom from the air around him. "Eliza, where I come from, there are rules about this sort of thing."

"About making love," she prompted.

"Yeah, that. And the rules are, a woman doesn't let a man make love to her unless she's married to him."

"You consider it a biblical matter, then," she said. "Fornication. A sin."

She was frustrating him with her simple logic.

"It's best forgotten by both of us," he said brusquely. "But first, I want you to know—I'm sorry."

"Sorry you made love to me, or sorry it's a sin?"

"I'm sorry I took advantage of you."

"I can't forgive you," she whispered.

Damn. "Why not?" he demanded.

"Because there is nothing to forgive. I wanted everything you gave me last night, Hunter, and if you say you're sorry, it ruins it for me. I don't want you to be sorry. I want you to be glad.'' She inhaled slowly, raised her voice. ''I want you to want me again.''

His body had an instant response, which he quickly concealed by turning back to the window. ''You didn't want that,'' he said. ''The things I did...the way I touched you... I made you desire me. I took your will away with my touch. It wasn't fair.''

She fell silent. He could see her reflection in the wavy glass of the window, and her face was set in thoughtful lines. ''Up until last night, I thought I had determined the sort of life that would be mine.''

''And what life is that?''

''The isolation of this island. The company of the wild things here. But then you touched me—made love to me. I don't care if they were tricks. You made me feel warm and alive and filled with wanting. If that's a sin, then I'm the worst of sinners. I'm not sorry, and I'd do it again at the slightest opportunity.''

''Well, it's not going to happen,'' he said, a cruel edge sharpening his voice. ''What if we made a baby?''

''What if we did?'' she said wryly.

''I'd never marry you, and you'd be saddled with a child all alone out here.''

His harsh statement kept her silent for much longer this time. He had told her the truth, which was the honorable thing to do. So why did he feel as if he had stepped on a kitten? The silence drew out with unbearable tension, and finally he went to the door, pausing before he left.

''Eliza?''

''I think I understand,'' she said slowly. ''Making love is a lot more complicated than it seemed last night.''

"You do understand," he said, not unkindly. "It was a momentary lapse."

She picked up her book and opened it to the black grosgrain ribbon marker. "A momentary lapse, then."

"Good night, Eliza."

She raised her face to him, and he noticed that she still wore that soft, make-love-to-me look he had seen in her eyes last night. The invitation lingered there, dangling in front of him like an apple in the garden of Eden.

"Good night, Hunter," she said.

"I never meant to hurt you," he said in a rush.

"You didn't hurt me."

"Yes, I did." He opened the door. "You just don't know it yet."

Fourteen

Eliza caught a fat hogfish for supper and tried to give all her concentration to preparing it. Instead, she kept thinking about Hunter. The memory of his touch kept her under a strange enchantment all day, yet he appeared to have forgotten their passion. He had spent the day working with both Finn and the scow, coaxing the horse to enter and exit the stall without fear. She had gone to check on them once, found them both wet, muddy, and ill-tempered, and so she had left them alone.

But she knew what was happening. Hunter was preparing to leave.

She shut her eyes and swayed with hurt. How could she have known it would feel this way to lose the man who had made love to her? If she'd known, she might have resisted him, protected herself from him. But that night, she had acted with a will not entirely her own. After seeing him help the runaway slave and learning that he'd set his own slaves free, she had given her whole trust to him, and it felt so wonderful to be able to do that at last. Trust was everything. She loved that she could trust him. She hated that she was losing him.

Hunter had tried to persuade her that their lovemaking had been wrong, a sin, something to atone for. A mistake. *I'd never marry you....*

She wouldn't argue with him. He was a man with a dark soul who planned to marry a proper lady for his poor, motherless children. She knew better than to try to change his intentions. But privately, she would forever treasure the night she had spent with Hunter Calhoun. They had made love under the stars, and in those few magical hours, her life had been transformed.

But change was inevitable. A force of nature. Her father and her life on the island had taught her that nothing lasted, nothing was permanent. The waves eroded the island itself; the seasons changed; the years brought a shifting of the landscape. Everything was fleeting, nothing lasted forever. Not even love.

As melancholy as that thought was, she knew she would always be grateful for the few stolen moments of searing sweetness she had found in Hunter's arms. But she also had the sense to realize that those secret hours were all she would ever get. To dream of more was foolish.

Yet that night, he challenged her hard-won wisdom with a sidelong look that made her heart skip a beat, a silky invitation in his voice: "Come away with me, Eliza. It's not safe for you here."

Part of her yearned to respond the way he wanted her to, but she shoved that hopelessly romantic dreamer aside and said, "Don't be absurd. No one will bother me."

"Is that what your father believed on the night they killed him?" he asked, abandoning his charm for ruthless persistence.

A shiver raced across her shoulders. Dark waves of memory surged up inside her, and because they were inside her, she couldn't escape them. A tingle of awareness tried to break through the dark, but she battled the memories. She didn't want to remember.

"Didn't you ever fear the men who attacked your father would come for you?" Hunter asked.

"Not until I agreed to work with your horse."

"You father's killers weren't witch-hunters," he said. "He was killed because of what he did for the slaves."

"What?" She nearly choked on the word.

"The men who killed your father must have found out about the fugitives."

She froze. "No. It was because of the horses. He was regarded with superstition and—"

"Eliza. They stopped burning witches two hundred years ago. But for the sake of keeping their slaves in shackles, some men would smother their own grandmothers."

The terrible logic of his claim shook her, but she could not deny it. Everything she had believed about her father's death was shifting. She felt the pain of losing him all over again. By bringing his suspicion about her father's killers to light, Hunter had turned her world inside out. She had thought, as long as she kept her gift with horses a secret, she would be safe. But Hunter had shattered that illusion.

"You don't know what you're talking about," she accused him, desperate to cling to her old beliefs.

"Oh, but I do. All too well. He was killed by slave-catchers."

"No." She pressed her arms to her middle, trying to protect herself. "That can't be."

"They're a brutal bunch," Hunter pointed out. "They hunt slaves for the bounty, and damn anyone who stands in their way."

"Slavery is that important, then," she said. "That men would kill to protect it."

"It's not just the slavery. It's a way of life. It's brought men everything they've ever dreamed of. They'll do anything to protect it. People don't want their lives to change, honey. That's a fact."

Eliza fled to the porch, letting the door snap shut behind her. When she heard him follow her out, she kept her gaze on the long purple shadows over the marsh. She couldn't imagine ever actually leaving this place. Flyte Island was the only world she had ever known. "Even if you're right," she said without looking back at him, "I'm not worried. They can't know about me."

"They will. This sort of news has a life of its own. When people—fugitives—learn that there is hope or possibility, that cannot stay hidden. Before long, slaves who want their freedom will know of you. Maybe not your name, but they'll learn where to find you, just as they once learned to find your father. You're hope, Eliza. Hope and possibility. It's only a matter of time before word gets out."

She thought of the wounded runaway they'd helped, and she remembered the look in his eyes when he had finally left the shore. Terror and exultation and triumph—if escaping bondage was his last act on earth, he would consider it worth the risk. And if he survived his journey, he would want others to follow.

Now, watching the cover of night settle over the far dunes, she swallowed hard, painfully. Living as she did, far from the world, she never considered that the island would be thought of as a place of hope. "That's why I have to stay," she said, the decision hardening her will. "Otherwise, who will help those poor people?"

"You won't help another soul if you suffer the same

fate as your father," he said harshly. "The location of the rendezvous will change. My brother will see to that."

She whirled to face him. "You have no right to interfere."

His smile held no humor, only sarcasm. "Too late. Ryan and I already discussed it."

"Well, if the rendezvous changes, then I won't be in any danger."

"Wrong. The slave-catchers knew of your father. Before long, they'll know you're cut from the same cloth. You have to leave the island." He was brusque and impatient with her, as if she were a slow-learning child.

Furious, she went back into the house. Yet despite his harsh words, she couldn't help thinking how empty this house, this island—her life—would be without him. Why hadn't she noticed that before? Why hadn't she known her life was barren? Had Hunter Calhoun done her any favor by showing her how lonely her existence was?

She should have known he wouldn't stay outside, content with his hammock and his flask of rum. He followed her boldly into the house and she felt his presence even though she refused to look at him. It was a phantom warmth, something she craved and needed as much as air.

He touched her shoulder and turned her. She wanted that touch too, the one that cast a veil of heat all over her body, made her lips tingle and reason fly out the window as if she had never had a lick of sense. When he caught her against him, everything inside her seemed to turn to warm liquid, and the response shamed her. It shamed her that in the midst of learning the true meaning of her father's death and the risk she herself entertained, she could not stop thinking about Hunter.

"Let go of me," she said, and wrenched away from him. But she couldn't escape the yearning. There was an ache deep inside her that had not been there before. Hunter Calhoun had put it there.

"You're forcing me to abandon my father's work and dishonor his memory," she stated.

"There's no honor in getting yourself killed."

"He tried to tell me," she said, thinking back to something her father had said. "He used to read me the letters of Lydia Child published in the *Abolitionists Gazette*. When she wrote of a slave who had died while trying to escape, he told me not to cry. Because some things are worse than dying."

Hunter cupped her chin in his hand. "I know that, Eliza. Lord, don't I know that."

She saw the pity in his eyes, the reluctance to be here with her. Jerking her head away, she retreated a few steps. "What would you do with me if I agreed to come away with you?" she demanded.

"What do you mean, *do* with you?"

The pity in his eyes turned to panic, and she almost laughed. "Would I fit into your tidewater aristocracy? Or would I be like the Irish Thoroughbred? Will you drag me somewhere against my will and try to tame me?"

He didn't exactly squirm, but she sensed his discomfiture. "Eliza—"

"You haven't thought that far ahead, have you?" she said. "I know you felt you had to ask, but the truth is, you have no idea what you would do with me."

"I'm sure as hell not leaving you here. Look, I'll hire you."

"*Hire* me?"

"To train my horses."

"Oh, there's a tempting offer," she scoffed.

"Think about it. You once told me you longed to go to California, like the Spanish bride. You could earn the price of your passage." He folded his arms across his chest. "Or was that just idle talk?"

He knew her too well, this harsh, angry man. He knew she had a dream, but he also knew the outside world frightened her. She never should have confessed her private wishes to a stranger. She had inadvertently given him power over her, and now he was using that power to push her into taking a step she feared. Dreams were safe, but they turned dangerous when you started to believe in them.

"Of course it was idle talk," she said, hoping he didn't notice that her voice trembled. "California is half a world away."

Fifteen

Eliza didn't want to see Hunter the next day, so she rose early and didn't bother with breakfast or coffee. She tiptoed out, sneaking a peek at him as she crossed the porch.

He resembled a warrior at rest, sun-gold hair tumbling over his brow, several days' growth of beard carving shadows along his cheeks and jaw. Did he look so enchanting to her because she had seen so few men? Or because of the way he made her heart sing when he touched her?

She had to stop thinking of him in this manner, she told herself brusquely. She had to stop thinking of him in any manner at all. She had to convince him to leave. Because if he lingered on the island any longer, she would beg him to stay.

Perhaps it is too late for that already, her heart whispered. She could not bear the thought of being without him. She would learn, then. She had learned to do without her father, hadn't she? The conversation last night had been absurd. She would not—could not—follow Hunter back to his world. He should have known better than to suggest it.

She walked fast along the path. No point getting all moon-eyed over this man. Today she would work the stallion into weary obedience, and at evening tide she would put him aboard the drover's scow and send Hunter Calhoun on his way. For good.

In the training arena her father had built, she lost herself in the work. It was the only thing that saved her. Finn occupied her entirely. Like Prince Ferdinand's flirtation with Miranda in *The Tempest,* she and the stallion were powerless to resist each other. The bond she felt with the stallion, the challenge and the affinity filled her. She drove him around and around the ring and when he was practically begging her for it, she mounted.

She rode bareback for a time, then reintroduced him to the bit. Sliding it between his velvety soft lips and up along his teeth, she murmured softly that this was something he knew, something he accepted, and with a quiet shock of recognition she realized that she sounded the way Hunter had sounded that night on the roof: tender, persuasive, sincere.

The horse didn't fight her, and when Eliza mounted again, he was beautifully and sweetly responsive. She worked him all day, and took him to the longest part of the beach where the sand had been pounded hard by the surf. There she discovered why he was considered a champion. He ran like the wind. Perhaps there were other equally fast horses, but she had never known an animal to have such heart, such joy in the act of running.

She bent low over the pumping neck, pressed her cheek to the huge throbbing artery of the stallion, and she too felt the joy. She let the speed steal her breath, and heard herself laugh with the pure clean pleasure of it.

Hunter Calhoun would be pleased; this much she knew. He had brought her a deranged animal. She would send him home with a champion.

Today.

Hours passed. The sun peaked, sank past noon and was headed toward sunset. Judging by the action of the waves, she knew the tide was coming in and that soon the scow would be afloat.

Sadness haunted her as she walked the stallion back to the settlement, stopping to put him in his pen for the night. This was not the raging, soul-tearing grief she had felt for her father. This hurt held the dull ache of eternity.

When she came upon the clearing, the first thing that struck her was the quiet. Had someone taken the chickens? Frowning, she went inside. At first glance she saw nothing amiss. Then her eyes widened as she noticed the empty shelves.

The books were gone. Shakespeare. Charlotte Brontë. The damaged Bible. The collection of illustrations. Every last one of them—gone. Two other items had been stolen as well—the locker containing the Spanish bride's trousseau and the crate with her father's mementos of his career in England.

She was so stunned by this turn of events that she sank to the old driftwood bench and stared at the puncheon floor in a terrible daze. She felt as she had one time when she had swum a pony out into the surf. The animal had panicked and had kicked her in a dozen places before she escaped him. The agony had consumed her, sucked all the air from her lungs.

It was like that now. Hunter Calhoun had removed from her house the only things that meant anything to her, and it was as if he had ripped her heart out.

She felt like an old, old woman as she made herself get up and go outside, down the path to the paddock area.

She got there in time to see him leading the stallion away.

That sight was like a slap of ice water, waking her up. She fairly flew along the path at him.

"What the hell are you doing, Calhoun?" she demanded.

His look was blurry and bemused. She instantly knew that he had been drinking.

"Oh, good," he said. "You're just in time to help me get the stallion aboard."

That had been her plan exactly, to put the stallion on the scow and send him on his way. But Hunter Calhoun wasn't satisfied merely to leave her be. He had to wreak havoc on her life as well. Dear God, and she had *trusted* this man? What sort of fool did that make her?

"I've brought a blindfold in case he gets balky. He's ready, isn't he?" Without waiting for an answer, he led the horse across to the mooring. "It's a calm sea this evening. We'll be at Albion before nightfall."

Peering into the box on the scow, she felt a jolt of white-hot rage. The scow resembled Noah's ark in miniature, with the Three Nymphs perched nervously on a rail, and Claribel tethered to the base of the tiller. Caliban paced up and down the beach, giving an occasional sharp bark of impatience.

"You've put my animals aboard," she sputtered.

"I couldn't very well leave them. They seem attached to you."

"I'm taking them back at once," she said, starting up the ramp.

"Don't do that."

"Why not?"

"Because I don't want to have to stop you. But I will if you don't cooperate."

"What?"

"It's my job to save you," he said, slurring his words. "It's the least I can do."

"I don't need saving."

He stopped, stock-still, and gave her a long, lazy look. "Oh, honey. Yes, you do." He stepped up on the ramp. "I didn't expect you to surrender easily. You want your things? Your animals? Fine, come aboard and get them."

She regarded him resentfully. "I'm staying." She pivoted away from him and strode back toward her house. If it was a battle of wills he wanted, she was determined to prevail. If he called her bluff and stole her things, perhaps she would pursue him to the place called Albion and reclaim her animals, bringing them home with her where they belonged.

She turned to give him a chance to call her back. Instead, she saw him easing the blindfolded stallion up the ramp as the sun settled low on the water. The sight hit her like a blow, but she refused to let herself feel the pain.

After they'd made love, he had accused himself of violating her. Now she realized it was true. He *had* violated her, though not in the way he thought. He had taken something much more valuable than her virginity. Now he expected her to follow him like a brainless gosling wherever he went. Did he think her belongings meant so much to her that she would follow them to a strange place? Then he didn't know her at all. Nothing was permanent. Nothing was worth hanging on to. She would learn to do without the things he had stolen from her.

Back at the house, she tried to go through the motions of her evening routine, but there were no eggs to gather, there was no cow to milk.

Night fell with its usual sudden hush. A blanket of dark hid the marsh and the dunes, muffling the sounds of the sea. Her loneliness burned deep. He had taken her books.

How dare he? The absence of the books left her alone with herself, truly alone, for the first time in her life. She didn't like it. It was a shock to realize she wasn't happy in her own company.

She couldn't sleep. Restless as a wild thing, she paced the floor. Then, finally, she left her bed and went out to the porch, settling into the hammock that hung empty in the shadows. Sleep came more easily than it should have, but it was a restless unsatisfying sleep plagued by confusing dreams.

Of him. She was transported up onto the lookout platform again, to that night filled with stars, and he was making love to her, and the feelings rising in her made her feel as if she would burst into flames. Hot, she was so hot, on fire for him, and the sweat raced down her temples and between her breasts until she nearly cried out aloud in pleasure and in pain.

The sensations were so real that, when she awoke in the middle of the night, she smelled smoke. A second or two of disorientation lingered, and then reality slammed into her.

Fire.

The roof was on fire.

Even before she could scramble out of the hammock, she heard shouts from the marsh and saw a flaming brand arc through the air. The bomb was a bottle filled with clear liquid—kerosene, she guessed—and stoppered with a rag set aflame.

"That'll smoke out the vermin," someone said.

Eliza slithered out of the hammock. *Slave-catchers.* The men who had killed her father. They had come back, this time for her. They must have pursued the runaway slave to the island.

Dear God, she should have listened to Hunter.

The flaming roof turned night to day. She was certain they would see her, but she had no choice. She could either stay and burn, or run and risk being caught. Her mind filled with terrible images of the marauders, she bent low and dropped over the railing of the porch. Behind her, the roof caved in with a hiss and a groan of ancient, wind-dried timber. On hands and knees she crawled toward the marsh, where the cordgrass rose in tall clumps through the mudflats.

She could hear the men talking. They hunted down fugitives in order to collect a bounty. Now she understood the icy fear of a slave on the run. She had no care for comfort, did not worry when she entered a hot pocket of hungry mosquitoes, did not heed the fact that she was drenched in mud. Her only thought was to get away. She moved deeper and deeper into the marsh, reaching the opposite edge, her feet finding firmer ground.

A rough-throated baying filled the air, and she nearly sobbed with terror. They had dogs, and Hunter Calhoun—damn him to the eternal fires—had sailed away with Caliban, who would have driven off the most ferocious of hounds. She had a vague notion of hiding in the deepest part of the woods, and made for the leeward side of the island. The hounds had scented her by now, she could tell, for their baying grew louder and more frenzied. She heard the rasp and crash of low shrubs being trampled. Casting a glance over her shoulder, she saw that the fire made a bowl of light in the night sky. A man with a long gun angled across his body ran toward her. She could see his bulk backlit by the flames.

Was this what her father had seen, just before he died?

She sucked air between teeth clenched in terror. Closer and closer the dogs came. She imagined she could hear the snap and snarl of them as they closed in on her. In front of her, the water lay like a pool of ink.

Her foot caught the upthrust knee of a cypress and she stumbled and fell, careening to a stop at the base of the tree. She tried to resist the impulse to climb, for the dogs would only keep her there until their masters found her. She felt the hot flow of blood from her foot and cursed, knowing the strong rusty scent of fresh blood would bring on the hounds that much faster. She scrambled across the dunes, making for the open water where she could throw them off the scent.

Her only hope was to plunge into the murk of the night waters, to endure the sting of saltwater in her wound, to lie low and pray she would not be found. It was a feeble plan, but it was better than staying around waiting to be captured.

She took a step toward the water, then another. The scarp of the dune was a high one. It was a long drop into the sea below, but she had to chance it. Another step, then another.

A swift shadow streaked out from the brush at the edge of the cliff. A hand clapped over her mouth. A strong arm clamped around her waist. And then the cliff gave way, and she was falling, falling, with the wind racing through her hair.

She didn't even have time to scream.

Part Two

...make yourself ready for the mischance of the hour...
—William Shakespeare, *The Tempest*, I, i

Part Two

Sixteen

❦

"I've never rescued anyone before," Hunter said, steering into the strong southerly current. He glared at the sputtering, cursing girl on the deck. "I wonder if it's always this difficult."

During the first hour of their escape from the island, she had not stopped talking. No, thought Hunter, thirsty for the rum he had already finished, she didn't talk. She whined. She ranted. She was ranting still.

"...no better than the Portuguese in Africa, capturing slaves. Who gave you the right to snatch me from my home? To steal my things and my animals and carry us off as if we were booty looted from a shipwreck?"

He adjusted the tiller. "Imagine," he said. "How dare I?"

"You can't force me to stay. I'll go home, see if I won't."

He'd had enough. Securing the tiller with a line, he thrust himself toward her, moving fast. Surprising her.

He shoved her up against the side of the pen and glared down into her face. "Listen. Because I'm only going to say this once. Your father was killed for helping slaves escape. Last night the slave-catchers burned your house to the ground. Lord knows what they'd have done if they'd found you.''

"Is that why you came back for me?''

"I didn't come back. I was lying at anchor, waiting for you to come to your senses. Which, I needn't point out, you failed to do.'' He knew he would never tell her how he'd paced the decks, wrestled with indecision until it was almost too late. He'd never confess what the sight of her burning house had done to him. "I couldn't let you wait around to be killed,'' he said brusquely.

"Who are you to make that decision for me?''

Someone who cares. He bit his tongue to keep the words in. Caring brought heartache. He was walking proof of that. "Someone who doesn't want you on his conscience.''

"And exactly what do you propose to do with me?''

He'd had plenty of time to think about it, but the ideas flew out of his head. When he looked at her now, when he smelled the wild heathery fragrance of her hair, all he could think about was what he had done to her that night. No matter how drunk he got he could still remember the taste of her mouth and the way her breasts had felt cupped in his hand. He could remember the startled sounds of delight she had made and could feel her legs wrapped unabashedly around him.

Hunter had lost count of the women he had loved over the years. But he knew there had never been anyone like Eliza.

"Well?'' She pushed for an answer. "Have you thought about that? Have you?''

"Of course I have,'' he lied, letting her go and pushing away from the pen. In truth, what *would* he do with such a girl? A feral woman, raised by her unconventional father at the edge of nowhere. The wild islands had been her classroom, a handful of books her tutors. In terms of horse sense, she was more learned than the most dedicated scholars at Old Dominion. But in terms of living, she was a babe in the woods. She had no idea how to get on in society.

"I'll pay you for the service you've done me," he said.

She plunked down on the deck and examined the gash in her foot. "You have no money. You said so yourself."

"When this stallion starts winning, I'll be flush. You'll be well compensated, I promise you that. You'll be able to book passage to California. It's what you've always wanted, isn't it?"

"I never pictured myself doing it," she said, wrapping a bandanna around her foot. "I never saw myself leaving the island." She stood up to grasp a shroud, and faced east to the low flat islands behind them. In the uncertain light of the coming dawn, there was little to distinguish them from sea or sky. "I can't see it anymore," she said quietly. "I can't see Flyte Island."

"Doesn't mean it's not there," he pointed out. In a way, he was glad she couldn't see her former home. The eerie glow from the fire had pulsed unnaturally into the night, illuminating the grief in her face. Now the shadows of dawn softened her drawn features. Still, he reminded himself, the woman had lost her home last night, lost it in a shock of violence. He wished he knew how to comfort her.

"Remember how you said you and your father used to dream of seeing California, the wild herds out there?" he said awkwardly. "I brought all your pictures and maps."

She held herself very stiff and straight as the rounded bow pushed into the low mist on the water. "It's easy to dream. Harder to face the dream coming true."

When they passed the tiny port of Cape Charles, a shrill

steam whistle sounded and a few fishing boats scudded by, shrouded in nets. The bay was opening up to a new morning. A vessel hove into view, emerging from the fog like a watery ghost.

"Get down, quickly," Hunter ordered her.

Eliza dropped to the deck and lay in the shadow of the stock pen. "Who is it?"

"Might be the scum who burned your place."

"Ahoy! What're you shipping?" came the demand from the boat. It was a skipjack, small and swift, flying enough canvas to outrun the scow in any wind.

"Livestock, and not a very good lot," Hunter said, sounding chagrined. He squinted through the fog, trying to see how many manned the skipjack. "And you? Out fishing today?" He already knew the answer to that. He saw no lines or weirs.

"There's been a slave escape from a place in Northampton County," a voice from the other boat said. "Handsome reward out for him."

Eliza closed her hand around a marlinespike, and Hunter's blood chilled. He had taken charge of keeping her out of danger. Reaching down, he snatched the pointed tool from her. "Haven't seen a soul, slave or free," he said loudly.

"My partner and I, we're after a lone runaway," one of the men explained. The bow of the sailboat angled toward the scow and cut cleanly through the gray water, drawing close with unexpected speed. "Young buck, crippled by a mantrap, last seen a bit north of here."

"Well, you're braver souls than I," Hunter said, "taking off after such a vicious character."

The man spat a stream of brown tobacco juice overboard. "You watch what you say, mister."

"You sure you only got livestock there?" the other

asked. "If'n you're telling the truth, you oughtn't to worry."

Hunter could see, by the ruffles in the water ahead, that he had a chance of catching the oncoming breeze if he could get there in time. But the other boat was steep-sided and sleek, quicker and more maneuverable than the ungainly scow. He had nothing to hide, though, and Ryan's ship was long gone. Still, he knew these two had burned Eliza's home and could well be the ones who had murdered her father. Elaborately casual, he unlashed his tiller and steered into the wind. "I'm not worried, gentlemen," he said easily. "Kind of you to inquire, though."

"Slacken sail!" The skipjack closed the distance fast, outfitted with plenty of canvas for fast runs to the big cities in the north. The sailboat hove in and out of the mist, finally emerging too close for comfort. The man on the deck held a long percussion shotgun pointed straight at Hunter.

"You hard of hearing?" the man demanded. "I said, slacken sail!"

Hunter was outmanned, outgunned and outmaneuvered. He had no choice. He grasped the mainsheet and gave it a quick jerk. The sail slackened instantly.

The pair of men on the skipjack worked with piratical precision. A grappling hook swung across, thunking against the side a few times before it grabbed hold. They pulled hand over hand, dragging the helpless scow toward them. The sailors were a weather-beaten pair, their hard faces creased with that special brutality of men who hunted slaves for profit.

Caliban planted his forepaws on the gunwale, black lips drawn back in a vicious grin. He didn't bark but made a far more threatening vibration deep in his throat. In the pen, the stallion whistled and thumped his hooves. Nervously the slave-catcher swung his weapon toward the big dog.

"Hold your fire," Eliza yelled, jumping up from her hiding place.

Hunter set his jaw. He wondered if she understood what a bother it was, keeping her safe.

"Well, now," the slave-catcher said, and despite the distance of several yards, Hunter could see the hard glitter in his eyes. "What have we here?"

Two sharply hungry gazes locked onto Eliza. Her wet dress hugged her form, showing the outline of her nipples, chilled to hardness, the tender curve of her belly and hips, the V-shape between her legs. Neither of them said a word. They didn't have to. They saw a woman, ripe for the plucking, and they wanted her in the crudest way possible.

Exactly as Hunter wanted her—and had taken her.

"Now I see why you ain't being so friendly," the man with the gun said. "Keeping the wench to yourself. Can't say's I blame you. I like a nice yeller bitch every once in a while myself."

Hunter felt a dull, quiet shock. Could these idiots possibly have assumed that Eliza was his slave?

"What's he talking about?" she demanded.

"Don't address your betters like that," he snapped at her.

"My betters?"

"Sit your scrawny ass down, woman, and shut your yap." Reaching forward, he shoved at her shoulder. She stumbled back, tripping over a coil of rope and plunking down onto the deck.

"Can't do a thing with poor Bertha," he said to the others, pasting on a long-suffering look. He deliberately used the name of the insane wife in *Jane Eyre* and hoped Eliza would catch on. "She used to be more biddable until the fever was at her. Addled her brains. Fried them, I think.''

"She fried her brains?" The sailor scratched his head.

"The fever did. Turns out there's nothing to be done." With a crudeness that came too naturally to him, he scratched his crotch to indicate the cause of the fever.

The slave-catchers exchanged a glance of distrust. Realization must have dawned on Eliza like the sun breaking through clouds. Squatting on deck, she strummed her lips, making an awful noise that caused the dog to tip back his head and howl. The men watched her with amazement. Their previous edgy lust gave way to disgust and, in small measure, a twinge of pity for Hunter for being saddled with such a creature.

Saddled with her. Almighty God, she was his now. His to keep, his to protect. And he was so inept at keeping and protecting anything.

His hand itched. Her Henry Rifle lay at hand, leaning in the shadows against the pen. He had to force himself to regain his patience. "I know you must be in a hurry to go about your business," he said. "I'm not looking for any trouble. Got enough of my own right here on this boat." He indicated the grappling hooks. "Here, I'll give you a hand with these."

Hunter slung one heavy iron hook overboard. The sharp point caught the rudder of the skipjack, yanking it off its mooring.

"Sorry," he said with a sheepish grin. "Didn't mean to be so careless." He reeled in the hook and slung it again, this time taking out a section of the gunwale. "I'm damn clumsy with this business—"

"Just leave it, you blamed fool," the slave-catcher said. "Damn your infernal hide. You disabled our steering."

"Have I, now?" Hunter asked.

Eliza's lip-strumming trailed off. She came up on her knees to watch.

"You'll have to give us a tow. Now, make fast that other hook," the slave-catcher ordered.

Hunter took up the heavy second hook. He could feel Eliza's eyes on him, pleading with him not to toss it to them. He sent them the most charming grin he could muster, the grin that had saved him from beatings as a boy and had won him impossible bank loans as a grown man.

"Gentlemen," he said, hefting the hook up onto his shoulder, "choke on it."

With that, he heaved the grappling hook overboard. The disabled skipjack foundered, sails luffing uselessly in the breeze. The current played havoc with her, swinging the bow wildly and causing her to wallow in a wave trough.

Gunshot exploded from the skipjack but the shot went wild, pinging harmlessly into the water. And Hunter calmly steered the scow out into the stream of the current heading into the bay.

Seventeen

Albion. In Latin the word meant "white," but Eliza's overwhelming first impression was of green. Green hills rising in ever-receding misty layers to the west. Green haze lying in the low valleys between the hills. Green trees taller than anything she'd seen on her low country island. Green murk at the fringes of the vast opening of the bay leading way up into the heart of Virginia.

The lushness of the area seemed vaguely decadent, as if it were about to burst from so much bounty. But decadence in the conventional sense had never bothered Eliza particularly.

While Hunter secured the lines to the ramp so the livestock could exit, Caliban barked excitedly and leaped ashore, toenails scrabbling over the weathered planks. Eliza felt nothing of the dog's sense of adventure. Overnight, her world had been transformed. The father she thought she had known had turned out to be a different person entirely. She took pride in the notion that he had secretly helped fugitives to freedom. Yet a part of her felt betrayed, because he'd hidden something so important from her. And the thing that he'd hidden had got him killed.

She felt foolish, having believed all this time that he'd been murdered because of his affinity for horses. But foolishness was not the cause of her broken heart. Hunter Calhoun was.

Even after an eventful night, a dangerous sail across the dark waters of the bay and an encounter with slave-catchers, he looked magnificent. The sunlight had a special quality when filtered through the tender green of the budding trees, and when it fell over him, his harsh masculinity was softened, so that he appeared almost vulnerable. His beard, nearly an inch long by now, had reddish strands amid the gold, and the ends looked so soft she had to fold her hands into fists to keep from touching them.

"Why are you staring at me like that?" he asked.

She stood up, preparing to help off-load the animals. "What do you suppose became of those men you left out in the bay?"

"With any luck, they couldn't repair their steering and were swept out into the Atlantic."

The thought that they might die created a strange coldness in her chest. Not regret, but discomfort, certainly. Hunter showed no emotion at all as he went about setting the ramp. After a while, he glanced at her again. "*Now* what?" he asked.

"I was just thinking about *The Tempest.*"

"That again."

"I never really thought about the ending. But you know, the story ends before they leave the island."

"So?"

"We never learn what becomes of everyone."

"Prospero goes back to his dukedom in Milan. Ferdinand and Miranda sail to Naples, where they live happily ever after as prince and princess. All the sprites and beasts are released from their enchantment. Make fast that line, will you?''

She obeyed sulkily. He didn't understand. As long as she stayed on the island, she didn't have to worry about the way things ended. Now, thrust into this strange place, she had to make her way through unfamiliar terrain, alien and green, fraught with peril.

Hunter went to the end of the dock and gave a shrill whistle. The chickens clucked and scolded. In the distance, a slender man started running toward them. Alarmed, she edged toward the scow.

''Eliza,'' Hunter said. ''You can't stay hidden away on that island forever. You belong in the world, not hiding from it.''

Perhaps he understood more than she knew. Her heart lurched at the sight of the stranger coming toward her. It was a youth, she saw as he drew near. She had never seen anyone quite like him. He was neither black nor white, but a melding of the two, with matted black hair that hung in long, twisted ropes from scalp to shoulder. His skin was the color of polished oak, his eyes the light gold of autumn leaves. His slight build gave him the look of a boy, but he had a peculiar musculature in his build, and a weary wisdom in his face that hinted he was older than he appeared.

''This is Noah,'' Hunter said. ''Runs the stables and races our horses. Noah, this is Miss Eliza Flyte.''

Noah sent her a brief nod, but clearly his interest was fixed on the gated pen in the scow. ''Well?'' he demanded.

Hunter said nothing as he slid back the bolt. Eliza took hold of Claribel's rope halter and led the milch cow ashore. Hunter opened the other side of the pen.

Noah shrank back, his fascinated gaze fixed on the blindfolded stallion. Hunter took the leading rein and brought Finn down the ramp. The horse's skin quivered, and his ears flicked with tension, but he walked obediently across the ankle-deep grass.

Hunter reached up and removed the thick cloth from the horse's eyes. "You were right. I didn't have to shoot him."

Noah's face lit with a radiant joy that nearly brought a smile to Eliza's face. "Praise the Lord," the youth said. "The horsemaster gentled him."

Hunter shook his head. "The horsemaster died some months ago."

Noah blinked in confusion. "Then who—"

"Miss Flyte," Hunter said, gesturing at Eliza. "The horsemaster's daughter."

The boy stared at her as if seeing her for the first time. "Ma'am, you're a wonder. Truly, a God-given wonder."

"He's a wonderful horse," Eliza said, relieved to find a topic in common with this intense, handsome boy. "He simply needed a special sort of training."

"Can you show me?" he asked. "Can you show me what you did?"

"I can indeed." She beamed, thinking that perhaps the world was not such a terrible place after all. Yet even as she smiled, fatigue rolled over her, and she had to turn away to stifle a yawn.

"Stable the horse and turn the cow out to the meadow by the bake house," Hunter said to Noah. "And see that the stallion gets a portion of sweetened oats. We'll put him through his paces later this morning."

"Yes, sir." Noah approached the stallion with a cool authority that pleased Eliza. The youth was clearly comfortable in the presence of horses. Finn's skin quivered and his ears twitched, but he was docile enough as Noah took hold of his lead. He hesitated, thought a moment, and said, "I reckon Blue will be mighty pleased to see the horse."

Hunter nodded curtly.

"Maybe," Noah said, speaking cautiously, "seeing the horse will help—"

"The boy's beyond any help," Hunter snapped. "Come with me," he said to Eliza. Without waiting to see if she complied, he strode across the broad, misty field—a lawn, she supposed, although she had never seen one. How lovely it was.

She tried to guess Hunter's mood. He was a different person, here on the mainland. He held his shoulders more tensely. He walked more stiffly. And he hadn't smiled since setting the slave-catchers adrift. He reminded her of Mr. Rochester, dour and secretive.

She shook her head, trying to banish her speculation, at least for a time. She wondered what he meant about his son being beyond any help.

He led her around a curve in the broad lawn. Immediately, she found cause for worry. "That is your house?" she demanded, staring at the huge white structure tucked into the cleft of two soft green velvet hills.

"It is." He didn't seem to notice her consternation.

House seemed such an inadequate term for the place. Columns soared three storeys from the marble steps of the front to the Greek-style pediment over the front entranceway. Row upon row of windows, each with a railed balcony, flanked the front. The first level had a veranda that wrapped around the entire vast structure. This was no house but a mansion, or a château, or an estate. Perhaps a villa or manor. But certainly not a house.

A long open drive with a parade of arching live oaks led the way to the front entrance. With each step, Eliza's sense of dread heightened. Though the breeze blew sweet with new growth, her chest felt tense, and it was hard to breathe. She inhaled laboriously, like a fish floundering on the beach. And still Hunter kept going, heedless of her discomfort.

The closer she drew to the house, the more she saw. Hand-carved scrolls crowned the front columns. A broad staircase led from the lawn to a railed porch that wrapped around the lower floor. Above a soaring portico were rows of French windows flanked by delicately carved shutters. She noticed something else as well. The white paint, which had appeared so stark and gleaming from a distance, was chipping and peeling. A few of the windows were cracked, and a few others had boards put up to cover the panes. Some of the shutters hung askew. An air of neglect haunted this once-fine white palace. She remembered what Hunter had told her about his life here, and about the death of his wife. Perhaps when he had lost her, he had stopped caring about the appearance of his home.

He went up the granite steps—the bottom one had a broken corner—and opened a tall door with a leaded fan-shaped lintel. Eliza stepped, wide-eyed, into a broad entry hall. The ceiling rose up all three storeys and a skylight of leaded, frosted glass let in a flood of diffused sunlight. Two staircases, each a mirror image of the other, curved up each side of the hall. Gilded double doors—all mysteriously closed—flanked the entrance, and twin narrow passageways led toward the back of the house. Though the hall was empty, with dust balls ambling across the wooden floor and cobwebs draping the woodwork in the corners, the sense of weary, spent grandeur stole her breath. Now she knew how Jane Eyre felt, getting her first glimpse of Thornfield Manor.

"Nancy," Hunter called out. "Nancy, I'm back."

He didn't turn to Eliza, didn't welcome her. And even

if he had, she wouldn't feel welcome in the haunted, shabby elegance of this strange house. A cavernous silence shrouded the place, yet in the midst of that silence, she heard a weird tap-tap, drawing closer. The click of old bones? The snap of dry tinder? She could not place the noise.

And then she saw Nancy.

The woman was old and stooped, her small black face suffused with an unexpected serenity. She wore a dimity dress and a crisply clean apron. At first Eliza thought she was leaning on a cane, but then she noticed that the tip of the cane was sliding along the floor and tapping against the baseboard. Nancy was blind, Eliza realized with a start, studying the deep-set, cloudy eyes. Blind as Mr. Rochester after the fire.

"Nancy, I've brought Miss Eliza Flyte home to stay a while," Hunter said, striding across the hall and giving her a hug. An unexpected lump rose in Eliza's throat. The tiny, dark woman and the big fair-haired man embraced, closing their eyes with an air of long affection.

"How do you do?" Eliza said nervously, raising her voice.

"I'm blind, girl, not deaf," Nancy scolded, but not unkindly. "Come here, so I can get a look at you."

She "looked" with a brief touch, taking Eliza's hand in hers and then trailing her fingers upward, lightly tracing the topography of her face. Once Eliza got over being startled, she pressed her mouth upward into a smile.

"You just a little bit of a thing," Nancy remarked. "But strong, I can tell." Her hand lingered in Eliza's hair, and a curious expression came over her face.

"Is something wrong?"

Nancy was quiet for several moments. She turned away.

"Let's get you something to eat, and then you need a rest."

"Thank you," Eliza said, feeling uncertain.

"Come on, then," Nancy said with a hint of impatience. Hunter started toward the front door.

"Mr. Hunter!" Nancy said sharply.

He froze, then turned to face her. "Ma'am?"

"Ain't you wondering about the little ones?"

"Of course." His face tightened strangely, as if something painful stabbed into him. "How are Blue and Belinda?"

"Off to their lessons at Bonterre." She spoke the name with a certain distaste. Addressing Eliza, she explained, "That'd be the Beaumont place up the road. I reckon they'll want to meet you when they get back this afternoon."

Hunter turned sharply for the door and left the house. Eliza stared after him a moment, baffled by his manner. What sort of father was so uninterested in his children?

"Papa?" a voice called, trembling slightly.

"Belinda, what's wrong?" Hunter asked his daughter. She was the one bright blossom in his life; she gave him a reason for emerging, at least once a day, from the fog of whiskey he usually hid inside. He bent down on one knee and held out his arms.

She came to him, her face curiously solemn for a seven-year-old's. "I have something to tell you, Papa," she said.

He held her for a few moments, moved by the pure sweetness of her scent, her voice, the warmth of her body. Over her head, he watched the stallion in the paddock adjacent to the stables. The last time Finn had been penned there, he had been caked in mud and possessed by madness. Now he stood placidly, flicking his tail at flies. Later this afternoon, Noah would begin working with him, and if things went well Finn would be taken out to the mile oval to see if he would race again.

Hunter tried to remember the last time Belinda had smiled for him, the last time he'd heard the sound of her laughter. It had been too damn long. Feeling awkward and unworthy, he picked her up in his arms. How light and delicate she was. How fragile, like a butterfly.

He kissed her golden blond curls. She had a great, beautiful mop of hair that more than compensated for the threadbare condition of her dress, which she was fast outgrowing. He'd have to ask her grandmother Beaumont if she could search her attic trunks for another of Lacey's childhood gowns. If he thought about it too hard, the idea of his little girl wearing her dead mother's dresses would make him insane.

"Tell me what's on your mind, sugar pie," he said, setting her down. "I'm all ears." He took his and waggled them, hoping to coax a grin from her. He wished she had dolls and fairy tales on her mind, but Belinda had left those behind two years ago, putting them to rest with the same solemn finality with which he had buried his wife in the family plot.

She didn't smile. If anything, she grew more somber still. "It's about Blue."

His heart took a dive, though he didn't let it show in his face. "What about Blue?"

"Well, he didn't come to Bonterre for lessons today. Master Rencher said he'd take a switch to him."

"Master Rencher will get his skinny neck wrung if he lays a hand on Blue." Hunter spoke mildly, but he was surprised by his own vehemence. The protective instinct his children roused in him was almost violent. Why couldn't he just love them? he wondered. Why was it so easy to be fierce, yet so hard to be simply affectionate? "So where did Blue go?"

"He climbed up to Uncle Ryan's old lookout platform and he won't come down."

"He'll come down when he gets hungry," he assured Belinda.

"He's been up there since early this morning," she said. Her eyes, round and blue as china plates, accused him with their complete lack of guile and calculation.

"What?"

"Up in the fort. He climbed up this morning, and he's still there."

Hunter's blood chilled. The ancient lookout platform, high in a loblolly pine overlooking the dock, had a perfect view of Mockjack Bay...and the landing at Albion.

Good God. Blue had been up there. He'd witnessed the entire scene at the dock. He'd seen Hunter show more interest in the stallion than his own children. Had heard him speak in harsh, hopeless tones.

The boy's beyond any help.

Damn. He'd really said that. And Blue had heard. The kid was troubled, but he wasn't deaf. And he wasn't an idiot.

Awash with guilt, he mounted one of the mares, not bothering with the saddle, and galloped down to the waterfront. As he rode, he imagined Blue huddled high in the pines, hearing his father dismiss him like an untamable horse only fit for the knacker's yard.

When he arrived at the dock, he saw Eliza on the scow, dragging her sea chest down the ramp. The huge dog waited on the dock, sitting back on his haunches.

A meal, a bath and a nap had done wonders for Eliza. Her curling black hair gleamed with blue highlights, and she moved with sprightly energy, pulling the crate along the dock. When she noticed Hunter, her face lit with a smile. "I'm glad you're here," she said. "This is too heavy for me to haul on my own."

"Noah will get it later," Hunter said curtly. He strode to the base of the huge tree, shaded his eyes and looked up.

"Blue!" he called. "Son, come down from there."

Eliza abandoned her efforts with the trunk. "Your boy's up in the tree?" she asked in amazement.

Hunter didn't reply. "Blue, come down at once," he said.

No response. But then, that was no surprise.

"It's dangerous for you to be up there. The nails have all rusted, and I don't think the boards will hold."

Again, no response.

Eliza went to the base of the tree. Caliban barked sharply, having spotted the boy. "Heavens, how long has he been up there?" Eliza asked.

"This is family business," Hunter snapped, fear for Blue coming out as fury. "You shouldn't be wandering the place on your own."

"Then *you* shouldn't have forced me to come here."

Ignoring her, Hunter angled his gaze up to the platform again. A pale, skinny leg swung idly off the edge of the rotted wood. Caliban whined, and Eliza shushed him.

"Damn it to hell, Blue. You'll fall from there, break your neck. Is that what you want?" he demanded, terrified. "Is it?"

Still no response. Blue's bare leg just kept swinging back and forth like a pendulum.

Hunter bit out an oath. "I'm coming up there, son. I'll carry you down if I have to." He grasped one of the rungs of the weathered handholds nailed to the trunk of the tree. The second he put his weight on it, the old wood broke into pieces that rained upon the ground. Clearly, Hunter's weight was too great to be borne by the ancient rungs. If he tried to climb up, he'd have no way of getting down.

"Goddamn it, Blue," he said in fear and frustration. "What'll it take to get you down from there?"

"A little more *savoir faire* than you possess, obviously," Eliza said, grossly mispronouncing the French. She moved in close with the purposeful precision of a Napoleon in miniature. Small, focused, intractable—those were the impressions she gave. You'd never know she'd been living a hermit's life on a remote island.

"Hello," she called pleasantly. "My name is Eliza Flyte. Your father's told me so much about you. I was wondering if you could help me, Blue. I was just on my way to see how the new stallion is settling in, and I was hoping you could come with me. There's something very special about this horse." She paused dramatically. "He talks."

Still no response. Hunter felt naked, vulnerable, his position as precarious as Blue's. Contrary to what Eliza had said, he'd told her virtually nothing of the boy.

"Oh, and after that," she said brightly, "your father promised he would have my special trunk delivered to my room. It's filled with—" She broke off deliberately.

The bare leg stopped swinging.

"Well, you'll see what treasures it's filled with when you help me unpack," Eliza concluded. "You won't want to miss them, I promise you that."

Hunter watched in amazement as the boy dangled both legs over the edge. With unhurried movements, he climbed down the handholds and landed with a gentle thud on the grass.

"Blue!" Hunter grabbed the boy, pulled him into his

arms. Blue had pine straw in his hair and he smelled of ocean breezes. "You scared the hell out of me."

Blue stood stiff and silent, neither pulling away nor leaning into the embrace. Hunter had been raised by a man who had no truck with showing affection. Jared Calhoun maintained that it wasn't manful to embrace even his own son. So Hunter had never learned to do it properly. Showing affection to his boy always made him feel awkward and strange.

Blue must possess a good measure of his grandfather in him, for he bore the embrace with his characteristic stiff aloofness. Hunter held him at arm's length. "Are you all right, son?"

Silence. But the boy peered past Hunter's shoulder at the woman standing behind him.

Hunter rose, frustrated. Control had slipped from him and he saw no way to take it back.

Blue tucked his hands shyly behind his back. He regarded her from the side of his eyes. The stance put Hunter in mind of the stallion that first morning on the island beach, wary and confused. The interest was there, but not the trust.

"Son, say hello to Miss Eliza Flyte," Hunter said, knowing it was futile.

Blue ducked his head.

Eliza caught his eye and sent him a dazzling smile that would have worked wonders on Hunter himself, had he been the reluctant one. "We'll have plenty of time to talk," she said pleasantly. "Your father brought me to live with you." She pressed a finger to her lower lip.

"She's come to be your...companion," Hunter said impulsively, thinking of Eliza's preoccupation with *Jane Eyre*. "Your governess."

Her eyes widened, but she recovered quickly, reaching

around behind Blue and taking his hand. To Hunter's astonishment, the boy didn't pull away. Eliza said, "I've never been to the mainland before. It's all completely new to me. I don't know my way around at all. Perhaps you'd show me where everything is."

To Hunter's further astonishment, Blue started walking. Hunter could only stare after them as, hand in hand, they headed toward the barn.

The little boy's hand fluttered within Eliza's like a small, timid bird. She knew better than to tighten her grip. That would only harm the fragile creature inside. She listened to Blue the way she listened to a frightened animal. She had to, because he had not spoken to her in words yet.

He kept his eyes downcast and his shoulders hitched up. Defensive, she thought. Self-protective.

But from what?

She dared to glance back over her shoulder. Hunter still stood by the dock. He faced the bay, feet planted wide, hands at his sides. In the midst of all that green—field, marsh, tall pines, the bay—he made a dark shadow that lay long against the surface of the water. Eliza had never seen a more lonely sight in her life.

The situation at Albion baffled her. Hunter's son, a beautiful, blue-eyed boy, hadn't smiled at his father, hadn't greeted him, had not even looked at him after descending from that dangerous perch in the tree.

The boy's beyond any help, Hunter had said.

Had Blue heard? And if he had, did he understand?

She knew instinctively that he was not simple or daft. One look into his eyes told her that. Behind the solemn, curiously adult facade lay a lively intelligence that lit up as he watched the big dog career across the yard after a mockingbird.

"Caliban never catches anything," she said, her voice betraying none of her thoughts. "Silly dog, he wouldn't know what to do if he did get a bird or a squirrel."

The boy didn't respond, but he brightened at the spectacle Caliban made. His back legs almost overtook his front as he raced over the lawn.

"My father used to say that dog was stitched together from mismatched parts—the legs of a pony, the body of a cow, the head of a dog and the wits of a dormouse." She grinned, remembering the day her father had brought Caliban home from Eastwick. The puppy's gangly legs had hung out of the crate and his fur had been a mass of gray-brown scruff. She had loved him instantly, dubbing him Caliban after the enchanted beast in *The Tempest*.

"The truth is," she went on, "he's part English mastiff and part Irish wolfhound. Irish, like the new stallion. And I promised you I'd show you how to talk to Finn, didn't I?"

Interest flickered in Blue's face. His steps quickened and he surged ahead of her in his haste to reach the barn. Inside the long, low building, boxes for the horses flanked the central aisle. At one end, there was a small dwelling or office and a tack and grooming room. She took down a lunge rein and looped it over her shoulder.

The stallion stood in the adjacent paddock under the sweeping outspread branch of an oak tree. Caliban caught the horse's attention, racing around outside the periphery of the enclosure with his jaw flapping low. The horse had grown accustomed to the dog and tolerated him well enough.

"Miss Eliza," Noah said, coming out of the office. "Hey, Blue. Did you come to see the stallion?"

The little boy nodded.

"He came right along, docile as you please," Noah said. "Tomorrow we'll put him with the other horses."

"I told Blue that Finn is a talking horse," Eliza said. "Come see, Noah."

The youth flashed her a look of suspicion, but followed them to the paddock.

"He speaks," she said matter-of-factly, "if you know how to listen." She lifted Blue and perched him on the top rail of the fence. It was a round beam, she noted with approval. Its shape prevented horses from cribbing the wood and getting colic. Already she was getting the impression that Hunter understood the needs of the horse farm far better than the needs of his son.

She entered the pen slowly but not hesitantly. "Watch the stallion," she said to the boys. "He's talking to me right now. See how he puts one ear back? Just one, not both. So he's not hostile. He's wondering what I want." She walked in a straight path toward him. "He's used to me now, so he'll let me put on this lunge rein. Watch his mouth—he keeps smacking his lips, so we know he's not worried about us being here. A horse won't act like he's eating if he's nervous."

She fastened the rein and, standing in the middle of the ring, prompted him to walk in a circle. Then she accelerated him into a canter. Both boys sat forward, clearly enthralled with the easy, flowing motion of the horse. Finn performed as she knew he would, responding to each command with smooth compliance. He had a fiery temperament but he also possessed the horse's ingrained will to please. When she finished the demonstration, the stallion followed her around like a dog, and she walked him straight to the fence where Noah and Blue sat enraptured.

"Glory be," Noah said, holding out his hand so Finn could inspect it. "A blamed miracle."

She stepped back and nodded encouragingly at Blue. "You can touch him. He likes to be scratched right under his jaw." Blue reached out, pressing his palm against the chestnut's big cheek. The horse leaned in to him, and Blue's hand rubbed firmly and affectionately under the jaw.

"You reckon I can ride him?" Noah asked.

"Aye. Hunter said you're the jockey."

Blue took his hand away. The horse swung his head closer, seeking more petting.

"This horse was a killer." Noah rubbed his thumb on the blaze of the stallion's forehead. "How did you heal him?"

"I expect you know a horse can't be evil, like a true killer. He was afraid. When a horse is afraid, it runs. When it can't run, it fights. Confined on that ship from Ireland, he was frightened by the storms for days on end. All he could do was fight."

Noah shook his head. "I swear, I don't understand all that, but I do know horses."

"That's what Hunter told me. He's very proud of you." She held out the long leather rein. "Lunge him for a while and ask him to work for you. He will."

"Yes, ma'am."

"We'd best get back to the house," she said to Blue.

Blue dropped to the ground and started toward the house. "I'll ask him to introduce me to his sister," she said. A little incredulously she added, "Seeing how his father assigned me to be the governess."

Noah hesitated, the rein dangling from a crook in his arm. "He won't do it," he said quietly.

"What?"

"Blue won't introduce you to his sister."

"Why not?"

Noah wet his lips nervously. "Don't you know?"

A chill of premonition touched the back of her neck. "Know what?"

"Blue doesn't speak. Ain't said a word since the day his mother died."

Hunter felt tired, and a thousand years old, when he came in from the stables later that day. Through force of habit he poured himself a glass of whiskey and drank two greedy gulps. It had been a long, strange day, beginning with the encounter with the slave-catchers and ending with—

A bumping sound from upstairs reminded him that the day wasn't over yet. He put the glass stopper in the decanter and went up the curved staircase, heading to the wing where the children's room was. Eliza had been given a room across the hall from them, and the bumping sound came from there.

He walked in to find both children standing by the old sea chest from the island. No one saw him come in. The room smelled musty from disuse, and old sheets still draped the sparse furniture. At one time, this had been a grand guest room, opulent with damask draperies and crystal vases filled with fresh flowers.

"Would you like to see my treasures?" Eliza asked them.

He remembered the night he had forced her to show him the contents of the locker. Reluctantly she had shown him the things that were important to her, revealed the things she dreamed about. How long ago that seemed, when they had been alone together in the driftwood cabin.

Now it already felt as if their time on the island had never happened.

But it had, and he recalled every moment, every shining look she had given him, every gasp of wonder when he'd held her in his arms and made love to her.

Discomfited, he cleared his throat. "I see you're getting settled in," he said.

"Papa!" Belinda said excitedly. "Miss Eliza's going to show us a treasure. Do you want to see?"

"I've seen her treasures," he said.

"Lift the lid, Blue," Eliza said, flushing at Hunter's tone. "Let's have a look."

The boy opened the chest eagerly and peered inside. With a theatrical flourish, Eliza lifted the old muslin and took out the jockey's silks that had belonged to her father, the old tankard and the gold mourning ring, and, finally, the gleaming pieces of the Spanish bride's dowry. She put the old moth-eaten wig on Blue, eliciting gales of laughter from Belinda, who gamely tried on the Monmouth cap.

"You make a right proper sailor now," Eliza said as the little girl preened. She showed them the book of maps and prints from the wild seacoast of California. "It's a faraway place," she said. "A magical place."

"Do you think we could go there?" asked Belinda.

A shadow fell over Eliza's face. "It's so far away, almost no one goes there." Then she brightened. "Here's what it sounds like." She held up the big conch shell. "Be very quiet, and you'll be able to hear the wind and the ocean."

The children put their heads together, pressing in close. Their faces shone with amazement. Eliza caught Hunter's eye, and for a moment he felt completely naked. In that one glance, he saw her understanding. She sensed the turmoil that boiled inside him with every breath he took. He adored his children with a ferocity that ached in his chest. But he didn't know—perhaps had never known—what to do with that love, except hurt.

Blue squatted beside the bed in the room he shared with his sister. He cast a furtive glance over his shoulder to make certain he was alone. He could hear Belinda and Miss Eliza—the governess—chattering like magpies across the hall, so he knew they wouldn't disturb him. Pressing his belly to the floor, he squirmed like a snake under the bed. Dust-mice scattered and tickled his nose. He held his breath, trying not to sneeze. He couldn't bear the idea of making a sound.

Reaching out, he groped in the dark until he found what he sought, feeling the smooth, dusty wood beneath his fingers. Inching back, he pulled it along with him, extracting it from its hiding place. It was a carved rosewood lap desk with brass fittings. His mama used to sit up in her bed, looking like a sunflower against a bank of feather bolsters, and write letters for hours and hours.

Blue hadn't looked in the box since the day she had told him to hide it. Although he had only been a baby of seven back then, he could remember exactly what she said to him. *Take it away and hide it, Blue.* Mama's voice had been harsh and whispery, because she was dying. *You must never say a word of this, Blue. Not a single word.*

When he had gone to see her the next day, to tell her he'd done as she'd asked, he had found the room shrouded in darkness. His papa sat beside the bed with his head in his hands and the sharp smell of whiskey on his breath. Blue didn't ask if his mama was dead. He just knew. And he did exactly what she told him—he never said a word.

Now he was a big boy of nine, and his hand looked big, almost grown-up, as he brushed it lightly over the surface of the lap desk and the brass hinges. In showing him the wonderful things in her battered old sea chest, Miss Eliza had inspired him.

Like Miss Eliza, he had a box full of secrets.

He wondered what would happen if he let them all out.

Eighteen

Eliza awoke but didn't open her eyes, because she didn't want the dream to go away. She was floating on a cloud, and everything smelled of dried rose petals and lavender, and someone, somewhere, hummed a song she had never heard.

It was all too delicious to relinquish. And yet a strange feeling crept over her—the feeling of being watched.

Her eyes flew open. At the foot of the bed, a shadow flickered. She blinked and shook her head. A trick of the morning light. She was completely alone in this strange, tall-ceilinged room.

And such a room it was. She realized her dream had been no dream at all, but the comforts she had encountered at Albion. The soft, floating cloud was actually a mattress—one stuffed with cotton rather than the dried milk-weed she had used on the island. The floral smells breathed gently from the bed linens themselves, and the sweet melody wafted in through the tall double doors that opened out to a balcony with a fancy plaster rail.

So this was his world, she mused. Hunter's world. He lived here in this vast, decaying place with a blind house-keeper, a cranky cook, two children and a jockey called

Noah. Eliza had not met anyone else yet. She guessed that it was either Nancy or Willa singing outside the window.

Supper last night had been a strained, uneasy affair. After Hunter's impulsive declaration that she would be the children's governess, she had taken the children in hand. In truth she was glad to do it, for she couldn't stand being idle. She discovered a deep fascination for the children. She had never known any before, and she felt a special affinity with them. Blue's silent watchfulness reminded her of the vigilance of a young fawn, curious yet cautious and ready to flee at any moment. Belinda's eagerness to please was puppylike, playful and guileless.

Eliza could not understand Hunter's attitude toward his children. She could tell he loved them, but he seemed uncertain as to what to do with them. She knew the rearing of children was considered women's work, and that children were to be kept in the women's domain. Yet she had grown up in the light of a father's love, not a mother's, and the warmth of that love lingered even now, because her father lived in her heart, always. It was so important to give a child that sort of love, she thought as she lay there in the comfortable bed. The sort that defied even death. She must get Hunter to see. She knew it would be a challenge—but she had never shied from a challenge.

Last night she had wondered what was going through his head as he watched her showing the children her treasures from the island. She had planned to ask him at supper time. But she and the children had gone to supper to find themselves alone. Hunter was nowhere in sight.

"Papa doesn't usually eat with us," Belinda explained matter-of-factly.

Because he usually drinks alone. Eliza's intuition filled in what the little girl hadn't said, either because she didn't understand or didn't want to know.

Eliza quickly discovered that Belinda, who was seven, had cast herself in the role of explainer of all things. She supplied answers to questions, sometimes before they were asked: "Grandfather Beaumont thinks Papa is a disgrace, and so he hired a tutor for us." "Blue doesn't like butter on his bread. He likes it plain." "My mama used to tell the cook what to fix for supper, but Nancy and Willa just fix any old thing they please." "When Papa gets worried, it makes him thirsty."

Eliza found the little girl delightful and charming. She found the boy...intriguing. His silence was an active, live thing. Not a void but something large and almost tangible. He and his sister had some secret rapport, so that with a single glance he could communicate with her. Like two wild creatures, they had created a mysterious means of talking without words.

"Blue doesn't like turnip greens," Belinda was wont to say. Or, "Blue wants to go look at the new stallion again."

Eliza had stayed awake late, wondering about these children. Recklessly she had accepted them as her charges. She was out of her depth entirely. Now she understood exactly how Jane Eyre felt, encountering her young charge for the first time.

She lay back against a bank of pillows and shut her eyes again. "Lord, help me," she whispered, "what have I done?"

Once again she had that uncanny sensation of being watched. Once again she opened her eyes, this time quickly enough to see a small bright head disappear behind the footboard of the bed, like a rabbit down a hole.

Eliza smiled and shifted to a sitting position. "Come on, then. I love a little company in the morning."

It was true, startlingly so. She, who had awakened so many mornings to the emptiness of the island, felt a small twinge of excitement to find herself in the presence of this little towheaded sprite.

Belinda reappeared, cautious and inquisitive as a kitten. She wore a wrinkled muslin gown and her hair was tousled, her face still soft from sleep. Eliza patted the bed. It was a big wooden affair, almost boatlike, with a canopy overhead and organdy curtains draped around. The little girl had to use a wooden step stool to climb up.

"Where's your brother?" Eliza asked.

"Under the bed," Belinda whispered.

"Do you think he'd like to climb up too?"

Belinda shook her head vigorously and cupped her hands around Eliza's ear. "I wasn't supposed to tell."

Eliza thought fast. "I was just pretending that this bed is a great ship upon the sea, and a storm's about to blow in. I'd hate for Blue to drown."

Belinda adopted the fantasy with the swift unquestioning acceptance of a true believer. She scrambled to the edge of the bed and held out her hand.

"Hurry, Blue!" she called. "Storm's coming! Grab on, and I'll pull you aboard."

"Watch out for that wave." Eliza flapped the counterpane dramatically. "We'll be swamped for certain."

Blue shot out from under the bed and leaped into the middle of the bedclothes.

Eliza didn't make a fuss over him. She shaded her eyes and gazed out to sea. "'Take in the topsail,'" she recited from *The Tempest.* "'Tend to th'master's whistle... Blow till thou burst thy wind!'"

The three of them sank deep into fantasy. Eliza enjoyed it immensely. Playing with the children was not so different from working with wild animals. She watched them and took her cue from them rather than trying to impose her will. Instinct told her not to press Blue with questions about why he never spoke. She knew it was up to her to find out where the hurt was coming from before she could figure out a way to heal it.

And she would. She didn't know when she had made that vow or how she would carry it out. But she could no more turn away from this silent little boy than she could the stallion Hunter had brought to her island.

"Blue," she said, "climb up to the topmast and signal to us if you sight land."

He jumped up and clung to the bedpost, shading his eyes as Eliza had done earlier. He waved his hand and eagerly bobbed his head.

"Land," Eliza called jubilantly. "We are saved!"

The three of them held hands and jumped up and down on the bed, churning through the mountain of bedclothes. A feather pillow tore open, and within seconds a snow-storm of white down filled the air. Eliza and Belinda yelled, "We are saved!" and Blue grinned from ear to ear.

They made such a ruckus that Eliza didn't hear the door open. All of a sudden Hunter was standing there, his expression thunderous. He had shaved his beard and groomed his hair, and he wore fawn-colored trousers, tall riding boots and a generously cut shirt. With a flurry of feathers cascading over him, he looked slightly magical, like a prince from another land.

Eliza and the children collapsed in a heap on the bed, as if they were birds shot out of the sky.

Belinda recovered first, squealing, "Father, look out! You'll drown in the ocean!"

"What?" He batted downy feathers away from his face.

"Hurry," she cried, raising up on her knees and clapping her hands. "We're in the middle of a terrible storm."

His jaw tightened. For a moment he looked completely

lost. Then he said, "Sorry, sweetheart. I haven't the time to play this morning. Now, go and get dressed, both of you, and then you can show Miss Eliza down to the dining room for breakfast."

Blue climbed out of the bed and headed for the door. Belinda followed him but paused before leaving. "Will you be having breakfast with us, Papa?"

"I've work to do. We've an exhibition race coming up, and then the yearling auction."

She nodded and slipped out. Eliza wished the child would stand up to her father, demand his attention, but instead she and her brother complied too easily, without question.

Eliza found herself alone with the master of Albion. She felt uncomfortably aware of her state. Her hair hung in an untidy braid, and she wore a borrowed night rail that was too large and had slipped down to bare one shoulder. His gaze seared like a hot brand on her exposed flesh, and she tugged the neckline up.

Everything felt different here. On the island, such things as nightgowns and dresses didn't matter. Yet in this strange mansion, an air of formality spun through the creaky old rooms like dust motes through bars of sunlight.

"The children shouldn't be allowed to get so wild indoors," he said.

"Why not?" She studied him for a moment. She hardly recognized him as the man who had brought his mad horse to the island. This man was stiff and angry, formal and excruciatingly correct. She caught herself thinking of the night they had made love and she'd been certain their souls had touched. It all seemed like a dream now. Perhaps it had never happened.

Her gaze dropped to his big hands. Oh, but it had happened. She remembered those hands.

"Because it's not proper," he said. "That's why not."

"When it comes to children, I have no idea what is proper and what is not," she said.

"Then in the future you should heed me—"

"But I do know," she went on as if she hadn't heard him, "that what makes a child happy is proper, and what makes him unhappy is not."

"You have a lot to learn, Eliza."

She got out of bed, her bare feet feeling the smooth wooden floor and stray feathers ruffling beneath them. Refusing to let this stuffy stranger intimidate her, she stood before him, fists on her hips. "So have you."

"You're a defiant article of baggage, Eliza Flyte."

She lifted her chin, wondering if she only imagined the reluctant admiration in his tone. But she had more pressing concerns than his opinion of her. "I want to talk about Blue," she said, watching his face closely.

He didn't move, but his whole body seemed to tense and brace itself in preparation for a blow. "I've business to look after this morn—"

"You've a son to look after." She swiftly crossed the room and shut the door.

"Don't do that," he said.

"Why not?"

His gaze flicked over her. "It's not proper."

She laughed. "Oh, and behaving properly has always been so important to me."

"Look at yourself." He yanked a drape off a tall, flat piece of furniture.

"A mirror," she whispered, intrigued. "I've never seen an actual mirror before." She caught a glimpse of herself in the oval cheval glass. She had seen her reflection in still water and in the shiny side of her black china teapot, but she'd never seen her entire self with such clarity. The image in the glass startled her.

"Look at me," she echoed Hunter, lifting her hand to brush a strand of wavy black hair out of her face. The stranger in the mirror did the same. She looked small and skinny in the overlarge night rail. Her face had a golden hue imbued by seasons in the sun. The color of her eyes startled her; she knew they were gray but she had never imagined the silvery depths of them. Her hair lay stark black against the snow-white nightgown. The thin fabric revealed the dark tips of her breasts and a shadow where her legs joined.

"Yes," Hunter said in a low voice, "look at you."

Watching in the mirror, she saw him come up behind her, bending his head to press his lips to the side of her neck.

Her head fell back in surrender. Lord, she had missed this, the feel of those big hands on her, the softness of his mouth kissing her. It was fascinating and deeply sensual to actually see the caress happening. His hands slipped around her waist from behind, hugging her against his hips. His hand skimmed upward, cupping her breast, thumb circling slowly, searchingly. When his other hand went downward, she lost the struggle to keep her eyes open. She closed them and dropped her head to the side, baring more of her neck and shoulder to his kisses. She felt herself floating away, and was sure she would open her eyes and see that the woman in the mirror was gone, having floated off to some distant place where sensation was everything and nothing mattered so much as the caress of his clever hands. And yet something tugged her, nagged at her, some issue unresolved.

In the kitchen below, Nancy launched into a new song, slow and mournful.

There was something suspect in the way Hunter handled her. His caresses seemed oddly calculated rather than spontaneous. He had never been manipulative with her, but he was now, and she thought she knew why.

Like a dreamer fighting wakefulness, she wanted to stay here in his arms even though she understood that he meant to distract her, nothing more. But inch by inch she fought her way back to reality. "You must...stop," she forced out between her teeth.

His hands didn't stop. "Don't you like this?"

"I..." She made herself open her eyes. The woman in the mirror looked different from the way she had a few minutes ago. Now she was flushed, full-lipped and heavy-lidded. Wanton and somehow used. "That's not the point." She wrenched out of his grasp and moved away from him so she could think more clearly. "You're clever enough to coax a reaction from a fence post, but that's different from my liking it."

He stared down at his trousers and set his hands on his hips. "You were more fun before you decided to join polite society. You've only been back to civilization for two days, and already you're starting to sound like a typical woman."

"You're the one who brought me here—against my will, I might add." She veered away from that accusation. There was no use arguing about matters that couldn't be changed. "You keep trying to distract me from talking about Blue."

His teasing grin disappeared. "What about Blue?"

"Why is he silent? Noah said he stopped speaking the day his mother died. Why is that? What happened?"

"The boy lost his mother." Hunter spoke slowly and distinctly, as if addressing an idiot. "He's grieving for her."

"How long?" she asked.

"It's been two years."

"That's far too long for him to be in this state." Before Hunter could stop her, she went on. "He's stuck somewhere in the middle of his grief, and he can't get out. You have to show him the way."

Without even moving, Hunter raised a defensive, invisible shield between them. "Don't you think I know that? Don't you think I agonize over my son? Don't you think I've tried to find a way to end his silence?"

"What have you tried, Hunter?" When he didn't answer, she asked again, "What?"

"I've taken him to every physician, every special tutor and school in the area. I've even considered sending him away to some institution."

"You can't cart Blue from place to place like a barn-soured horse," she said, even though she could see his temper starting to boil. "He needs *you*. When was the last time you played with your children?"

"Oh, for Chrissake—"

"You can't remember, can you?"

"I'm with them constantly. They spend hours at the arena or the mile track."

"It's not the same. They're observers. You should be with them."

"And what the hell do you know of this? What makes you an expert on my children?"

"I've learned to watch, Hunter. To listen and watch."

"That might work on a horse, but not a boy." His eyes were as hard and cold as cut emeralds. "Christ, you were raised on an island like a wild animal—"

"Get out," she said, her voice so low with rage that she was almost whispering. "Now."

Even Hunter seemed to realize he'd crossed the line

with his callous remark. He took a step toward her. "Eliza, I didn't mean—"

"Yes, you did." His remark had pierced deep. She felt as though she were bleeding in some secret place. "Now, get out, and I'll see to your children."

"How come you picked all the bits of ham out of your eggs?" Belinda asked at breakfast.

Eliza, still shaken from her altercation with Hunter, dabbed at her lips with a napkin. "I never eat ham."

"Don't you like it?" Belinda dug hungrily into the mound of fluffy eggs and diced ham.

"I've never eaten it."

"You didn't eat the roast last night, either," Belinda said. "But you ate all the nasty greens and oysters and corn pone. Why is that?"

Blue ate more slowly and thoughtfully than his sister. Eliza could feel his attention fall on her like a sunbeam. She knew the answer she gave to Belinda's question was important. She knew better than to lie to children.

"I don't ever eat meat," she said. "Only fish and shell-fish."

"Really?"

"Really."

"Not even venison sausages? Not even fried chicken or rabbit stew or pork chops?"

"No. None of that."

Belinda took a gulp of heavily sweetened tea. "Why not?" she persisted.

"Well, I suppose it's because when I was a girl like you, I lived all alone on an island with my father. I didn't have any children to play with, so I spent all my time with animals."

"You lived all alone?" The blue eyes widened almost comically.

"That's right. Sometimes drovers came for the horses, but most days it was just me and my father. So I made friends with the animals."

"How did you do that?"

"It took a lot of time, and a lot of patience, and most of all, a lot of watching."

"What were you watching for?"

"I had to figure out a way to talk to them."

"Silly. Animals don't talk."

"They certainly do. Not in words, but they've always got something to say." She sneaked a glance at Blue and saw that he was rapt with attention. "I had deer that let me pet them, and squirrels and rabbits that ate from my hand, and birds that would roost on my shoulder, and baby ducks that followed me everywhere I went. The milch cow came when I called her, and all the wild ponies let me ride whenever I wanted."

Belinda dropped her fork. "That's a whopper!"

Eliza solemnly crossed a hand over her chest. "It's true. All of it. So that's why I'd never eat the flesh of an animal. It would be like eating a friend."

"Eeuw," Belinda said delightedly. "I bet Master Rencher would be all stringy and greasy."

"Who's Master Rencher?"

"The schoolmaster at Bonterre." She made a face, then slathered a square of corn bread with gooseberry jam. "So why do you still eat fish and crabs and oysters?" she demanded.

Eliza laughed. "I never did figure out how to talk to an oyster." She made a pinching motion with her hand and nipped playfully at Blue's ear. "And can you imagine making friends with a crab?"

Blue looked stunned at first. Then he ducked away from her, but not before she'd detected a twinkle in his eye and the beginnings of a smile.

They ate in companionable silence for a time. Eliza fell deep into thought about the strange turn her life had taken, and what it meant, and what was in store for her.

"Can we meet the animals from the island?" Belinda asked, setting her rumpled napkin on the table. "The ones that talk to you?"

"Of course."

"Hurrah!" Belinda jumped up.

"Dishes first."

"Huh?" asked Belinda.

"We have to clean our dishes," Eliza explained.

"But Willa and Nancy always do the dishes."

"Willa and Nancy didn't dirty them. We did."

Belinda beamed, thinking this was a new game. "Oh!"

Eliza got a tray from the sideboard. As she was stacking the dishes, she saw with a start that Blue's plate was not empty.

He had carefully and thoroughly picked out every bit of ham.

Hot and thirsty, Eliza flopped down on the grass under one of Albion's huge, twisted live oaks. She uncorked the cider jug and took a long drink, then passed it to Blue. "Share with your sister," she said, mopping her brow. "You children will wear me to a frazzle," she added, leaning on her elbows and looking up at the canopy of leaves. She had almost said "You'll be the death of me," but she couldn't be careless with phrases like that, not under the circumstances. "You've given me no rest all day."

"You said we could play with the animals," Belinda pointed out.

"Yes, I did. We milked Claribel, and we fed melon rinds to the chickens, and made a bed for Miranda in the barn loft—"

Caliban came bounding up and dropped a well-chewed stick at her feet. The huge dog's tongue lolled out one side of his mouth, and his sides fanned like a bellows with excitement. He was the children's favorite so far, because he was such a clown.

"Look," Belinda exclaimed, "Caliban still wants to play."

"He always wants to play," Eliza said with mock exasperation. She flung the stick halfheartedly. It spun high above the lush green lawn. While the big dog bounded after it, Eliza drank more cider. Nancy had given them a big jug to take on their outing.

"Why is he called Caliban?" Belinda asked.

"Because he's so big, and he's not very pretty. Caliban is the name of a monster in a play called *The Tempest.*"

"Is he a very bad monster?" The little girl watched the dog take off after a dragonfly.

"He was naughty sometimes, but in the end he was sorry. My father used to tell me he was a lost soul."

Blue tucked his knees up to his chest, making a ledge for his chin. He took an idle sip of the cider and stared across the lawn at the riding arena, where Hunter and Noah were putting the stallion through his paces. The Irish Thoroughbred held a special fascination for Blue. She had noticed that right off.

"Where is your father now?" Belinda asked.

Eliza should have seen the question coming. "He's up among the stars," she said.

"What?"

Belinda was a literal thinker, Eliza realized. She must remember that. "He died," she said. Two simple words. So inadequate to express the loss she had endured.

"My mother died too," Belinda said.

"I know."

"Do you think she's up among the stars too, Miss Eliza?"

"Oh, yes. You must miss her very much." She tried to discern some reaction from Blue, but he merely kept his chin planted on his knees and stared straight ahead.

Belinda drank some of the cider, wiping her chin carelessly with the hem of her frock. "Everything was different when Mama was alive."

"I'd like to hear all about her sometime," Eliza said.

"Papa doesn't like us to talk about her."

"How do you know that?"

"Well, every time I ask him something about Mama, he gets terrifically gruff and thirsty."

Eliza did not press the child to say more. She was getting a strangely accurate view of this sad, damaged family. Her instinct to heal ran strong with these children. Stronger even than her instinct to save the stallion when she thought Hunter Calhoun was going to shoot it. This urge to connect and protect was powerful, and it sprang from a place inside her that she hadn't even known existed.

She wondered if this was the same urge that fueled a mare's fierce protectiveness of a newborn foal, or the dramatic performance of the piping plover that would lie in the sand and pretend to be wounded to distract a predator from her young.

Eliza wanted to touch Blue, to hold him close, but she restrained herself. The same mare that wouldn't let a foal leave her side would later drive a yearling from the herd, only allowing it to return if it came back on the mare's terms. She had no idea how things worked between a woman and child, but she decided to follow her instincts in this.

"Let's go look at the stallion," she said, getting to her feet and dusting off her dress.

Blue and Belinda scampered along beside her as she crossed the broad meadow to the mile oval.

"Papa made this," Belinda explained as they walked together, Caliban bounding off far ahead of them. "He and Noah spent weeks and weeks. They got so dirty."

If the house had an empty, neglected air, the riding facilities had a feeling of abundance. The quarters that housed Noah and two grooms were neat, the hedges trimmed around the front door. The barn was clean and well supplied with cedar shavings, hay, grain and alfalfa. The round pen and new arena had been stoutly built. There was a small building with a high roof which she recognized as a starting gate. She had never seen one, but a drawing in the Rarey text and in her father's fireside descriptions of the Derby races back in England gave her a clear picture of the narrow chute.

At the side of the oval, they climbed to a wooden viewing platform. Noah was mounted on the stallion, and Hunter stood watching with a flag tucked under one arm.

"Hello," Eliza called, waving to them.

The horse pricked his ears and pawed at the ground, but settled at a low word from Noah. Eliza was pleased to see the rapport between horse and rider. She was far more interested in Hunter, though. Unlike Noah, he did not look happy to see her and the children. She had not forgotten his cruel remark to her this morning, but she didn't want the children to see her anger and hurt.

"I see you've got him under saddle," she said.

"He's a beauty," Noah said, pressing the stallion to a

smart canter. "What do you think of that, eh, Blue?" He passed by the platform with a special smile for Blue. The younger boy smiled back and held closer to the rail, enraptured as Noah rode by. Caliban ran partway along the track, then broke free, veering off to dig in the sandy fringes of the marsh.

Hunter joined them, hoisting himself up to the platform. He looked flushed and triumphant. "I do believe we have our racehorse back," he said.

"You're a fine jockey, Noah," Eliza remarked.

"The best in Virginia," Hunter said, pretending she had spoken to him. "Noah used to hire out to other horse owners, but he won't have to do that anymore if the race and the yearling sale are successful this summer."

Noah beamed with pride. Then he tucked up his legs, and the stallion bolted forward in a flat-out gallop. Noah tightened the reins and fought to hold him in, but Finn clamped the bit in his teeth and yanked control away from his rider. Noah could do nothing but stay high in the stirrups, elbows low on the pumping neck as they careened around the turn of the oval and flew along the backstretch with a speed and grace that made Eliza's chest ache.

"Noah's going to have to get him under control, get him to quit stealing the bit," Hunter murmured, but a taut, cautious joy softened his comment.

Belinda clapped her hands. "He's the fastest horse in Virginia, Papa. Maybe in the whole wide world." She flung her arms around his upper thigh and rested her cheek against him. "I'm glad you went on that fool's errand," she declared.

Blue ducked his head. Eliza was certain she'd seen him smile.

"Who said I was on a fool's errand?" Hunter demanded.

"Grandfather Beaumont."

"Such a surprise." He ruffled her yellow hair. "Speaking of Grandfather Beaumont, why aren't you two at lessons today?"

Still clinging to his leg, she leaned back and tilted her head to look up at him. "It's Saturday. We never have lessons on Saturday. And tomorrow is Grandfather Beaumont's picnic. Absolutely everyone will be there. Aunt Delaney and Uncle Ernest and Francine and her new baby, and all the cousins too." She smiled blissfully. "No lessons, and a picnic. You'll come, won't you, Papa?"

His smile faded and he freed himself from her grasp. "I don't know, sweetheart—"

"Papa, please. You must. You completely must."

Eliza held her breath, watching him prepare to rattle off his excuses. She could just hear them now—too much work to do here, horse buyers coming from out of town, two mares about to foal... He was so easy to read when it came to his children.

She wondered about the true cause of his reluctance. She'd heard enough to understand that his late wife's family did not approve of his enterprise or the way he was raising the children. Was it that, or had she been correct earlier in accusing him of avoiding his own children?

"Pleeease," Belinda said.

Even Hunter couldn't seem to resist the appeal in her blue eyes. He patted Belinda on the head. "I suppose I will, then."

"And Miss Eliza too?"

He froze, clearly unprepared for the question. He regarded Eliza with an impersonal stare for a moment, then said, "Why not? Since she's your governess, she'll surely want to come along."

"Hurrah!" Belinda tugged at her brother's hand.

"Come on, Blue. Let's see what Caliban dug up. I bet it's buried treasure."

Eliza peeled off her smile the moment the children were gone.

Hunter planted his fists on his hips and glared right back at her.

"You had no call to say what you did this morning," she said.

"Nor did you."

"I was criticizing your manner with the children. You attacked my upbringing. There's a difference."

"Is there?"

"Yes. I can't change what's past. But you can change. You can be a better father to Belinda and Blue—"

"Damn it, woman, I told you. I am a good father to them."

"You don't let them talk about their mother."

"I don't forbid it, but they shouldn't dwell on tragedy."

"They're so young, Hunter. They need to know what their mother was like. They need for you to tell them."

"I don't have anything to tell my children about their mother that they don't already know."

They both fell silent, watching Noah exercise the horse. Its hooves struck the surface of the track in a heartbeat rhythm. Together with the waves on the distant shore and the wind in the trees, it made a strange music, punctuated now and then by Belinda's laughter or a bark from Caliban.

Hunter's big hands gripped the rail of the reviewing stand. "Look, Eliza. Maybe you had it easier than I thought out on that island for all those years."

"What do you mean by that?"

He laughed humorlessly. "Come to the picnic tomorrow, and you'll see."

Nineteen

ᦱ᥇᥇ᦱ

At noon the next day, Hunter waited in the foyer for Eliza to come down. The house was fragrant with the smell of Willa's biscuits, which would be their contribution to the Beaumonts' picnic.

Blue and Belinda waited out front with the buggy. Though Bonterre lay only a mile down the road, Hunter wanted to drive. There were still some things his pride would not permit, and arriving at his in-laws on foot was one of them. He had only one cart horse, an elderly and cantankerous Morgan mare. He couldn't afford better. Every possible resource was for the Thoroughbreds.

Blue and Belinda wore their Sunday clothes. They shone like newly minted coins, the very sight of them bringing a smile to his lips.

He caught himself thinking about Eliza's accusation earlier. Was it true? Did he deliberately avoid his children and look for excuses not to be with them? She had been vehement in her meddlesome insistence that he spend more time with them, that he speak to them of Lacey. The idea was preposterous. Didn't Eliza see that?

No, she didn't see anything but his children—two broken-winged birds she felt duty-bound to heal. She didn't know them. Didn't understand.

Upstairs, a door opened and shut, and Eliza came down the staircase on the right. His stomach lurched when he saw her. She looked both terrible and beautiful. She had clearly taken pains with her appearance. Her hair, freshly washed, gleamed brightly, and her brown homespun dress was clean. But she was barefoot, her clothes old and threadbare.

The eager expression on her face told him she had no clue about the reception she would get from the company at Bonterre.

"I'm ready," she said with a big smile. "Where are the children?"

Hunter didn't take his eyes off her. "Willa!" he yelled, loud enough to make Eliza jump.

The cook came hurrying in. "You need something?"

He still didn't look away. "Take Miss Eliza upstairs and find her something to wear," he commanded.

Eliza's eyes widened as if she had stepped on a tack. "I am wearing something."

"People in these parts dress up for picnics." He spread his arms and turned in a circle, showing off his tailored blue frock coat and the emerald silk waistcoat beneath. "See?"

"I see a man with the pride of a peacock," she snapped. "No, wait. That would insult the peacock."

Willa gave a low whistle. "Girl, you look like a field han—oh." She eyed Hunter guiltily. "I reckon I can find something." She met Eliza halfway on the stairs. "Come on, girl. Let's get you fixed up."

Eliza turned and aimed a look of loathing at Hunter, prompting him to call out, "And Willa, don't forget the shoes."

At the first landing, they turned right, heading for the suite of rooms that had been Lacey's domain when she had lived at Albion as his wife. How long ago that had been. Another lifetime.

He could still picture those rooms, though he had not opened the door to them since the day Lacey had taken the children and left.

"I married a tobacco planter," she had said tearfully when he had announced his plan to turn Albion into a horse farm. "I am a planter's wife. I simply don't know how to be anything else."

"We'll work together on this, Lacey. It'll be our own family enterprise. It'll be good, you'll see."

How naive and simple he had been back then. How full of hopes and dreams.

His plea to Lacey had simply insulted her. "I am taking the children to live at Bonterre," she announced. "When you come to your senses and decide to be a planter again, I shall consider forgiving you."

She had taken crate after crate of her gowns and petticoats with her, but had left much behind—the older stuff that had fallen out of fashion. He knew this because he allowed Willa and Nancy to help themselves to whatever they wanted from Lacey's rooms. He reckoned he was the only man in Virginia whose servants wore silk gowns from the Maison de Lumière in Paris.

Without even realizing he had taken out his flask, Hunter unscrewed the cap and took a swig.

"Ain't going to help you none to show up tipsy," Nancy scolded, coming into the foyer with her shuffling gait.

Resigned, Hunter put away the flask. "Woman, how do you do that?"

"No trick to it. I hear you pacing like a caged wildcat

and I know you going to be wanting the whiskey. Why ain't you left yet? Them biscuits'll get cold."

"Willa is putting a new frock on Eliza. And shoes." He shook his head. "Christ, I should've let her show up at the picnic barefoot and in rags."

"Folks at Bonterre'd eat her alive and suck the marrow out of her bones."

"It would serve her right." He brought his fist down on the newel post. "I didn't expect her to want to stay."

"Then you shouldn't have dragged her off that island."

Hunter gently touched Nancy's shoulder. "I had to, honey. It wasn't safe there anymore."

"And you think it's safe here, for a girl like that?"

"Like what?" He scowled. "She's just a tad ignorant, that's all."

Nancy stiffened, and he could feel her probing attention as if she were looking at him. "That's all?" Her clouded eyes were still curiously alert, her face compassionate. "I see."

"She's supposed to be in Norfolk waiting for a ship to California."

"What's California?"

"It's a huge place far in the west, across a distance as wide as the Atlantic. To sail there, you have to sail southward, nearly to the bottom of the world where the sun never shines and the ice never thaws."

"And this girl don't want to do that."

"She does," he said. "She told me—"

"So let her go."

I can't. I'm not ready yet. He took a deep breath and wondered if he could get away with a sip from his flask. "I need her to stay until I remarry," he told Nancy.

"Ha. Who you going to marry?"

"I guess I can find a wife now that Albion's out of debt."

"It ain't Albion I'm worried about, boy. It's you."

"I'm fine," Hunter insisted. But of all the people in the world, Nancy was the one he was least able to deceive. "Honey, I'm doing the right thing with Eliza. The children took to her. *They* need her. No call to send her away tomorrow."

Nancy snorted. "She doesn't want you to do that any more than you want to." She reached up and cupped his cheek the way she had been doing since he was a baby. "Girl's just been driven out of the only home she ever knew. You let her bide a while here. I expect she'll be ready for a change by and by."

"I'm ready for something," Eliza announced from the top of the stairs. "Though I'm not certain what."

In a decidedly feminine rustle of skirts, she descended. Hunter stared at her as if she were a stranger. Her hair was pulled sleekly back and plaited, the plaits pinned in a neat cluster at the nape of her neck. She wore a dark blue dress that was quite plain—exactly what you would expect a proper governess or nanny to wear.

As she descended the stairs, the toes of her shiny black tap boots peeked out from the hem of the skirts. It felt eerie, seeing Lacey's dress again. He could not recall the last time he had seen Lacey wearing this particular gown, but he could picture her so clearly—that smooth, almost haughty carriage, that upright posture bred into her at Miss Porter's School in the north.

"I've decided I'm not angry with you anymore," Eliza said, grinning at him. "Willa explained that you're being kind and helping me fit in."

"I've seldom been accused of kindness," he said.

What Eliza lacked in finesse she made up for in enthusiasm. She nearly slipped a couple of times on the stairs, but she clung to the rail and laughed at her blunders.

"These shoes will take some getting used to. They pinch terribly."

He held out a hand to steady her. "I think they're supposed to."

"And what would you know of ladies' shoes?" she asked.

"I've heard enough complaints."

"Here," Willa called, hurrying down the stairs. "You'll be needing a hat." The straw hat had a wide brim, and it made Eliza's face look like the middle of a flower. Hunter felt a hitch of emotion as she gazed up at him with a radiant smile. "I had no idea a picnic was such a grand affair," she confessed.

"Around here, a picnic's never just a picnic." He held the front door for her, catching a whiff of gardenia fragrance as she walked past.

"Your wife had beautiful things," she said to him. "Thank you."

He didn't reply. Nor did he make a comment when she nearly fell backward trying to get into the buggy. He caught her against him, and immediately started to feel the way he had yesterday morning in front of the mirror. Damn the woman.

Laughing at herself, she landed in the seat beside Belinda.

"We've been waiting and waiting," Belinda said. "So we made friends with the mare, just like you showed us."

"The horse is mean," Hunter warned her. "She bites."

"Not anymore," Belinda said. She and her brother exchanged a conspiratorial look.

"You're all turning strange on me," Hunter grumbled.

He sat on the driver's banquette and flicked the reins. The Morgan started forward.

"Blue," said Eliza, "maybe you would like to sit up beside your father."

"It's not safe," Hunter said, his objection swift and automatic.

"Nonsense." She helped Blue climb up. "He's probably old enough to take the reins."

Hunter studied the small silent boy beside him. "Ask me," he said softly. "Ask me for the reins, son." As soon as the words were out, Hunter wanted to reel them back in. Why did he do this, time and time again? Why did he keep hoping, when it was clear there was no hope?

Blue stared up at him, his face blank. His eyes, as clear and as deep as the sea, begged for a turn at the reins. But he said nothing.

"One word," Hunter said, because he couldn't help himself. "Just say 'please,' and I'll let you drive."

Blue looked away and faced straight ahead at the worn dirt road.

"You look real nice," Belinda said to Eliza. "Your hair is so curly and pretty."

Hunter's stomach twisted. Ever the peacemaker, Belinda was always quick to change the subject or turn the attention away from Blue's affliction. Belinda would do anything to stave off a confrontation. She was protective of Blue, as fierce in her own way as Hunter was in his. Who were these children?

He felt unworthy, undeserving of them. Perhaps, he thought wildly, they weren't his at all, but two enchanted creatures. Each time he looked at them, he felt a strange sensation that they could not possibly belong to him. They were too beautiful. They were something left by the fairies one night; perhaps they weren't real children at all, but changelings come to make mischief on his life, and one day they would leave.

Then he studied Blue and saw the pain locked in the boy's eyes. It was like looking into a mirror. Blue was his son, and the boy bore the wounds of that.

"Thank you for that compliment," Eliza said to Belinda. "This dress belonged to your mother."

"Really? I don't remember it. Mama had lots and lots of dresses."

"Which ones do you remember? Tell me about them."

Hunter bit his lip to keep from telling her to shut up. She had been doing this since the moment she'd met Belinda, encouraging the child to dredge up memories of her dead mother. It was morbid, yet Belinda seemed to relish her recollections of small details, everything from the way the light struck her mama's hair when she sat on the veranda to the design of her favorite cameo necklace.

"And she used to sing us a song, a special song in the nursery at night," Belinda mused. "But I can't remember it. Something about a blanket of stars."

The back of Hunter's throat itched for a slug of whiskey. He flicked the reins to urge the horse faster. Mamie Beaumont would surely have a nice big vat of her planter's punch made up for the guests. He salivated just thinking of the sugary liquor. But as hard as he tried, he couldn't keep out the memories. Belinda had been just five years old when Lacey had died so horribly, yet the little girl had an uncanny memory for details. She recalled colors and smells and sounds with razor-sharp accuracy. And she had a way of phrasing things that made Hunter remember too.

"...a blanket of stars and a wagon hitched to..."

"The moon?" Eliza guessed.

"Maybe."

Blue shifted in agitation and drummed his fingers on the rail of the cart.

"Do you remember the tune?" Eliza prompted. "You could sing the tune and the words would come back to you."

Belinda heaved a sigh and slumped back against the seat. "Can't."

"Maybe your father or brother remembers the song," Eliza said.

Hunter shouldn't have been surprised by her suggestion. He shouldn't have been surprised that once she asked it, he recalled every word and every note of the lullaby. *Come away and fly with me, to the top of the highest tree, in a wagon hitched to the moon, a blanket of stars to keep us warm. Past the clouds and past the sun, all the way to heaven, here I come.*

Blue fidgeted restively on the seat beside him. The boy remembered the song too. But neither of them would speak up, Hunter knew. They would both keep the memories and the words and even the music buried deep.

"I know a song," Eliza said brightly. "Would you like to hear it?"

Belinda clapped her hands and bounced in the seat. "Yes! Yes, please!"

Eliza launched into a strange song set to a vaguely Celtic melody. "'Come unto these yellow sands, And then take hands: courtsied when you have and kiss'd the wild waves whist, Foot it featly here and there; And, sweet sprites, the burthen bear.'"

She had an untrained and curiously appealing voice. Not sweet, but a slightly husky croon that intrigued him. Hunter caught Blue glancing back over his shoulder at Eliza. The boy had never taken this much interest in someone.

"That's one of Ariel's songs from *The Tempest*," she explained.

"Who is Ariel?"

"A sprite."

"What's a sprite?"

"A forest spirit. He lives under an enchantment. In the end of the play, the old wizard sets him free."

"Will you tell us the story of *The Tempest?*"

Eliza laughed. "I can recite it from memory. And yes, I'll tell you both, a little each night at bedtime. Would that be all right?"

"Yes!" More bouncing on the bench. The Morgan flattened her ears peevishly at the motion.

Hunter scowled at the road unfolding in front of the horse. Things were spinning out of control. He had no idea what might happen from one moment to the next. He didn't like this, didn't like it at all. He didn't like what Eliza was doing to this family. To him.

She was making him feel again.

His sanity depended on holding himself at a distance, and she kept drawing him back. Closer to her, to home, to his children. Closer to the secrets in his own heart. He would have to resist her harder, because if he gave in to her, he'd be lost. Then she would leave—he had promised her California—and for the second time, he would lose the woman he loved.

He nearly choked on the thought. He didn't love Eliza Flyte. He barely knew her. The magical, strange, compelling night he had spent making love to her was supposed to be expunged from his memory. He wasn't supposed to think about it. She was a stranger with no knowledge of the world he lived in. Loving her could only lead to disaster.

His shoulders grew taut with tension as he drove nearer

to Bonterre. The neighboring plantation was not quite as beautiful as Albion had been in its prime, but it was impressive nonetheless. The brick mansion crowned a green knoll, and the lawns and yards swarmed with guests and servants rushing here and there in pinwheels of color. The sun rode high in a clear sky that held the burning promise of summer.

This was the world he had been born to, the world his children were born to. When he had tried to leave it and make his own way, everything had fallen apart. That had been his mistake—trying to leave. He had to get back to where he belonged. He had delayed long enough.

As he surveyed the elegant company, Hunter wondered if it was cruelty or something else that had prompted him to bring Eliza today. *They'll eat her alive and suck the marrow out of her bones,* Nancy had promised, and she had been right. He had only to look at his sister-in-law Delaney or Lacey's cousin Francine in their ruffles and lace, to see what Nancy meant.

He knew of nothing quite so charming, nor quite so lethal, as the well-born women of Virginia. Their bite was more poisonous than the sting of an adder, a lingering sweet venom that could kill a person slowly, with unimaginable pain.

He got down from the buggy and lifted Belinda from the passenger bench. Before he could help Eliza, she had hopped out of the cart, and Blue had jumped to the ground.

"There's Sarah Jane," Belinda yelled, running off to play with her second cousin. Blue trotted after her. Hunter found himself alone with Eliza. "Well," he said. "Welcome to Bonterre. I'll try to introduce you to everyone."

"As the governess?"

"I reckon so."

"Fine." Head held high, she walked toward their hosts.

Hunter waited by the buggy for a groom, then caught up with Eliza. He introduced her to Lacey's parents, Hugh and Mamie, and then to the extended clan that made up the Beaumont dynasty: Trey, the eldest son, possessed his father's relentless drive and ambition. Ernest, the younger brother, was a charming, laconic ne'er-do-well. Ernest's wife, Delaney, had a sharp-eyed awareness of the least little slight. An array of cousins rounded out the family, all deeply concerned about the current state of fox hunting and the price of tobacco in Richmond.

Delaney took Eliza by the arm. "You're just a perfect gem," she said. "Where in heaven's name did Hunter find you?"

"I lived all my life on Flyte Island," said Eliza. She didn't seem intimidated by Delaney's keen looks and probing questions.

"The children are quite a handful, aren't they?" Delaney prompted. "Tell me, my dear, how are you getting along with young Theodore?"

Hunter pivoted away to the punch table. Lacey's family was scandalized by the way he was raising his children at Albion, a place that had turned its back on tobacco to embrace a questionable enterprise. Yet his in-laws weren't too proud to buy his horses or bet on them, he noticed.

Ever since his first yearling sale, a number of belles had begun to primp for him, from Josephine Jefferson herself to Tabby and Cilla Lee Parks of Norfolk. Women with money, social standing, looks. He had best stop delaying and choose a wife. His kids needed a mother. Their re-action to Eliza was proof of that.

He caught his gaze wandering to Eliza. A bevy of in-quisitive neighbors and cousins clustered around her, their voluminous white party gowns enclosing her like a blossom in a hornets' nest. He had to stifle the impulse to rescue her from being sucked into their midst.

But Eliza was strong in ways he was just beginning to discover, so he walked away—to get something to drink.

Twenty

As a hired governess, Eliza knew she was not supposed to be enjoying herself, but she couldn't help it. Was this the oddest gathering in Virginia, or were all picnics like this? Was there really a game called croquet, or had this strange group invented it specially for the occasion? She had no idea, but hitting a wooden ball through hoops struck her as the height of weirdness.

She loved it. She loved whacking the silly ball, and later on she loved the game of blindman's buff even though she wound up tangled in an azalea bush while the other guests laughed uproariously. She loved mumblety-peg too, having no idea that ladies weren't supposed to play games with knives. As it turned out, she threw Ernest Beaumont's hunting knife better than anyone else, and doubled over with mirth to see him, hands tied behind his back, trying to extract it from the ground with his teeth.

Then there was the talk, which was far less enchanting than the party games. The picnic guests spoke endlessly of nothing at all. It was uncanny, the way a pair of grown women could yammer on about the quality of a fabric or the merits of a curling iron for thirty minutes without ceasing. Even more uncanny was the way the men spoke to each other, swaggering about and describing their fox hunting exploits or tobacco crop, each trying to outboast the previous one.

So this was the world she had missed by living on the island.

"Miss Eliza, you must be exhausted from all the games," a young lady said, linking arms with her. "Come and get a drink of lemonade with my sister and me." It was Miss Tabitha Parks of Norfolk. She and her sister Priscilla had taken a special interest in Eliza. They insisted on being called Tabby and Cilla.

"The men are about to start jumping their horses," Cilla said. "It's entirely too tedious."

Eliza thought she might like to see the jumping, but the sisters were being kind, so she allowed herself to be swept along with them.

"Tell us what it's like, being a governess," Tabby said.

Eliza took a cup of lemonade from a servant. She smiled her thanks, but the serving girl kept her eyes downcast, and didn't see.

"Yes, tell us," Cilla prompted.

"I've only just started," Eliza confessed. "It's quite different from *Jane Eyre*, though."

The sisters exchanged a blank look. "Jane who?"

"Never mind." Cilla leaned in conspiratorially. "Is it entirely too grotesque, looking after a boy who won't speak?"

A flash of maternal protectiveness, the likes of which Eliza had never felt before, momentarily blinded her. "I beg your pardon?"

"Well, you know. The boy, Theodore. Do you suppose he's simple, or touched in the head—"

"He's a beautiful, lovable boy," Eliza broke in, "and I'll thank you to remember that."

"There, there," Tabby said placatingly. "Cilla didn't mean any insult. What we *really* want to know is this— What is he like?"

"Blue?"

"No, Hunter Calhoun, of course!"

Eliza smiled, knowing her heart was in her eyes, but not caring that they saw. "He is wonderful, and annoying, and funny, and sad, and...wonderful."

Tabby fanned herself vigorously. Cilla nearly choked on her lemonade. "Heavens to Betsy," they exclaimed in unison. "You're in love with him!"

Eliza's face heated. She wasn't quite sure what she was embarrassed about, but these women seemed far too interested in her feelings for Hunter. "I never said—"

A flurry of excitement erupted on the lawn where the jumping course had been set up. Trey Beaumont came charging in on a lathered and clearly distressed roan hunter. The horse was prancing and tossing its head as Trey hauled hard on the reins. A froth of spittle formed at the corners of the horse's mouth.

Eliza set down her cup of mint lemonade. She picked her skirts up to the knees and raced across the lawn. "Slacken the reins," she called to the rider. "Do it now."

He must have been so surprised by the command coming from a woman that he obeyed. Eliza positioned herself in front of the horse and made a soothing sound in her throat. The horse shook his head violently, nearly cracking his skull against hers. "There now, easy," she said, and took the reins. The roan momentarily settled. "Sir, dismount quickly."

The bewildered man got off the horse, and it sidled in agitation. "I don't know what came over him."

Tabby and Cilla Parks arrived, breathless with excitement. "Miss Eliza," Tabby said. "You ran right out in front of that horse. You could have been killed."

"I'm fine." Eliza held fast to the reins and ran her hand up the length of the roan's skull, absorbed in watching the ears.

"But we didn't finish our conversation," Cilla said. "And it was just getting interesting."

Eliza ignored them as she coaxed the horse to lower his head.

"He's my best jumper," Trey Beaumont said, "but he's not been himself."

Eliza handed him the reins. "Hold him still, and I'll show you why." She took a lace-edged handkerchief from the sash of her gown. Carefully, she probed into the horse's ear. The Parks sisters looked as though they might faint. Even Eliza grimaced when she extracted a small hornet.

"This gives new meaning to a bee in the bonnet," said Trey. "How can I thank you, Miss Flyte?"

"You needn't thank me at all." For the first time, she noticed the initials *LBC* on the fancy—and now soiled—handkerchief. "Just listen to your horse, Mr. Beaumont. He will always tell you what's wrong."

A light smattering of applause sounded, and she was surprised to see a group of onlookers. Tabby and Cilla fluttered their fans. "We had no idea, Miss Eliza, of your hidden talent. How on earth did you get so good with horses?"

Eliza chafed beneath the glare of attention. "I've worked with animals all my life."

"Really?" Both sisters closed in on her. "Do tell."

There was no point in lying or covering up. It wasn't as if she was ashamed of her past, who she was and the way she had been brought up. Eliza said simply, "My father was a horsemaster in England, and he taught me everything he knew.''

"My God,'' said Trey Beaumont. "She is the horse-master's daughter.''

Delaney Beaumont gasped. "But you said you were governess to Hunter's children.''

"I confess it is a new enterprise for me.''

"Imagine that. To go from taming horses to training children. You are truly a woman of many talents.''

Eliza stared into her magnolia-blossom face. "You have no idea.''

"I think I do, Miss Eliza.'' Delaney's smile held no warmth. "I think I do.'' She turned sharply and walked away with her nose in the air.

People certainly were strange, Eliza reflected. What a variety of personalities she had encountered, just here at this party. Perhaps she shouldn't be surprised. Every animal she had known was an individual with its own unique foibles and idiosyncrasies.

She headed down a manicured slope of lawn past an area where a group of men stood around, smoking and drinking, laughing loudly. She wasn't surprised to see Hunter among them. He was easy enough to spot in a crowd. Taller by half a head than most, and with his golden hair gleaming in the afternoon sunlight, he cut a striking figure. The sight of him caused a queer tightening of her stomach, and she had to tear her gaze away.

Heavens to Betsy, the Parks sisters had said. *You're in love with him.*

It wasn't supposed to be like this, Eliza thought. She was supposed to forget what had happened on the island. Hunter certainly had. Now that she was getting a glimpse of his world, she understood why he had said *I'd never marry you.*

He wasn't being cruel, just realistic. He had been born and raised to marry one of these gorgeous ladies. He'd already done so once, and tragedy had ended it. Now he would find another mate, and he would select her from the opulent, fan-fluttering group of ladies on the lawn.

It was interesting that among people, the females strutted and performed for the males, not vice versa as in nature. Here, the garish plumage belonged to the ladies; the flirtatious behavior came from them. Eliza found it all faintly ridiculous and unnecessarily coy. She could not imagine performing like that to catch a man's attention. On the island, she had caught Hunter's attention without even trying.

She heard shouts and splashing down by a pond fringed with cattail reeds. On the bank, Belinda and a group of little ones threw rocks and skipping stones in the water. Some of the boys had stripped down to their breeches. They swung on a rope out over the water, then shrieked as they dropped in.

Smiling, Eliza approached the group. Even Blue seemed excited, clapping his hands as some of the older boys jumped in. "Would you like to go swimming?" Eliza asked.

He nodded eagerly.

"You do know how to swim, don't you?" she asked.

Another nod.

"Here, let me take your shirt and shoes so they don't get all muddy."

As the boy peeled off his shoes and socks with gleeful haste, she stood back and thought, *Talk to me. Tell me why you're so silent, Blue.* She wanted to know. She wanted to hear his voice, his laughter, perhaps a song he knew.

"Now the shirt," she said, holding his shoes and stockings.

He peeled off the white chambray shirt and tossed it to her. Then he turned and ran down to the pond. Eliza watched him for a second, then called out sharply, "Blue!"

He froze, hunching up his shoulders. She walked up to him and gingerly took his hand, her throat thick with dread. "My God," she whispered. "My sweet God."

The little boy's back was striped with angry red welts. "Who did this to you, Blue?" she whispered, keeping her voice down to preserve the boy's dignity. "Who was it?"

His face clouded. Then he wrenched away from her and ran to the pond, grasping the rope and swinging himself wildly out over the surface before dropping in.

He stayed underwater a long time, long enough for Eliza to take a step in the direction of the pond. Then suddenly he broke the surface, his light brown hair slicked back and his lips parted in a grin.

Eliza fought against the thoughts she was having. Surely not. Surely Hunter Calhoun, for all his troubles, did not beat his son. He didn't show affection for the boy the way Eliza ached for him to, but he was gentle enough, if remote.

Today in the buggy he had prodded Blue to speak up. How many times had Hunter done that? How many times had he begged the boy to speak, and been ignored? Enough times to drive him to violence? Did he get so frustrated that he hit his son?

Turning on her heel, she hurried off to find Hunter. She was like the wooden mallet on the croquet green, scattering the men with her brazen approach. She supposed there was some rule or regulation about a woman marching into the midst of men who were busy smoking and drinking, but she didn't care. "I need a word with you," she said to Hunter, unable to look left or right, afraid she would start railing at him right away.

She could hear low murmurs rippling across the ranks of onlookers.

Hunter wore the laconic smile of a man who had just spent a pleasurable hour in the sun, drinking whiskey with his cronies. He spread his hands in mock helplessness. "Only three days at Albion, and she's already bossing me around," he said.

The others laughed. Eliza turned and strode away, heading for a rose arbor in the side yard. She stalked to the tall trellis, fragrant and alive with the rumble of bees, and then set her hands on her hips.

"Do you beat your son?" she demanded, when Hunter caught up to her.

His lazy affability vanished like the dew in the angry heat of the sun. "What?"

"I asked, do you beat your son?"

"Damn you," he said. "It's bad enough you come waltzing into our lives—"

"I didn't waltz anywhere. If you recall, you dragged me bodily from my home."

"While it was burned to the ground by men who would have burned you right along with it if they'd found you," he reminded her.

"You haven't answered my question," she pointed out. "Is it because I've found you out? Because you beat him until his back is red and bruised from the blows?"

"What the hell are you babbling about?"

"Blue!"

Hunter took a menacing step toward her, pressing her against the roses that climbed up the arbor. The sickly sweet aroma filled her senses, and she couldn't take her eyes off Hunter's furious face.

"You look at me, goddamn it," he said, "and you listen well, because I'll only say this once. I would never—ever—raise a hand to my son. Never have, never will, so you can take your crazy notion somewhere else."

She refused to flinch or look away, though she wanted to. His words filled her mind. She thought of the way he was with Belinda and Blue, and she suddenly knew how terribly wrong she had been to assume he had hurt his son. Drunk or sober, Hunter Calhoun was, if anything, overly cautious. He would not lay a hand on his children. It was almost sad, the way he took pains to avoid touching them.

"I had to ask," she said, "because Blue's been beaten."

He scowled and didn't let up pressing on her. "What the hell do you mean?"

"When he took off his shirt to go swimming in the pond, I saw that he'd been beaten. There are terrible welts on his back, and—"

He gave her one final shove as he pushed off and strode toward the pond. "Blue!" he bellowed. "Blue, get the hell out of the water. Blue! Where the hell are you, boy?"

The child came slogging out of the pond, eyeing Hunter askance. Eliza wondered how often Blue had seen his father drunk, and if he always regarded him with this heartbreaking suspicion and regret. Hunter took the boy's hand and turned him, and when he saw the marks on his back, his eyes blazed with fury.

"Who did this to you, son?" he demanded. "Who beat you?"

Blue stared at the ground. The other boys ceased their shrieking and chasing to watch.

"You tell me, son," Hunter said in an urgent hiss. "I want to know who did this."

Blue continued to stare at the ground. Eliza knew the boy would not speak. She swept her gaze around the half circle of youngsters.

"We need to know what happened to Blue," she said to the group.

"It was Master Rencher," said a small, chubby boy, jerking his thumb toward a group of men talking in the shade. "He laid into him during lessons 'cause Blue wouldn't speak up."

Hunter said a word that made the boys turn pale. He stalked across the lawn so swiftly that Eliza had to run to keep up. "What are you doing?" she demanded.

Hunter didn't answer. As he walked toward the tutor, he peeled off his frock coat and rolled up his sleeves.

A thin, elegant man with the clear, pleasant speech of a scholar, Rencher sat on a garden chaise with some of the older men, laughing and smoking. Hunter didn't even give him a second to prepare. He grabbed Rencher by the collar, dragging him from the chaise and hauling the surprised man to his feet.

"You son of a bitch," Hunter said between his teeth. "You goddamn son of a bitch."

His fist smashed with a sickening crunch into Rencher's face. Blood spurted in an arc, spraying over Hunter like a crimson fountain. The tutor fell after that first blow, curling into a ball on the ground and trying to protect his face with his hands. Hunter drew back his foot to aim a kick at his ribs and kidneys.

From out of nowhere, Blue raced in, dripping wet. He flung himself at his father, grabbing his hand and tugging desperately. His face begged Hunter to stop.

Eliza watched with her heart in her throat. She wanted

so badly to help. But all she and the rest could do was stand by and watch them.

At his son's touch, the fight seemed to go out of Hunter. He backed off, stepping away from the trembling, whimpering man on the ground. Then he grabbed Blue with one hand, Belinda with the other, and started walking away. He didn't even look to see if Eliza followed.

Hugh Beaumont hurried toward them. "See here, Calhoun—"

"I gave your goddamn tutor the sack," was all Hunter said. He didn't look left or right as he headed straight for home.

Blue lay facedown on the bed, wrinkling his nose at the smelly poultice Nancy had put on his back. They'd made him and Belinda go to bed early, right at sundown, and he knew it was going to be a long time before he slept.

He was mad at himself. He should have been more careful with his shirt, but he'd forgotten all about the stripes from Master Rencher's cane. Thanks to him, his papa had thrashed the schoolmaster in front of everyone. Grandfather and Grandmother Beaumont would shake their heads and click their tongues and say things like *He can't control himself when he gets like that.... Whatever will become of the children?*

They were always saying things like that.

Restless, Blue peeked at his sister. She lay sound asleep. Very quietly, he got out of bed, went to the open window and stood looking out at the deep purple shadows in the yard. The breeze smelled of new grass and flowers.

On the sill was a glass canning jar containing the butterflies Belinda had caught at the picnic. Cousin Francine had tied a bit of muslin over the top of the jar so Belinda could take them home.

He picked up the jar and peered inside. They were so pretty—two of them with yellow and black splashes on their wings. As he looked closer, he saw that the edges of the wings were ragged and powdery from beating helplessly against the glass. Although they were beautiful and Belinda loved them, they were prisoners inside that jar. If they didn't stop beating their wings, they would probably soon die.

Blue set down the jar and untied the string, removing the bit of muslin. The butterflies stayed inside.

Go. He didn't speak aloud, even though he wanted to.

Then a gust of wind came, and the butterflies stirred, rising fast out of the jar and flying out the window. Blue watched them until they were little wild specks against the night sky, swooping like leaves on the breeze. Then he turned and went back to bed.

Twenty-One

"I want to talk about Blue," Eliza said.

"I want another drink of whiskey," Hunter murmured, balancing an empty glass on his drawn-up knee.

They sat on the front veranda. It was twilight. Willa had already put the children to bed and a hush had settled over the farm. Evening birds haunted the high branches of the live oaks, and a light breeze rustled through the leaves. A steam packet slid by on the distant quiet waters. With the sun melting into a pool of gold on the bay, it should have been a scene of tranquility. But instead, Hunter felt edgy with unspent rage. Eliza looked anxious and upset, twisting the fabric of her blue picnic dress.

"You've had enough whiskey," she said.

"You sound like a goddamn temperance scold."

"I sound like someone who cares about Blue. Lord knows, somebody needs to."

He lost his breath as if she had knocked the wind out of him. Damn the meddling woman. "I care about my son," he said. "I've loved him since the day he was born and I held him in my arms and thanked God for the blessing. You've known him a few days. So don't go thinking you know what's best for him."

"I know you care. So much that you nearly killed a man today. But that's not the kind of caring Blue needs."

He swiveled away so he didn't have to look at her. "What the hell do you know about what Blue needs?"

"Not much. That's why I want you to tell me more about him. I want to know everything." She put her hand on his sleeve, her fingers resting lightly, like a timid bird. "Please."

It was the *please* that did it. That, and the fact that she touched him. He turned to her, his heart on fire with the need to tell her everything, the need to get it out.

"He stopped speaking the day his mama died," Hunter said.

"That much I know. How did she die?" Eliza asked.

He dragged in a deep breath, feeling a sharp ache in his chest. "In a fire," he said, and when Eliza winced, he added, "It was an accident."

"How did it happen?"

He could tell from the expression on her face that she was really asking *why* it had happened. He had never explained it all, beginning to end, to another person. But he wanted to now. Needed to. "I suppose the trouble started when Lacey moved back home to Bonterre," he said quietly. "She left me the same day the French spinet piano did. The furniture was carted off to auction to pay the debts my father left. She was so mortified that she took the children on foot, marching straight across the meadow to her father's house." He stared into his empty whiskey glass. "And I did what any typical Southern gentleman would do—I started drinking."

"Why?"

"It blunted the pain of having my family taken away. People gossiped that my pride was hurt by the shame of poverty. In truth, it was Lacey who suffered from the shame."

"Was Blue all right?" Eliza asked.

He nodded. "He still talked, if that's what you mean."

"I need to know what made him stop," she said softly.

With elaborate care, Hunter turned the glass around and around in his hands. "I don't know why, but she took to closing herself up in her room and writing long letters nearly every morning. That's what Blue used to tell me. You'd never know it, but he was a big talker. Every time he saw me, he'd tell story after story."

Hunter paused and pinched the bridge of his nose, squeezing his eyes shut. "He used to tell me all about his day. He said his mama wrote letters for hours and hours in the mornings, and then she would seal them up and send a houseboy down to the landing with them for the afternoon packet. I never paid much mind. Lacey always did write with a fine hand, so I reckoned she was just corresponding with friends to while away the hours.

"But Blue never told me what happened the day she died. I had to get the story from a servant girl who was scared out of her wits. While sealing one of her letters, Lacey was careless with the wax and flame. You have to understand, my wife was a beautiful woman, vain about her figure and devoted to fashion. She wore whalebone stays and a cage of steel hoops beneath her skirts. When the sealing wax dropped on her skirt and was ignited by the flame, those hoops became her prison."

Her jaw dropped in horror. "You mean she couldn't get out of her burning clothes?"

He stared thirstily at the bottom of his empty glass. But tonight he knew no amount of whiskey would blunt the memories, so he simply set down the glass and continued. "I'm told her screams weren't heard at first because she had shut the door to her room in order to write in private. When they found her, most of the clothes had burned away." He swallowed hard and looked into Eliza's strange, misty eyes, as if to find peace there. "She had no hair left to speak of."

"Oh, Hunter. I'm so sorry."

"By the time I was summoned, she had been put to bed. I found her whispering to Blue—she didn't have much of a voice left. The Beaumonts said he refused to leave her side. I was stunned when I saw her, so close to death." His beautiful Lacey. What a shock that had been. "She did recognize me, but I couldn't understand what she was trying to say. Blue seemed upset, so I told him to wait outside with his sister."

Hunter forced himself to go on. "There was nothing left of Lacey. But as Blue walked past her bed, his little face all wet with tears, her hand shot out. At first I thought it was a reflex, like a death shudder, but she grabbed his arm. It scared the hell out of him. Her hand was all wound in a bandage that was oozing. And she looked Blue in the eye and said, 'Remember your promise.'"

"What promise?"

"I have no idea. She was delirious. Just hours from death. I don't know why she grabbed Blue like that. Don't know what she was trying to tell him. He was terrified. She was a sight—nothing like the mama he knew. Hair burned off, face red and blistered. Her lips barely moved. He ran out of the room, and that was the last time he saw his mother alive."

Hunter planted his elbows on his knees and shoved his fingers through his hair as if to weed out the memories, but it was no use. They were a part of him. "Lacey was out of her mind from the injuries and the laudanum the doctor gave her for the pain. I didn't know what to do. So

I talked to her. I talked about anything and everything. My dreams of turning Albion into a Thoroughbred farm, the way she looked to me the first time I kissed her... I tried to bring up every pleasant memory that lay buried in our past. I'll never know if she heard me or not."

Eliza wept quietly in a way that he had never been able to do. She hadn't known Lacey, but she knew how to grieve. He got up and faced out toward the darkening yard, filled with remembrances of that night. "When I ran out of talk, I didn't know what else to do. So I sat down at her bedside and held her poor burned hand until she died."

"I hurt for you," Eliza whispered, her step soft on the porch as she came up behind him. "Oh, how I hurt for you."

"That's why I didn't want to tell you this," he said. "That's why I never think of Lacey these days. Sometimes I see her smile in Blue's eyes or hear the echo of her voice in Belinda's laughter. I can't stand that."

He had grimly swept her out of his life. But Lacey's legacy lingered. Blue was left with open wounds, struck mute by shock and grief. Belinda, who had been just five when it happened, had hazier memories of her mama. Hunter would never, ever forget. Some nights, when he closed his eyes, he could still see his wife's charred and blistered body. Could still smell the burned flesh and hair, still hear her rasping, rattling breaths as she struggled to stay alive for just a moment longer.

Crushing the heels of his hands into his eyes, he tried to erase the images, but they stayed inside his head, forever branded on his memory. He swore, grabbed his glass and pushed past Eliza as he went in search of more whiskey.

She stood in front of him, blocking his way. "That won't help you."

He gave a short, sarcastic laugh. "Don't be absurd. Thinking you've found the root of my problem is a mistake."

"But you just told me everything I need to know," she said, her small face somber in the twilight. "You just told me where all the troubles in this family come from."

Something inside him, something the whiskey hadn't reached yet, seriously considered her words. He had a swift, compelling image of seeing her on the beach with the stallion for the first time. She had said almost the same thing. *Find out where the fear is coming from. That's where you begin.*

He had built a fortress around his heart. Here she was with her chisel, taking it down, bit by bit. And each time a piece fell away, it hurt. He felt more cold and exposed.

"Get the hell out of my way," he said between his teeth.

She planted herself in the doorway, pushing her palms against the door frame and looking him straight in the eye. "Your wife died two years ago and you've been drinking ever since. Don't you think that if the whiskey was going to work, it would have by now?"

"I don't drink because I want it to work," he said. "I drink because I want to forget."

"You can't simply forget about the children," she said.

"I'm good to my kids. I love them."

"They need more—"

"What the hell do you know?" he growled. "You never even met a kid until Blue and Belinda."

"But I know what it's like to lose someone," she replied, practically whispering. "Don't you get it, Calhoun? My father was everything to me. He was Prospero. The wizard. He made the world turn around me. And when I lost him, I lost everything I ever loved."

"Damn it," he said, pointing an unsteady finger. "You're nothing but trouble. I want you out of my life." It was true, he needed to be away from her. Away from her rain-colored eyes and her earnest looks, and her unsettling way of peering into his soul and seeing the things he tried to keep hidden.

But he was like the stallion on the beach, wanting to be away from her yet drawn to her at the same time. Later he would blame the whiskey, but at the moment he didn't try to resist the urge to touch her. It was more than an urge; it was a need, like the need to draw the next breath.

He put out his hand and watched it waver a little drunkenly as he reached for her. He touched her face first, that smooth pale cheek, and with the pad of his thumb he traced the shape of her full lips. She didn't move, didn't even blink, as she stood in the doorway with the house obscured behind her and the falling dark of twilight throwing her features into velvety shadow. The darkness merely made his other senses more acute. He could feel the smooth texture of her skin and he could hear the way her breathing stopped for a few seconds, then continued in soft shallow puffs. His exploring thumb continued past her lips, over her chin and down to skim over her vulnerable throat. She was so delicate there, tender as a new flower. His hand looked big and rough against her throat, but she bore his touch without flinching, and even seemed to warm beneath it.

"I'm not supposed to be doing this," he whispered. "I told myself I wouldn't do it again."

"Then why are you?"

"Don't ask. Just…let me…" He quit trying to explain, quit trying to rationalize. He pulled her forward, tight against him, and his mouth found hers. She tasted as sweet as he knew she would, and her body felt pliant against his. Unlike the other women he'd known, she didn't pretend not to want this. Her surrender now, like the night on the roof, was total. She swayed against him, her body as graceful as a willow in a breeze, and she opened her mouth. No pretended coyness or lessons from finishing school governed her response. No one had ever told her to slap a man away, to tell him no, to giggle and blush. And he loved it. God, how he loved the feel of Eliza in his arms, a woman who didn't have designs on him.

But she had expectations, he thought, his hands skimming up and down the length of her. She expected everything from him.

And that, ultimately, was what made him push her away. He actually groaned when he let go of her, the sound of a man being hit in a fight.

"What's the matter?" she asked.

"We've been through this before." He turned away and sat on the steps of the veranda. The fireflies came out, vague secretive flashes in the low shrubs of the yard. "You're in the world, Eliza, and it's a bigger world than your island. What you do matters now."

She sat down beside him. "Is that why you don't want me here?"

"I never said I didn't want you here."

"But you don't."

"You never wanted to come to Albion. You want to go to California."

"California can wait. It's not going anywhere. Once I met your children, I wanted to stay, at least for a while."

"Why?"

"Because they're so little and they need me."

"Fine. They have needs. So tell me what they need."

She moved away from him on the step, pushing back to lean against the pillar. "They're stuck, Hunter. They've lost their mother, and they have to grieve for her. They have to feel the hurt before they can get over the grief.''

"You don't know what the hell you're talking about. What makes you the authority on motherless children?''

She regarded him steadily until he started to squirm.

"That's different,'' he said, frustrated. "You never knew your mother. You didn't know what you lost because you never had it.''

"I know what it's like to be hurting inside,'' she said. "I know what it's like to be fearful. That's what I see in Belinda and Blue. Especially Blue. They can't get over the hurt.'' She took a deep breath and braced both hands on the step behind her. "They can't, because you won't let them.''

"What?'' He laughed harshly. "I can't believe you dared to say that.''

"It's about time someone did. Others might shrink from your temper, but not me. You've already said you don't want me around, you're shipping me to California. So I have nothing to lose, do I?''

"I don't have to listen to this.''

"You're right. You don't. You can stand up right now and go into the house and drink some more. And tomorrow when you wake up, everything will be the same. Blue won't be speaking. Belinda will hide everything she thinks and everything she feels. And you'll be too drunk to notice.''

An explosion built inside him, but didn't erupt. He felt himself seething with rage, yet he was riveted by her candor and her boldness. "And what,'' he asked with exaggerated politeness, "would you suggest I do?''

"To start with, you have to let them remember their mother.''

"I've never stopped them from remembering.''

"Not in so many words, no. But every time Belinda mentions her or asks you something about her, you cut her off. Change the subject to anything but what is on her mind and in her heart. Perhaps that's why Blue doesn't speak at all. Because you don't really want him to, because you're afraid he'll speak of his mother."

"That's horse shit." He stood up so fast his head swam. He held the railing to steady himself.

She stood up too, pinning him in place with her determination. She was fierce, this strange small woman. "Let them know it's all right to remember, and to speak of her."

"Why the hell do you think that will change things?" he snapped. "Their mother died a horrible death. Do you think if I tell them to grieve for Lacey, things will change?"

"Will they change if you *don't* tell them?" she shot back.

The air between them crackled with tension. No one had ever affected him like Eliza. No one had ever challenged and provoked him as she did. She was pushing him to be a better man than he was capable of being. But she didn't understand. Like some racehorses, his best wasn't good enough.

"Look," he said, "I won't deny the children have cottoned to you. They like you, Eliza. They like you because you don't act like other adults." He watched her bridle defensively. "Don't get mad, you know that's a compliment." He thought of the women at the picnic today, strutting around and flirting and trying to get his attention. "You know damn well it is."

"What are you saying?"

"That if you think you can fix whatever's wrong with my kids, I won't stand in your way."

"They're not wild horses," she said. "They're children. I can't simply lead them around an arena until they decide to follow me." She pushed a finger at her lower lip, deep in thought. "Do you have any drawings or photographs of their mother?"

Panic thumped in his chest. "I reckon I have a few."

"When was the last time you or the children looked at them?"

"We don't look at them."

"Why not?"

"Are you daft, woman? Blue would just turn away, and Belinda would bawl and ask a lot of questions."

"Maybe you should let them."

"Maybe you should mind your own damn business."

"But you just said I could—"

"I didn't say I'd help you," he interrupted. "Now, move out of my way. We have a lot to do tomorrow. The exhibition race is coming up, and I want to enter the stallion in it. I'll need your help training him."

"Only if you promise to show them the photographs."

"Are you blackmailing me?"

She smiled with false sweetness. "Think of it as a bargain."

Twenty-Two

Eliza suspected Hunter was thinking about what she had said about the children, but he pretended the conversation had never taken place. Fine, she thought. In due time, she would get her way. Though she had little experience with children, she knew about loss and remembrance and things that go unspoken. She knew she could reach them.

Already they followed her everywhere like twin shadows, slipping along arbor paths in the garden or through the reeds at the water's edge. She loved the wonder in their faces when she pointed out the ring in the water where a fish surfaced, the zigzag path of a honeybee going from blossom to blossom, the rise of a loon out of the reeds and into the clouds over the bay. She loved the way they were startled and impressed by the things of nature, and the way they threw themselves into new experiences with total exuberance.

One day they were standing at the edge of the dock, looking out at the water on an overcast morning. A pastel-colored mist fused the sea and sky, creating in them a drifting sensation, as if they had floated away from the rest of the world.

"Look at that ship!" Belinda cried, pointing to the

deepwater lanes far out in the bay. The boat appeared translucent, insubstantial, as if it wasn't real. "It's a la-teen-rigged bark, just like Uncle Ryan's ship." She cupped her hands around her mouth. "Uncle Ryan! Come back!"

Eliza stroked the little girl's soft hair. It wasn't Ryan Calhoun. His ship flew a bright red topsail. And she knew why. She felt a shudder of apprehension when she pictured Captain Calhoun, sweeping in like an avenging angel to rescue a fugitive slave. If it weren't for the feud between abolitionists and slave-catchers, her father would still be alive, she thought bitterly. But no, she mustn't resent the abolitionists. The blame lay with the system of slavery, not those who defied it.

"I don't think that's your uncle's ship," she said. "And it's too far away. They can't hear you."

The three of them stood on the dock, watching the boat sail toward the misty horizon. Then it disappeared grad-ually, growing more and more faint, like a ghost fading from the light.

"I always worry when a ship goes," Belinda said. "If I can't see it anymore, how do I know it's still there?"

Eliza smiled, but the child was in earnest. She sat down on the edge of the dock, patting the planks so the children would sit down too. "I'll tell you how you know," she said. "Because when it leaves our view, someone else on the opposite shore can see it eventually. So even though it's out of your sight, it's in someone else's."

"Really?"

"I promise. If I were on Flyte Island right now, I would probably see that bark. And when I couldn't see it any-more, I'd know someone on another shore could."

Belinda plucked a daisy and started dropping petals, one by one, into the water. Blue stared at the horizon, clearly preoccupied with the departing ship. After a time, the morning mist burned off, giving way to the sharp clarity of a summer afternoon.

An idea nagged at Eliza, but she heard loud whinnying from the barn and stood up. "We'd best be going. Willa had the idea of planting flowers at the racetrack to make it look nice for all the guests who come to the race. Would you like to help?"

"Yes!" Belinda jumped up. Blue did too, even faster, and ran along the sandy track that bordered the streambed and the beach. He loved the horses, Eliza realized. Loving something was the key to healing. She kept watching the boy, looking for a sign. The way he had stared at the departing ship filled her mind. She went and fetched the wheelbarrow full of rosebushes Willa had dug from the garden, and made her way to the mile oval.

Noah and Hunter were working with the stallion. She could see instantly that Finn was balky and reluctant to enter the starting gate. After tossing his head sharply a few times, he sidled away to browse in desultory fashion in the grass that fringed the track.

Noah, seated high with his knees tucked in jockey position, looked at the sky as if asking for divine guidance. Hunter inspected the gate, pushing his fingers through his golden hair as he was wont to do when frustrated. He looked annoyingly good today, she thought, even though he had probably spent the previous night pursuing his favorite pastime of drinking. She couldn't understand it. He nearly made himself sick with drink, yet the next day he could always get up and work like three men instead of one.

He wore fitted riding breeches and a plain shirt. As she watched, he took a dipper of water from a jug and drank it, letting the droplets sluice down the front of him. Then he peeled off the shirt and slung it over a fence rail. Eliza hoped the children hadn't noticed her staring at their father's bare chest, glistening with sweat. She hoped he hadn't noticed how lonely she was for him.

"You can get started digging in the roses, right here at the entrance to the racetrack," she said to Blue and Belinda. "A lot of important people will be coming to see the Thoroughbreds run, and we want to impress them." She knew enough of the racing world to know that, to the gentry, appearances were everything.

She tried to compose herself as she approached Hunter. He barely glanced at her, but said, "He won't take to the starting gate today."

"What's the matter?"

"We can get him to back in," said Noah, "but he won't come out."

She walked slowly around the apparatus. Finn had proven himself tractable going in and out of stalls, and this was no exception. Noah was able to bring him into the gate. But then, when Hunter released the bar, the horse bridled and balked.

Eliza set her hands on her hips and studied the track. The long, straight sides of the oval had been beaten smooth. It appeared to be the ideal racing ground. A short distance to the east lay the beach, where waves broke on the shore and blue herons stood one-legged in the shallow surf. To the north, a fringe of green brier nodded and shimmered in the sea breeze. The meadows of Albion bordered the other two sides of the track. In the high rippling hills beyond, the white house gleamed, its flaws invisible from a distance.

The horse had never looked better. Under Noah's constant care, he had gained weight and bulk and muscle. His _____ _____ to a high sheen by constant grooming.

But the flare of fear in his countenance troubled Eliza. As she watched, the fear intensified and the horse turned his head sharply to the side.

"Lead him out of the gate," she said to Noah.

Then she went in and stood there, thinking hard.

"What are you doing?" Hunter asked.

She'd nearly forgotten he was there. "I'm trying to see what the horse sees."

"But—"

"Hush. I need to concentrate." Didn't he know by now that he should trust her when it came to training a horse?

She felt the breeze in her hair and face, and smelled the salt-heavy air and the rotten-sweet aroma of wrack that washed up on the beach. Heard the shimmering chimes of the wind in the wax-myrtle trees. And saw a dead branch bobbing, bobbing, at the distant north end of the racetrack, preparing to drop off.

Looking at it, she laughed.

"What is it?" Impatience edged Hunter's voice. He was anxious about the upcoming exhibition; she knew it. He wanted the stallion to perform, to make him proud, to bring legitimacy to Albion.

"Come with me," she said, walking down the track. Hunter peppered her with questions, but she enjoyed keeping him in suspense.

When they reached the end of the track, she pointed at the precariously swaying branch of deadwood. Sun and wind had bleached the branch to the color of bone. Two dark knots, like malevolent eyes, marked the end of it. "We've got to get that down."

"What for?"

"Because the horse is afraid of it."

He snorted humorlessly. "That's absurd."

The wind caught at the pale, bare wood, causing it to

nod ominously up and down. "See?" she said. "It looks like a—a snake, or a dragon, doesn't it?"

"Looks like a dead tree."

She glared at him. "Do you really want to question my judgment in this?" she demanded.

He heaved a long-suffering sigh. "I'll fetch an ax. I'm going to have to hack through the brush to get to the dead tree."

Over the next hour, he worked up a fine sweat, and when he emerged from the brush, his torso was raked by scratches. "There," he said, gesturing at the place where the huge branch used to be. "I slew your dragon. Are you happy now?"

"That depends," she said, trying not to laugh. But he did look comical, scratched and cranky and unkempt.

"On what?"

"On what the stallion thinks," she said, then turned and went to plant flowers with the children.

She was right, of course, Hunter conceded. The dead tree must have looked alarming to the horse—surely one of the densest of all God's creatures. If Finn had the wits of Eliza's laying hens, he would be considered gifted. Once the offending object was removed, the stallion stood calmly in the starting gate. He lowered his head and distended his nostrils, blowing calmly into the dust.

Hunter and Noah exchanged a glance. "Ready?" he asked the boy.

Noah gave a brief nod.

Hunter shoved back the barrier.

If he had blinked, he would have missed it. But he didn't. The stallion shot out faster than a stone from a sling. Hunter had never seen any start so swift, and the promise didn't end there. The stallion thundered hell for leather around the track, his great body stretching to its limit, his head focused and determined with the single-minded absorption of a true champion. The savagery that had made him so difficult had been transformed into pure energy on the track.

Hunter didn't have to check the timing in order to know that he'd never seen a horse run faster. He tilted his face to the sky and shut his eyes tight, feeling elation rise like the sun, warming him with rare shimmers of hope. Could it be that finally his fortunes were turning?

The slowing tempo of hoofbeats alerted him that the run was finished. Noah would have to walk the stallion now to cool him down. Behind him, Hunter heard a familiar low whistle. He was already smiling when he turned.

"Did you see?" he asked.

His cousin Charles strode across the yard toward him, hands outstretched in an expression of wonder. "Lord Almighty, I saw. Can't believe my eyes."

"Believe, cousin. It's the Irish Thoroughbred I wrote you about. It's going to race in the exhibition run before the yearling auction."

"This is the horse that went mad?"

"The very one."

"What happened to you?" Charles asked, eyeing him up and down. "Have you been in a fight?"

Hunter picked up his discarded shirt and dabbed at the stinging scratches on his chest, shoulders and back. "Not in the way you think," he said, putting on the shirt. Ever since his confrontation with Eliza after the picnic, they had been locked in a battle of wills. She claimed the children needed to reminisce about their mother, to weep over her picture and grieve for her. He couldn't make Eliza understand that they had all been grieving for two years. No good could come of probing deeper into the wounds. The best solution for all concerned was for him to settle on a new wife and concentrate on Albion. That was the only way to get on with their lives.

He shook off the thought. His cousin's visit provided a welcome distraction.

Charles Calhoun's green eyes glittered merrily. He lived in Richmond, where his father used to manage the business end of the tobacco trade. One day, about seventeen years back, Charles's father had simply got up and left. Charles had been just thirteen at the time, confused and frightened by the sudden abandonment. His mother had taken to her bed that day and hadn't been the same since. Like a young Odysseus, Charles had stalked his father, tracking him westward into the misty wooded hills of the Blue Ridge.

He'd found his father in the arms of a Shawnee Indian woman. They lived in a cabin with a new baby and too many dogs, and his father had been too drunk to recognize the sallow-faced young man with the straggling new beard as his first-born son. Charles had returned home to Richmond, reporting to his mother that his father was dead. Then, in accordance with family tradition, he had taken his first drink of whiskey and hadn't stopped until he was wildly drunk. That night he had begun a love affair with his mother's maidservant, and less than a year later the girl died giving birth to Noah.

It was no rare thing for a man of the south to have fathered a mulatto child. The relationship was no secret, particularly if that child turned out to be as handsome as Noah was, and had a special talent, as Noah did with horses. Hunter supposed it was no great matter in Charles's mind, but Charles had always been fond of parties and socializing and wasn't given to searching his soul.

He never wondered if there was something he should be doing for this boy who had been born into the world because of him.

The matter wasn't for Hunter to decide. Lord knew, he had a hard enough time being father to his own legitimate son. Charles was not a bad person, but a careless one, raised as he was in a climate of infidelity. Years ago, he and Hunter had vied good-naturedly for Lacey's hand in marriage, and Charles had cheerfully backed off when she favored Hunter.

"Cousin Charles!" Belinda shrieked with delight. Dropping her trowel, the little girl came tumbling pell-mell across the yard, Blue at her heels. The two of them rammed smack into Charles, who staggered back with exaggerated surprise, laughing and hugging them. They adored him, because he laughed easily and sang songs and never told them no. Hunter looked on proudly, thinking how beautiful his children were. Belinda was as fair and pale as the dawn, and Blue had his mother's dramatic intensity. Like Lacey, he was keen-eyed and driven, filled with secrets.

"Look at you," Charles said, holding them at arm's length. "Blue, you're getting taller than a bean stalk, and I swear, Miss Belinda, you're even prettier than your own mama."

"Was she?" Belinda leaped on the comment. "Was she pretty?"

"Don't pester your cousin," Hunter warned. He felt Eliza's silent censure, but ignored it.

"They're not pestering me," Charles said. He chucked Belinda under the chin. "Your mama was just about the prettiest thing in Virginia, honey, and now that honor belongs to you. And who is this?" he asked, focusing a sharp interest on Eliza.

"This is Miss Eliza," Belinda said. "She's our governess."

"You don't say." Charles took Eliza's hand and bent gallantly over it.

"I do so say," Belinda objected. "Didn't you hear?"

"I heard." He caught Hunter's eye and winked. "Well done, cousin. Well done indeed."

Eliza watched the play of sunlight on Charles's shining dark hair, and Hunter watched her. His gut twisted with an unpleasant twinge. What was it he didn't like about this moment? The genuine warmth in her smile as she said "How do you do?" or the clear pleasure in Charles's eyes when he smiled at her? Or the way he kept hold of her hand and brushed his thumb lightly over her wrist?

Hunter grabbed Charles by the shoulder and drew him away from Eliza. "It's been too long since your last visit, you old sinner," he said. "Come and inspect this horse of mine."

He felt Charles straighten his shoulders as they approached Noah. The youth had slowed the stallion to an easy walk, back and forth at the end of the track.

When the boy saw his father coming, his face drew into sullen and wary lines. The two of them had never known each other well. When the boy was a baby, Charles had given him to a wet nurse at Albion, and he had been raised here, neither family member nor slave, but an uneasy guest who worked hard to earn his keep. Eventually he had found his place by proving himself gifted with horses. His small stature and keen sense of timing and control made him the best jockey in the county.

"Mister Charles," he said formally.

"Noah, you're looking fine. Just fine up on that big old Irishman."

"Thank you, sir." Noah turned the horse away. "I'd best keep him on the move so he doesn't get a windgall."

"I thought you were going to shoot this horse," Charles said to Hunter, his admiring eye checking out every inch of the stallion.

"I thought I had to," Hunter admitted.

Eliza and the children had finished planting the flowers at the front of the track. He hadn't thought flowers could improve the place, but the color added a festive air. Now Eliza took her charges out to the beach. They scurried about, collecting shells and letting the waves chase them. He wondered if his children had always been this playful. He couldn't recall Lacey cavorting on the sand with them, ever.

"Noah convinced me to get help from the horsemaster of Flyte Island," he said to Charles.

"I always thought that was a tall tale."

"Turns out it wasn't. But once I got to the island, I learned that Henry Flyte died last year."

"So what did you do?"

Hunter gestured at Eliza, who had picked her skirts up to her knees to let the waves splash over her bare feet. "That's his daughter."

Charles slapped his forehead. "Goddamn it, Hunter, where does your luck come from?"

Hunter laughed, genuinely baffled. "What the hell do you mean, luck?"

"You get this stallion for a song, and then its trainer is a goddess who winds up looking after your kids. Most would call that luck."

"A goddess?" Hunter said. "You think she's a goddess?"

"Look at her."

Both of them looked. Unaware of their scrutiny, she

frolicked in the waves with the children. Her black hair flew like ribbons on the wind, and she laughed with a ready joy that was infectious. She made the very picture of beauty in full flower—natural, unrestrained, untainted.

Hunter forced himself to tear his gaze away. "I know what she looks like."

"And?"

"And she's the horsemaster's daughter. She's weird, Charles. Raised all alone out on that island. She's got some crazy notions."

"What sort of crazy notions?"

That love is something that happens regardless of who you are or what you think you want, he thought. That two people pleasuring each other is a natural expression of that love.

He gritted his teeth to keep from speaking aloud. He could never confess his thoughts to anyone, not even Charles.

"Unconventional ideas." He recalled the flurry of speculation that had erupted around her at the Beaumonts' picnic. "She has no idea what society is like."

"Lucky girl."

"She wants to go to California."

"That's not so weird. A few years back, everyone on earth wanted to go to California."

"She's not interested in gold. She and her father always meant to see the unsettled land on the north coast. Some of the Spanish land grants turned out to be fine horse country."

"So when's she going?"

"I convinced her to stay and look after the children until—" Hunter had to swallow, for his throat suddenly went dry "—until I find myself a wife."

"You're finally going to do it, then."

"I reckon it's past time. The kids need a mother. Belinda's getting to a girly age, and Blue—well, Blue's not getting any better."

"So who're you going to marry?"

Hunter shook his head. "I've got a few prospects in mind. Those two Parks sisters from Norfolk—"

"Tabby and Cilla?"

"Yeah, those two."

"You can only marry one of them."

"I know that, numbskull." He didn't admit that he had never been able to tell them apart. Pale and conventionally pretty, they made themselves available to him every chance they got. For the life of him, he couldn't say what sort of girls they were, except that they were wealthy and had nice manners and held the admiration of society.

"You could do worse," Charles murmured.

"True."

His cousin turned and started down the track toward the house. "But then again," he said over his shoulder, "you could do better."

Blue wondered if he should show Miss Eliza what he had found on the beach. On the one hand, it was special to have something secret and perfect all to himself. But on the other hand, what good was having a secret if you were the only one who knew about it?

He frowned, trying to reason it out. Sometimes, reasoning made his head hurt.

He sat with his bare feet buried in the deep warm sand. Behind him on the track, he could hear the stallion running. Boom*boom,* boom*boom,* like a heartbeat. Only lots faster. Finn was so fast that he could go places no one else could, like maybe to heaven...and back again.

Miss Eliza and Belinda held hands and stood in the surf,

giggling when the waves shushed over their bare feet. They didn't care when they got their dresses wet. He liked that about Miss Eliza. She wasn't fussy about clothes the way most grown-ups were.

Blue got up and walked over to her, holding out his hand. She turned to him with that open, easy smile that made him feel good inside. "What is it, Blue?" she asked. "Did you find something?"

She talked to him all the time. She asked him questions, but she never waited for him to speak. She never smacked him when he didn't give her an answer.

He dropped his treasure into her hand.

"A sand dollar," she exclaimed, bending down to show it to Belinda. "Look, it's been lying in the sun a good long time. See how bleached-out it is?" She held the round shell on the flat of her palm. "I bet you didn't know there's a secret inside a sand dollar."

Blue perked up. Belinda shook the shell and held it to the light. "What kind of secret?" his sister asked.

"Five white doves," Eliza claimed.

"Inside the sand dollar?" Belinda wrinkled her nose. Blue frowned skeptically. "Let's see," Belinda said.

"I'll have to break the shell to let them out. We have to make sure that's all right with Blue."

He took the sand dollar and thought very hard for a few minutes. In the background, he could hear his papa talking to Noah in a low, friendly voice. Papa talked to Noah all the time.

Blue moved swiftly. He slammed the sand dollar down on a large, flat rock, breaking the shell to pieces. At first, all he saw were little white bits, like tiny bones.

Miss Eliza picked out five pieces shaped like birds in flight. "The doves were inside the sand dollar," she said, "and Blue let them out. He set them free." One by one, she lay the tiny pieces on the palm of her hand. "Would you like me to keep them safe for you, Blue?"

He nodded and watched her drop the bits of shell into her apron pocket, treating his discovery as if it were the most important thing in the world.

Blue made up his mind. He would show Miss Eliza his other secret. The big one. The one he was never to say a word about.

Twenty-Three

~⊸⊸⊙⊙⊛~

Eliza stood outside the door to Hunter's study. A low rumble of male voices, punctuated by an occasional burst of laughter, drifted from behind the closed double doors. Cousin Charles had proved to be a merry addition to the household, bringing laughter to the empty halls of Albion. She liked him quite a lot, though he seemed a bit young and frivolous, occasionally even furtive in his manner. He had a slender build, refined features and good manners. She knew he admired the way she looked, and she wanted to be moved by that; she tried to be. If she could manage to feel the same sharp sting of attraction for some man other than Hunter Calhoun, she could convince herself she wasn't falling in love.

But alas, as handsome and charming as Charles was, and as gratified as she was by his admiration, it wasn't the same. Like Jane Eyre, she was doomed to yearn for a man who had no place in his life for her, a man she could not have.

Impatient with her thoughts, she rapped sharply at the door.

"Come in," called Hunter.

He and Charles sat on opposite sides of the desk from

each other, with racing logs and breeders' books spread out in a mess across the surface. Charles puffed on a cheroot and Hunter swirled whiskey in a cup. She could see with a glance that he was not drunk. She hated the fact that she knew him well enough to tell the difference.

"Miss Eliza," said Charles, "I do declare, you get prettier every day."

She grinned. "I don't, but your compliments do." She turned to Hunter. "The children are in bed and want you to say good-night."

He rose from his seat. When she had first started this nightly practice, he had balked, claiming that telling them good-night after supper had always been sufficient. But she was determined to draw him into their lives, and bringing him upstairs to the nursery each night was part of the process.

"Your voice should be the last thing they hear before they go to sleep," she had said. "Your face should be the last thing they see."

"Bossy little thing, isn't she?" Charles observed as Hunter went to the door.

She suspected that, though Hunter would never admit it, he actually enjoyed seeing them bathed and snuggled up to their chins in their little beds, for he came readily enough. She hoped he wouldn't change his mind tonight, when he saw what she had done.

Hunter never knew what to expect when he walked into his children's bedroom. Eliza showed them new things each day, from a starfish to a pheasant feather to a jar of fireflies to a sprouting sweet pea. She drew upon their natural sense of curiosity and wonder in a way that seemed to come easily to her. The lessons they learned from her were the simple, profound laws of nature—that everything was connected to everything else, every cause had an effect, every action had a reaction. He couldn't remember whether or not Lacey had that sort of ease and intuition with them. It bothered him that he couldn't remember.

"Look what we did, Papa," Belinda said. "Are you surprised?" She bounded to the foot of her bed.

He felt as if all the air had been sucked out of him. There on the wall between the two small bedsteads hung a large sepia-toned portrait of himself and Lacey and the children.

It was the only picture that had been made of them as a family. He remembered the day they had sat for the portrait. It was full summer, the lawn lush and the peach trees heavy with fruit. The photographer, a fussy nervous man from Baltimore, had exclaimed over the beauty of Lacey's gown and hair, the effervescence of the children.

The children wore white, their hair neatly brushed. Lacey and Belinda were seated—Lacey kept shifting uncomfortably on the photographer's low stool—while he and Blue stood behind them. He and his wife regarded the camera box with smooth-faced dignity. Belinda and Blue weren't smiling, yet their eyes danced in the lively way that children have even when they've been told to keep still.

He remembered the birdsong that day. He remembered the smell of the wind off the bay and the way the summer air felt on his face. He remembered the fleeting prettiness of Lacey's smile and the laughter of the children when the photographer announced that he had finished his work.

Up to that point in his life, the world had been good to Hunter Calhoun. For a young man who had never done particularly well at his studies and had never been forced to do anything other than breathe, he had a good life, an easy life.

Too easy. Perhaps that was the problem. Only days after the photograph was taken, his father had died, the will had been read and the creditors had come to call.

Nothing in Hunter's golden life had prepared him to face bankruptcy. He'd listened to the advice of the bankers, his father-in-law, his neighbors. And then he had done as he pleased, freeing the slaves, ceasing the tobacco operations and starting a horse farm.

The rash enterprise had cost him Lacey and the souls of his children.

"We hung it up special, right between our two beds," Belinda was explaining, oblivious to his agonized thoughts. "That way, Mama's close to Blue and she's close to me."

Hunter couldn't look at his daughter. If he did, he would see Lacey's wide blue eyes and cupid's-bow mouth. Instead, he glared at Eliza Flyte. "Take it down," he said in a low, angry voice.

"But, Papa—" Belinda began. She lapsed into silence when Eliza put her hand on her shoulder.

"The children wanted a picture of their mother in this room." Eliza motioned toward the door. "Blue, Belinda, go and see if Nancy will give you a glass of water before bed."

The children slipped out, clearly aware that there was to be a Discussion.

"I said, take it down—or I will," Hunter ordered.

She moved between him and the picture on the wall. "Why?" she demanded.

He couldn't believe she didn't understand. "Because it's morbid, that's why. It's disheartening. Every time they come into this room, they'll see her—"

"They'll see her whether her picture's on the wall or not," Eliza said softly.

"It hurts them to look at her," he blurted out.

"You're wrong. You won't let them finish with their feelings for her. They have to grieve, and they have to heal. You're not letting them do that."

"How the hell would you know?"

"Because I've been watching you. I've spent practically every waking hour with the children, and it couldn't be clearer. They're afraid to stop pining for their mother because they think that's the first step in losing her forever."

"Isn't it?" he demanded, surprising himself with the question.

Her eyes narrowed. "You seem to think so." She sat down on one of the little nursery beds. "When my father died, I wept and raged for weeks," she said.

He studied the angle of her slender neck, the sweet curve of her cheekbone, and in spite of himself he wanted to touch her.

"But mostly," she admitted, "I was afraid. Not of being alone. Not of never seeing him again. I was afraid I'd forget. Terrified. One day I woke up, and I couldn't remember the sound of his voice. Another time, I tried to think of what his hands looked like, and I couldn't make a picture in my mind. I was losing him bit by bit. Do you know how frightening that was?"

Hunter felt a fullness in his throat, and he couldn't speak. Eliza was so honest, so open. Didn't she know people weren't supposed to talk about things like this?

But his heart responded to what she was saying. He knew exactly what it felt like to forget the shape of someone's fingers or the sound of her laughter. Some days, he could picture Lacey sitting in her salon sipping tea from a china cup, and others, all he could see was a blistered and wheezing carcass on a bed, a bandaged hand grasping for his. He swallowed hard, but the thickness in his throat wouldn't go away.

"I felt," Eliza said, "as if my father was being stripped away from me, layer by layer. Little details that didn't seem important when he was alive were suddenly all I had left of him. The way he'd set his elbows on the arms of his chair before telling me a story. The look on his face when he whistled a birdcall. Those things kept fading away one by one. I took to sleeping in his nightshirt because I thought some part of him lingered there."

She drew in a deep, pain-racked breath. "Then one day, I tried his birdcall. There was a little wren in the trees on the west side of the island I wanted to coax over. I whistled, just like my father used to do. And the bird came to me. It alit right on the ground not five feet from me."

Her eyes were damp and distant, and Hunter wanted to look away from them, but he found himself spellbound by her honesty and her agony.

"And you know what I discovered in that moment?" she asked, but didn't wait for an answer. "He never left me. My father never left me. He can't be taken from me, even if I have trouble picturing his face or remembering the sound of his voice." She touched her chest gently with her open hand. "He's here, and he'll always be here, in a place that will never let him go."

Hunter felt humbled and astonished by the depth of her love for her father. Had he ever loved his father in that way?

Jared Calhoun had been less a father than a figurehead, marching through life, not looking back to see who followed. He had been a formidable man, worthy of respect. But he had never taken his son to a marsh and taught him birdcalls.

And what of Lacey? Did she live in his heart, or was

she merely a fading memory? He suspected, to his horror, that she was the latter.

That was why he slept badly at night. That was why he drank.

Belinda and Blue came back into the room, bounding into their beds. "Can we keep the picture up, Papa? Can we?" Belinda asked. "Can we, Papa?"

He felt them all looking at him. Waiting. He could think of only one way to clear the stinging thickness from his throat. He gave a curt nod, then left the room to find something to drink.

When Eliza had first come to Albion, she had been overwhelmed by the number of books in the library. Hunter claimed there had been many more in the past, but auctioneers had sold many of the more costly volumes to pay off debts and back taxes. Even so, dozens of books lined the shelves of the long, narrow study. She got a bit dizzy each time she went there to find something to read.

It was late, and her candle was guttering low in its brass holder as she perused the shelves. She had finished some books by Jane Austen—_Northanger Abbey, Pride and Prejudice_—that had nearly made her swoon with fascination. She had enjoyed the dark, ironic works of Daniel Defoe, though _Robinson Crusoe_ had made her ache with missing Flyte Island. She thought tonight she might read a nonfictional book—the essays of Rousseau or Emerson, perhaps.

In a breath of wind from the doorway, the candle flame wavered against the wall of books. Startled, Eliza looked up.

"Blue?" she said, climbing down from the step stool and hurrying across the room. "Blue, it's very late. What are you doing awake?"

The boy slipped furtively into the room. In his arms, he carried a large wooden box.

"What is it, Blue?" she asked.

He set the box next to the lamp on the battered oak library table. When the light wavered over it, she could see that it was of dark, polished rosewood with brass fittings.

"May I open it?" she asked.

Blue stepped back, holding out his hand, palm up.

Slowly she lifted the lid. It was an enchanting piece, cleverly made. It had a slanting tooled-leather surface with the letters *L.B.C.* embossed in gold. Lacey Beaumont Calhoun? At the top was an array of ink jars and pen nibs. "It's a lap desk," she said. "Where did you get this, Blue?"

He stuck his finger through a satin loop of ribbon at the edge of the tooled leather. The surface of the lap desk folded back, exposing the interior of the box.

She raised the flame in the lamp. The stale smell of dried lavender and old wax struck her as she looked at the contents. "What is this, Blue?" she asked.

No answer.

She flipped through the stack of folded letters—the ink fading—that lay within. Her gaze swept over some of the writings, and what she saw chilled her blood. Dear God, how long had Blue been keeping this secret?

"Have you read these?" she asked.

He shook his head. *No.*

"Do you want me to read them?"

No response.

"You've had these since your mother died, haven't you?" Her heart broke at the burden he'd carried, but she made herself smile down at him. "How very brave you've been to keep these for so long. Shall I keep them for you now?''

A clear, emphatic nod. *Yes.*

She shut the lid on the box and said, ''Then I shall, and you never have to worry about what's inside here ever again.''

He drew in a long breath, shuddering with relief as he did so. And then she saw it—a single tear sliding down his cheek. The sight shocked her, and for a moment she couldn't speak, couldn't move. Then she set aside the lamp and pulled Blue against her.

''Shh, it's all right,'' she said, cupping his head to her chest. ''Hush, my sweet boy. It's all right now.''

Twenty-Four

❧❧❧

Eliza stood in the middle of the sandy arena, locked in a stare-down with a stubborn mare. The horse was one of the yearlings to be offered at Albion's annual sale. Excitement was mounting in the region, for the horses Hunter had sold last year had proved to be of the highest quality. Buyers from far and wide would be arriving for this year's sale. Word had it that important buyers from England and Mexico would attend.

Hunter and his cousin worked tirelessly, hoping for a huge success. She suspected that Hunter was driven by something deeper than commercial ambition. The sooner he rebuilt his fortune, the sooner he could attract a new wife and mother for his children, and the sooner Eliza could go to California for—

For what? The question kept nagging at her. It had been one thing to sit by the fire each night and look at the lithographs of the west coast and dream. Actually making the journey was another matter entirely. But that was the choice she had made. It was the promise she had made to herself. Her father had always wanted to see California. She owed it to him to see for herself.

The matter at hand, however, was this mare. She was a

beautiful Thoroughbred, her breeding evident in a haughty, royal spirit. Her dappled lavender-gray coat shone brilliantly in the sun.

But she was aggressive, and defensive with people and with other horses. In her current state, she'd never attract a buyer.

"Come on," Eliza said in a soft voice. A horse couldn't understand the words, of course, but the inflections were part of the language Eliza had learned from her father. "Come on, you want to follow my lead." Then, very deliberately, she shooed the animal away with a toss of her cotton rope.

The mare sidled back, but she wasn't a fearful horse, and she came on like a wave, stiff-legged, head down. With one powerful shove, she knocked Eliza backward into the sand.

Eliza landed with a hard thud. She felt the air leave her lungs and sat there dazed, her knees drawn up. It was a good thing she had decided to wear breeches today, she thought. Otherwise, her pose on the ground would appear quite improper.

To add insult to injury, the mare danced away, kicking up sand. It showered Eliza, sprinkling the brim of her hat and trickling down her back. She coughed and shook her head, then levered herself up. She fluffed out the fabric of her shirt, trying to get rid of the grains of sand.

"Boy!" called a light female voice.

The mare lifted her tail and loped off to the opposite end of the arena.

"Boy!" the voice called again.

It took Eliza a moment to realize someone was talking to her. She spied two young ladies seated high in a carriage with a formally dressed African driver. A liveried black servant stood behind them, holding a fringed umbrella over their heads.

The Parks sisters of Norfolk, Eliza realized as she approached them.

"Do you mean me?" she asked, laughing.

"Why yes, boy. We wanted to know where we might find Mr. Calhoun."

Eliza spread her arms. Grains of sand dropped from her sleeves. Then she removed her hat. Her hair, which had been tucked up under it, came cascading down. "It's me, Miss Tabby, Miss Cilla. Eliza Flyte. We met at the Beaumonts' picnic."

She thought it amusing that they'd mistaken her for a boy. The sisters exchanged a shocked glance. Miss Tabby recovered first. "I'm certain I don't remember."

"Sure you do," Eliza said. "I'm looking after Hun— Mr. Calhoun's children."

"And his horses too," Miss Cilla murmured. "You're a person of many talents."

Eliza laughed and pointed her toe, bending low with mock ballroom formality. Cousin Charles had taught her to dance in preparation for the huge party Hunter would host in honor of the exhibition race and yearling sale. "Thank you."

Tabby whispered something to Cilla. "We really shouldn't chat too much longer. Hunter invited us for tea and lemonade this afternoon."

Eliza got a funny feeling in her stomach. Lately he had been actively courting women and introducing them to his children. In fact, Blue and Belinda were having their baths right now, getting cleaned up for the visit. The idea of parading them around like this Thoroughbred mare left a bad taste in her mouth.

"Mr. Calhoun is probably waiting for you at the

house." She tried to keep her smile in place. "I hope you enjoy your visit."

"I'm certain we will," Miss Tabby muttered. "Driver, to the main house," she said grandly, and the carriage rolled away. The two sisters put their heads together again, talking and casting glances over their shoulders at Eliza.

What a pair of goose-brains, she thought, then turned her attention back to the mare. It took her most of the afternoon, but eventually she had the horse halter-trained. By the time Hunter arrived at the arena, she was proudly leading the mare in circles. The horse had a naturally impressive gait and stance.

"How does she look from there?" she asked, knowing the mare looked good.

"Fine," he said, but he seemed distracted. "You can turn her out to pasture now." He pulled back the gate, and Eliza led the mare past him. She could tell from the subtle slur in his voice that he hadn't been the one drinking tea.

"Did the children enjoy their visit with Miss Tabby and Miss Cilla?" she asked. *Did you?*

"That's what I want to speak to you about," he said.

She let the mare loose in the pasture and slung the lead rope over her shoulder. She was hot and sweaty, gritty with sand from working all afternoon. The sun had tanned her forearms dark gold. In comparison to Hunter in his finery, she felt like a ragamuffin. "So speak," she said.

They walked together to the covered well, which stood in the shade outside the bake house.

"Blue wouldn't say a word, of course, and Belinda spoke only of this project you're building with them. This toy boat, or some such silliness."

Eliza refused to flinch at his accusatory tone. "Blue speaks to no one, and Belinda speaks to everyone. If you didn't want to hear about the project, you should have changed the subject. And if these ladies reject your children based on this meeting, then they're not worth courting anyway."

"You think not?" He handed her a dipper of water from the well.

She paused to drink greedily, letting the water trickle down her chin and the front of her shirt. She wiped her mouth on her sleeve. After Blue had shown her what was in the rosewood lap desk, she had come to understand why the little boy never spoke. But she was trapped in silence now too. She could never tell Hunter what she had learned.

"Your children deserve better," she said.

"And what about me?"

She set down the dipper and leaned against the rim of the well. All the fatigue of a hard day's work gathered in her shoulders. "I have no idea what you need, Hunter Calhoun."

His finger traced a droplet of water down her throat, his touch both familiar and unsettling. "What I need and what I want are two different things."

She shivered despite the heat of the day, and took another drink to soothe the dryness of her throat. Another drop of water trickled like a tear down her neck and disappeared into the top of her shirt. His gaze followed the path of the droplet, and the heat of his stare scorched her.

"You have to explain certain things to me," she said. "Trying to make sense of your society is impossible for me."

"Don't you know why I've been avoiding you?" he asked. His voice was liquid and warm, all the rough doubts smoothed out by whiskey. "Can't you guess?"

"Tell me," she said.

He held her with both arms, his hands cupping her shoulders and then tracing down her arms. "It's because

I have a duty to Albion and to my children. They need a mother, and it's my job to find her. I can't concentrate on the search if all I can think about is you.''

She swayed toward him, desperate for his touch. "That's a problem."

He touched her breasts through the shirt, and she caught her breath, letting her eyes drift half closed.

"Oh, yes," he said, lowering his mouth to hers. "That is a problem."

He kissed her the way she had been dreaming about for weeks, only instead of feeling a warm wave of delight, she felt herself burst into flames. It was too painful, too intense. She wanted him too much. Yet even though the sharp yearning stabbed at her, she could not force herself to push him away. She kissed him hungrily, a long devouring kiss that satisfied nothing, yet promised everything.

He pressed her against the river-rock edge of the well, parting her legs with his thighs and fitting himself between. She wound her arms around his neck and marveled at the wonder she felt when he touched her. How was this possible? How could she want this haughty, troubled, whiskey-drunk man with such intensity? And why him, only him?

If he made love to her right now, this instant, on the grass in full light of day, it would not be soon enough. "Please," she whispered fervently against his hungry mouth. "Please."

He must have thought it was a plea to stop, for he groaned and pulled away. His eyes were bright crystals, the emotion trapped deep inside where she could not reach it. Despite the whiskey, a sharp lucidity hardened his features.

Eliza supposed she could be wrong, reading so much

into his expression, but something unspoken passed between them.

"I'd best go." He jerked his shoulder in the direction of the old overseer's residence, which now housed Noah and the newly hired grooms.

"The children have made something very special," she said. "This evening at sunset, it'll be ready. You might want to see for yourself."

"Fine."

"We'll be down at the dock."

"Don't wait for me," he said.

"You know we will."

Just when she thought he was turning to leave, he put out his hand, tipping up her chin to hold her gaze. "Promise me something, Eliza," he said.

Anything, she thought, loving his touch. But she had the presence of mind to say, "That depends on what you're asking."

"Guard your heart. Don't depend on me to do it, because I won't."

"I don't know what you mean."

He skimmed his thumb down her arm, pressing the pulse at her wrist. "Oh, honey," he said. "Yes, you do."

When Hunter headed down to the landing at sunset, the first thing he noticed was that the children were dressed in their Sunday best. It reminded him that he never took them to the nearest church at Exmore, leaving that duty to Nancy and Willa. Folks probably looked askance at him for letting the servants take his kids to the Negro church, but he ignored the disapproval.

He had been ignoring disapproval for a good long while.

Three more days, and the exhibition and yearling auction would be upon them. Excitement ran high, buzzing through his bloodstream in a way the whiskey never could. The stallion was perhaps not at the peak of his form, but he was close. He was the fastest horse Hunter had ever seen, and he had seen plenty, having traveled from the Union Course racetrack in New York to the Metairie Course outside New Orleans. An impressive performance by Finn would bring a fortune in stud fees and stimulate interest in the auction. If all went well, he might just turn a profit for the first time since inheriting Albion.

He owed much of it to Eliza Flyte. The thought of her troubled him and he slowed his steps, in no hurry to see her at the dock. But he saw her in his mind's eye anyway, all bathed in golden sunset colors, her hair an inky stream, her eyes deep with wanting him.

It was getting harder and harder to keep his distance from her. She was so unspoiled, so unconventional. This afternoon at the well, he had amazed himself by pulling away from her when everything inside him wanted to take her, possess her, fill himself up with her and pour himself into her. When he was on the island she had been good for him, bringing calmness to his soul and clarity to his thoughts. When it was just the two of them, he felt clean and new, as unspoiled as she, as if the sins of the past had never happened.

He was greedy for that feeling again. But it was a false feeling. He was a tainted man, a man who had sinned in the past and taken on responsibilities he couldn't ignore simply because he happened to be obsessed with the horse-master's daughter. The only thing to do was keep his distance, and when the time was right, send her to California.

Yes, that would be her reward. He would spend some of the profits from the yearling auction to buy her a stateroom on a ship bound for the west coast.

When he neared the water's edge, she smiled at him,

that open, breath-catching smile that said so much and concealed so little. He had told her to guard her heart, but he was not certain she had the first idea of how to do that.

"Papa!" Belinda jumped up and ran to him, grabbing his hand and tugging him out to the dock. "Papa, come see. We've made a wonderful thing."

"I can't wait," he said, smiling down at her.

This precious little girl needed a mother. It was as simple as that. She was too good. She demanded nothing and forgave everything. He didn't deserve her, but she deserved a mother who would raise her to be a perfect Virginia belle. But Lacey had been a perfect belle, he reflected uncomfortably. Did he really want his daughter to turn out like Lacey?

He honestly didn't know what was best for his children, couldn't make the choices that needed to be made. That was why he needed a wife, to share in those decisions, to help bear those burdens.

Blue led the way down the dock. Unlike Belinda, he didn't have a spring in his step, but a smooth dignity that was almost eerie in a boy his age.

A crudely built toy boat awaited at the end of the dock.

"See what we made," Belinda said. The hull was fashioned from a hollowed-out block of wood. Its sail had been fashioned from a handkerchief with lace around the edges. "It's fine, sweetheart. Very pretty."

She dropped her chin to her chest in an uncharacteristically bashful pose. "It's in honor of Mama," she whispered.

The dart struck deep into unsuspecting flesh. He could never get used to hearing her speak of Lacey. "You'll have to explain what you mean, sugar pie." He kept his voice light, although he wanted to choke Eliza. She kept hammering away at this business of grief and loss, making it the center of his children's lives. It was morbid, pure and simple, the way she fed their obsession with Lacey.

"We painted it special for Mama. I did the stern and Blue did the bow."

Hunter hunkered down on the creaky wooden deck and inspected the paint job. Belinda's paint was sunny yellow on the outside of the hull, a reflection of the face she showed the world. Blue's was a neutral indigo color that said nothing.

For the inside of the hull, Belinda had used a dark angry scramble of violet swirls interspersed with slashes of black and brown. Blue's choices, in contrast, were surprisingly light and clear, with puffy clouds of pastel.

Then Hunter saw something that brought a lump to his throat. In neat, precise writing, Blue had penned a message inside the boat: *It's all right.*

It was as close as Hunter had ever come to understanding his children. Eliza stood back, her hands clasped, blinking fast as she watched them.

"We've brought some things." Belinda flipped open the lid of a wicker basket. "These go in the boat."

She and Blue squatted on the dock, taking out their carefully preserved objects and placing them in the homemade boat.

Lacey's things.

A mother-of-pearl comb carved with three roses. An imported pen with a sterling silver tip. A tiny old-fashioned china shoe, the one she had kept dried lavender in. An ivory-ribbed fan of painted silk.

Each object was something Lacey had owned and treasured. Each one was an inexorable reminder of her, evoking a specific memory of a moment, a look, a scent. He saw her eyes, peeking over the edge of the fan, her long curls spilling down from the comb, the pen pressed thoughtfully against her lower lip as she considered what to write. He could smell the dried lavender of her bed linens, which exhaled the fragrance when he made love to her.

Hunter pinched the bridge of his nose, fighting a fury and grief too sharp to bear. The children seemed calm as they arranged the objects carefully in their boat. Finally, Blue put in a small branch of dogwood blossom.

Belinda held a card, thickly glued at the edges with sealing wax. On the front she had written *Mama*.

"No one is allowed to read this," she said solemnly. "No one but my mama." She pressed the card briefly to her lips and put it in the boat. "We're ready for the candle," she said to Eliza.

Eliza's cheeks were wet as she knelt down beside them. Hunter thought her tears would upset the children, but Blue and Belinda seemed more interested in fitting the candle into a holder in the stern of the boat, which was shielded from the wind by its tiny sail. Crickets buzzed in the grass at the water's edge. Eliza lit the candle, and Blue lay belly-down on the dock.

"Careful," Belinda cautioned, sliding the boat over to him. "Don't let anything spill out."

The boy held the boat gently in his two hands, then slowly lowered it to the water.

"Wait," Hunter said, speaking past a terrible ache in his throat. "Wait, son." He never even thought about what he was doing. It was automatic, like putting a wounded bird out of its misery. He simply twisted off his gold wedding band, the one engraved with Lacey's initials, and dropped it in the boat.

Blue looked at him for a long moment, then turned away, setting the little craft on the surface of the water. The sun was gone, lingering like a bruise on the clouds behind them. The bay reflected the color of hammered gold, lightly ribbed by a southerly breeze. At first the boat sat idle, then turned lazily into the wind. Blue reached down and gave it a shove.

The candle flame wavered, then flared a little. A swirling current caught the tiny boat, carrying it away from the dock.

No one moved or spoke. The four of them kept their gazes riveted on the light, growing ever fainter as the breeze and current carried the toy boat out to sea. At last, after what seemed like a long time, darkness and distance swallowed the speck of light and there was nothing more to be seen.

"'Bye, Mama," Belinda whispered. She reached up and took Eliza's hand. The two of them turned and started back toward the house. They walked slowly, not looking to see if the others followed.

Blue stood up. Hunter, still seated on the dock, told himself to hold out his hand to his son. But at that moment, something exploded inside him with the force of a dam bursting. Finally, after all this time, a deep and terrible grief came out of him, wild and uncontrollable. He erupted into sobs that racked and hurt and shook his entire frame.

Then, through the harsh tremors of his sobs, he felt something—a hesitant touch on his shoulder, delicate as a butterfly alighting there. The sensation froze Hunter completely. Weeping, tears, sobs, shaking—everything froze.

He felt the breeze on his face as he looked up at his son. Behind Blue, the first stars of the night came out. Blue tilted his head slightly to one side, gave the tiniest of smiles and whispered, "It's all right now."

Hunter wouldn't let himself look away from his son's face. "Say it again, Blue. I want to hear you say it again."

"It's all right," Blue said aloud, no longer whispering. "I wanted you to know, it's all right."

Hunter slid his arms around his boy. How strong and slender Blue was, how warm and vital. He smelled of grass and fresh air. "Ah, Blue, Blue," Hunter said, "I've missed hearing your voice. I've missed that so much."

They held each other for a while, and then with the darkness came the realization that it was time to get back to the house. They walked home hand in hand, to find that Eliza had already put Belinda to bed. The little girl lay in the bars of moonlight that slanted through the window. She sent them a sleepy smile.

Blue didn't need any help getting ready for bed, but Hunter stayed anyway, watching the boy's quick, efficient nightly routine. Blue hung his clothes on a peg and put on his nightshirt. Then he climbed into bed and Hunter tucked him in. "Will you sing the lullaby, Papa? You know the one I mean."

"Sing it," Belinda urged, completely unsurprised to hear Blue speak. "Please sing it."

Hunter softly sang the words he had always known: *Come away and fly with me, to the top of the highest tree, in a wagon hitched to the moon, a blanket of stars to keep us warm.*

Blue joined in, his voice as sweet and clear as sunshine. *Past the clouds and past the sun, all the way to heaven, here I come.*

"Good night, Papa," Blue said, closing his eyes.

Hunter kissed both children. When he left their room and gently shut the door behind him, his feet didn't even feel the floor.

Part Three

Lest too light winning
Make the prize light.
—William Shakespeare, *The Tempest*, I, ii

Twenty-Five

"**W**hy, Miss Eliza, you aren't wearing your breeches today," said Tabby Parks with a flutter of her fan.

Eliza laughed and smoothed her blue skirt. "I wouldn't think of it, not on a day like today."

She and Tabby and dozens of others stood on the broad meadow that formed a green apron around the mile oval. Excitement crackled like heat lightning through the summer air. The day of the exhibition had arrived, and people had traveled far, some even from across the sea, to bid on Albion yearlings.

Tabby waved her fan thoughtfully. "You mean, you won't be working as a stable boy today?"

Eliza caught the sharpness in her tone. "Ah, I see what you're trying to do. Charles—that is, Mr. Calhoun—told me to watch out for remarks like that. I didn't believe him, of course, but I see he was correct."

"Remarks like that. Whatever do you mean?"

With a smile, Eliza explained, "He said there would be those who look down on me because I wasn't brought up a planter's daughter and schooled in dancing and manners. He said—and I vow I did not for a moment believe this—

that there are those who actually judge a person by the sort of clothes she wears. Can you imagine?''

"Heaven forbid," Tabby said. "I'd best go find a seat." She all but ran away, and Eliza had to bite her lip to keep from laughing.

Hunter's quest for a proper wife amused her even as it broke her heart. They were all such silly hens, running around and clucking about nothing. In the evenings after supper, sometimes she and Hunter sat on the porch and discussed it. He was serious about taking a wife, and she felt disloyal being amused by the whole process—but sometimes she couldn't help herself.

She had made up her mind, after that day at the well, to take his advice and guard her heart. He could not have been clearer. He had told her, in words and in deeds, that he would never marry her. Her job was to help him with his children, and she had done her best. When Blue had entrusted her with his secret, she had felt the love and pride she imagined a true mother would feel. She could think of only one thing to do with the rosewood lap desk. She had taken it to Lacey's room, where Hunter never ventured, and had placed it in an armoire beneath a dusty old jewel case.

The ceremony with the boat and candle had brought Hunter and Blue to their knees, but it had been a cleansing pain, a baptism by fire. Like steel from the crucible, they had both emerged stronger. Blue had taken to speaking again, though he would probably always be a shy, reserved boy. But he was back—well and truly back—from the dark place where his soul had dwelt for so long.

Maybe Hunter would not even need a new wife, she mused. The children were doing so well now.

But that was just fanciful thinking, she forced herself to admit. He was a creature of this strange and haughty society where every gentleman required a suitable wife. Once he found one, convention would be served. Nothing lasted, including the love she felt. It would heal and leave a scar, but after a while it wouldn't hurt so much.

"Miss Flyte?" A strange, exotic-looking man approached her. He had very dark hair, a bushy mustache beneath a prominent nose and a courtly air as he bowed from the waist. "I am Simon Vega, from California." She stood there in amazement. He tucked his flat silk cap under one elbow and said, "I work for Roberto Montgomery, of Rancho del Mar. Mr. Calhoun sent a wire some weeks ago to the landline office, regarding his auction."

Her thoughts darted in confusion. Had Hunter brought this man here as a way to get rid of her, or to give her the dream she had once confessed to him? "I've read that California is a beautiful land," she said uncertainly. "I've seen pictures, maps, of a place called Cielito."

He smiled. "A little heaven, and the name of a favorite dance. It is the name they gave to many areas in the old days. Most of them deserve it." The smile sharpened as he grew businesslike. "You have a great reputation as a trainer of horses. My client, Don Roberto, is a wealthy man. He would be pleased to employ you...if that is your desire."

Hunter had arranged this, she realized. Did he know what was in her heart and in her mind, or was he simply through with her?

"There is no need to reply right now," Simon Vega said. "You must be given time to consider it. The herds are nothing like this, of course." He gestured at the racehorses. "Most are reclaimed from the wild. Don Roberto would give you a bungalow by the sea," he added, then put on his hat and bade her good day.

She had to find Hunter, had to explain to him that

dreams were safer when they were locked in her heart. But he'd never understand, because he was a different sort of dreamer. He believed in making dreams come true.

She found him with his bright head bent over the proffered hand of a woman she didn't recognize. Something about her told Eliza she was not one of the usual silly hens. She wore a gown of deep burgundy velvet that accentuated the lush curves of her figure. A hat with a wide brim obscured her features, and a wealth of golden-brown hair spilled down her back. Rather than giggling and waving her fan, she looked Hunter in the eye and spoke earnestly to him. Eliza wasn't sure how she knew, but she sensed an intimacy between them.

Her stomach churned as she walked away.

What did she expect? she wondered. That he'd marry the governess? Such unlikely things only happened in books.

Ah, but it hurt, wanting him and knowing she'd never have him. He had been hers for that one brief, magical night, a night she could not forget. Why hadn't she realized back then that it would be the only time he would touch her like that, love her like that? In her naiveté, she had thought it was the beginning of something.

She was wiser now in so many ways. Too wise to get her heart trampled.

"That's his sister-in-law, you goose," said Charles, planting himself in front of her to stop her retreat.

"What?"

"You know very well what, Miss Heart-on-her-Sleeve. The woman Hunter's talking to. It's Isadora Peabody Calhoun, Ryan's wife." Charles took her arm and led her toward the woman in the velvet gown. "Come and meet her. She's one of those damn Yankees. But she is wonderful."

Eliza tried not to feel relieved. "Charles," she said hesitantly. "What was it like when Hunter's wife was alive?"

He blanched. "Why do you ask?"

"I simply wish to know," she said awkwardly, stung by his heart-on-her-sleeve remark.

A bead of sweat trickled down Charles's temple. "She was so damn lonely," he said through his teeth.

"Mrs. Calhoun, you mean," Eliza said. She pictured Hunter's wife pining away, desperately writing love letters, day after day. "Lacey."

"Yeah, and the hell of it was, he never even noticed because he was so caught up in his horse trades. She needed him so bad, and he never even knew—" Charles broke off, wiped his brow with a handkerchief. "Enough said. Let's go meet my Yankee cousin."

Unlike anyone Eliza had met in Virginia, Isadora had a direct, intelligent manner and an air of confidence. "How do you do?" she asked. "I have been perfectly frantic to make your acquaintance. It's such a blessing, what you've done for Blue. We've been so worried about him."

"It was Blue's doing, not mine. I don't think you have to worry anymore." Eliza watched the children race with a pack of youngsters across the lawn. "They're remarkable children."

"They're lucky to have you."

A commotion of shouts and whistles erupted in the yard adjacent to the barn. Hired footmen clustered around a gleaming black hired coach. A compact, dapper man with a brass-handled cane and bushy white side-whiskers stepped out and strolled toward the oval, accompanied by an equally elegant lady.

"Heavens be," Isadora exclaimed. "That is Lord Alistair Stewart and his daughter, the Lady Margaret."

"Someone of importance?" Eliza asked.

"I should say so. He's quite the figure in racing. A true institution in the sport, known for having a perfect memory of every race in the past half-century."

Eliza wondered if Lord Stewart had known her father. It was strange to think that he'd had a life in England so long ago. She wanted to ask the Englishman if he'd ever heard of Henry Flyte, but she felt awkward and bashful. Before long she lost sight of Lord Alistair as others arrived from Louisiana and Saratoga and other far-flung places.

She walked down toward the pen at the starting gates, where the jockeys and horses waited to race. Here, the tension was drawn taut, not so much with high spirits but with nerves. The jockeys, mostly young black men, walked their horses slowly, many of them speaking to the stallions in low tones. Eliza spotted Finn and Noah right away, and her stomach lifted in anxiety.

Both horse and jockey looked fit to be tied. Noah seemed wound up like a coiled spring, and the stallion kept flattening his ears and pawing the ground. It wasn't a good sign. The animal might be unpredictable in the gate and race.

She went to them, holding out a folded garment. "I've brought you something, Noah," she said.

His head came up quickly, in unison with the horse's. It was almost comical the way the two of them had taken to each other. Their temperaments were the same. They were both smart and quick and high-strung, which could be virtues, or spell disaster, depending on other factors.

She handed it to him. "My father wore this in the Epsom Derby. Why don't you try it on?"

He shook out the short silken jacket. The yellow fabric rippled on the afternoon breeze. "Miss Eliza, are you sure?"

"Of course. In his day, my father was quite the rider,

or so he used to tell me. I never saw him race. I'd be honored if you'd wear his silks today.''

"I will, then," the boy said, beaming. "I'd be purely proud to wear this.''

She held out the jacket while he put his arms in the sleeves. Specially tailored to fit close and neat, it might have been made for him. He was small and compact, much as her father had been. The sleeves were a little short, but he didn't complain. She stepped back, her heart swelling with emotion. "Look at you, Noah," she said. "Just look at you." On impulse, she leaned forward and kissed his cheek.

The other jockeys hooted and hollered with good-natured derision. Despite the deep brown color of his skin, she could see him blush to the tips of his ears. He looked handsome in the yellow jacket, the tight trousers and fitted boots.

In the midst of the excitement, the gentleman from England stopped. "The stallion's remarkable," he commented. "Remarkable indeed. If reports of his gifts are true, his fame will spread." He eyed Noah. "I say, haven't seen that cut or color in a quarter-century, perhaps longer.''

Eliza's chest tightened. She forced herself to speak calmly. "Sir, these jockey's silks once belonged to a man called Henry Flyte.''

The pale, sharp eyes narrowed, and Lord Alistair thumped his cane on the ground. "Henry Flyte, you say? Why—"

"He was my father," she added in an eager rush.

"Your father, you say?" The pale eyes shifted away.

"His most famous race was on a horse called Alea-zar—"

"Pardon me, miss. I must go and find my seat." Lord

Alistair stabbed his cane into the ground and pivoted away.

His evasiveness puzzled her, but before she could follow the Englishman, Charles arrived.

"All that's missing," he said to Noah, "is the cap."

Noah's pride seemed to collapse in on itself and he appeared to withdraw and grow smaller. He lifted his shoulders up around his ears.

"Hello, Charles," Eliza said.

"Sir," Noah mumbled.

Father and son were incredibly awkward with one another. Charles's posture was stiff as he entered the pen and crossed to Noah, holding something out.

"I thought you might want to wear this as well," he said.

It was a leather jockey cap with a buff-colored visor. Hesitantly, Noah took it. "Thank you, sir." He ran his thumb over the stitching on the back. Eliza craned her neck to see the embroidery. In small, careful stitches of green silk were the letters *NC*.

"That stands for Noah Calhoun," Charles said.

The boy's eyes flared wide. Charles put his hand on his shoulder and gave it a brief squeeze. "Good luck in the race."

He left immediately, strolling the grounds with a mint julep in one hand, a cheroot in the other and a well-dressed young woman on each side of him.

A bell clanged, and Eliza saw the stallion shiver in response. Finn remembered this. The horse had raced a hundred times before, in Ireland. He remembered this.

With his heart in his eyes, Noah put on the cap and led the stallion to the gates.

Eliza was glad she hadn't eaten breakfast that morning. Her stomach was so jumpy she knew she couldn't have kept anything down. When she saw Hunter waiting at the numbered gate, she grew doubly nervous.

He held the stallion's head as Noah mounted. The boy looked small and athletic in the racing stance, his legs tucked up and his chest bent low over the horse's back. Hunter drew aside the door of the starting gate, watching every move the stallion made.

Eliza held her breath. Thank goodness her father's racing days had ended before she was born, for she was not made to endure this heart-pounding anxiety. The horse's behavior was hard to read when he was confined to this small space, but he didn't sidle or balk. His ears stayed pricked forward, his eyes on the oval track.

"You all right, Noah?" Hunter asked softly.

"Yes, sir."

"You look mighty handsome up there, son."

"Thank you, sir."

"Ride like the wind, Noah. I've seen you do it. Ride like the wind."

"I aim to, sir."

Hunter and Eliza and the other handlers moved away from the box. The starter climbed up on his platform, pistol in hand.

Eliza and Hunter shared a look, and all the noise and confusion of the riders and horses faded to nothing.

"What?" Hunter asked. "Why are you looking at me like that?"

"Like what?"

"Like you're pleased with me."

"I am pleased with you. It was very nice, the way you just spoke with Noah."

"I know how to be nice."

"Yes, you do." Before she said too much, she walked toward the reviewing stand. The first bench had been cordoned off with a garland of white flowers. It was reserved for the host of the race and his family.

Charles and the children waited there. Blue and Belinda, dressed in summer finery, clutched the front rail and kept their eyes riveted to the track. When Eliza walked past, Belinda jumped up and down. "Here, Miss Eliza! Sit with us. You must, you must."

Before Eliza could shake her head and slip away, Hunter took her by the elbow and steered her to the bench. "You heard the girl, Miss Flyte," he said with laughter in his voice. "You must."

She ignored him, but smiled down at the children. "This is quite an honor."

"Noah and Finn will take First Place," Blue said with unquestioning confidence.

"Do you think so?"

He grinned at his sister. "They must."

Charles took a sip of his drink and made a face. Then he brought out a flask from his boot and added more whiskey. He held out the flask to Hunter, who looked at it for a moment.

Blue and Belinda stared at him.

"Not now, Charles, but thank you," Hunter said.

Eliza didn't realize she had been holding her breath until it all came out in a rush.

"Riders ready!" the racing master called. Every sound died. Even the wind seemed to be holding back, waiting for the start of the race.

The starter lifted his pistol toward the sky.

Noah drew fully into a tuck on the stallion's back. The boy's grip on the reins tightened and then slackened. Eliza was close enough to see the horse's skin quiver and contract, acknowledging the presence of the rider.

The pistol exploded.

Gates shot back, and the horses and riders surged forward. The spectators all came out of their seats. Eliza could feel them behind her, the benches groaning with their movements. A deafening chorus of pounding hooves filled the air.

Eliza stayed frozen in place. She could not have moved to save her life.

The stallion came out of the gate like a bullet from a gun. Noah tucked and bent his head low over the pumping neck. Finn and the boy moved as one being—the barrier between horse and rider blurred.

But victory was not assured. This was a race of champions. Some of the horses and riders were experienced racers, and immediately a sorrel and a black pulled up. In the backstretch, the sorrel pumped ahead of Finn. There was a mad scramble for the first critical curve in the racetrack. The rider who dominated that curve would dominate the race. The sorrel, the black and Finn aimed like arrows for it. Noah tried to hold him in, but Finn ripped control from the boy and flew off, his speed so great that he nearly had Noah standing up in the saddle.

Noah's yellow jacket gleamed in the sun, and even from a distance Eliza imagined the shudder of wind over the garment as he drove the stallion to shattering speeds. He took the curve only a fraction of a second ahead of the sorrel. Then it was a flat-out battle to the finish line, stretched across the end of the track.

The sorrel and Finn kept the lead, but they came on with identical speed. They moved, Eliza imagined, like twin steam engines or the opposite wheels of a locomotive. They were that fast, that relentless.

"A tie," someone shouted. "There's going to be a tie!"

For the first time, Eliza relaxed on the bench. Hunter

sent her a glare of annoyance. "How the hell can you be so calm when there's going to be a tie?" he demanded.

"There won't be a tie," she said simply.

"How do you—"

"Watch. Just watch."

It was something she had noticed about the stallion early in his training. He had a peculiar sense of the finish line. Her father had explained to her once that some horses were compelled, by instinct or by training, to get there first. The ancient knowledge of the herd governed the horse's behavior. An aggressive stallion like Finn had the drive and instinct to pull ahead of the pack.

No matter how focused a horse was, Eliza knew, it would always be aware of its surroundings. Herd animals relying on flight for defense had a strong need to know where everything was in the space around them.

If there was a sorrel charging neck and neck beside the stallion, Finn would know it.

Eliza's fists clenched in her lap. Only a few lengths remained before the finish.

At first, she feared she was wrong, for nothing changed. The horses ran in perfect tandem, almost as if they were harnessed together. But then, just as her heart began to sink, something happened.

Later, folks would whisper that it was magic, or the work of the supernatural possessing the horse from misty Ireland. Folks swore up and down and crosswise that they actually saw all four of the stallion's hooves leave the ground at once and shoot forward, a full length ahead of the sorrel. For years to come, spectators would tell their grandchildren of the day they saw the Irish horse fly.

In truth, Eliza simply recognized that the stallion's heart had done the work. Heart. Spirit. Her father called it different things, but what he meant was the will to win.

The Irish Thoroughbred surged across the finish line and kept going. Noah uncoiled from his crouch, ripped the cap off his head and sent it sailing jubilantly through the air. The stallion slowed gradually, sand flying and then settling, to make way for the rest of the herd.

Hunter stood on the bench, hollering like a wild man, his fists raised to heaven and his face shining with triumph. In a frenzy of congratulations, he and Charles thumped one another on the back. Then Hunter jumped down from the bench and picked up Blue and Belinda, hugging them close and then letting them scamper off into the milling crowd. Finally he grabbed Eliza so swiftly she had no chance to think, and swept her into an embrace that took her breath away.

"We did it," he said, spinning her off her feet. "We did it."

She felt the heat of several stares on them, and pushed away, knowing her cheeks were on fire. "You'd best go and see Noah."

He was laughing as he stepped back. What a different man he was in triumph, with the darkness gone from his eyes. Here was a man who had seen the fulfillment of a dream. Victory seemed to add inches to his stature. He braced one arm on the rail and vaulted over, striding across the racing oval to Noah.

Eliza felt the joy of triumph too, but it tasted bittersweet in her mouth. She had wanted this for Hunter, and for the children and Noah and Albion. But the price of his success was her departure. There was now no reason for her to stay.

As she tried to exit the reviewing stand, Charles stopped her. "Where are you off to?"

"I—"

"Aren't you staying for the auction?"

"I don't think so."

"There's a banquet and a ball tonight."

"No, Charles, I'd rather not."

"Why not?"

She gestured at the crowd, the ladies in their beautiful gowns, the men in frock coats and gleaming top hats. "I don't belong here. You know that."

"You had as much to do with Finn's race today as the horse himself."

"Is the horse coming to the ball, then?"

He laughed. "No, but if he had a smile like yours, I'd find a way to bring him." He took her hand, leading her toward the house. "You're coming."

"No."

"I'll arrange everything."

"Charles—"

"Oh, sweetie, don't waste your breath. Haven't you figured it out by now? I don't take no for an answer."

Twenty-Six

~~~❧✦❧~~~

"I don't know what's lining up faster," Ryan Calhoun said to his half brother at the ball that night. "The mares for your stallion's stud service, or the belles for your hand in marriage."

Hunter lifted his glass in salute to the bevy of ladies who paraded past, their sharp-eyed mamas trying to direct his attention to their daughters. "A couple of years ago, everyone declared Albion was a ruin. Now look at them." He beamed at his guests, all vying to be seen at the victory ball. Men and women who would not have deigned to be caught here when the place was bankrupt now crowded the dance floor. Even his father-in-law, Hugh Beaumont, had made an appearance, and had offered cordial—if not heartfelt—congratulations on the success of the auction.

"This is sweet," Hunter admitted. "My my, but this is sweet."

He felt Ryan's gaze as he drained his glass of whiskey and held it out to a hired servant for more. But Ryan said nothing. Half brothers, they were too far apart in age and distance to be truly close. Hunter was the elder by twelve years, and Ryan's address, most of the year, was in the realm of Neptune. Still, Hunter knew him well enough to feel his disapproval.

"Your Yankee wife must be dragging you to too many temperance meetings," he joked.

"I didn't say anything."

"You didn't have to. You're staring at me as if I just farted in church."

Ryan straightened the tie of his puce silk neck cloth. "It's not my place to judge you. Lord knows, I have enough flaws of my own. But if you don't slow down on the whiskey, you'll miss your own party."

The servant arrived with another drink. Hunter took an unapologetic swig. "I'm celebrating, little brother."

"There was never any question of that. I always knew you could make a success of horse racing. Finding that lady trainer was surely a stroke of luck, wasn't it?" Ryan had never mentioned meeting Eliza on Flyte Island the night she'd helped the escaping slave. People of the Underground Railroad never spoke of their doings.

"I'd have shot Sir Finnegan if it wasn't for her."

"Everything got better once you brought her to Albion," Ryan pointed out. "Funny how that works." Then he bowed from the waist. "If you'll excuse me, I think I'll go dance with my Yankee wife."

Hunter watched him find Isadora in the crowd and take her hand. She turned and smiled at him, and that smile had the power to light the world. What an odd match those two were—red-haired Ryan oozing Southern charm, and tall, straitlaced Isadora, whose intensity and ruthless intelligence intimidated most people. But when they were together, the match seemed perfectly right.

Hunter wondered if Lacey had ever regarded him with that depth of affection. He couldn't recall, but he supposed that if she had, he'd remember it.

He tossed back the whiskey and set aside his glass. Enough woolgathering. The tides of fortune had turned for him, and brooding about the past was no way to celebrate. As he strode toward the dance floor, he ran a gauntlet of eligible ladies. There were the daughters of Señor Montgomery's agent, neighbors and visitors from all over the Tidewater region, and Lady Margaret Stewart from England. Like the Thoroughbred in his stables, these elite young ladies had been selectively bred and trained for a specific purpose—to marry well and to carry on the way of life that was so cherished by them all. Two years ago, women of their class had recoiled from Hunter with scandalized whispers. Now they preened and strutted to get him to ask for a dance.

He chose Tabby Parks because she had dark hair.

She giggled as he bowed before her, and he wondered if there was a polite way to let her know he'd changed his mind. It was too late. What was one waltz anyway? He'd had enough whiskey to make the identity of his partner cease to matter.

"What a wonderful night for you," Tabby said, and he had to admit her voice had the smooth warmth of honey. "How very proud you must be."

"I reckon I am," he said. "I've put a lot of hard work into this."

"You'll be wanting to restore Albion soon, then," she said.

"Restore it?"

"Of course. Replant the tobacco fields, refurbish the house, buy some new darkies—"

He laughed, cutting her off abruptly. "God Almighty, I just got rid of that way of life."

She ran her tongue lightly over her bottom lip. "But think of your children, Hunter. They've been raised like wild Indians. It's time they settled down. Theodore's old enough to be sent away to school, and Belinda needs to learn her needlework and deportment..."

At that point, he stopped listening. Tabby had no notion of what his children needed, and no inkling of his plans for Albion. Neither did her sister Cilla, nor Lady Margaret, nor Miss Martin of Williamsburg. He danced with each in turn, favoring no young lady over the others.

As the evening wore on, Hunter had to force himself to make the terrible admission that his success wasn't enough. The money, the fame, the admiration of women, the esteem of his peers—none of it meant anything to him. He had always thought that if he saved Albion, his life would be complete. He had set out to build a horse farm, and to do it without slave labor or becoming beholden to any other man. He had accomplished that—but now what?

His thoughts kept drifting, as they so often did, to Eliza. What was it Ryan had said about her? *Everything got better once you brought her to Albion.* It was so true. Quietly, without really explaining what she was doing, perhaps without even meaning to, she had turned his life around. She had tamed the madness from his horse, but, more importantly, she had brought his children out of their mire of despair. Blue and Belinda would always bear the scars of losing their mother, but the joy was back again. They embraced each day with an exuberance Hunter had not seen in them since before Lacey had left.

Could he ever thank Eliza for that? Was there any way?

He supposed not. A simple thanks would sound too trite and inadequate. He wished there were something he could give her, offer her, say to her, to let her know how important she was to him.

But what?

As he danced with a beautiful, smiling woman in his

arms, he wished Eliza had come to the ball. It startled him, how much he wished that.

The only thing she had ever asked of him was the freedom to travel to distant California in search of a dream. Now he could afford to buy her passage to the distant Pacific coast. He should want her to have what she wished for, even though the thought of sending her half a world away simply emptied him. For once in his life he had to look beyond his own selfishness. He had torn Eliza from her world with the promise that he would help her embark on a new life. It was time to let her go.

The decision didn't please him, yet having it settled in his mind had a certain calming effect. He put more effort into making small talk with his dance partners, even coaxing a smile from Miss Bondurant, who was petrified of him.

In the middle of the dance, she peered over his shoulder and asked, "Who is that with your cousin Charles? I don't recognize her."

Hunter led his partner in a turn that allowed him to see Charles dancing with a petite young woman in an ice-blue gown. He wasn't the only one craning his neck and staring. Practically everyone in the room was.

He tried not to stumble and tread on his partner's feet, but the shock made him clumsy. "Sorry," he muttered, moving to the edge of the dance floor. "I'd best get you to safety." With a self-deprecating grin, he delivered her to her mother and then turned to gawk at the newcomer.

It was Eliza Flyte, of course, but an Eliza he had never seen before.

Festooned in a blue satin gown, she was an enchanting creature, small and slender, with glossy black curls caught up in fancy combs. She wore long white gloves and carried a lace fan on a ribbon at her waist. Blue slippers showed occasionally beneath the full, shimmery gown. Everything about her was remarkable, from the vivid beauty of her face, to the sound of her laughter, to the compelling energy of her dance step.

She was the sort of vision adolescent boys conjured in their minds when they thought about the girl they'd like to marry. She was the woman grown men dreamed of when the girls they did marry turned out quite different from their adolescent fantasies. She was the beauty little girls pictured when they wondered what they would be once they were all grown up.

She was Miranda, daughter of Prospero, a creature of myth and air, stardust and seafoam.

He had definitely had too much to drink. He went to the punch bowl and gulped down several cups of mint lemonade to counteract all the whiskey he'd consumed. Then he ran a hand through his hair, straightened his neck cloth and walked across the dance floor to Charles and Eliza.

"Pardon me," he said in his most charming drawl. "But I do believe I'd like to break in."

"Go away," Charles said, never taking his eyes off Eliza.

"That's hardly the polite reply, cousin," Hunter said, trying to be good-natured.

"Who ever said I was polite?" Charles twirled sharply, presenting his back to Hunter.

"Oh, for heaven's sake," Eliza said, laughing. "You're like a pair of little boys." She extracted herself from Charles's grasp and turned to Hunter.

She fit in his arms as if she had been specially fashioned for his embrace. They moved well together, her small steps easily keeping up with his. The fancy dress offered a dazzling view of her bosom, the cleavage deep, the tops of her breasts prominent above the scalloped neckline.

"You're staring," she said with laughter in her voice.

"Do you blame me?"

She laughed again. "I really don't think it's considered proper."

"I assure you it's completely improper, but I can't help myself." He splayed his fingers over her back, amazed that his hand was able to span her waist. "Who the devil did this to you?"

"Your cousin Charles. The one you just accused of being impolite. The one you just banished from the floor."

"Charles did this? He must be a man of hidden talents."

"It was Charles and Willa, with some help from Belinda and Blue. The dress belonged to your late wife, and Willa altered it and added some trim." She bit her lip. "I hope you're not vexed about the dress."

"Hell no, I'm not vexed. Lacey had enough dresses for five women." He didn't recall his wife in this blue dress. But then, he didn't recall her in *any* particular dress. Yet he knew he'd never forget the way Eliza looked tonight. "I had no idea you were this—" He hesitated, trying to rephrase the comment.

"You had best stop there," she said. "Anything you say will surely get you in trouble. You're so charming when you don't speak."

Lord, but he liked her. Liked this laughing, teasing, beautiful girl.

"You have to admit," he said, "you do look different."

"I feel different. My father used to play tunes on his mouth harp or hum them, and he taught me some dance steps, but I had no idea it was like this."

"Like what?"

"So beautiful," she said, her eyes sparkling with wonder. "So…magical. Everyone looks lovely. The music sounds like nothing I'd ever imagined. It fills this room. Every corner of this room, all the way up to the rafters. Why didn't anyone tell me music was like this?"

The ensemble—on a dais at the end of the room, under the shell-shaped half dome of the ballroom—put out a sound that was liquid and full and sweet. It stunned him to realize she was hearing music for the first time. He and the other guests took the simple country tune for granted.

"From now on, and forever after, I'll always imagine the angels in heaven when I hear music." She tilted back her head, exposing the arch of her throat, and laughed aloud as they turned swiftly together. "No wonder dancing was invented," she said exuberantly.

He speculated about how long it would take her to realize she had become an object of speculation. Already, after only this one dance, he could feel the attention of everyone in the room. The men, of course, could barely contain themselves, their eyes hard and avid as they awaited a chance at her. The women stared too, though with a different sort of sharpness.

"Miss Flyte, I think it's only fair to warn you," he said.

"Warn me about what?"

"I think you're going to be very popular with the gentlemen tonight."

"Is that a bad thing?"

"Only if you let someone take advantage of you."

"You'll have to explain that one." Mischief glittered in her eyes.

"Compromise you."

"Ah. You mean like you did on the roof that night."

The mere reminder created an uncomfortable heat between them. "Goes to show you that even a man you trust can't be trusted."

"And you're saying there are others like you?"

"There are others worse than me."

She laughed again. It was remarkable, amazing and slightly appalling to see her blossom with self-assurance like this. From wide-eyed recluse to society belle was a giant leap, but she seemed to be taking it in stride. "Don't worry about me. I really don't think I could be taken advantage of or compromised without my consent."

He wanted to explain that a determined man could snap her will like a dry twig. But now was not the time to describe something ugly. Let her have this one special night. He would watch out for her.

A foolish notion. Because he wanted to eat her alive.

"I met your Mr. Vega," she said abruptly. "The man from California."

"And...?"

"And I realized that dreaming about something is quite different from actually doing it."

"You mean you really don't want to go?"

She stared at a spot over his shoulder. "I honestly don't know," she whispered.

He was reluctant to let her go, but he couldn't very well monopolize her the entire night. He decided to let Ryan have the next dance. Of all the men present, his half brother was the least likely to have any untoward thoughts. Ryan adored his wife too much to even consider it.

They traded partners in the middle of the contra dance. Isadora was nearly as tall as Hunter, and her merry eyes grew merrier as she studied his face. "Don't sulk, Hunter," she teased in her funny, flat, Yankee voice. "You look like a baby that's had its sugar-teat snatched away."

"Ah, but I have, sister dear."

"The horsemaster's daughter has turned out to be the belle of the ball."

"True." He sought Eliza out with his gaze, and his hold on Isadora tightened.

Her smile disappeared. "Oh, heavens be, say it's not so."

"What's not so?"

"You've made love to her, haven't you? You've already taken the poor girl."

"What—"

"Don't lie, Hunter. Remember who I am. Your bossy sister-in-law, formerly an old maid. Old maids are lied to more than any other sort of woman, so we know what a lie sounds like. We recognize a young woman in love for the first time too."

His step nearly faltered. "What are you saying? That you think Eliza's in love with me?"

"It's possible. When I see her looking at you, I see myself three years ago, looking at—"

"At my brother, Ryan?"

Her generous mouth twitched with a rueful smile. "At Chad Easterbrook." The dance ended, and she kept hold of his arm, bringing him to the side of the room where the tall French doors stood ajar to let in a breeze.

"Who's he?"

"A man I once thought I loved."

"But you didn't," he said urgently. "Not really."

"As it turned out, I mistook a certain starry-eyed attraction for true love." Her smile softened. "I didn't know the difference until I met your brother."

"And you think Eliza is wrong now."

"I think she's very naive. She's led a sheltered life. Whether she's right or wrong is for you to discover."

He watched Eliza spin past as the dance set changed.

Her skirt swirled like a pinwheel and her head tilted back as she laughed at something her partner said. She was vibrantly beautiful, blossoming under the golden heat of the chandeliers and lamps of the ballroom, and under the attention of hordes of inquisitive friends and neighbors.

A brief solemnity came over Isadora. "I'd say the sheltered part of her life is over."

Eliza had never worn shoes for so long in her life, and she discovered that she did not much care for it. The dancing slippers pinched, and after several sets she begged for a rest. Her partner, a Mr. Martin, grabbed both of her hands and begged her for another chance.

"Oh, for heaven's sake, it's not you. If you must know, my feet hurt."

"Forgive me, then. I had no idea." Gallantly he swept her along to a velvet-covered bench at the side of the room and held her hand while she sat down. He was so earnest as he sank to one knee before her that she didn't dare to laugh, though he looked comical. "Shall I go for help? Can I order a servant to bring something?"

She felt the stares probing at them, and she flushed. "Truly, there's no need. If I could just get these slippers off, I'll be fine." She bent down and unbuttoned the cross-strap.

"Miss Flyte!" Poor Mr. Martin looked as if he might faint.

"Sir, if the sight of a bare foot offends you, then you'd best look away."

As she slipped off the confining slippers, she heard, quite clearly, a series of gasps and whispers all around her. Her faux pas was serious indeed. But where was the sense in mincing around with tortured feet all night while pretending to have a good time?

She searched the crowd for Hunter, but so many revelers pressed close that she couldn't find him. She knew she must brazen it out on her own. She squared her shoulders and stood up, pushing the slippers under the bench with her foot. "It's not as if I've stripped myself naked," she stated baldly to the people watching her. "My feet hurt, and Mr. Martin was kind enough to keep me from getting an injury."

"My feet hurt too, Mama," a young lady whispered. "Can I—"

"Certainly not," came the hissed reply.

The orchestra struck up a lively reel. Eliza had no idea what to do now that she had managed to offend everyone in the room. Help arrived in the form of a smiling Cousin Charles, who elbowed his way toward her and took her by the hand.

"May I have this dance?" he asked.

She let out a breath of relief. "I'm honored, sir." She laughed at herself. It was exactly how they spoke in *Jane Eyre,* but it felt strange to be in a situation that seemed like something out of a book. Jane would not have taken off her shoes, but then again, Jane was just a character made of ink and paper.

They went into the reel with a lively step, and the music and light surrounded and possessed her. She forgot all about the fact that she had just committed a highly improper act. Didn't these people understand? She had never heard music before.

"I suppose after this," she said breathlessly, "I am going to have to hide myself away in shame."

"I wouldn't worry about that," Charles said, a darkly amused gleam in his eye.

"Why not?" She passed behind him and emerged on the other side, eyeing him with growing suspicion.

"Because you're no ordinary young lady."

She laughed. "There are those who would dispute that I'm a lady at all."

She sailed through the reel, loving every moment of it. Now that her feet no longer hurt, she skipped as if walking on a cloud, and changed partners with the smoothness of a practiced lady. It was an enchanted night—the music, the food, the smiling faces. Never could she have imagined such an experience. Charlotte Brontë had written of stiff, formal affairs with currents of gossip undermining every moment. It wasn't like that at all.

She found herself wishing Hunter would reclaim her for a dance, but he had gone off to a doorway with a group of the older men to smoke cigars and talk business. She was determined to show she could have fun without his constant company.

Dance after dance spun by, and she felt like Cinderella in the fairy tale—except that she had discarded both slippers and didn't care a fig about getting either of them back. She forgot to watch for impending disaster—until the couple behind them in the set slammed into them. With a little shriek, the young lady tumbled back. Eliza noted vaguely that it was Tabby Parks, and that she sprawled on her backside with very little grace.

"I am so sorry," Eliza said, holding out a hand.

Tabby sputtered like a wet cat. Ignoring Eliza's hand, she grabbed her partner and lurched to her feet, tottering away on shoes that looked as if they fit even more tightly than Eliza's had. No wonder she was so cross.

"Now I understand why all the ladies carry fans," Eliza whispered to Charles. "Dancing is a hot business. Oh, Charles. Did I disgrace myself entirely?"

He chuckled. "No, only partially. Miss Tabby will survive, I'm certain. They say a cat has nine lives."

Eliza escaped the dance floor. Spying a gap in the crowd, she darted outside onto the brick-paved veranda. In the relative coolness and privacy of the night, she felt a mortified heat high in her cheeks. As she strolled down a garden path, she tipped back her head to enjoy the night breeze. She stopped short when she noticed a knot of ladies, young and old, clustered in the glow of torchlight near the stone fountain in the middle of the garden.

"…has managed to offend everyone present, right down to the lowliest servant."

Eliza stopped and stood completely still. She recognized Miss Cilla Parks's scandalized voice.

"Personally, I think he should dismiss her immediately. What a disaster for those poor little children. They'll be the laughingstock of Virginia, running around barefoot and speaking so strangely. Did you know we saw her wearing breeches?"

"Really?" someone asked.

"She was dressed like a boy. What can he be thinking, letting a creature like Eliza Flyte mingle at his affairs as if she were one of us?"

Eliza stepped into the circle of torchlight. "Maybe you should ask him," she said, smooth fury in her voice.

Mrs. Merriwether Martin sucked in a shocked breath. "This is a private conversation."

"But if I'm the topic," Eliza said, trying not to let her humiliation show, "then surely I should be privy to what is being said."

"Brave girl," Tabby Parks murmured, snapping her fan shut. "I'm sure I wouldn't want to hear it."

"If you're rude enough to discuss me behind my back—"

"It's not rudeness," Cilla interrupted, her eyes wide with innocence. "We are concerned about Hunter. He's been a friend and neighbor for many years, and it worries us when a stranger comes into his life and begins... changing things."

Changing things, she thought. Like turning the tide of his fortune. Getting his son to speak after two years of silence.

"Just who are you, anyway?" Tabby asked.

More kindly, Lady Margaret inquired, "Who are your people, dear?"

Eliza thought the question absurd. "I've not kept a pedigree on myself, if that's what you're asking. Breeding matters with horses, not people."

Feminine gasps all around. "Believe me," Mrs. Martin intoned, "it matters to Hunter Calhoun."

"How do you know?" Eliza asked.

"Because we understand him in a way you never could. All we were suggesting, Miss Flyte, is that perhaps you should limit your training to Hunter's horses, not Hunter's children."

The bald statement reverberated across the veranda. The blow hit Eliza harder than she ever could have anticipated. She knew there were those who thought her strange, an outsider, someone who didn't belong in this closed and close-minded society. But she had dared to believe that, in time, acceptance would come.

Her understanding of the situation crystallized. Any number of young ladies were lining up to snare Hunter. They saw her as a threat. Nothing she did or said could convince these society belles that she wasn't a barefoot bumpkin whose presence would bring about the ruination of a good man.

She really didn't care what these anserine creatures thought of her. But she did care about Hunter and his children. Was she a mortification to them? Would Blue and Belinda suffer ridicule because of her?

"Excuse me," she stated, forcing into her voice a conviction she did not feel. "I'll let you line up for Hunter like mares to the stud. I understand he's about to commence a new breeding program."

A gale of outrage followed her as she crossed the veranda, marching around to the back of the house to let herself into the kitchen. Amazingly, she kept her composure until she lit a candle in the kitchen, then felt despair tear at her soul.

She held the edge of the big scrubbed wooden table and sank down to the bench. It was madness, trying to fit in to this society. She didn't want this at all, not for any price. She understood females being combative to defend their territory. That happened in nature all the time. But until tonight, she hadn't understood what it was like to be the challenger.

Hearing a step on the threshold of the kitchen, she looked up. Moonlight framed Nancy's decrepit form, her abundant white hair. "What you doing here all by yourself, girl?" the old woman asked.

"When I'm by myself, I don't get into trouble." Eliza stood and took Nancy's hand in hers. "Sit with me."

Nancy's eyes, as deep and unseeing as the night itself, crinkled at the corners in a smile. She took a biscuit from the jar on the table and handed one to Eliza. "Always helps to eat something."

"I should have stayed away from the ball. It's not the sort of affair for me."

"Liar," Nancy said, not unkindly.

"Nothing escapes you, does it?"

"Not with a house full of folks and hired servants running everywhere, talking their fool faces off."

Eliza took a bite of the biscuit. "I loved it, Nancy. The music, the food, the dancing—I never wanted it to end. But these people... They know I'm not one of them, nor would I ever try to be."

Nancy finished the biscuit and dusted the flour from her hands. "Ain't no point in trying, honey. That ain't the path to happiness."

"Then what is?"

The old woman slowly rose from the table. "You'll find it, girl. Or it'll find you."

Eliza helped Nancy to her room. Then she checked on Blue and Belinda, touched by the untroubled beauty of their sleeping faces. Belinda's tiny fist was curled like a bud upon her pillow. Blue clutched his own close against his chest, his breathing soft and even. She bent and kissed each child on the forehead, feeling love for them swell in her heart. It ached, because she knew she couldn't love these children the way a mother could.

Walking slowly, on bare feet that still felt the phantom rhythm of the orchestra, she made her way to bed, seeking a sleep that would not come.

Twenty-Seven

Long after the company had gone home or found their way to one of the guest rooms, Hunter stayed awake. He had drunk more whiskey than a sailor on shore leave, but its effects disappointed him. Tonight, he felt everything. He felt every poke and prod and nuance of emotion. He felt things he had been numbing himself against for years.

Unable to contemplate sleeping, he went out to the barn. Every stall was occupied with racehorses. Things were as they should be. For once, he could breathe a sigh of relief about his state of affairs. He wasn't bankrupt, his children were learning to embrace life again. He could take his choice of women to be his wife and stepmother to Belinda and Blue.

He stood poised on the brink of success. At last, everything was as he wanted it.

Except that nothing felt right. And he knew exactly why—Eliza Flyte.

She had left the party without even telling him. She had just slipped away.

He stood in the broad corridor that ran down the length of the stables, listening to the gentle nickering of the horses, and thought about Eliza. It was all he did these days, or so it seemed.

Finn put his head out of the box and nipped sleepily at Hunter's sleeve. Idly Hunter fitted his shoulder under the stallion's muzzle and scratched the smooth chestnut cheek. Finn responded with a contented rumble low in his throat. When Hunter had first seen this horse, the idea of anyone actually being able to touch—not to mention ride—him was unthinkable. Now he was a champion, the star of the hour, and probably the most valuable horse in Virginia.

The stallion nodded his great head and Hunter stepped away, holding him at arm's length. The velvety lips rolled back playfully, going for his ears and hair. The horse's grassy breath blew hot in his face. In spite of himself, Hunter laughed softly.

"Kissing on the mouth," said a thoughtful voice from the doorway. "Now that's something my father never tried with his horses."

With a startled snort, the stallion swung his head toward Eliza. The movement made Hunter stumble back, slumping atop a bale of hay. Moonlight cast her in shades of blue as she stepped inside the barn.

"What are you doing up?" he asked. "It's the middle of the night."

"It's an hour 'til dawn," she corrected him. "I couldn't sleep."

"Neither could I," he admitted.

She looked incredibly beautiful to him, a creature of moonlight and mist. A white cotton nightgown swirled like a cloud around her ankles. She wore her black hair loose, falling abundantly over her shoulders and down her back. Shadows hid her face, but he sensed that her attention was riveted on him.

"Why couldn't you sleep?" he asked her.

"Everything has been happening so fast. It's all so new and exciting," she said. "When I was standing at the banquet table at the party tonight, I was at a loss. There was too much there, Hunter. Too much to sample. I simply couldn't make up my mind where to begin. I feel the same way about everything else these days."

He chuckled, intrigued by her honesty and lack of pretense. "Really?"

"Really. Why couldn't you sleep?"

He hesitated, wondering if he should lie to her. No, he thought. She wasn't easy to lie to. And so he said flatly, "Because I couldn't stop thinking about you."

She stiffened, suspicion prickling over her almost visibly. "What do you mean?"

"Exactly that. Everyone went to bed, and I should have gone as well, and slept soundly on the knowledge that Albion is about to enter a period of prosperity. Instead, I found myself thinking of you."

She turned away and went to the doorway, speaking over her shoulder. "We should change the subject."

"Fine." He sat forward on the hay bale. "Did you enjoy the party?" he inquired.

She hesitated, then said, "It was completely amazing." She twirled around, hugging herself, and the nightgown belled out around her. "I felt like Cinderella going to the ball." She stopped spinning to face him.

"There will probably be plenty more dances now."

"Not for me there won't be."

A chill stole over him despite the balmy warmth of the night. "What do you mean? Didn't you like it? Didn't you have a good time?"

"I liked it, I danced with plenty of charming gentlemen, I had a good time, and if I'm ever tempted to go to a ball again, you have my permission to shoot me."

He planted his elbows on his knees. "I don't understand you." He was only half joking.

She came toward him, moving like a wraith through a stream of blue moonlight, and stood in the center aisle of the barn. "I wouldn't have missed tonight for the world. I saw so much, learned so much." She ducked her head. He could hear her drawing in a long slow breath like a swimmer before diving into deep, cold water.

"One of the things I learned was that this isn't my world."

Panic knocked at his chest. He wanted her here. He *needed* her here. "Give it time, Eliza—"

"It can never be my world. I feel the same way when I study a herd of horses. I'm the outsider, looking in. I can understand what's going on, and can even take part if I'm careful and I watch my behavior, but I'll never think and feel as they do. I'll never be one of them." She lifted her head so that the light traced the clean line of her profile. "You and I belong to different species."

"Come here." He held out both hands to her.

She hugged herself protectively. "I can't."

"Why not?"

"Because...well, that's one thing I've learned from being here in your world. It's not proper. A woman doesn't just go around wantonly making love to men."

"Who said I expected you to make love to me? Wantonly?" He stood up, knowing he shouldn't, knowing he couldn't help himself. "Dance with me, Eliza. There's no harm in dancing with me."

Before she could answer, he caught her in his arms, humming the first few bars of a waltz. She gasped in surprise, but instead of pulling away she let him hold her, grasped his hand and rested her other hand on his upper arm. They danced in the barn, with cedar shavings under their feet and the moonlight streaming down through the central skylight. Each detail of the moment stood out in sharp relief—the sound of her breathing and the warm smell of the horses, the clarity of her eyes and the way the light fell over her hair, the feel of her small, hard-working hand in his.

"You've been drinking whiskey," she whispered.

He stopped humming but kept dancing. "I always drink whiskey."

"More than usual tonight, I think."

"You're probably right. Tonight...I needed to forget."

"Forget what?"

"How much—" He paused and stopped dancing to weave his hand up into her thick black hair. "How much I want you," he finished just before lowering his head and settling his mouth over hers.

A better man would have stopped. A better man would have backed away, warned her to go to her room and lock the door. A better man would have done everything in his power to keep from hurting her.

But Hunter knew himself all too well. There wasn't much good in him, and here was the proof. He had ruined this girl by taking her innocence, and then, instead of trying to make amends by helping her get on with her life, pointing her in the direction of her dreams, perhaps arranging a proper marriage with the right sort of man, he did nothing but follow the dictates of his body and his heart.

And she made it so easy for him, this strange, fey girl who had never heard music until tonight. She fell into his kiss, curled up into his embrace and convinced him, with the softest of moans and a helpless, whispered endearment, that she wanted him as much as he wanted her.

Without breaking the kiss, he swept her up into his arms

and took her into the barn office. Shadows haunted the tall cases of breeder journals and the long desk strewn with notes. With a sweep of his arm he cleared the desk, not caring when important papers swished to the floor and a pewter ink jar fell with a clatter. He laid her down on the old oak desk that had been his father's, and even through the fog of his desire he saw a dark irony in the situation. This desk, where his father had made and lost a fortune in tobacco, this desk where his father had signed the papers selling people Hunter loved to the slave traders, was about to know the heat of an illicit passion.

Stop me, he thought, pressing Eliza back on the cleared surface. *Stop me.*

She placed her palms flat against his chest, under his shirt, her touch lingering over his heart. He knew then that she wasn't about to stop him.

He tried one last time, forcing out the words. "This shouldn't be happening. Not here, not like this."

"Then where?" she whispered, her lips already full and slick from kissing. "And how?"

"You are so beautiful," he said. "You should be taken on a bed of softest down, with coverlets of silk and flowers all around."

She traced her finger down the front of him and lower, finding the shape of him through his breeches. "Should such things matter to me?"

"Do they?"

"I don't think so." Dropping back her head, she bared her creamy throat to him. He kissed her there, where a powerful pulse matched the rhythm of his own desire. "No. Nothing matters but you," she whispered.

He tugged the ribbon at the neckline of her gown and drew the garment off her, baring her entirely to the moonlight. Reclining on the long desk, she resembled a pagan offering, a beauty so precious and rare that only the gods were fit to receive her. Her body held the fresh promise of an unopened bud. He was the only man ever to see the pearlescent gleam of the moonlight on her breasts. The only one to taste the fullness of her lips. Like the time on the island, he was going to use her, destroy her, and he didn't even care. Long ago, he had lost himself, lost who he was, lost his direction in life.

For now he had but one purpose, and that was to do justice to the innocent gift of her trust and her passion. She made it easy, for she offered no protest. She watched him peel off his shirt and bend over her, and when he kissed her breasts, she gasped with pleasure and lifted herself toward him. She tasted of the secret springs of womanhood, and she did not resist anything, not his hungriest kisses, not his boldest caresses, not his most intimate touch.

She drew from him a long, patient eroticism he never knew he possessed. He held his own desires at bay, compelled to seek her pleasure before his own. He kissed her in all the most sensitive places of her body, and she responded with an abandon that made his heart soar. He felt every ripple, every quiver, every held-back disbelieving breath. This was so new to him, *she* was so new to him.

She objected to nothing and encouraged everything. With both hands she undid the side buttons of his breeches and took them off, sighing with pleasure at the sight of him. Her touch was as frank and bold as her stare. No one had ever trained her to be modest or coy. No schoolgirl notions inhibited her responses to him. Her touch was fire, everywhere, branding him, lifting him to heights he had never imagined.

He stood at the end of the desk and slid her toward him, leaning forward to gently impale her. They joined in a slow, lingering bond that made the world catch fire. The rich heat of loving her enveloped him, and for the first time in his life, physical pleasure became an emotion he could actually feel in his soul. She was special, this woman he had dragged kicking and screaming into his world. Every moment with her was a new discovery.

The rhythm of his strokes matched the rhythm of her shallow breaths, and he kept his eyes open, watching her. He covered her hands with his and held her pinned down on the desk, a helpless victim of the pleasure he could see rippling over her in waves.

His name burst from her, and her spasms completely robbed him of control. He flung himself into the abyss with her, letting the pleasure roar through him, collapsing on her as he claimed her mouth with his, imprisoned her hands in his and filled her with all that he was.

Long moments stretched out, and he knew he should move, but he couldn't. Never had he felt such emotion in making love, and it was all due to Eliza. He had done nothing special, nothing but admit the truth about his desire for her. He had always enjoyed sex and taken pleasure in it, but until Eliza he had never thought of it as a form of worship.

Still joined, they fit together and breathed as one, mouth to mouth, breast to chest. He couldn't believe he was still kissing her. He felt as if they had survived some disaster together, a shipwreck or hurricane, and they were the only survivors on earth.

With a groan, he pulled his mouth from hers and tried to rise.

She caught him fast against her. "Don't go."

He laughed, letting her feel the rumble of his throat against her smooth shoulder. "Oh, love. Do you think I want to?"

"Then stay. Just for a few moments longer."

"You're comfortable like this?"

Now it was her turn to laugh. "You've put ideas into my head."

"What sort of ideas?"

"You've got me thinking about that bed of swansdown and the silk coverlets."

"Ah, honey," he said, wishing the moment would go on, wishing he wasn't drunk so he'd remember every detail. "I'd make you a bed of clouds if I could." Inch by inch, he took himself away, kissing each part of her goodbye as he left—face, shoulders, breasts, belly, thighs. He found her rumpled nightgown on the floor and handed it to her. Then he pulled on his breeches and propped himself on the side of the desk.

"It's getting light," he observed, nodding at the unglazed window. A silvery thread appeared on the horizon, very low, just touching the waterline. A rooster crowed, a piercing lonely sound in the misty dark before dawn.

"We've got a busy day ahead." Reluctantly he pulled her heavy hair out of the neckline of her gown. "And," he said, leaning forward to kiss her, "plans to make."

"Plans?"

He laughed quietly and kissed her again. "Something about a bed of softest down—"

"Hunter." She put her hands on his shoulders and pushed back, solemnly studying his face.

"Yeah?"

"You don't seem to understand…why I came looking for you tonight."

He grinned. "Sure I understand, honey."

Her eyes glittered in the coming light. Tears? He panicked. He never knew what to do when a woman wept.

"I've made a mess of this," she said softly. "It was

stupid of me to go looking for you in my nightgown, but I wasn't thinking. I just wanted to get it over with.''

''Get what over with?''

She took a long, shuddering breath. ''Telling you that I'm leaving.''

Something inside him turned to stone. And then he laughed. ''You're joking.''

''You know it's the right thing to do. You're the one who brought Mr. Vega here, with the invitation from Don Roberto.''

''But that was before—''

''Before what?''

''Marry me,'' he said, the command rushing from him in a single breath.

She blinked, and all trace of her tears went away. ''What?''

''I said, marry me. And you'll note I didn't ask it.'' He grabbed both of her wrists, his big hands swallowing hers. The impulsive idea surprised him as much as it did her. ''I can't let you walk out of my life.''

Her face shone with elation. But just as quickly, the light in her eyes dimmed. ''I don't fit in here, Hunter. We've spoken of this before.''

''We'll build our own world to fit us, Eliza. We can do it. I know we can.'' He lifted her hands to his lips and covered them with kisses. ''Marry me. The hell with what anyone says. Marry me.''

She shut her eyes. ''I don't know what I'm feeling,'' she whispered. ''I don't know whether it's terror or excitement.'' Then she opened her eyes and laughed with a pure, clear joy that filled his heart. ''Yes. Yes, I'll marry you, Hunter Calhoun.''

Twenty-Eight

Hunter wanted everything to be perfect when he and Eliza told the children, but more than that, he wanted everything to happen fast. He wished all the guests would depart, but many of them lingered, talking over their horse trades and the racing season to come. Only in the darkest moments, when even whiskey wouldn't give him amnesia, did he admit that the need for haste stemmed from his gut-level worry that something might go wrong.

His friends and neighbors would be mortified by his choice of a wife. They expected him to choose an heiress, a polished gem from finishing school, not a barefoot island girl with no pedigree. But he meant what he'd promised Eliza about making the world fit them, not the other way around.

All day long, events had conspired to keep them apart. There had been meetings with horse buyers, shippers, speculators. Several of the foreigners stayed on, including Montgomery's man Vega, and the Englishman and his daughter. After supper, perhaps there would be time for them to steal up to the nursery and tell Blue and Belinda their news.

He dressed with special care in a black silk frock coat

with split tails, a dark green waistcoat, a snowy white shirt and onyx studs. He could think of only one reason for his unusual fit of vanity. He wanted to be the suitor Eliza read about in all the novels she loved so well.

Except that he knew he'd be a very nervous suitor. He refilled his whiskey flask, sliding the flat silver vessel into an inner pocket of his frock coat. He could hear the children giggling upstairs, and the sound of their voices calmed his nerves a little. How excited they would be when they learned Eliza was going to be their mother.

A gift, he thought. That was what Eliza needed. He planned to order a wedding band from the jeweler in Norfolk, yet he suddenly wanted something to give her today. But what?

A piece that had belonged to his mother, he decided, striding out of the master bedroom. He'd given Lacey all his mother's jewels years ago. They'd had to sell off the more costly items, but there was one piece Lacey had always refused to wear. A brooch. Lacey had declared it vulgar and gaudy.

Eliza would think it was perfect, because the brooch was in the shape of a seashell. Hunter remembered it from his boyhood. It had a shell of hammered gold and an emerald in the center.

He hurried into Lacey's old suite of rooms where she'd spent so many hours doing some mysterious ritual called her "toilette." Long muslin dust cloths draped the furniture, creating a haunted, neglected air. He hadn't seen the inside of the armoire in years, and the door creaked as he swung it open. There, on the shelf, rested the familiar jewel case of bird's-eye maple, coated in finger-smeared dust.

It sat atop a rosewood box. Hunter wouldn't have noticed the rosewood box at all, except that it was curiously dust-free, as if someone had placed it there only recently. He set aside the jewel case and took out the box.

Lacey's lap desk. He had given it to her for their first Christmas. He set it on the draped bed and flipped it open. There were her initials, embossed in gold on the tooled leather surface. Almost idly, he folded back the leather writing surface, and was surprised to see letters there. A good-size stack of them. It was a little eerie finding this, like hearing a ghost whisper in his ear. Frowning, Hunter picked up a random letter and started to read.

At first the content of the letters, penned in a bold and disconcertingly familiar hand, confused him. What was this about, these words of illicit love and constant yearning, these frantic, furtive plans, his name rendered as a mysterious *H?* As he read on, the confusion gave way to something worse. Betrayal swept through him like a forest fire. Holy Christ, how could he not have known? How could he have been so stupid?

Hunter Calhoun did the only thing he knew how to do well. He took out his flask and started drinking.

"You look exactly like a princess," Belinda declared, admiring Eliza's dress. "Is there going to be another party tonight?"

"Not exactly. Some of the guests have stayed over, but—" She broke off. Best to wait for Hunter to give them the news together. "We just want everyone to have a wonderful time." She twirled in front of the mirror. Willa had made over one of Lacey's gowns with fitted sleeves, seed pearls on the bodice and a scalloped hem. "Do you think this is too fancy for supper, or just right?"

"Just right." The little girl stood on the bed to straighten the tortoiseshell comb in Eliza's hair. "Where is your brother?"

"He was reading, and he fell asleep," Belinda said. "He thinks all these grown-ups are purely boring. So do I."

Eliza laughed, but a wave of nervousness rippled through her. After supper, if the hour wasn't too late, she and Hunter would tell the children what they planned. It was frustrating, having to maneuver around houseguests, but she would not allow herself to complain. Once she married Hunter, such things would be expected of her.

"I'm hungry," Belinda said, lying back on the bed.

Eliza gave her part of a biscuit left over from the afternoon tea she'd been too tense to eat. Belinda ate the biscuit, and the next time Eliza looked at her, the child was sound asleep. She smiled. It was just as well, she supposed. The children would be wakeful enough once they heard the news.

Eliza took one last look at herself in the mirror. She didn't appear any different, but everything had changed. Just for a moment, she let herself think about the night before. It might have been a dream, making love with Hunter in the barn office, except that her body stung with delicious aches everywhere he had touched and loved her. She wondered if the secret joy she felt showed on her face. She wondered if people would notice.

Her last task before she went down to supper was to put on a pair of shoes. After the dancing last night, she had sworn she would never wear them again, but now that she was to become a proper wife, she must submit to them. The shoes with spool heels, which Willa had salvaged from Lacey's old things, were even more uncomfortable than dancing slippers.

Eliza forced herself to walk smoothly to the top of the stairs. Garlands of flowers had been woven through the banisters, and the entryway smelled heavily of roses. Yet in the wake of the party, a curiously solemn air pervaded the house. She looked out the window at the landing. Across the bay, the lighthouse beam flickered in the twilight.

A sense of foreboding scuttled over her. Lifting her skirts so she could walk faster, she hurried to the dining room.

Like the entryway, it was festooned with flowers and haunted by the shadows of the fast-falling night.

And empty—or nearly so. Lord Alistair Stewart and his daughter Margaret were engaged in what appeared to be a heated conversation, which ceased abruptly when they saw her.

"Pardon me," she murmured. "I didn't mean to distur—"

"Nonsense, my dear girl, come in." The English nobleman waved his hand impatiently. "We were having a glass of sherry before supper."

Eliza declined with a shake of her head. Lady Margaret, who was as pretty as a long-stemmed rose, held a pair of gloves knotted in front of her. "Father and I were just commenting on your remarkable gift with horses."

"If patience is a gift. That's all it is, really." Eliza thought about the way Lord Alistair had reacted to her questions about her father the day before. Recognition had flashed in his eyes, she was sure of it. "Sir," she said hesitantly, "I do wish you could tell me something of my father's career in England. Please, it would mean so much to me."

"I knew *of* him," he said carefully. "There was a time when every horse fancier in England knew of Henry Flyte." He finished his sherry. "He was a most remarkable trainer and a gifted jockey."

"And my mother?" she asked with her heart in her throat. "Did you know her as well?"

His glass wobbled as he set it on the sideboard and exchanged a glance with Lady Margaret. "Miss Flyte, perhaps you'd do me the favor of giving our regrets to our host. My daughter and I must make ready to leave on the morning packet. I've appointments in Richmond tomorrow."

Eliza couldn't help herself. She pursued the gentleman and his daughter to the door. "If you can recall anything," she said, "anything at all, it would mean the world to me. You see, I never knew my mother."

Lady Margaret, who had been white-faced and silent, stopped in the doorway. "Father, don't you think—"

"No," he said.

Eliza sent Lady Margaret a pleading look. "You must know how important this is to me. It's as if half of me has been missing all my life."

Lady Margaret turned to her father. "She has a right to know."

His face reddened, and he cleared his throat. Moving as if his bones hurt, he held open a French door. "We must go where we can speak in private," he said.

Burning with curiosity, Eliza accompanied the Englishman and his daughter to the garden gazebo. The iron filigree dome atop the gazebo created twisted shadows on the lawn. Lord Alistair leaned on one of the columns as if in need of support. "Henry Flyte had a rare gift with racehorses, but off the mile oval he had a reputation for being…impulsive."

Eliza discovered that she couldn't breathe as this man spoke of her father. She listened with her whole being, fascinated by this part of her father's life that had been a mystery to her for so long.

"He was known to be a womanizer, I fear," Lord Alistair went on. "And then he lost his heart to one particular woman—or so went the gossip in the Haymarket."

"My mother?"

He nodded.

"Then you *did* know her—"

"Certainly not." He spoke sharply, then seemed to catch himself. "You see, she was a woman who—she worked, er—" He seemed truly at a loss.

Lady Margaret went to her father's side. "Just tell her, Father."

He stiffened his spine. "It was said that she was extremely beautiful. She came from Jamaica, and she worked in a brothel."

Eliza absorbed the words like a blow. They didn't hurt so much as numb her. A brothel was a place where women entertained men for money. Beyond that, she knew nothing else.

But the Englishman wasn't finished. "She was a quadroon, Miss Flyte. That means she was one-quarter African. She had been a slave in Jamaica, and had escaped to London."

A slave. Her mother had been a slave. The idea was so extraordinary that Eliza reeled in shock. All her life, she had thought of her mother in the vaguest of terms—a woman with a gentle face, a soft voice, dark hair and eyes like Eliza's own. The word *slave* changed the picture entirely. She imagined a captive woman, forced to work to the brink of desperation, then compelled to run for her life. Had her mother been like the man Eliza had helped on Flyte Island? Had she been frightened, abused, wounded by a mantrap? The idea of her mother's suffering was unbearable.

"Her name," Eliza said. "Do you know what her name was?"

"I'm afraid I don't. The last anyone in racing circles heard, she had died in childbirth, and Henry Flyte had disappeared."

So much of her father became clear to her in that moment. At last she understood why he had been so protective of her and so circumspect about her mother. She now knew why he had secretly devoted himself to the cause of abolition. He *was* Prospero, she realized. He had built a world of his own creation where his word was law. But like the wizard's spells, it was all an illusion.

"I'm terribly sorry, Miss Flyte," said Lord Alistair.

She studied him and then his daughter. "Sorry for what?" she asked. "I wanted to know the truth. You told me, and for that I thank you. I am the same person I was just moments ago when you offered me a glass of sherry."

"In the eyes of any thinking person, that is true. You won't find me spreading gossip," he vowed, "but this is Virginia, where people like your mother are held in bondage."

A chill streaked up Eliza's spine. She was a free person of color, as Noah was. Which meant that marrying Hunter was against the law. And despite the assurances of Lord Alistair and Lady Margaret, Eliza had long known of a force faster than light. And that was gossip in the Tidewater region.

Eliza thought it strange that Hunter was not in the dining room with his guests. Stranger still that she felt so utterly calm. The very air around her seemed a thick substance, muffled by shock. She checked on the children, finding Blue asleep in his bed, an open book face-down on his chest. She took away the book and covered him up, then carried Belinda to bed. The little girl protested sleepily when Eliza took off her dress. "Is it over, Eliza?" she mumbled. "Did I miss supper?"

"It's over, sweet thing," Eliza whispered, and Belinda tucked her fist under her chin and went back to sleep. What a blessing that she and Hunter had not announced their plans to the children. Because now, of course, those plans had changed.

Night had fallen, and she could hear a low murmur of conversation from downstairs. She fetched a lamp, holding it steady in front of her, watching the golden glow waver over her bell-shaped gown. She found herself thinking of the Spanish bride who had died so young, never having found her bridegroom.

Swept by a strange melancholy, Eliza noticed the door to Lacey's room was ajar. No one went in there. She herself had only ever gone there once, and that had been to—

"Oh, dear God," she whispered, and rushed into the room.

It was too dark to see. She lifted the lamp high and stood in the musty shadows until her eyes adjusted. And then she saw a movement by the bed. It was Hunter, standing over the rosewood box filled with the letters to his late wife.

"Hunter," she said in a rush, "I'm so sorry—"

"Ah," he said. "So it was you who hid this away. I wondered. They say the husband is always the last to know." The whiskey added a whip-crack of contempt to his voice. "Where did you find this?"

No more lies, she thought. Lies and silence had poisoned this family. The truth might hurt, but then the healing could start. "Blue had it," she stated, aching for the little boy who had stood at his dying mother's bedside and accepted the terrible burden of Lacey's secrets. "After the...accident, his mother told him to hide it away. And she said—oh, God—she said that he must never say a word. That's why Blue didn't speak for so long.''

"Goddamn faithless bitch.'' Hunter's oath seared the air. "I hope she's burning in hell. Where are my dueling pistols? I'll send Charles to join her.''

Eliza nearly dropped the lamp. The letters were from Charles, then. She had not recognized the handwriting, but Hunter had. Charles. Yes, it made sense that the tender, frivolous letters had been penned by him. *She was so damn lonely,* he'd said of Lacey. *She needed him so bad, and he never even knew...*

"I won't let you hurt Charles,'' she said, moving in front of the doorway.

Hunter laughed bitterly. "When I'm sober, I'll thank you for that.''

She exhaled silently in relief. The lamp hissed into the quiet room, and an occasional burst of laughter came from below.

"He's a good man, my cousin Charles,'' Hunter said. "Looks after things for me. Farm, horses, wife... Tell me, when you're my wife, will he look after you too?''

Her mouth dried, and every thought evaporated from her head. Long moments stretched out until she finally found her voice. She picked up the lamp and went to the door. "I can't marry you, Hunter.''

Hunter slammed his palm against the doorjamb, blocking her exit. He smelled of bay rum and whiskey and despair. *"Why?"* he asked.

She ducked away from him, for it was too hard to think straight when he was near, and she couldn't talk to him when he was drunk. "I learned, only today, that I am a person of color.''

He loosened his cravat and scowled. "What color?''

"My mother was a quadroon. She used to be a slave in Jamaica, and then she escaped to London. I don't know what her name was, only that she died giving birth to me." She watched Hunter's face closely. He bore the news with a cold stoicism that hid everything he felt. His scowl softened, then deepened, but he said nothing. "Does that shock you?" she asked him. "Disgust you?"

Hunter whipped off his cravat and wadded it into a ball. "Hell's bells, woman, why do you think this changes anything?"

"It changes everything."

"Horseshit. How do you even know it's true?"

"It's true." She knew it in her bones. She knew it from the way her father had lived his life. She knew it from the way he had died.

"Then we won't tell anyone."

She laughed incredulously. "That's absurd. The news will spread. A great number of young ladies will greet the news of our engagement with disappointment."

"So?"

"So your friends and neighbors will search for any reason to discredit me as your bride. It was a simple matter for me to find out about my mother. Anyone else could do the same." Like a seriously wounded victim, she felt too numb to feel anything for the moment. Things were ending before they had a chance to begin. She knew what would happen if she dared to marry one of their own.

"Who the hell cares what other folks say?" he demanded. "I thought we settled that last night."

"But last night it wasn't illegal for us to marry. Beyond that, you have to think of your children. Can you imagine what it will be like for them when word gets out?"

Even Hunter had no answer for that. In that one moment she saw all of their moments together, from the first day when he had landed on her beach, to the instant she had walked in this room to see the hatred in his eyes.

"I wanted to know who my mother was," she said. "I had no idea it would change the course of my life."

"It's safer not to know some things." His gaze shifted to the barn. A light burned in the solitary bunk where Noah lived.

Hunter said no more. He took out his whiskey bottle and put it to his lips. She had no idea whether he even knew she left the room.

Part Four

Be free, and fare thou well.
—William Shakespeare, *The Tempest*, V, i

Twenty-Nine

❧ ☙

Leaving wasn't so hard, Eliza reflected as she slowly awakened to face her final day at Albion. People did it all the time.

She blinked at the slant of light through the window. She could tell it was still morning by the position of the sun. Tucking her knees up under her chin, she tried to put some order to her thoughts, but it was no use. How could she think when her heart was breaking?

"Get up, get up," sang Blue, bounding into the sun-flooded room. "Don't sleep the day away."

She blinked and rubbed her stinging eyes, and couldn't help smiling at the two moppets who had climbed onto her bed. "I suppose you'll make sure of that," she said.

"Aye aye, sir." Blue stood on the mattress, grasping the bedpost like the shroud of a sail and peering out the window. Out in the yard below, Albion was a hive of activity, with guests leaving and horse buyers arranging transport. The landing at the end of the dock was crammed with yachts and steamers. Beneath loads of luggage, servants staggered between the house and the carriages.

"Another storm's coming," Blue announced dramatically.

"A storm, a storm," Belinda shrieked, falling unquestioningly into the familiar fantasy.

Watching the children, Eliza fought tears. She'd known true happiness with this damaged, love-hungry family, but now her time here was over. Blue halted in his play, as if sensing the downward shift of her mood. "What's the matter?" he asked quietly.

Belinda held still too, waiting for the answer.

"I…" Eliza looked helplessly from one eager, anxious face to the other. She took a deep breath and began again. "I'm feeling a little sad today."

"You'll make it better," Blue said earnestly. "You always do."

"No, *you'll* make it better," she said. "Come here, you two." She held out her arms.

They dove into her embrace, one child on each side, snuggling against her chest. How dear they were, warm as puppies, loving her with complete abandon. The woman Hunter eventually chose to be his wife would be lucky indeed. After yesterday's revelations, he might swear off women for a good long while, but he would get over his disillusionment one day.

He'd left Lacey's room in a rage last night. She'd heard him in the stables, and by the light of a three-quarter moon she'd seen him riding off to the high meadows in his elegant evening clothes. Eventually, he'd have to make his own explanations to the children.

"I need you to help me today," she said with a cheeriness she didn't feel.

"Help you do what?"

"Pack my things."

Blue caught on first, pulling back to eye her suspiciously. "What for?"

"For a trip."

"Where're we going?" Belinda asked. "Are we taking the mail packet?"

Blue shushed her and turned on Eliza. "You're leaving us, aren't you? You're going to California."

She smiled, loving this angry, beautiful child. "I am, Blue. I'm going off on a very long trip."

"No!" Belinda burst out. Her eyes filled with tears. "You can't, you can't, you can't," she wailed. "You have to stay with us."

Eliza struggled to hold on to her composure through the storm of Blue's anger and Belinda's grief. When she got them to calm down, she said, "Remember what I said when I first came here? I said I could only stay a while." She caressed Belinda's soft curls, twirling one around her finger. "Everything is so much better now. You are both such wonderful, remarkable children. My work here is done."

"Is that what we were?" Blue demanded. "Work? Like the stallion?"

His insights, for one so young, always amazed her. She could understand why he would think that. She had trained a mad horse and sent him off with Noah when he was calm again. She helped the children with their grief—now they assumed she would walk away from them as well.

And they were right. They were absolutely right.

Perhaps it was some flaw in her makeup, but it was the only way she knew how to live her life. Everything was short term. The world in which she had grown up had changed with the seasons, altered with the storms. Restless waves consumed the shifting dunes of Flyte Island. Nothing was permanent. Experience had taught her how to survive.

But not how to stay.

"Let me tell you something about the stallion," she

said, choosing her words carefully. "He will always be with me, no matter where I go. In my heart and in my mind, I'll keep him safe and sound. It's the same with the two of you, only my feelings are much, much stronger. I feel such an incredible love for you that it doesn't matter how far away I go. Part of me will always be with you."

They didn't believe her. She could tell by Belinda's trembling chin and Blue's fierce scowl. "You'll be gone," the boy said. "Not part of you—all of you. Gone."

"When you're older, you'll understand. I'm like the ship that sails to a far-off shore. You can't see me, but I'll still be there. I'll still love you." She took each of their hands. "I'll carry that love wherever I go."

"What's going to happen to us?" Belinda asked.

"You'll be fine," Eliza assured her.

"But what's going to happen?" she persisted. "Are we going back to Bonterre for tutoring, or—"

"Not unless you want to. Your father has made a big success of Albion. If you like, you can have a tutor here. I imagine that, in time, your father might marry again."

"No," Belinda cried. "I don't want him to marry anyone unless he marries you."

The words hammered into her and they hurt. Because that was exactly what she had been thinking. But she was no seven-year-old expecting wishes to come true. She was a grown woman who'd had a taste of this world and discovered that she didn't fit in, no matter how much she loved Hunter Calhoun.

"Sweetheart," she said gently, "your papa needs someone who knows about being a wife and a mother. Not someone who knows about horses."

"But you know everything," Blue snapped. "Everything important."

"That's why it's not a good idea for me to stay here

any longer. It will just make leaving harder." She threw back the covers and got out of bed. "Now, please. You have to help me make plans for all the animals I brought from the island."

"Are you taking them with you?"

"Just Caliban." Hearing his name, the big dog belly-crawled out from under the bed and thumped his tail on the floor.

"How come he gets to go?" Blue asked.

"Because he's been mine since he was old enough to leave his mother, and I'll get too lonely on my trip without him."

"Won't you be lonely without us and Papa?"

"Of course," she said. "But I can't take you with me."

"Why not?"

"Because you have to stay here, at this wonderful farm your papa has made, and you have to live the life he's given you."

"I want to go to California with you," Blue insisted.

"No, you don't. You don't want to leave Nancy and Willa and Noah and all the animals. You'll write me letters, and maybe one day you'll come to California and visit me."

"And what will you be doing?"

Missing you. And missing your father more than food or air or life itself.

She bit her lip and went to the clothespress, choosing a day gown of plain muslin. Over their protests, which grew louder and louder, she put her things in a traveling trunk. There was so little she wanted to take with her—some items of clothing, her two books, the Spanish bride's things. A feeling of incompleteness nagged at her. Something was missing, but she couldn't decide what it was.

When she shut the lid with a musty thud, the children sobbed openly.

Eliza wasn't certain she could hold her own emotions in check, but for the sake of the children, she had to. "Come here." She held out both hands. "Come and help me say goodbye to everyone."

They found Nancy and Willa in the kitchen. Belinda wrenched free of Eliza to slam herself face-first into Nancy's apron.

"She's going away," the little girl wailed. "Eliza is going to California!"

"I know, honey," Nancy said, her unseeing eyes cast down. "I know. I reckon sooner or later everybody goes away."

Eliza hugged them each in turn. "I'll miss you," she said, trying to memorize the old, wise faces of these two women. With quiet strength they had endured at Albion, faithful to Hunter even when he could barely afford to feed them.

Eliza took the children outside, into the heavy lush air of high summer. The perfume of magnolia and camellia rode the breeze, and magpies chattered high in the live oaks that lined the front drive.

She tried not to hold the children's hands too tightly. Blue and Belinda had so much promise. She had to step out of the way so they could fulfill that promise. Her presence would only hold them back, and if she stayed until they got older, she knew the day would come when her mother's background would be revealed. Right now, they were too young to feel the sting of gossip and censure, to know what the whispers and titters meant when friends and neighbors saw Eliza. She knew how it felt to be the outsider. She never wanted Blue or Belinda to feel that ostracism, ever. For their sakes, she had to leave.

And for the sake of her own heart, she admitted. Too much of it already belonged to the children, and far too much to their father. If she stayed any longer, there would be nothing left of her. Loving Hunter and his children would consume her entirely.

In the barn, she spent a quiet moment with Finn. The stallion nuzzled at her shoulder, and she stroked his neck thoughtfully. "That was quite a ride you took me on, Sir Finnegan," she said, then turned to Noah. "Take care of him, Noah."

"Yes, ma'am," the youth said. "I surely will."

Charles came out to the yard, his shirt askew, as if he had dressed in haste. "Is it true, then?" he asked. "You're leaving."

She nodded, hoping her composure would hold. "Off to California to find my fortune."

"Some of us wish you could have found it here," he said.

"Ah, Charles. You know better than that."

Belinda's chin started trembling anew.

Charles went down on one knee. "Guess what happened in the hayrick last night?" he asked, snaring the children's attention.

"What? What?" Belinda broke away from Eliza and grabbed her uncle's hand.

"A litter of kittens was born."

"Really? Can we see? Can we?"

Bless you, Eliza thought. She needed him to do this, to create a distraction so she could say her goodbyes and not worry that they would grieve.

"The mama cat is very tame." He stood up with a twinkle in his eye. "She'll let you get very close."

"Hurrah!"

Eliza held out her arms. "One last hug and a kiss," she said.

They flew to her, nearly unbalancing her as they wrapped their arms around her. The unexpected strength of their embraces always startled her. A child's love was fierce, she thought, squeezing her eyes shut. There was no stronger force in the universe.

She tried to inhale the essence of them, their smell of sunshine and green grass and milky, childlike sweetness. Would she remember this smell? Would she always cry when she thought of it? Leaving them like this, she felt like the piping plover guarding her nest, wounding herself in order to save her brood.

"Goodbye, my sweet loves," she whispered. "Be good, and write me lots of letters."

They looked glum again, so she set them away from her. "You'd better get to the barn before the mama cat moves her litter."

"Goodbye, Eliza," Belinda said. "I love you."

"I know, sweetheart. I love you too."

The little girl ran across the lawn toward the barn. Blue broke away without saying anything. Eliza wanted to call out to him, to ask him to forgive her, to assure him that she wasn't betraying him by leaving him. But he was so young, and it was time to let go. Charles opened his mouth to chastise the boy for rudeness, but Eliza shook her head, shushing him. Blue's acceptance would come when he was ready, just as it had in the matter of his mother's death.

She stood looking at Charles, and finally said, "Hunter found the letters."

"Letters?"

"The ones you wrote to Lacey. She kept them all in a box, and yesterday he found them."

His face went ashen. "He'll kill me."

"I don't think so. But that is between the two of you. You're both decent men. You both loved the same woman, and now she is gone. I have to believe you won't let it destroy your friendship." She looked over his shoulder at the busy dock. "I have to go."

Charles took her in his arms, burying his face in her hair and then pulling back to kiss her square on the mouth. "Lordy, I've been wanting to do that for a damn long time," he said.

"Aren't you in enough trouble already?" she asked, pushing him away.

"Then a little more won't matter. Did you like it?"

She laughed, her heart hurting. "I daresay half the county has dreamed of being kissed by you."

"Did you like it enough to stay?"

"Ah, Charles. You know I can't."

He studied her hard. "You're right. You'd have to become someone else entirely."

"Either that, or we'd have to refashion society. Though somehow I can't imagine Eudora Bondurant dancing barefoot."

Their laughter was tinged with wistfulness. Charles glanced at Blue, who lingered in the yard. "Goodbye, sugar pie. Send us a letter from California."

"I will."

He joined Blue, taking the boy's hand. She watched them growing smaller and smaller on the lawn as they walked away from her. Just before they turned on the path to the barn, Blue wrenched away from Charles and came racing back to her.

"Eliza," he called. "Eliza, wait!"

He slammed into her and hugged her hard, harder even than before. "I thought if I didn't say goodbye then it wouldn't be real," he sobbed into her skirts.

"Shush, darling," she said, stroking his bright sun-warmed hair. "Shush now. You've said the sweetest good-bye of all, and now I can go and know you'll be fine."

He stepped back. "Eliza."

"Yes?"

"I love you."

She looked one last time at his dear, adorable face, into the eyes that had locked in so many secrets for so long. "I love you too, my sweetest boy. I always, always will, no matter where I go."

He turned and ran then, and she was glad, for it hurt too much to linger over this. She went out to the landing, where the mail packet was moored, the smell of steam and hot oil wafting up from the fiddley. The decks of the steamer were laden with bales of tobacco from the tide-water plantations along its route to the port of Norfolk. The crew took on firewood from the stack at the end of the dock. Eliza put two fingers in her mouth and whistled for Caliban, who came bounding across the yard, his jaw low and his tongue flapping. She shooed the dog onto the boat, assuring the crewmen he was friendly.

Then she walked down the dock, aware of every detail. The tread of her footsteps on the wooden planks. The liquid lapping of the water against the pilings. The sound of a herring gull wheeling overhead. The rise of a rockfish in a ring of sunlit water.

It was a moment that would forever be frozen in time for her. She knew that, for as long as she lived, she would remember this. It was like a dream, vivid and clinging past dawn. The day she embarked on her new life. The day she would fulfill her father's destiny.

"Eliza, wait."

Hunter's voice stopped her cold. She stood facing the end of the dock, hearing his approach. He was hurrying.

"Eliza, look at me," he said. Then, without waiting for her to respond, he took her by the shoulders and turned her so she couldn't avoid looking at him.

He still wore his evening clothes.

"Hunter—"

"No, let me say this. What Lacey did has nothing to do with you. The idea that Blue stayed mute for two years because she told him not to say a word was so appalling that I couldn't think straight. The fact that you didn't tell me about the letters Blue kept hidden all this time— I realize you did that because you didn't want me to be hurt." His grip on her upper arms tightened. "Forgive me," he said. "Forgive all the things I said."

"Ah, Hunter." She drew strength from the love in her heart. "There's nothing to forgive."

"Then stay, Eliza. Stay with me."

She bit her lip to keep from flinging herself at him and shouting yes. Instead, she forced herself to cling to cold reason. She stared at him, this weary gentleman in his rumpled finery, his haggard face stubbled with whiskers, his eyes old and tired and desperate, red from drinking.

"I wasn't myself yesterday," he said.

Her throat hurt unbearably as she swallowed. She thought of the bleary accusations, the darkness that emerged from his soul, lit by the whiskey. Drinking created a place within him that she could not touch. The whiskey put up a wall and kept his heart from its full commitment.

"You were," she said, forcing the words past her aching throat. "You were yourself, Hunter. You belong here, on the farm you built, among the people who know and accept you as you are. That's why I have to leave. I have to find a place where it doesn't matter who my mother was."

"Don't you get it?" he said. "I don't care. You're still Eliza. The woman I made love to under the stars—"

"Stop," she said. "This isn't helping."

He made a hissing sound of pain. "You don't love me enough to stay."

"I love you—and the children—enough to leave." She paused, taking his hands away from her arms. His touch was too sweet, reminding her of moments when they had been so close that nothing else mattered—not the drinking, not who her parents were, not the way the world worked.

"Oh, for Christ's sake," he said. "Don't tell me—"

"Listen," she said. "We both know this can't work. Hunter, we live in a world that can't accept our love. You know what would happen if I stayed. The mere fact of my existence is a disgrace in people's eyes. These are the people we have to live among. Your children have to grow up with their children. I won't burden them with my presence."

"If people find you objectionable, then they're the ones who are wrong, not you."

"That may well be, but we can't change their thinking." She clenched her hands into fists at her sides to keep from reaching for him, to keep from begging for one last touch, one last kiss. "You can't take your children away from their home or leave this place you've worked so hard to build," she said softly. "And I...I can't stay."

"You can, goddamn it, but you won't," he snapped. "Your father taught you a lot of things, Eliza. He made a unique and brilliant woman out of you. But there's one thing he forgot to teach you."

"What?" she asked, flayed by his contemptuous tone. "What are you saying?"

"He forgot to teach you that some things last."

"What?"

Furious, he paced the dock. From the corner of her eye, she could see the crewmen finishing up with the wood.

"Oh, he taught you all about change. Everything changes—the seasons, the shore, the cycle of life and death. You learned those lessons well, Eliza. Too damn well. So well that you can't even conceive of a love that lasts forever, a love strong enough to endure people's gossip. The first thought of a snub, and you're running away like—like a wild thing."

Like one of the wild ponies, she thought. The creatures that lived out at the edge of the world. She was one of them—a flight animal.

"There's another thing my father taught me, 'What strength I have's mine own,'" she quoted from *The Tempest.* "He trained me to respect myself. Enough to walk away when it's the only option I have."

The steamer whistle blew three loud blasts.

Hunter's body jerked as if he had been shot. He grabbed her by the shoulders and hauled her against him.

And then he kissed her. He had done so many times before, but never with this fury and this fire. She felt it seething from him as his mouth claimed hers. His tongue plundered her, moving smoothly in and out of her in an echo of the passion they had shared. The fierce possession of his embrace made a mockery of her objections. She felt herself bending back, overwhelmed as the banked fires of her own desire sparked to life.

She pushed at him, trying to resist, but suddenly the pushing fists opened of their own accord, and she buried her fingers into the fine fabric of his dress shirt. His whisker stubble burned her face. She knew she would bear the marks of it for days to come. She didn't care. She knew only that she loved this man with all that she was. But it wasn't enough.

Perhaps he was right about her father. Like Prospero, he had conjured a life out of thin air, and though it was idyllic, it was contrived, artificial. It had left a hole in her; he simply didn't know how to make something last.

Hunter's brutal kiss went on and on, a sensual assault that made her whimper with wanting and frustration.

The steamboat whistled again, its shrill impatience screaming across the bay.

She managed to wrench away finally. One last look at his weary, red-rimmed eyes. One last look at his moist, love-bruised mouth. One last look at the big hands that knew how to touch her with such fierce tenderness.

She tried to speak, but had no idea what to say. *Good-bye.* She pressed her fist to her mouth to keep in the sobs.

"Stay," he said. "It's not too late to change your mind. Stay."

"I...can't." The tears spilled freely now, and she didn't bother stopping them. "You know I can't."

With that, she picked up her skirts and ran to the end of the dock, boarded the steamer—and did not allow herself to look back.

Thirty

Hunter Calhoun quit drinking early that next day, and he held to this state of temperance for all the weeks that followed. He went about his business, and business was good. Better than good, it was extraordinary. Finn won the Fairmont Stakes and the Dominion Derby. He proved so prolific that he was booked to stand stud for the next three years.

At least one of us is finding satisfaction, Hunter thought as he watched the stallion trotting up and down in the breeding yard, awaiting a mare in season.

Hunter had plenty of opportunities with women lately. Young ladies of all shapes, sizes and stations came to him. Some tendered extraordinary offers. A widowed English countess vowed she would buy him a noble title if he married her. A French courtesan offered sexual favors he thought existed only in the imagination. A New York railroad heiress devised an entire racing syndicate to entice him into marriage.

Most of the women were beautiful. Many were kind and sincere. Several even genuinely liked his children. He could have taken his pick of any of them.

But he didn't. Because none of them was Eliza.

Each time he danced with a woman, he remembered what it was like to hold Eliza, to love Eliza, and he couldn't imagine the point of holding anyone else. So Hunter Calhoun, once a notorious rake, had reluctantly become the picture of temperance and abstinence. His cronies gave him no end of trouble about it, but he didn't care.

He would never care what people said.

"Papa, come look," Blue yelled from the barn. "Trinculo caught a mouse!"

Hunter went inside to admire the catch. The little cat, born the day Eliza had left, had become Blue's special pet, and quite the fierce hunter. One of its littermates, a gray tabby, had been adopted by Belinda.

"Eeuw," she said, coming over to see. "A dead mouse." She stroked the tabby, which wore an absurd lace collar and doll bonnet. "Sugar Pie would never kill a mouse." She held the cat out to her father. "Her bonnet's come undone, Papa. Can you tie it for her?"

He took the chagrined cat in his lap and carefully made a bow beneath its chin, then handed it back to Belinda. She leaned over and gave him a loud, smacking kiss on the cheek. Laughing, Blue did the same. Both children played at his feet, giggling.

You should see me now, Eliza, he thought. You'd be proud of me.

He spent hours each day with his children, who were growing more fearless and smarter and stronger with the passing of the season. He hadn't touched a drop of whiskey since the day she'd left.

Over the summer, people had flocked to Albion, a name now famous in horse-racing circles. Everyone wanted to meet the man whose horse was the reigning champion. At one time, this prosperity and acclaim would have meant everything to Hunter. It would have meant a dream fulfilled. But lately…it didn't matter. Not nearly as much as sitting in the barn and watching his children play, or reading them a bedtime story each night. Not nearly as much as remembering Eliza, and the way he used to feel when he was buried so deep inside her that he was no longer himself, but a creature that existed only for the purpose of loving her.

He wondered how long it would be before he stopped thinking about her. As it was, he awoke each morning with her image in his mind, and fell asleep each night with that same image clasped to his heart. He spent practically every waking moment thinking about where she might be just now, what she might be doing.

Was California the fulfillment of her dream?

Was it as beautiful and as fertile as she had wished?

Had she found what she was looking for there?

Did she think of him as often as he thought of her?

Hearing a whistle from the coach yard, he went to see who had arrived. A fancy closed carriage, gleaming black and pulled by a pair of matched black geldings stood in the yard.

Charles leaped out, sporting a fancy new hat and a big grin. "The north parcel's ours, cousin," he said. "The bank approved the loan. By this time next year, the farm will double in size."

"Good work." The development would have meant the world to Hunter at one time, but now the enthusiasm came from Charles.

It was strange, but no animosity festered between Hunter and Charles. After the first confrontation about Lacey—the encounter had entailed a fistfight and some harsh words—they rarely spoke of her. Hunter had his pride, but he also understood Lacey. She had thrived on attention, and when Hunter's attention turned to the horse farm, she had felt utterly abandoned. If she hadn't fled to Charles it would have been someone else.

Hunter supposed the thing to do was to challenge his cousin to a duel, possibly gun him down in defense of Lacey's honor. But he had learned that honor was only worth fighting for if you knew what was at stake, and in the case of Lacey, he had never known. He and Charles settled into a cautious but cordial arrangement.

He had seen real growth and compassion in his young cousin, particularly with regard to Noah. The boy needed a father; finally Charles could fill that role. The two of them had taken over the day-to-day operation of the farm, giving Hunter more time with his children.

Belinda and Blue came racing out to greet Charles. "You're back!" they cried. "What did you bring us?"

"I have something special for you," he said in a conspiratorial voice.

"What is it?" Belinda asked. "What?"

He handed each child a parcel wrapped in oilcloth. "It's chocolate from Switzerland. Have you ever tasted chocolate before?"

They shook their heads. He opened one parcel and gave them each a bite. Brother and sister swooned comically in ecstasy. "More!" Blue exclaimed. "Can we please have some more?"

"Save some for Noah, you greedy creatures," Charles said, going off in search of his son.

They finished half the chocolate, and started a game of tag in the yard, laughing with joy. Each time Hunter thought of Blue's two years of silence, he thanked God for Eliza, who had found a way to set him free.

He turned and looked out at the green, rolling, fertile acres of Albion. In the patrician world of Old Virginia, the land was everything, perhaps the only thing. Men lived for it. Some died for it. Hunter had labored over it for years, and at last he could claim success. He had it all. The paddock of champion horses. The jockeys and grooms busy at their training. The foals and mares in the high meadows. The children laughing lustily as they played on the lawn.

All this had happened thanks to his hard work—and just a touch of magic from the horsemaster's daughter.

He had chased this dream for so long that seeing it fulfilled seemed anticlimactic. But it wasn't even that. Sometimes he questioned whether it was the right dream, after all.

He walked across the dusty track to Charles and Noah. Father and son were deep in conversation in the shade of a live oak. They made a fine picture, the two of them, and it struck Hunter that they looked to be more a part of this place than he had ever been.

Odd.

Charles clapped Noah on the shoulder. "Finish eating that Swiss chocolate. We've got work to do," he said.

Noah's face darkened a shade, but he grinned in pure pleasure. Being at the top of his sport made things like the color of his skin and which side of the blanket he was born on cease to matter. He had attracted the notice of the racing circuit, and inspired pride in the man who had sired him. And through it all, he managed to maintain the joy in riding a fast horse, and that, more than anything, made him a true champion.

"Wait a minute," Hunter said, a sudden decision seizing hold of his heart. "I want to talk to you both." He hunkered down in the shade and looked at his cousin and Noah. "I have a proposition to make."

Part Five

Let us not burden our remembrances
With a heaviness that's gone.
                    —William Shakespeare, *The Tempest,* V, i

Thirty-One

They called her La Llorona, because she looked so sad. When she caught one of the Spanish wranglers or Anita the cook watching her, Eliza tried to remember to smile. And truly, she told herself, she had much to smile about and plenty to be thankful for. Her ship had arrived in San Francisco Bay at the height of the harvest season, and the new land seemed to open its arms with promise. She had a bank draft from Albion Farm which she'd found in the carpetbag she had brought from Virginia. She hadn't asked for it. She certainly hadn't expected it. But the generous payment from Hunter Calhoun had proved to be her hope for the future.

A woman with more pride and less common sense might have torn the draft to bits and cast it to the four winds, but a woman alone in search of a new life could not indulge a fit of pique. Nor could Eliza part with something Hunter had given her, for she understood that he had loved her in his own fashion.

Roberto Montgomery, whose agent had seen her work in Virginia, had brought her to the vast and ancient Rancho del Mar, comprising five thousand pristine acres along the coast beside a busy deepwater harbor. The area was exactly as the old, yellowed lithographs had depicted it—sweeping vistas, a dramatic seacoast, endless free range over strange, scrubby grasslands, and yellowed hills where the herds ran wild and no Anglo or Spanish person had ever set foot.

She lived in a small wooden-frame house by the sea, where the thunder of waves filled the night and migrating gray whales spouted as they passed. A short distance away lay the training grounds where she worked each day with the horses, some of them imported from far places, but most culled from the huge herd of wild mustangs. The horses were not so different from the island ponies she had left behind. Yet these were larger, swifter and in brisk demand from the ranchers and settlers in the area. Using the age-old methods she had learned as a child, she culled mares and yearlings from the herd, gentling them in the manner of her father.

It was a way to survive in a beautiful, empty land. It was a way to fill her days, so that the sleep of exhaustion would fill her nights.

But often, in the many quiet moments that came over her, Eliza found herself thinking of the past. Of Blue and Belinda, and the music of their laughter in the morning. Of Hunter, and the way he touched her heart. Even in his most desperate, tormented moments, he always touched her heart.

At such times, tears would fill her eyes and sometimes outright sobs would cripple her, doubling her over with an agony she didn't think would ever end. And when the ranch hands saw her like that, they whispered of La Llorona and made the sign of the cross.

One day in early December, when a blustery wind skirled down from the heights and rippled across the glassy bay, she sensed a special energy in the cool air. She was used to change and here it was, changing seasons again.

She patted the neck of the mare she was leading and found more evidence of the season. The young mare's coat had thickened into a dense mat of warmth for the coming winter. As she brought the horse along the narrow track that hugged the craggy coastline, a chill wind blew her dress against her legs, and she smoothed her hand down the front of her ungainly silhouette.

Another change. On that final night, in the moon-washed barn of Albion, Hunter Calhoun had given her a parting gift, this one more precious and profound than anything she could imagine. He had given her a baby.

The prospect brought both a thrill of joy and a shiver of fear to her. She felt lost, inadequate, incapable of being the sole person responsible for another human being. Then she would think of Belinda and Blue and realize that it was so easy to love a child. Here in California, she didn't fear being questioned about her lineage. Some of the children who raced around Rancho del Mar owed their heritage to Spaniard, Indian, Anglo and probably African as well, she supposed. It mattered to some Californians, of course; it always would. But this vast land was so different from insular Tidewater Virginia. For the baby's sake, she told the Montgomerys that she was a widow. More she would not—could not—say.

It had been wrong of her, she thought sadly, to think that love didn't last. It was the most permanent bond anyone could forge. Perhaps if she had realized that before, she might have stayed, made a life with Hunter, even dared to brave the censure of those around them.

In the distance, a sharp bark sounded. Caliban went bounding across the broad meadow toward the landing that gave access to the ranch storehouses. She followed the racing speck of the dog to the water's edge—and dropped the mare's lead rope.

Ships were a common sight in the deep, clear harbor of Rancho del Mar. The powerful Montgomery family had an international reputation, and traders came from far and wide to do business with Don Roberto. But this was not just any ship.

This ship flew a red topsail.

She made a small sound, the cry of an animal in pain. And then she started to run.

By the time she reached the landing, the ship's boat had arrived ashore. Two small figures ran toward her. She went down on one knee and flung out her arms. Blue and Belinda flew to her, and she filled her arms with their warm, ecstatic bodies.

"We're here," Belinda crowed. "Uncle Ryan brought us on his ship. We've come to see you!"

"Are you surprised?" Blue asked.

"I'm flabbergasted," she said. "I can't believe you're here."

She looked up over their heads and saw Hunter standing on the dock. Her heart seized with terror and elation. "Go and say hello to Caliban," she said to the children. "And there's a very nice lady named Anita who will give you something to eat at the big house."

Laughing with joy and stumbling on their sea legs, the children went racing up to the house.

Hunter came toward her, looking tall and handsome and terribly grave. He appeared exactly the same and yet completely different. His eyes were so filled with love that she couldn't speak.

"It's no good," he said in that low, slow drawl she remembered so well. "I missed you too much—" He broke off as the wind blew and showed her prominent belly. "Good God, Eliza."

Tears poured unchecked from her eyes. "Surprise," she whispered.

He gathered her into his arms with such aching hesitation that she cried even harder, burying her face against his warm shoulder.

"I love you," he murmured, kissing her hair. "I love you."

"Ah, Hunter," she said unsteadily, "I love you too, and I always will." She tilted her face up and welcomed his kiss, tasting tears and salt air and everything she had missed about him. "You knew that, didn't you?"

"Yeah. I think I did."

"Loving one another has never been our problem, has it?"

"Honey," he said desperately, pulling back. "I stopped drinking. I don't drink anymore, ever. The whiskey made me crazy—I didn't realize that until I stopped. It kept you away from the place where you belong."

"And where is that?" she asked.

"Right here," he said, taking her hand and pressing it to his chest. "Right here in my heart. I can't be without you, Eliza. I was a fool to think I ever could."

She shut her eyes, feeling the strong, steady beat of his heart against her palm. Yet she couldn't help remembering the stifling social gatherings of Tidewater Virginia, and a shadow passed over her hope. "Hunter, some things haven't changed. I'll always be the horsemaster's daughter, whose mother was a runaway slave."

"How can you think that would change the way I feel?" he demanded. "I love everything that you are. Every drop of blood that runs in your veins. Though I never knew your parents, I honor them, because they made you."

She tried to stop crying. "You are an amazing man, Hunter Calhoun. But society isn't ready for a love like ours. I'll never fit into your world."

He kissed her eyelids, each in turn, and she opened them to look up at him. "That's not why I came here," he said.

"Then why?"

"I came to stay."

"Here?"

"If you'll have me. All of us. Me and the children. We can get a place of our own, make a new start out here. This isn't your world or mine either. We can build a new world together."

"How could you leave Albion? All your work, your dreams—"

"Albion wasn't enough, not after I found you. Charles and Noah run the farm as well as I ever did, maybe better. After you left, the dream became my purgatory. I tried to put on a good face, go about my business, but it didn't work. Nothing works without you."

"You can't mean that," she said. "How can you give up everything you've built?"

He smoothed his hand over her belly, and a look of wonder suffused his face. "Building it is better than having it, Eliza. I learned that from you."

The stark, sweet honesty of his admission struck her, then penetrated so deeply that it almost hurt. "Do you mean that, Hunter?" she asked softly.

"Hell's bells, woman, of course I mean it."

Epilogue

Cielito, California
1858

Blue Calhoun started riding early that day. He loved the cool sharp air of morning when the sea mist snaked across the meadows and nestled in the crevices between the hills. He loved the muted quiet before the start of another busy day, and he loved the eager strength of Stephano, his favorite horse, one he had tamed and trained all on his own.

And lately, he loved the sight of Sancha Montgomery, who was thirteen years old and so pretty it made him dizzy just to look at her. She had a habit of coming out early, barefoot and with her skirts swishing around her ankles, to walk along the path that marked the boundary of their parents' property. It was almost as if she knew his habit of riding out early. He loved talking to her; she was so easy to talk to. Someday he might tell her his biggest secret: that for two years, he didn't speak. She probably wouldn't believe him, though, because he talked all the time now.

His father had bought a claim north of Rancho del Mar,

and he'd built a huge, rambling white house and a barn and arena even larger than the one at Albion. Breeding and racing were not so important out in the wilds of northern California, but there would always be a need for horses, and already everyone in the area knew where to get the best—from the Calhouns.

Blue brought Stephano down to a walk and kept his eyes peeled for Sancha. A swift wind cleared the mist from the cliff's edge and there she was, dark hair and red dress, arm raised to wave a greeting. He waved back, feeling a little charge of excitement, because she and her family would be coming for a visit today. In fact, he had to hurry back in order to help organize the celebration, and so he angled his horse homeward, watching the clouds blow away as the sun rose higher.

Down in the yard behind the house, preparations were already under way. It was Belinda's tenth birthday, and she had insisted on a huge and lavish fiesta. Long tables were set up under the shade trees. Three-year-old Henry, whom everyone called Hank, waddled along behind poor old Caliban. The elderly dog preferred to spend his days sleeping in the sun, but he showed a weary tolerance for Blue's energetic half brother.

Belinda and Anita wrestled with a long tablecloth that kept blowing in the wind. His father and Eliza came out on the porch, walking hand-in-hand, heads bent together as they laughed at Hank's antics. Eliza was so pretty, even prettier than she had been when Blue first saw her, shading her eyes and looking up at him in the tree house at Albion. He remembered liking her instantly then, and feeling a gentle unfurling in his heart, and thinking that one day he would tell her the things hidden inside him. And he had, and the miracle was, she and his father had understood.

He was old enough now to know that their love and approval protected him far better than any enforced silence.

His parents' voices drifted up to Blue, a soft assurance that the world they had made was the place where they all fit.

For a moment, an ominous cloud obscured the sun, and Eliza cast up a worried eye, probably fretting that Belinda's birthday would be spoiled by rain. But after a few moments the cloud drifted out to sea.

Life was like that, Blue supposed, a mixture of dark and light. You had to learn to wait until the sunshine broke through. And if you were patient, it always did, no matter what.

Afterword

Dear Reader,

The story of the mysterious stranger with the power to heal is a favorite of mine, and one I find myself returning to again and again. In this particular time in history, the stakes were quite high. The Underground Railroad is described by Page Smith as "one of the most remarkable clandestine operations in all history," and Chesapeake Bay, located so temptingly close to the Mason-Dixon line, provided a route to freedom for many slaves. The escape described in this novel is based on actual events. The story of Hunter and Eliza was an amazing journey for me, and like the best of journeys, the outcome was a mystery until I discovered what Blue learned in the end—that nothing less than love and commitment will bring us to the place we belong.

As I began working on my next book, *The Hostage,* my travels and research led me to another unique and dramatic setting. Islands have always fascinated me. Each is a small universe unto itself, with its own drama and pathos. I was delighted when a small, obscure historical reference led me to a place called Isle Royale, an island in Lake Superior.

I envisioned a woman fleeing for her life in the midst of the great Chicago fire of 1871, and suddenly the character of Deborah Sinclair appeared. An heiress to a mining fortune, she believes her future is set, until she is kidnaped by the wild, mysterious Tom Silver, who brings her face-to-face with her worst fears…and her deepest desires.

* * * * *

Please watch for
THE HOSTAGE
in May of 2000.
Until then, happy reading.

Warmly,
Susan Wiggs
P.O. Box 4469
Rolling Bay, WA 98061-0469

*From one of America's best-loved authors…a story
about what life, joy and Christmas are all about!*

DEBBIE MACOMBER

Shirley, Goodness and Mercy

Greg Bennett knows he's made mistakes, hurt people,
failed in all the ways that matter. Now he has no one
to spend Christmas with, no one who cares.

Greg finds himself in a church—and whispers a simple
heartfelt prayer. A prayer that wends its way to the
Archangel Gabriel, who assigns his favorite angels—
Shirley, Goodness and Mercy—to Greg Bennett's case.
Because Gabriel knows full well that Greg's going to
need the assistance of all three!

Shirley, Goodness and Mercy shall follow
him…because it's Christmas.

On sale October 22, 1999, wherever hardcovers are sold!

MIRA

Look us up on-line at: http://www.mirabooks.com   MDM529

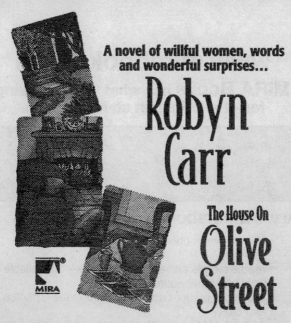

*From one of America's
best-loved authors...*

DIANA PALMER

comes a passionate, provocative story

Paper Rose

Tate Winthrope once boldly came to Cecily Blake's
rescue. Her devotion to him knew no bounds, but the
fiercely proud Native American refused to consider a
mixed marriage, and their passion remained unfulfilled.

But years later, when Tate's in trouble, it's Cecily who
comes to his rescue, attempting to shield the man
she loves from a devastating secret that could
destroy his life....

**"The dialogue is charming, the characters
likable and the sex sizzling..."**
*—Publishers Weekly
on ONCE IN PARIS*

*On sale mid-November 1999
wherever paperbacks are sold.*

MIRA

Visit us at www.mirabooks.com   MDP539